WITHDRAWN
MENASHA'S PUBLIC LIBRARY

The Night Ranger

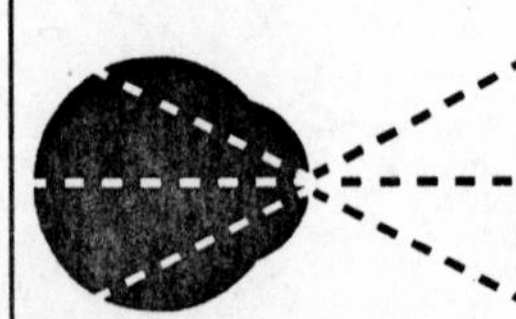

This Large Print Book carries the Seal of Approval of N.A.V.H.

The Night Ranger

Alex Berenson

WHEELER PUBLISHING
A part of Gale, Cengage Learning

Detroit • New York • San Francisco • New Haven, Conn • Waterville, Maine • London

This is a work of fiction. Names, characters, places, and incidents either are the product of the author's imagination or are used fictitiously, and any resemblance to actual persons, living or dead, businesses, companies, events, or locales is entirely coincidental.

While the author has made every effort to provide accurate telephone numbers and Internet addresses at the time of publication, neither the publisher nor the author assumes any responsibility for errors, or for changes that occur after publication. Further, the publisher does not have any control over and does not assume any responsibility for author or third-party websites or their content.

Wheeler Publishing Large Print Hardcover.
The text of this Large Print edition is unabridged.
Other aspects of the book may vary from the original edition.
Set in 16 pt. Plantin.

LIBRARY OF CONGRESS CATALOGING-IN-PUBLICATION DATA

Berenson, Alex.
The night ranger / by Alex Berenson.
pages ; cm. (Wheeler publishing large print hardcover)
ISBN 978-1-4104-5494-2 (hardcover) — ISBN 1-4104-5494-0 (hardcover)
1. Intelligence officers—Fiction. 2. Undercover operations—Fiction.
3. Americans—Africa, East—Fiction. 4. Large type books. I. Title.
PS3602.E75146N54 2013b
813'.6—dc23 2012044888

Published in 2013 by arrangement with G. P. Putnam's Sons, a member of Penguin Group (USA) Inc.

Printed in Mexico
2 3 4 5 6 7 17 16 15 14 13

For Joey,
whose adventures were only beginning

Prologue

Dadaab, Kenya

Not that Gwen Murphy would tell anyone. She pushed the idea away as soon as it came. But the refugees were starting to creep her out.

Gwen lay on her cot, pretending to sleep. Outside the walls of the trailer she shared with Hailey Barnes, the Hagadera refugee camp was coming to life. Diesel engines rumbled in the distance as the morning's first supply convoy arrived. Closer, two men shouted to each other in their clicking African language. "Happy Birthday," Gwen murmured to herself. Her twenty-third. The first she'd spent outside the United States, much less in Africa.

For twelve weeks Gwen had volunteered for WorldCares/ChildrenFirst, an aid agency that offered food and medical care to Somali refugees. The Somalis came to Kenya to escape famine and war. Hundreds of thousands lived in Hagadera and other camps around the town of Dadaab in eastern Kenya. At first the mission had seemed simple to Gwen. Feed the hungry, shelter the homeless, protect the innocent. But the longer she stayed, the less she understood this place.

She tried not to think about that, either.

Her alarm beeped. She gave up the charade of sleep, opened her eyes. Seven-thirty a.m. Rise and shine. Across the trailer, Hailey's cot was empty. Hailey always left before Gwen. She claimed she liked to watch the sun rise. Gwen thought she might have something going with Jasper, the ex-Marine who ran security at their compound, but Hailey denied they were anything but friends. I just like the place when it's quiet, she said.

Gwen wrapped herself in her thin cotton blanket, reached for her laptop. WorldCares housed its workers in a walled compound at the edge of the Hagadera camp. The compound had its own electricity and water and wireless service, not great but enough to download email.

She found twenty-two new messages on her Gmail account, mainly birthday greetings. Her little sister Catelyn had sent a picture of them by the Golden Gate Bridge, one of Gwen's favorites, from a trip to California the year before.

> Only four more weeks of do-gooding! Can't wait for you to get home so I can buy you a 3 a.m. Egg McMuffin — hinting at an epic night on that trip. Tell Hailey The Heartbreaker I said hi! Owen and Scott too! Happy 23rd! XOXO C

Next up, from her mom:

> Daddy and I will call today but if you're busy or we don't get through I want you to know how much we love, love, LOVE you! And we're so proud of you, what you're doing over there is so great . . .

So great. If they only knew. Gwen signed off, pulled on sweatpants and a long-sleeved shirt for the walk to the bathroom trailer. On her first morning here, she'd made the mistake of stepping out in boyshorts and a thin cotton tee. She hadn't gotten ten steps before a crusty forty-something woman intercepted her.

"This is a refugee camp, not a gentlemen's club," the woman barked in a thick British accent. "We respect local sensitivities. As I don't doubt you're aware, you have a very pleasant body" — somehow "pleasant" sounded like an accusation — "but if you want to dress like a Russian whore I suggest Moscow. You'd do well."

Whore? Moscow? Gwen wanted to argue but instead hustled back to her trailer. She later learned the woman was Moss Laughton, the logistics director for WorldCares. Moss's moods ranged from bad to worse. Still, Gwen had grown to like her after that initial run-in. Maybe because they couldn't be more different. The British woman had short spiky hair and was shaped like a potato. She didn't care how she looked or what people said about her. And she wasn't afraid to yell. She once described her job to Gwen as trying to keep the stealing to a reasonable level. And failing.

Gwen decided to give herself an extra-long, extra-hot shower this morning. Moss wouldn't be amused. Moss said any shower more than three minutes long was a waste of time and water. But it wasn't Moss's birthday, was it?

The Hagadera camp was one of three giant refugee centers near Dadaab, an overgrown village on the dusty plains of eastern Kenya. The camps opened in 1991, when Somalia's government first collapsed. For most of their existence they'd held fewer than one hundred thousand refugees. But since 2009, drought and war had caused hundreds of thousands of Somalis to flee their homes. With nowhere else to go, they trekked west across the desert toward Kenya. Along the way, bandits stole from them and raped them. If they were too weak to walk, they got left behind. And not for the Rapture. They died of dehydration or starvation. Hyenas and lions dragged away their corpses. Even when they reached Kenya, they weren't safe. The Kenyan police demanded bribes and threw the Somalis back over the border if they didn't pay. But enough refugees got through that half a million now lived in the camps, in endless rows of tents that studded the land like anthills. Some received sturdy white tents that looked like they belonged in an upscale camping expedition. Abercrombie and Kent: Journey to Dadaab. The others built their own shelters out of plastic sheets and scraps of wood. Vast open plains surrounded the camps, but the Kenyan government refused to expand them. So the tents were crammed into ever-smaller plots as new refugees arrived. Each was a miniature city of refugees, with a city's problems.

Gwen hadn't known any of this when she'd come to Dadaab three months before, with Hailey and Owen Broder and Scott Thompson. The four of them had just graduated from the University of Montana, in Missoula. Gwen had grown up in western Montana, lived there her whole life. She was ready for a change. An adventure.

Then Scott said he might go to Kenya to work for his uncle James helping refugees. Gwen was surprised. Scott had never struck her as caring. In fact, when it came to women, she knew firsthand he was exactly the opposite. But he told her that James ran a charity called WorldCares. "We can go to Africa for a few months. Beats hanging around here," he said. "Plus when we're done, we'll go on a safari. Watch lions getting it on. You know they have sex for like two days straight." Scott sounded at least as enthusiastic about the lions as the refugees.

That night she Googled Dadaab. The pictures shocked her. She couldn't believe people still starved to death. Of course, anorexia, but that was different. Anyway, the point was that the refugees were starving. United Nations says 750,000 Somalis at risk from famine, the headlines said. Worst food shortage since 1991. Babies with bellies swollen from hunger. Women with arms like sticks. Gwen decided right then that she'd go. Do whatever it was that aid workers did.

When she told her family about her plan, she figured her mom — and certainly her dad — would put up a fight. Aside from a few weekends in Canada, she'd only been out of the United States once, on a spring break trip to Cancún. But they didn't. "It'll be good for you," her mom said. "Broaden your horizons."

Then Hailey decided to come, too. She told Gwen she wanted a better shot at med school. She'd applied her senior year, but her test scores weren't great and the only place that accepted her was in the Caribbean. "This stuff looks great on your résumé," Hailey said. "In the interviews, too. 'When I saw little Dikembe come back to life, I knew I wanted to be a healer.' I don't have to tell them that the kind of healing I'm talking about is dermatology. Laser skin peels for five hundred dollars a pop."

"Isn't that a little cynical?"

"It's a lot cynical. But doctors make mucho dinero and, unlike you, I can't afford the luxury of being an idealist."

"I'm not rich."

"Gwennie, rich people always say that."

Finally, Owen joined up. He didn't have to explain why. Gwen knew. He'd had a terrible crush on her for two years. Though he wasn't a stalker. More a hopeless romantic.

He gave her longing looks when he thought she wouldn't notice. She wished she found him attractive. But he was curly-haired, soulful. Gwen didn't go for soulful. Gwen went for jocks. Jerks. Like Scott. Scott was about six-two, two-fifteen, with sandy blond hair and broad shoulders and a ridiculous six-pack. Scott could dunk. Gwen had seen him. When Scott wrapped an arm around her, she felt held. She was starting to rethink Scott and all the Scotts of the world. One had given her a bad herpes scare a few months back. But for now she was still in the jock-jerk camp.

Back in her trailer, post-shower, Gwen tugged on cargo pants and boots and a black T-shirt that she knew flattered her. Though, in truth, she would have looked good in sackcloth. She had the honey-blond hair and long lean legs of a Dallas Cowboys cheerleader. She stood out absurdly in the camp's crowds, an alien from Planet Beautiful.

But her looks hardly mattered here. The refugee kids wanted to touch her hair, sure. Their parents wanted more rations, a chance for an American visa. When they realized she couldn't help, they moved on. She was just another aid worker here, unworthy of special attention. The realization unsettled her. She wondered if she was seeing what life would be like when she was sixty.

She walked to the WorldCares canteen, a concrete room with a gas-fired stove and two oversized refrigerators. Posters of missions covered the walls, smiling black and brown children surrounding white volunteers. Owen and Scott sat at a wooden table, spooning up oatmeal from chipped bowls.

"Oatmeal?" They hadn't had any yesterday. Gwen poured a cup of coffee, busied herself brewing a fresh pot. Leaving the coffeemaker empty was a great sin at WorldCares. As Moss had made sure she learned.

"Bunch of Quaker Instant came in yesterday," Owen said. "All kinds. Apples and cinnamon, brown sugar and whatever —"

"Pepsi's getting a nice tax deduction on that, I'll bet," Scott said.

"Pepsi?" Gwen didn't get it.

"They own Quaker. Stuff's about to expire, they can't sell it, so they give it to us, write it off at full price. Everybody wins."

"I get it." Just because she didn't know that Pepsi owned Quaker didn't make her stupid. Or did it? Other people always seemed to know things she didn't. But then, she'd never tried very hard in school. Around sixth grade, she'd realized that boys would do her homework. She didn't even have to fool around with them unless she wanted to. They were happy to be near her. This band, the Hold Steady, had a song called "You Can Make Him Like You." And it was true. All the way through college, where she'd barely graduated with a 2.1 in sociology. Even that had required her to flirt with a professor senior year so he would let her retake her final. Not that she'd slept with him. He was old. And married. But she'd gone to his study hours dressed in her cutest gray yoga pants, the ones that cupped her ass perfectly, and made sure to lean over his desk and let him see the black thong poking out where her T-shirt didn't reach. She knew that her moves were obvious, and she knew he knew too. But she'd learned that men didn't care. They could be fully aware they were being played and still enjoy the game. No doubt he was filing her image away for later, when he was having boring sex with his wife for the millionth time.

So she'd gotten her C's, and she was a college graduate, nobody could take that away. But she wondered if she should have studied a little harder. For this trip she'd bought a Kindle, loaded it with a bunch of famous books she hadn't read, *The Great Gatsby* and *Invisible Man* and whatever.

She'd forced her way through them, too. But she had to admit she didn't really enjoy them. Maybe she should have tried *Twilight* and *The Hunger Games;* a lot of her friends liked those.

"What's happening today?" Gwen said. Besides my birthday. She wondered if they'd forgotten.

"I'm meeting with James about that reporter coming next week," Owen said.

"What's that?"

"Yeah, from Houston. He wants a list of talking points for everybody, make sure we're all on message about the mission. Talk about our local partners, how we do more than just hand out food, all that stuff."

"Spin, in other words," Scott said. "Make sure WorldCares gets mentioned along with CARE and MSF and the big boys. Publicity means donations. So if you have any questions about what we're doing over here, keep them to yourself."

Gwen had come to Dadaab imagining herself hand-feeding starving kids, handing out bowls of soup to grateful villagers. She saw now that she hadn't had a clue how refugee camps operated. Only the most recent arrivals were hungry. A massive operation existed precisely to keep the refugees from starving. In that narrow sense, the camps worked. The Somalis who lived here ate better than their countrymen across the border — or the Kenyan villagers who lived nearby. Many refugees sold portions of their food rations in local markets.

At the same time, the refugees were stuck in legal limbo. Kenyans didn't want Somalis any more than most Americans wanted Mexican immigrants. As far as the Kenyan government was concerned, the camps were too large and had been open too long. So Kenya didn't allow the refugees to own land or work legally. They weren't even supposed to leave the camps, although as a practical matter the Kenyan police couldn't stop them. Most of all, the government didn't want the refugees organizing for political rights or citizenship.

So the refugees couldn't work or farm. They were warehoused in relative safety, and they would never starve. But they were basically prisoners. Like prisoners, they spent much of their time chasing freebies. Their requests ranged from the petty — *My ration of cooking oil was short last week* — to the heartbreaking — *My brother disappeared at the border two months ago. Can you help me find him?* If you weren't a doctor, opportunities for genuine heroism were few and far between at Dadaab.

Recently, Gwen had been spending her time with kids. The average Somali woman had six children, and the camps didn't have nearly enough schools to accommodate them. The girls stayed close by their mothers. The boys played with raggedy soccer balls and pretended to shoot one another. WorldCares had boxes of donated children's books stored in the back of its warehouse. They'd arrived a few months before, but no one knew what to do with them. The kids couldn't speak English, much less read it. The boxes sat untouched as the food deliveries came and went. Just thinking about them depressed Gwen, made her think of all the books she hadn't read.

About a month before, she had gone into the warehouse and grabbed the first book she found, a copy of *Where the Wild Things Are.* She took the choice as a sign. All the books she could have picked, and she'd come up with one she remembered. She took it to the front gate and stood outside reading until a boy wandered over to listen to her. Since then she'd come out every day, picking a different book each time. Some days only a couple kids showed up. Some days, twenty or so. Only one, a tiny boy named Joseph who had the whitest teeth

Gwen had ever seen, understood more than a few words of English. He had taken upon himself the role of translator. Gwen figured he was adding his own commentary, because he often had the kids laughing at stuff that wasn't supposed to be funny.

"How about you?" Owen said, back in the canteen. "Any big plans today?"

"Joseph gonna be helping you with your reading again?" Scott said. "He told me last week that you got through *The Cat in the Hat* all on your own."

Gwen didn't bother answering. Scott had come by her trailer two nights before for a quick-and-dirty. She hadn't been in the mood. Since then he'd been snippy. Guys like him hated being told no.

"Such a dick," Owen said. "By the way, happy birthday." He reached into the messenger bag he always carried, handed Gwen an oversize envelope.

"Seriously?" Scott said. "Please don't tell me you've been carrying that for three months to give to her. That's weird, man."

Bringing a card for her all the way from the United States did verge on weird. But Gwen wasn't giving Scott the pleasure of hearing her say so. "It's called being thoughtful," she said. She wrapped an arm around Owen's shoulders, kissed his cheek. She was surprised to feel the muscles in his upper back. Three months unloading trucks had toughened him up.

"Of course he remembered," Scott said. "You've been talking about it for weeks. I wanted to pretend that we'd forgotten just to see what would happen, but your hero here wouldn't dream of it. Bet he's got a poem for you in there. 'The White Rose of Kenya.' *She walks through the camps like a stripe on a skunk. With every step, she makes refugee hearts leap. Too bad it's their stomachs that are the problem.*"

Despite herself, Gwen laughed.

"Or would it be a limerick? *There once was a girl in Dadaab. Whose mouth I want on my —*"

"That doesn't rhyme."

" 'Knob' doesn't rhyme?"

" 'Knob' is a really gross word in that context."

"Corncob. Baby, Owen will make it rhyme. He'll make sweet love to you Dadaab-style. Pour surplus cooking oil all over your body and lick it off." Scott going on like Owen wasn't even there. Managing to mock Owen and Gwen and their work all at once.

"Such a dick." But even she could hear

the flirty undertone in her voice. Scott was arrogant and cruel. But he was also hilarious, sometimes even at his own expense. Whereas Owen just stared at her with those deep brown eyes. *I love you,* the stare said. *I'll be good to you forever if only you'll love me back.* Why didn't men understand that unrequited love was a bore? She was half afraid to open his card.

Owen walked out, not quite slamming the door.

"Poor baby," Scott said. "I think I hurt his feelings."

"Sooner or later, he's going to kill you in your sleep. And half the girls in Missoula will cheer. What are you doing today?"

"Talking to my uncle, and then I think Suggs and me are going for a drive."

Suggs was a Kenyan who worked as a fixer for WorldCares, part of the cost of doing business for Western aid agencies and journalists in Kenya. If a food convoy ran into a roadblock, fixers negotiated the "toll" to free it. If the police claimed that WorldCares needed a permit for an electrical generator, fixers found out whether they wanted a bribe, were enforcing a real law that no one knew about, or both. If a refugee showed up at the compound claiming to be a tribal leader, fixers found out how important he was. WorldCares had three fixers. But Suggs was the best. He handled the trickiest jobs. He had a big belly and what seemed like an endless supply of brightly colored polo shirts. Kenya's version of Tony Soprano.

"A drive?"

"To Witu. See what's happening over there."

Witu was a satellite camp that had sprung up about fifteen miles from Hagadera. Its growth had taken the Kenyan government and the aid agencies by surprise. Thousands of refugees now lived there. Gwen had never seen it, but from what she had heard, the place was a mess, run by Somali gangs.

"I thought we didn't deliver there."

"We don't. The guys who do, you know how they do it? The drivers don't even turn off their trucks. They park at the edge of the road and the guards toss food off the back. Like they're feeding sharks or something."

The fact that aid workers could be attacked by the people they were trying to help was something else Gwen hadn't realized back in Montana. "So why go?"

"I wanted to check it out myself. Anyway, we'll be ready." Ready being code for armed.

"Any excuse to carry a gun like a real man." Agencies like WorldCares hired armed guards to protect their trucks, but aid workers weren't supposed to have weapons.

"Actually I'm hoping they capture me, rough me up. Work me over, you know what I'm saying? It's not gay if you're a hostage."

"All you frat boys are a little bit gay. Why you hate women so much."

"Use and hate aren't the same, beautiful. Happy birthday. I don't have a card for you, but I can give you a present when I get back. You'll have to unwrap it yourself."

"Such a charmer."

Scott gave her his usual toothy pleased-with-himself grin and walked out.

She spent the morning emailing everyone who had sent her birthday greetings. It was noon when she walked out of the WorldCares compound. "Going to read," she said to Harry, one of the gate guards. The guards hung out in a wooden shed with a screened window and a rough painted sign that said "STOP HERE!!" They looked friendly enough in their white short-sleeved shirts, but Gwen knew they had rifles tucked under a blanket.

"Yes, Miss Murphy." She couldn't get him to call her Gwen no matter how often she asked.

She crossed the dirt road separating the compound from the camp. The refugee families had lit fires for their midday meal, and a sour diesel odor lay over the tents. Firewood was hard to find around Dadaab, so most refugees used scraps of trash wood soaked in diesel. During her first weeks at the compound, Gwen's throat had been scratchy and sore. Now, for better or worse, her body seemed to have accepted the smoke.

Moss had warned her against going alone into the camp. So she read beneath an acacia tree just a few feet from the road, its knobby roots running almost to the edge of the first row of tents.

Only a couple boys were waiting for her. Joseph wasn't among them. Gwen wished he would show more regularly, but she couldn't make him. She didn't even know who his parents were, much less where they lived. He seemed to understand that she had no real authority. Gwen had no way to test him, but he was clearly smart. Besides his command of English, he was a natural ringleader. The other boys looked to him for guidance. In the United States he'd be in a gifted program. Here he had Gwen reading him children's books.

Growing up, Gwen had never had to share

a bedroom. Her parents had given her a Nissan Pathfinder on the day she passed her driving test. Used, but still. She knew she was lucky, that she had a head start over the kids who lived in the trailer parks north of 90 and worked night jobs to help their families pay the rent. But even those kids had winter clothes and three meals a day. Unless they got pregnant and dropped out, they were guaranteed twelve years of school, a chance at college. Everybody back home had at least a chance to live a better life.

Now she saw with her own eyes that millions of people, some crazy number, had no shot at all. She didn't have a head start over Joseph. They weren't playing the same game. He would never be anything but a refugee. He'd be lucky to learn to read. Doubly lucky if Somalia ever calmed enough for his parents to take him back to the village where he'd been born. More likely he would remain on the streets of this camp until he joined a gang and disappeared. Gwen wondered if she wasn't being mean to him and the other boys by showing them books about the United States when they would never have a chance to go.

Today she had brought a thick comic book that she'd pulled at random from the warehouse. It was called *Maus* and looked like it was about cats and mice. As she reached the tree, more shoeless, stick-legged kids came running over, chattering at her. Her regulars. Even after a month of reading, she couldn't keep them all straight, though she knew that the littlest one called himself Guster, and the tallest Nene.

"I brought a good one today," she said. "Lots of animals." She sat against the tree, folded her long legs underneath her. She loved this moment, the feel of the rough trunk against her back, a book in her hand. The noise of the camp faded and the kids circled up and she read. But by page three, she had a sinking realization that *Maus* wasn't about mice at all.

Not that it mattered. The kids weren't paying attention. Without Joseph to translate, they were losing focus, arguing. Guster got up and ran around the tree, yelling. She snapped the book shut. "I'm leaving unless you behave." They ignored her, and she knew the language barrier wasn't the reason. They didn't care. "You know, this is why you're never going to amount to anything."

She was joking, but she wasn't. Another lesson of the last three months. She felt terrible for these refugees. Especially the kids. Yet she felt something else too, the feeling she tried to keep down. She hated the way they lived, the dirt and smoke. The way they bred kids they couldn't support. The fact that instead of standing up for themselves, they had run away from their own country to this place, where they depended on handouts from white people to live. Would Americans have done that? Did the refugees even want to go home? Or were they content to live here, helpless as baby birds chirping for their next feeding?

Then she'd remember Joseph, and her anger would turn to shame. She'd had every chance. They'd had none. Now she judged them. She couldn't square her feelings, this anger and heartbreak jumbled up. The kids circled around her and the tree. She stood. The sun was high now. Her face flushed under her hat. The heat and the smoke dizzied her. "All of you. Enough. Enough." They kept running, spinning around her. She reached out, clenched her hand around Guster's skinny arm, pulled him close. "Listen —" She saw at once she'd grabbed him too hard. He yelped and looked up at her with such hatred that she felt an almost electric shock tear through her. She let go and he tore off into the mess of tents and disappeared as the other kids shouted at her.

She spent the afternoon in her trailer. She

plowed through *Maus* start to finish and then tried to distract herself with *Cosmo* and *Elle* and *Yoga Journal.* She had the magazines stuffed in her backpack like a twelve-year-old's porn stash. She shouldn't have lost her temper. She should have let the kids run themselves out and then gone back to her stupid reading. She just wanted to help and she didn't know how. She couldn't deliver a baby or dig a well. She couldn't even unload the trucks. A forty-pound bag would knock her over.

Where was Hailey, anyway? Her best friend had deserted her. On her birthday. She lay on her cot, buried her face in her pillow until she heard footsteps enter the trailer.

"Gwennie? Happy birthday."

"I have a headache."

"No, you don't." Hailey tugged at her legs. She had no choice but to sit up. She fake-swiped at Hailey's face and Hailey responded with a long hiss. In the bars in Missoula, they made a striking pair. Hailey's dad was black, her mom white. She was tall and light-skinned, with big brown eyes. Guys liked her. Lots of guys. Hence Hailey the Heartbreaker.

"Where have you been?"

"Taking care of cholera patients. Which

basically spells cleaning bedpans. I told you I'd be at the hospital today." She held a canvas bag.

"You did?" Gwen felt stupider than ever.

"Come on, tell Dr. Hailey."

"I can't even." But she did.

"So you grabbed his arm," Hailey said when she was finished. "Trust me, that kid's been through worse."

"It's not that. Do you know what this is?" She held up *Maus*.

Hailey flipped through it. "The Holocaust, right? The mice are the Jews and the cats are the Germans."

"How do you know that?"

"I don't know, some world history class I took freshman year, maybe."

"Well, I didn't."

"Gwen. I don't know how to say this straight out without sounding condescending, but you are not dumb. You just never bothered to study."

"It's the same."

"It's not. If you were dumb, you wouldn't be upset about any of this."

"This place —"

"Look, we're not the Army or anything, we're not even getting paid. We're volunteers, we're doing our best. If nothing else, we're witnesses."

"Witnesses to what? I can't even get anyone back home to understand what's going on here. They send these dumb emails like *God's work, keep it up,* and that's all they want to know."

Hailey unzipped her bag. "Time to put the pity party to bed. Guess what I have in here."

"Hailey, I'm serious —"

"You want your birthday present or not?" Hailey reached into the bag and pulled out a bottle of Patrón and a jar of margarita mix. "Do not ask what I had to do to get these."

"Tequila?"

"Come on. Let's drink our sorrows away. Just like real aid workers. And if Owen or Scott stop by, I'm telling them to get lost."

It was a fun night. The next morning, Gwen's head was screaming, but even so she felt better. She came into the canteen, choked down a glass of water. Owen and Scott sat at the center table spooning down oatmeal, a replay of the day before. Neither looked glad to see her. She liked that.

"So Scott wants us to take a run to Lamu," Owen said.

Moss had told Gwen about Lamu. She made the place sound like paradise. It was an island a few miles off the Kenyan coast, on the Indian Ocean. Turquoise-blue water and an old port. But the Somali border was only about fifty miles away, and not long before, bandits had attacked a resort close by. They'd killed an English tourist and dragged his wife back to Somalia, where she'd died in captivity. Since then, most Westerners had stayed away. "Isn't it too dangerous?"

"You said that yesterday when I told you I was going to Witu."

"Just because you didn't get killed doesn't mean it was smart."

"Suggs says we'll be fine. We drive to Garissa and then southeast so we don't get too close to the border. Get to Mokowe in two or three hours, that's on the coast, and from there it's about a twenty-minute speedboat ride."

Gwen wished she didn't have such a nasty headache. "What do you think, Owen?"

"It's probably okay as long as we have Suggs. Maybe we go one morning, stay a couple nights, drive back in the afternoon. I was talking to an MSF guy last week and he said it really is great. Plus all the millionaires are staying away, so if we go now we'll have the place to ourselves."

Owen's confidence was reassuring. Aside from his doomed love for her, he was a levelheaded guy.

"When?"

"Next week," Scott said. "Before the rainy season starts."

"What about the reporter? Aren't we supposed to be here to talk to her?"

"She'll be around a few days."

"I'll talk to Hailey about it." Gwen just trying to buy time now.

Scott smiled. "She's in. Said it sounded great."

Then Gwen knew that she was going, whether she felt like it or not.

The Land Cruiser had the usual supplies that African roads demanded. A full-size spare tire and a spare for the spare. A plastic jerrican of gasoline, two of water. Twenty yards of tow rope and two-by-fours to provide traction if the truck got caught in mud. A jack and a repair kit with every tool a mechanic might want.

"Looks like we're going across the continent, not on a two-night holiday," Owen said. The four stood by the Toyota, waiting for Suggs. It was just past dawn. The air for once felt crisp, the stink of diesel gone. Gwen saw why Hailey liked this hour.

"When did you start saying 'holiday'?" Scott said. "It's a vacation. Or maybe research."

"Research for what?" Hailey said.

"The book I'm writing. Still trying to pick a title. Which do you like, 'I Heart Refugees' or 'Kenya on Three Handouts a Day'?"

"Shouldn't you read a book before you try writing one?"

"I don't see why."

"You know what I love about you, Scott?"

"Nothing?"

Hailey laughed. "You think you know how ridiculous you are, but you have no idea."

Suggs walked across the compound's central courtyard toward them. He had a big man's rolling gait, short wide steps. He held a thermos and wore a bright orange polo shirt and lime-green pants. A pistol on his right hip completed the outfit.

"He planning to play eighteen at the Dadaab country club?" Scott said.

"I can never tell whether he's riffing ironically off the African-fixer look or embracing it," Owen said.

"That is a very good question."

"Ready?" Suggs said.

"As we'll ever be," Scott said.

"We'll be in Mokowe in four, maybe five hours."

"Then the boats?"

"They will be happy to see you, I promise.

Real Americans with real American money. Every Kenyan's favorite."

"I feel so loved," Owen said.

No one argued when Scott took the front passenger seat. The other three sat in back, Owen in the middle, splaying his legs for maximum thigh-to-thigh contact with Gwen. Suggs shoved his gun under the driver's seat and out the front gate they went. Gwen had a knot in her stomach, a mix of excitement and nervousness. She remembered feeling this way at her junior prom, knowing she'd be losing her virginity before the night was through. More than six years had passed since then. Amazing.

"What are you thinking about?" Hailey said.

"How glad I am to be on this trip with all of you. Even Scott."

"The Wisdom of the Barbie," Scott said.

Suggs stopped at the guardhouse to register their departure. But he seemed to hear something he didn't like from Harry. They had a short, heated conversation in Swahili. Then they rolled out to the dirt track that led around the camp to the main Dadaab road. At this hour the camp was mostly quiet. A little boy, maybe four years old, stood naked by the side of the road, peeing, his face creased in concentration on his task. Suggs stopped and yelled something. The boy looked up and grinned and waggled his penis, sending a stream of urine side to side. Suggs honked and rolled on.

"We are the worst aid workers ever," Owen said.

At the intersection of the camp track and the main road that led to Dadaab, Suggs turned right. Gwen didn't get it. She had always thought Dadaab was left.

"Aren't we going north?" Owen said. "Back to Dadaab and then west to Garissa and then make a left and head southeast."

Suggs pulled over. "The guard, he says the Kenyan police have a big roadblock up there. This way goes south past Bakafi and then west and then picks up the same road to Mokowe. No tarmac" — the Kenyans called pavement tarmac — "but I think it's safe. The bandits stay closer to the camps, between here and Garissa. To the south there's no place for them to hide. You'll be in Lamu by noon."

"We were going to stay on the main roads," Scott said. "That was the plan."

Suggs looked them over. "You think I want to be kidnapped? They kidnap you, they ransom you. You're Americans, right. They kidnap me, they —" He put a finger to his head and pulled the trigger. "Nobody going to spend so much money feeding me" — he laughed a big man's laugh, ho-ho-ho — "Suggs is telling you, this way is safe. But you decide for yourself."

"It's fine by me, if it's okay with everyone else," Scott said. "What do you think?"

"You trust this guy?" Hailey said.

"I trusted him with my life last week when we went to Witu. He's talked convoys out of roadblocks, all kinds of stuff. He's worked for WorldCares for years. Yeah, I trust him."

"Well, I believe what he says about not wanting to get kidnapped. Nobody likes a fat hostage," Hailey said. "I'm in."

"Owen?"

"Okay." Though Owen didn't sound sure to Gwen.

"Gwen?"

She wanted to say no, take me home. But she knew what would happen. They'd come back in three days and tell her what a great time they'd all had and how lame she was for missing out. Scott would be merciless. "Let's go."

"All right." Suggs put the Land Cruiser in gear and they rolled away from Dadaab down the soft red dirt road.

And the real nightmare began.

Part One

1

Dadaab

James Thompson's voice rose. Again.

"There are people who say we can't do anything about this. Americans who say that. That we should let these Africans fend for themselves, starve for themselves. That they did it to themselves by having so many kids. That we can't afford to help them. You know what I say to that?"

"Tell me," Paula Hutchens said. They were in Thompson's office at WorldCares headquarters at Dadaab. Like the rest of the compound, the room was unadorned, the furniture simple and thrifty. A poster behind Thompson showed a black girl running hand in hand with a white boy.

"I say letting kids starve is not in keeping with our principles. And I'm not afraid to tell you it's racist. If these children had white skin and not black, you think anyone would be saying, Let them die? Let me tell you, we've forgotten how lucky we are. Even worse, we've forgotten the duties, the obligations, that come with that luck."

Thompson stopped speaking. He leaned forward in his chair, stared at Hutchens like he could see through her. Hutchens had only met Thompson a few hours before, but already she was getting used to that look. The man had presence.

Thompson was in his late forties, with broad shoulders and thick lips and meaty hands. He wasn't tall, but his bulk made him formidable. He looked like a bailiff. Or a pit boss. When he got excited, he spread his hands and raised his voice. He sounded like an old-time preacher. In reality, as he'd told Hutchens, he came from a family of railroad workers. He ran WorldCares/ChildrenFirst as a secular organization, no proselytizing allowed. "We're here to feed the hungry and help the sick. We look after their bodies. Their souls are their own business, as far as I'm concerned."

Hutchens could already see that James Thompson would star in her feature on the aid groups at Dadaab. Fine by her. She was a reporter for the *Houston Chronicle.* Normally she covered the mayor, but the paper had reached into its not-so-deep pockets to send her on a ten-day reporting trip to

Kenya. Roy Hunter, the *Chronicle*'s publisher, had taken an interest in Dadaab after his daughter read a book about Somali refugees. Every few months, Hunter called the paper's editor and demanded a series on something that had caught his attention. Deep-sea fishing in the Gulf. The potential for hypersonic passenger jets. HOUSTON TO HONG KONG IN TWO HOURS? IT'S POSSIBLE!

The editor knew better than to argue with the man whose name graced his paycheck. He looked for a plausible excuse to send a reporter to Kenya, and found it in WorldCares and other Texas-based aid organizations working in Dadaab. Now Hutchens was working on a series tentatively called "Texans with Heart." It had been "Texans Who Love the World" until Hutchens pointed out that the title sounded like a bad porn movie.

She couldn't claim to know much about the issues over here, but she'd done some research on WorldCares before she'd come over. The group had grown a lot in the last few years. After meeting Thompson, she saw why.

He leaned forward now, lasered in on her with those blue eyes. "What do you think, Ms. Hutchens?" He had a slight southern accent that took the edge off his ferocity.

She hated when sources tried this tactic. Reporters didn't have much going for them anymore. Her job security and prestige had evaporated years before. But she still had the privilege of asking the questions, not answering them. "About what?"

"About this. All of it."

"I'm a reporter. My job is to tell your story. In any case, I just got here."

"With all due respect, ma'am, that's a bunch of junk. People look to you for advice. They want the newspaper to tell them what to think."

"I've never noticed that, Mr. Thompson. Though the idea does have a certain appeal."

"I'm not joking. I'm serious as a heart attack. I'm publishing a book next spring. Called 'The Children Will Lead.' I want the world to know. It's a crime to let these people suffer. And I'm not saying do everything for them, I'm not saying that at all. I'm saying work with them, build something together."

"I get it." Her digital tape recorder beeped. She decided to bring the interview to a close. For now, anyway. She had a feeling that Thompson wasn't done talking, and might never be. "I'd like to see a little bit of the camp itself today, if that's possible. You know, since I got here this morning, I've hardly seen a refugee."

"Today may not work. We don't like to send people out late in the afternoon for security reasons. But tomorrow morning, sure." Thompson settled back in his chair. "And you'll still be here when my nephew and our other interns get back, right?"

"When will that be?"

"Two days, three at most."

"I should be here, yes."

"I think they'd give you a really good perspective. The four of them just graduated college and they've been here three months working seven days a week. Finally I told Scott, that's my nephew, take a couple days off before you burn out. They went to Lamu."

"What's Lamu?"

"Island just off the coast. Amazing place. So I hear. Never been myself."

"I look forward to talking to them." She slipped her recorder into her computer case.

"Feel free to talk to anyone you might like on our staff. I've told everybody to do their best to answer your questions. Open-door policy."

"I appreciate that."

A heavy knock on Thompson's door,

which was in fact closed. Hutchens turned around to see it swing open. The guy who ran security — she couldn't remember his name, something weird — strode in. "I'm sorry to interrupt, but something important's come up." He looked at Hutchens.

"I was just leaving."

"No, please. Whatever he has to say, I don't mind you hearing."

The security officer hesitated. Then: "It's the interns. Your nephew and the others. No one's heard from them."

"What about Suggs?"

"Not him either."

"That can't be. They were going to call when they got to Mokowe."

Open-door policy or no, Thompson realized she'd just heard something she shouldn't have. "Ms. Hutchens, can you go back to your trailer for a few minutes, let us sort this out?"

Hutchens sat forgotten for the two hours, as the sun set and the compound's lights kicked on. Through her screened window, she heard hushed, urgent voices. Finally, just as she was about to head back to Thompson's office and demand to know what was happening, a heavy knock rattled her door. Thompson stepped in.

"There's really no way to keep this from you. My nephew and the others, plus the Kenyan driving them, they've disappeared. Their phones are off, they didn't check into the hotel in Lamu, their Land Cruiser didn't reach Mokowe."

"An accident?"

"Unlikely. Someone would have called us. It's possible" — he hesitated — "it's possible they've been kidnapped."

"I'm so sorry." She was, too. But the reporter in her had one thought: *Great story. And all mine.*

"I have to ask you not to write about this. Or tell your editors."

"I can't do that, sir."

"Their safety —"

"If they've been kidnapped, then every aid worker in Dadaab is at risk, every tourist in Kenya. They have a right to know." The right to know. Every reporter's most sacred cow.

"At least give us time to make sure. Try to get them back quickly and quietly."

Hutchens considered. "Look, Houston's nine hours behind, it's morning there. Tell you what, I won't do anything today. But tomorrow morning there, afternoon here, I have to call my editors and tell them." What she didn't tell him was that she planned to spend the night and morning putting together a biography of the four volunteers and Suggs. This story would be big.

"That's the best you can do."

"It's more than I should do."

"I've never understood until now why people don't like reporters."

"Sorry you feel that way." Over the years she'd had a lot of practice saying those words. They never worked, and they didn't this time. Thompson pursed his lips in disgust and turned away, slamming the door to her trailer as he went.

2

North Conway, New Hampshire

John Wells ran.

Over the river and through the woods. Wearing only a T-shirt and shorts despite the cold. His legs burning but his breath level and easy. His heart pumping twice a second and more. Tonka, his boon companion, a stride behind, matching him on four legs.

The trail curved through grizzled trees in the low mountains outside North Conway. Gray wallpaper covered the late-afternoon sky. Wells kept his head down to watch the roots and dips in the trail. He hurdled a puddle left from rain two nights before, landed clean, ignored the twinge in his left leg.

For Wells the woods offered a special sorcery, the magic of leaving himself behind. The missions, the kills, the towns and villages with names he could barely pronounce. He had lived in a world that few Americans outside the military ever saw, the North-West Frontier and the Bekaa Valley and the other red zones. Running here, he worked up an honest sweat, not the stink of tension and sleepless hours. These runs set him free from the question that had plagued him since the Arghandab: Had he acted justly? Francesca didn't bother him. Alders did.

Though in some ways the question didn't matter. The word once writ couldn't be undone, et cetera. No one else could help him answer, not Shafer, not even Anne. So Wells ran.

Back at the farmhouse he found Anne in the kitchen, squatting beside the open cabinet under the sink, which was full of dirty dishwater. Two wrenches and a penlight were laid on a rag on the floor. Wells squatted behind her, smoothed her hair away, kissed her neck.

"What seems to be the problem, Officer?"

She was a cop in the North Conway Police Department, though she was thinking about joining the state police, which investigated many murders and major crimes in New Hampshire. She and Wells had been together almost three years. In the last few months, she'd stopped asking if he thought they should marry. Maybe she thought he risked his life too casually to commit to a marriage, much less a family. Maybe she had her own reasons for taking marriage off the table. He couldn't bring himself to ask. He was happy to be with her this way for as long as she would let him.

She was past thirty now, and the New Hampshire winters had given her hints of crow's-feet and wrinkles that city girls didn't get until their forties. But her jeans and sweaters hid a supple body and strong legs. Wells loved watching her walk. At the moment, though, she wasn't happy to see him.

"Why don't you go take a shower and let me fix this."

"I can help."

"Like you know anything about plumbing. If I weren't here, you'd have done what you always do. Tossed in a bottle of Drano, and if that didn't work, bought the really strong stuff, and if that didn't work, called the plumber. It's bad for the pipes."

"I'm feeling very emasculated." Though Wells had to admit that aside from chopping wood, he wasn't particularly handy around the house. His survival skills were more primal.

"Where'd you and Tonka go?"

"The usual."

She turned around, nuzzled against his neck. "You smell good. Like the woods. Tell you what. If I can fix this quick enough, maybe I'll join you in the shower."

"Give me a chance to regain my manhood."

"Something like that."

She didn't join him. While he was soaping up, he heard the phone. He showered quickly and then brought up logs for a fire in their bedroom. She found him just as he kindled it. "Trying to prove you're not completely useless around the house?"

"That obvious?"

"Yes. As a matter of fact. Evan called."

"Evan my son?"

"Is there another Evan? Said it was important."

That's impossible, Wells almost said. Just before his last mission, he had visited Evan in Montana. He hadn't seen his son in more than a decade and wanted to reconnect, explain his absence. Evan had smashed that hope in the time they needed to finish a cup of coffee. He'd made clear that he hated the CIA and viewed Wells as a professional vigilante at best, a war criminal at worst.

Wells had left Montana figuring that they wouldn't talk again for many years. If ever.

Wells couldn't imagine Evan had woken up today and had a change of heart. He had no idea what his son might want. Not money. His stepfather was a doctor and they lived well.

"Maybe somebody's pregnant and he doesn't want to tell his parents," Anne said.

"I don't see him coming to me for that. I don't see him coming to me for anything."

She handed him her phone.

Despite everything, he knew Evan's number by heart.

"Hello?"

"It's John." "John" seemed safer than "your dad."

"Thanks for calling me back so fast."

"Everything okay?"

"How are you, Dad?"

The falsity of the last word churned Wells's stomach.

"Let's talk about why you called."

But Evan didn't seem to know what to say next.

"Something wrong with Heather?" Wells finally said. Wells's ex-wife, Evan's mom.

"You know on the news, those aid workers, the ones kidnapped in Kenya?"

"Sure." The story had taken over the media in the last seventy-two hours. Four American volunteers taken hostage. Dragged into the heart of darkness, most likely by Somali bandits. The cable networks couldn't get enough of it. The fact that the two women were so photogenic didn't hurt. If you were going to get kidnapped, being pretty was the way to go. Plus they were all friends, recent graduates of the University of Montana —

Wells realized why Evan had called. "You knew them?"

"One of them, mainly. Gwen Murphy. I'm friends with her sister. Catelyn."

"Friends."

"Good friends."

Words that could mean anything. Wells didn't push.

"Catelyn's freaking out," Evan said.

"I can call some people down at Langley, ask them to watch it. They probably already are." Wells had resigned from the CIA years before, but he'd stayed entangled with the agency. As a rule, the CIA avoided involvement in overseas kidnappings unless the victims were government employees or the crime had clear political or terrorist overtones. But given the media attention that this case had received, Wells imagined the agency was working its contacts inside the Kenyan security services.

"Dad — John — it's been five days and Gwen's family is going crazy. Nobody has a clue. Nobody's seen them, nobody's sent any ransom stuff. Brandon, that's her dad, he's talking about getting on a plane, going over there. Even though everybody says that wouldn't help."

"It wouldn't." It would add to the circus. The grieving father, wandering through the camps, passing out pictures as camera crews tagged along. Have you seen this woman? The irony that many people at Dadaab had lost their own children would be lost to the viewers, though not the refugees themselves.

"I told Catelyn about you and she got really excited. She thought — she thought maybe you could look into it yourself."

The words gave more away than Evan had intended, implying that he'd never mentioned Wells to the girl before now. Wells tried to pretend that didn't bother him. In a way neither of them could have anticipated, Evan had suddenly seen the value in his father's skill set. Wells found himself both flattered and angry. "Kidnappings are tricky, Evan. I'm not an expert in them. Or Africa. I'm sure the Murphys are talking to people who are."

"They can pay. They have money."

"It's not about that."

"Please, Dad. Please."

With those three words, Wells had no choice. Evan was using him. So? Parents existed to be used by their children. "Look. I'll talk to the family, the Murphys, and if they want me involved, I'll do what I can."

"I promise, they want you. They know who you are. I reminded them about the Times Square thing."

Several years before, Wells had stopped a terrorist attack on Times Square and briefly become a national hero. But his recent missions had stayed secret, and memories were short. "They remembered that?"

"Wikipedia. Anyway. I'll tell Mr. Murphy to call you. Thanks, Dad."

"Glad to be of service." Wells wasn't sure whether he was being sarcastic.

"So?" Anne said. Wells explained. She took his right hand between hers, squeezed his palm and traced its lines, half masseuse and half fortune-teller. "Had to have been a hard call for him."

"It didn't sound hard."

"He's a smart kid. He knows what he did. You're in his life again, whether he likes it or not."

"Maybe. Or maybe he's hoping to get laid. Not that I blame him. If his friend Catelyn looks anything like her sister."

"Please don't tell me you're going to turn into a dirty old man."

The ringing phone saved him from answering.

"Mr. Wells? This is Brandon Murphy. Thank you, thank you, for agreeing to do this." Murphy sounded fevered. Wells wondered if he'd slept since he'd found out his daughter had been taken.

"Tell me what you know."

Murphy explained that James Thompson, the head of WorldCares, had called four days before — late evening in Montana, morning in Kenya. Thompson said the four volunteers, along with a Kenyan employee named Suggs, had gone missing the previous day.

"From what I've read, they were headed for Lamu Island, is that right?"

"It was a few days off." Murphy sounded defensive. The sleazier cable hosts liked mentioning that the volunteers had been on their way to a vacation. An ultra-luxury resort island off the Kenyan coast, Nancy Grace said. Just the four of them, *relaxing.* She made *relaxing* sound like code for *having an orgy.*

"And Gwen told you in advance about the trip."

"She was nervous because of those kidnappings a while back, but Hailey —"

"Hailey Barnes —"

"Yes. Hailey thought it would be fine. And that's her best friend. Gwen, she's a beautiful girl and she's not dumb, but she's not a leader, you understand. Basically she operates on instinct, listens to the people around her."

"I understand."

"Scott, that's James Thompson's nephew, he pushed, too. The trip was his idea."

"And were Scott and Gwen boyfriend and girlfriend?" Nancy Grace had hinted as much.

"You know, kids that age, they don't necessarily use those words."

"But they had a relationship."

"Yes. So back to your initial question, we knew she was going. She emailed on the morning they were leaving. She did that most days to let us know she was okay. Morning for her, the night before for us."

"Her message that morning was routine."

"Yes. And we asked her to email us when she got to Lamu, which would have been overnight for us. But when I woke up the next morning and checked my Gmail I didn't see anything. I figured, okay, she'll send something soon. Or maybe Lamu doesn't have good Internet. I checked during the day and I didn't hear anything. I was getting nervous." Murphy paused, breathed deep. "Then, afternoon in Missoula, early in the morning over there, Thompson called. He said he didn't want to worry me but no one at WorldCares had heard from any of them since the previous morning. Including the driver, this man Suggs. He asked if Gwen had checked in with us."

"Did he say he thought they'd been kidnapped?"

"Not at first. He said his security officer had checked with the hospitals and the police and the Interior Ministry and hadn't heard anything, but they'd check again in the morning when the offices opened. That maybe the police detained them for some reason. I brought up kidnapping. Me. Not him. Like he didn't want to mention the word. He said yes, that's also possible. I got angry, told him he was supposed to be keeping my daughter safe. He said he understood how I felt, that his nephew was with her and that he hoped they'd all be back safely very soon."

"Then what happened?"

"We couldn't sleep, of course. I emailed all her friends here, asked anyone if maybe she'd emailed them, but she hadn't. And we called Hailey, Owen, their parents, and they hadn't heard anything either. Then, a couple hours later, James Thompson called back, said that they'd double-checked with the police and that we had to assume the worst. His exact words. We must assume the worst, he said. I'll never forget that. Because the most irrelevant thing went through my mind. Assuming makes an ass out of you and me. That's what I thought at that moment. I'm a fool." Brandon Murphy fell silent. Wells waited. There was nothing to say. Finally, Murphy spoke again. "The next news we got was maybe twelve hours later."

"So this is close to two days after she left the camp for Lamu —"

"Yes. So much time wasted, and I don't understand. Anyway, Thompson called back, said the Kenyan police found their SUV on a dirt road about a hundred miles south of Dadaab. That they were gone and that the police assumed they'd been taken over the border. To Somalia."

"Did he say anything about damage to it, the SUV?" Damage, as in bullet holes or bloodstains.

"No, and I didn't ask. I guess I should

have. I did ask whether the police had found evidence that anyone had been hurt. He said no."

"That's good."

"And then the media got wind, and since then, the last three days have been crazy. The police are helping us, they moved the TV trucks off our block, but if we leave, it's like sharks."

"My son said you haven't received a ransom demand."

"No." A single word that carried a world of despair.

"And you've been in touch with Thompson since he told you about the SUV."

"At least twice a day. But he says it might be weeks before anybody makes a demand. Even months. He says that doesn't mean anything except that they may be moving the hostages to somewhere they consider more secure."

"More secure" no doubt translated into "deeper in Somalia," but Wells saw no reason to say so. "You spoken to anyone besides Thompson? Either in the U.S. government or the Kenyan?"

"A woman at the embassy named Kathy Balfour. Not sure of her title, but I could find it for you. She said they were pressing the Kenyan police. She put me in touch with an officer in Nairobi, a colonel. Russell Mesuru's his name. He told me the case is their highest priority."

"What about the FBI or the agency?"

"I've been talking to an FBI agent, Martina Forbes — she's in Washington. She said they work with the CIA and their first step is they try to trace cell phones and computers, that kind of thing. They're already working that angle but they've gotten nothing so far. The next step is probably a ransom demand, she said, but they prefer to let the host country take the lead unless they have no choice."

An answer more forthcoming than Wells expected. And the FBI had been surprisingly aggressive considering that the aid workers had disappeared only five days before. The publicity was having an effect.

"But I have a strong impression that the Kenyan police don't have much chance of finding her even if she's still in Kenya. And no chance if she's in Somalia. Do you think I should go over there?"

Murphy was probably right about the skills of the Kenyan police, though Wells didn't want to upset him further. "Not right now. It might attract even more attention, make matters worse. Have you talked to anybody who specializes in these situations?"

"A place called Kroll. In New York. They told us they manage negotiations and payments, not rescues, that until we got a ransom demand it didn't make sense to involve them. I'll spend everything we have to get Gwen back, but since they said they cost like ten thousand dollars a day, I figured I'd hold off for now. More money for ransom, if it comes to that."

"But WorldCares must have kidnapping insurance."

"The way Thompson explained it to me, it covers volunteers as long as they're in the camps or working on assignments. Like an aid convoy. Not on vacation. And since everyone in the world knows they were headed to Lamu —"

Murphy broke off. Someone must have told him that Somali kidnappers often asked for ransom payments of millions of dollars. Without insurance, the family might lose everything.

"So you think I can be helpful," Wells said.

"Your son says you're the best at this."

"East Africa is not my area of expertise."

"Mr. Wells, my wife hasn't slept in four days. I mean, not one minute. She blames herself, she blames me, she blames everybody. All night last night she paced around the bedroom counting her steps. She got to twelve thousand and then told me she wanted to jump out the window. I would have called an ambulance but I know it just would have made the reporters even crazier. You want me to beg you, I will. You want me to pay, name your price."

"You don't have to beg. Or pay. Just email me a note saying that I'm your representative over there and you authorize me to find your daughter."

"Of course. And I'll tell Jim Thompson you're coming."

"No." Wells wanted to meet the head of WorldCares on his own terms.

"All right." Though Murphy sounded uncertain. "When do you think you might go?"

"Tonight, if I can find the flights."

"Mr. Wells. Thank you, thank you."

"I'll do my best. I can't promise a miracle. She might be dead already, you understand?"

Murphy wasn't listening. "God bless you." As if Wells had already saved his daughter.

Wells hung up, called Ellis Shafer, his old boss at the CIA.

"John. Word travels fast."

"What?"

"That's not why you're calling?"

Wells waited. He knew from experience that silence was the only way out of these conversational cul-de-sacs with Shafer.

"The big man is out. At the end of the year. I speak of the capo di tutti capi. The one we call Vincenzo."

Shafer was being cute because this was an open line and because he liked being cute. Vincenzo was Vinny Duto, the CIA's director. Wells didn't like Duto, but part of him would be sorry to see the man go. The informal arrangement between Wells and the agency might not survive a new regime.

"What's he doing?"

"Eight ball says running for the Senate. You were right, John. He's looking at the big one and he needs some real-life political experience."

"Does he even have a party? Or a state?"

"Democrat of Pennsylvania. I know he appears to have arrived on this planet a full-grown sociopath, but he was in fact born in Philly."

"Democrats aren't going to vote for him. He was neck-deep in rendition and all the rest." As Wells and Shafer knew personally.

"He can't run as a Republican. Too liberal on the social stuff. Guess he figures aside from the ACLU types Democrats don't care about rendition any more than Republicans. He's right, too. He's got a shot."

"Let's see how he does the first time somebody asks him a question he doesn't like." Duto was not exactly warm and fuzzy. Over the years, he had learned to check his temper. Still, he was a man used to giving orders and having them obeyed, and that attitude was hard to hide.

"Don't be surprised if he calls to say bye. I think he's getting sentimental. He's got me on the calendar for a valedictory lunch. I'm not sure if I'm the main course or just an appetizer. So what's up?"

Wells explained, not mentioning Evan.

"I've only been following it on TV, but I'll see what we have and call back."

Wells spent the next half hour arranging travel. Nairobi was more than seven thousand miles away, and no nonstops ran between the United States and Kenya, not even from New York. It was already past six p.m. He would have to catch an overnight from Logan to Heathrow. Then he'd be stuck in London several hours until he connected on a night flight to Nairobi. With the time difference, he'd arrive the morning after next. A lot of lost time, but he couldn't do better without a private jet, and even that would save only a few hours.

Wells booked the tickets under his own name. No reason to be tricky. His diplomatic passport would let him carry a pistol and ammunition and, maybe most important of all, a wad of cash big enough to get out of trouble. Or into it, if necessary.

With the flights arranged, Wells grabbed his backpack, sending Tonka into hiding. The dog knew what the pack meant. Wells kept his pistol and cash and other unmentionables in a locked trunk in the bedroom closet. He took fifty thousand dollars, the Makarov two passports, and a satellite phone. He hesitated for a moment and then grabbed a handful of other goodies that might be tough to come by in Kenya. Finally, the vintage Ray-Bans that Anne had given him before his last mission. He kept them locked up so he wouldn't lose them. They were lucky.

Anne had disappeared into the spare bedroom while he packed. She came back with copies of the email from Brandon Murphy designating Wells as his representative, plus a pile of stories and blog posts about the kidnapping and the world of the camps at Dadaab. "Background."

Wells kissed her.

His cell trilled. Shafer. "Tell me."

"None other. So I have to tell you this one is tough. On a bunch of levels. As far as we can tell, no single group over there runs these kidnappings. The goal is to grab people, get them onto Somali soil, so the Kenyans can't get them very easily. After that, as long as you can keep paying your guards, you can hold them basically forever. Somalia has no real central government, no police, no legal authority to step in. Sometimes, these boats that get taken in the Gulf of Aden, the shipowners pay to get their vessels back but not the sailors themselves. So the sailors are held for years, until either the kidnappers take pity on them and let them go, or else they cut their throats."

"We don't interfere."

"You know that since 1993, Black Hawk Down, we prefer to pretend Somalia doesn't exist. We'll hit anyone linked to AQ with drones when we get a chance, and we know some groups involved in piracy, because we can identify vessels and the ports they operate from. But the west side of the country, the Kenyan side, it's just gangs, mostly. We don't have much. The Kenyan police have given us a few names, but no photos or locations or anything real. Frankly, we don't pay much attention, because mainly it's Somali-on-Somali violence. No ships, so no shipping companies complaining."

"No white people."

"You said it, not me."

"You have any good news, Ellis?"

"I have one piece of advice. Think about playing up the Arab thing. Kenya and Somalia are close to the Arabian Peninsula. There are businessmen there from Dubai and Lebanon. Stick to Arabic when you can, wear the right clothes, you'll stand out less."

"Makes sense."

"And I'll put in a word for you with the COS" — chief of station — "in Nairobi. Name's Tania Roddrick. For all the good it'll do."

"Know much about her?"

"She's young, only been there three years. Speaks Swahili. Ambitious. African-American. On the surface she has a good relationship with the Kenyan government, but I don't know how deep it goes." What Shafer really meant was *Be careful of her,* but neither man needed the words spoken out loud.

"Anything else?"

"Just my gut, but I'm not sure the Kenyans are that interested in solving this. Kenya's thoroughly sick of those camps. A few dead volunteers might be what they need to close them."

"Wonderful world."

"Indeed. John. Mind if I ask why you're sticking your nose in this? Besides boredom and a vague desire to do good."

"Evan." Wells explained the call. Shafer already knew the backstory.

"Good enough, then."

"For once nothing sarcastic."

"He's your son. I get it. Anything I can do, call me."

"Thanks, Ellis."

"I'll drive you to Logan," Anne said.

"You don't need to do that."

"I'll drive you."

At the front door, Tonka blocked him. "I'll be back soon. I promise." But the dog wouldn't move, and after a minute of negotiating and scratching behind the ears, Wells had to drag him aside. Wells tossed his pack into the back of his Subaru WRX and settled into the passenger seat, letting Anne drive. The flight was leaving in four hours, and even with his fancy passport and first-class seat he didn't have much time. The shortest route was nearly straight south on 16, but both he and Anne preferred to dogleg southwest to 93 and make up the extra miles with speed. Like him, she had a heavy right foot.

She drove expertly, singing the WRX along the tight curves of the White Mountain Highway. They kept a companionable silence until the interstate. Then she reached over, squeezed his arm. "What are you thinking about?"

"The hostages. How terrifying this has to be. I'll take a firefight any day. This, you try to negotiate, to explain yourself, establish a rapport. None of it matters. Sooner or later they'll punish you just to prove they can."

"Kurland."

The name carried Wells to an underground cell in Saudi Arabia. He hated thinking about Ambassador Kurland. Sometimes he wondered if life was anything more than the accumulation of regrets. "Kurland, yes. But I think it must be even worse for women. The fear of rape."

"Any man tries that with me, I'm gonna make him pay. Even if it gets me killed."

Anne still didn't see what this kind of captivity meant. What if ten men and not one are holding you? What if they tie your legs apart, make sure everybody gets a turn? "That's a happy thought," Wells said.

They were coming up fast on an SUV, a big Ford that didn't belong in the passing lane. Anne didn't bother to slow down or hit it with her brights, just slid by at ninety.

"You wish you were coming?" Wells said.

"Yes and no. Mainly I keep thinking about that Makarov of yours. How it's a lousy pistol and the magazine is too small and it almost got you killed last year. You need to lose it, get something better. But you have this idiotic attachment to it. This sentimental streak I see in you sometimes. I saw you stuff your Ray-Bans in the pack."

"*You* gave those to me."

"I'm glad you like them. But they're just glasses. And the Makarov's just a pistol and you need a better one."

"You get in these spots, it's not a video game. You're in close, and whoever shoots first wins. As long as your gun doesn't jam, and believe me, that thing never jams. Muzzle velocity, caliber, that stuff doesn't matter. It's for basement soldiers. Guys playing Battlefield 3."

"You're telling me extra rounds wouldn't have come in handy last year. Or more stopping power. I don't mean an assault rifle. I'm talking about a better pistol."

She was right, he knew. "I'll think about it."

"When you get back, that might be your Christmas present. If I'm allowed to call it that."

Wells, who was one-quarter Muslim by

birth, had taken Islam as his faith on his first mission for the agency, when he'd gone undercover in Afghanistan to infiltrate al-Qaeda. Over the years, his attachment to the religion had waxed and waned. His relationship with Anne fell outside its bounds. She wasn't Muslim and they weren't married. But his faith had returned in other ways in the last few months. He was praying every day, avoiding pork and alcohol. He'd even signed up to audit a class on Islam at Dartmouth, his alma mater, a way to learn more about the religion's cultural and theological foundations.

"My stocking will be heavy with a Glock."

"If you're lucky."

"You're my Christmas present. Every day of the year."

"Listen to you. Getting soppy."

"The way to a man's heart is through his trigger finger." He rested a hand on her thigh.

The evening rush was done when they hit Boston, and Anne pulled up to the curb at Logan two hours before his flight. "Be careful over there. And come home quick."

"I will. I love you."

She pointed at her eyes, touched her

heart, pointed at him. "Now go."

He went.

3

Near the Kenya/Somalia border

Even with the hood blinding her, Gwen knew the others were close. The heavy black sack allowed only flecks of light, and Gwen wasn't even sure if those were real or her imagination. But she heard Hailey humming tunelessly, Owen clearing his throat. More than anything, she wanted to see them. At least talk to them. But she'd learned her lesson.

Five days before, a few hours after they'd been brought here, wherever *here* was, a man warned them not to talk. She'd been hooded then, too. The drawstring was pulled tight around her neck, chafing, a constant wordless warning. She was in a hut, she knew that much, and her right hand was handcuffed to a chain that seemed to be attached behind her. They were left alone for a while, and then a man walked into the hut with heavy flat steps. Gwen thought he was a big man. Like Suggs.

"Nod if you can hear me," the man said. The words seemed silly. Of course they could hear him. But Gwen nodded.

"Good. You don't speak unless spoken to." He had a soft British lilt, like lots of Kenyans. Gwen had always liked British accents. No more. "If you need the toilet, say toilet. Elsewise, you stay silent. Stay silent and we'll take off your hoods. If not, they stay on. And I promise, they don't get easier. We're going to take care of you. Not hurt you. Do what we say and everything will be fine."

He walked out with those heavy jailer's steps. Gwen listened to him go like she could see with her ears. Then nothing. Someone murmured in a language she didn't know. So much she didn't know about this place. She wasn't even sure whether night had fallen. The hut was hot and stifling, and the hood made judging the passage of time nearly impossible. She was exhausted but couldn't sleep. A while later, she closed her eyes. She imagined Thanksgiving with her family, sitting in her aunt's dining room, the house warm and bright. Outside, her cousins ran around playing football, tackling each other too hard. When she was thirteen, her uncle Conor nearly sliced off his thumb cutting the turkey. He'd been working hard, straining at the big leg joint, and the knife slipped away and cut into the webbing of his palm. He raised his eyebrows and grinned as the blood pulsed out. Gwen had been just old enough to notice that he'd topped off his scotch glass all afternoon. Her dad tied a dish towel around Conor's hand to stop the bleeding and drove him to the St. Patrick emergency room downtown.

The kicker came the next year, when Conor brought out a new toy, a power carving saw. Her dad couldn't lay off. *You want to chop off your whole hand? Slow-cook it, serve it with the yams?* Conor waved the saw like a baton and muttered about know-it-all doctors until her dad retreated to the living room to watch the Lions. *Is he really going to cut off his hand?* Gwen asked. *Only if we're lucky,* her dad answered.

But now she wished she hadn't thought about her family. Soon they'd hear about what had happened. She knew how desperate they'd feel. Three years before, her sister Catelyn had swerved for a deer on US 93, wrapped her RAV4 around a tree. She was put into a medically induced coma to relieve the swelling in her brain.

Gwen refused to leave Catelyn's bedside for forty-eight hours, until her dad told her if she didn't take a nap he would ask the docs to sedate her. All along she bargained silently with God — *Let Catelyn live and I'll go to church every week / never speed again / stop fighting with my mom / be a better sister.* She couldn't help herself, though she was certain that God didn't make deals like that. And of course she hadn't kept her promises, even though Catelyn came out of the coma four days after the accident and recovered completely.

Until now those days had been the worst of Gwen's life. Her parents probably felt the same. But at least they had known Catelyn was being cared for and wasn't in pain. This time, they wouldn't have those certainties. They would be in hell, thanks to Gwen's own foolishness. Let's go to Lamu! What a great idea!

She wanted to cry, but she bit her lip so she wouldn't. She had to control her emotions, focus on the reality of this place. She leaned against the rough brick wall, counted to one hundred and back to zero. Up and down and up and down. The air in the hut cooled. Her back ached and her legs cramped. Her belly was empty and her mouth was dry. They hadn't given her any food or water. In the infinite darkness she pressed her lips tight and rasped her tongue against her teeth. Weirdly, she wasn't scared. Not at the moment. She was sure she would be in the days to come. But for now she was just deeply physically uncomfortable.

She remembered her sixth-grade teacher, Edwin Granger, explaining the rule of three: three minutes without air, three days without water, three weeks without food. Granger had been teaching them state history, the Johnson party. The Johnsons were pioneers trapped by an early-season blizzard in the Bitterroots. They would have been Montana's version of the Donners, only they got lucky and caught a thaw and found their way back to the plains.

The story stuck with Gwen in part because Granger had creeped her out so much. He had pockmarked skin and jet-black hair that she knew now must have been dyed. In September he treated her like everybody else. By June she couldn't escape the way he looked at her. Fortunately, he didn't try to touch her, never even said anything inappropriate. But his squinty blue eyes had stayed with her. Her first taste of unwanted male attention.

Granger lingered over the tale of the Johnsons. *I want you all to understand the power of these mountains,* he'd said. Gwen wasn't impressed. Everybody in Montana knew that blizzards could hit the Bitterroots as early as in October. The Johnsons should have waited for spring. Instead, only the blind luck of a warm December saved them from their own stupidity. Otherwise they would have been sharpening axes like the Donners. *What's for dinner, honey?*

Now Gwen knew what had happened to all the pioneers who hadn't made it. One big mistake and then a couple small ones. For example, *Let's go to Lamu.* Followed by *Forget the main road.* Just like that the wagons were stuck in axle-high drifts with the snow still coming. And all the Africans in the world couldn't dig you out. Not in three days or weeks or years. Suddenly she was back in Granger's class. She needed water, she was so thirsty. She raised her hand and said, *I'll do what you want if you just let me get a drink, whatever you want.* He said, *Wake up,* but with a British accent. She tried to stand, only her hand was stuck in the desk —

She opened her eyes, but she was still in the dark. Nothing made sense. Then she remembered the hood. Strange to wake to darkness. Someone reached behind her neck. She twisted her head in panic. "Easy," a man said, the same British accent she'd heard the night before. The drawstring loosened and the hood came up, the fabric rubbing her face —

And she saw. Until this moment, she hadn't realized what a gift sight was. Even though all she saw was a windowless brick hut maybe twenty feet square, lit by a battery-powered lantern that barely cut though the dirt in the air. The hut was warming. It must be morning, so somehow she'd slept for several hours. A coat of dust covered her tongue. Her joints were stiff and cramped from the hours against the wall. She felt like she'd been stuck in the worst seat in coach on the longest flight of her life.

At least their kidnappers hadn't split them up. The others already had their hoods off. Scott sat against the back wall, with a nasty purple bruise on his cheek from the beating he'd taken during the kidnapping. He caught her looking at him and winked. She thought she'd imagined it. Then he winked again. Had to prove how cool he was. A frat boy to the end. Gwen knew she should be furious with him. This trip had been his idea. Still she was glad to have him. She felt somehow that nothing too terrible could happen with him here.

Owen sat directly across from her. He smiled when he saw her looking, but the grin felt forced. Painted on, by the worst painter alive. She hoped he wouldn't do anything dumb to prove that he wasn't afraid. Hailey was closest, a couple feet to her left. She gave Gwen a half-nod, nothing more.

They were all held the same way, their right hands chained to posts set in the walls about eighteen inches above the mud floor. The chains were maybe four feet long, so they had some flexibility to move. They could even stand. And Gwen was relieved to see that the kidnappers had set bottles of water beside each of them, the big two-liter kind.

Still, the hut was miserable. A musky smell filled the room, not just sweat but something richer, murkier. She had noticed it in African men before. Pre-kidnapping Gwen would have wrinkled her nose and walked straight out. But new Gwen could already imagine a place worse than this. A shorter chain. A hood that never came off. Worst of all, being alone.

Finally, Gwen focused on her captor. As she'd guessed, he was a big man, six feet tall and heavy. Fine. And wearing a disguise, a full-face Joker mask. She understood that he didn't want them to recognize him. But she couldn't imagine why he'd chosen this particular mask. She wasn't sure she wanted the answer, either.

"You see the water beside you," he said. "Drink it carefully. It's all you get for the day."

"What about food?" Owen said.

Gwen didn't know whether Owen had forgotten the warning about speaking or simply wanted to test its limits. Either way, he'd made a mistake. The Joker squatted beside Owen, grabbed the water bottle. And then carefully, deliberately, unscrewed the cap and stood and tipped the bottle over. Gwen couldn't have imagined how closely she could focus on such a simple act. The stream of colorless liquid flexed thick and thin as it poured out of the bottle's plastic mouth. Inside the container, air bubbles rose and popped. Gwen felt herself reaching with her free left hand for her own bottle, feeling its heft. Three days without water. Did that rule apply in a hut that would be a hundred degrees by the afternoon?

When the Joker stopped pouring, the bottle was still half-full. Owen shook his head, stared at the floor. The Joker set the bottle down. He seemed to smile behind his mask, though Gwen couldn't be sure.

"You can live a long time without food. As my people will tell you. Months. Water is what you need. I hope I don't have to explain again. No speaking unless spoken to. I'll see you tomorrow. Don't be late." He laughed, a rich velvety sound, *Oh-oh-oh,* and walked out.

This man was enjoying himself, Gwen thought. He was performing, the surest sign of his power. He didn't care that they hated him. He knew they would have to choke down their hate. She saw now: This was what it meant to be powerless. Something else, too: The refugees must feel this way all the time.

After a while they reached for their bottles, sipped in silence. Casually, Gwen checked out the guard. He sat beside the black blanket that covered the doorway on a cheap plastic chair that slumped under his weight. He was young and rangy and tough. Scott, with his pumped-up arms and thousand-crunches abs, might have had a chance against him. If Scott weren't chained to the wall. If the guy didn't have a pistol in his hip holster.

For the next three days, the hoods stayed off, and every morning they got two liters of water.

■ ■ ■ ■

Then they made a mistake. Gwen made a mistake.

She was sure Sunglasses was asleep.

Three guards watched them in shifts. The overnight guard wore wraparound sunglasses and was the nastiest of the three. He didn't speak, not even hello or good-bye. He didn't like to be bothered about the bathroom. Maybe he was just angry that he'd drawn the overnight shift. Gwen called him Sunglasses. Not out loud, of course.

On that fourth day of captivity, Gwen decided she needed to talk to Hailey. They were all in the same room, and yet the others might as well have been a thousand miles away. So she held her pee the whole afternoon and evening. By the time Sunglasses came in, she couldn't think about anything except how much she had to go. Sunglasses checked their chains, as the guards did each shift. Then he went to his chair and dimmed the electric lantern. Gwen closed her eyes and waited, counting to one thousand and back down. She was sure she would have fallen asleep if not for her aching bladder.

Finally, she opened her eyes. She felt

wrung out and empty. When she moved her head, she saw streaks of red and white, like her brain couldn't keep up with her eyes. She hadn't known until now that she could be this tired and still be awake. The others were quiet. Gwen looked at Sunglasses. He slumped in his chair, legs kicked out, arms loose. His breathing was slow and deep. He was out.

Still, she counted another five hundred. Her heart pounded so loudly she had the crazy fear it might wake everyone in the room. Finally, she leaned toward Hailey, making sure her chain didn't clank. For a second, less, she hissed, the sharp ugly sound that she and Hailey used at crowded parties to get each other's attention.

Hailey opened her eyes. Pure 200-proof panic filled her face and then she focused on Gwen. "Hailey."

Hailey raised a finger to her lips.

Gwen nodded at the chair where Sunglasses slept. "He's out." She realized that she'd been so focused on getting to a moment where she could speak that she hadn't thought about what to say. "How are you?"

Hailey shrugged. Like, *You woke me to ask me that?* She was right, too. Sick or well hardly mattered.

"Better question. Did Suggs set us up?"

Suggs had been taken with the rest of them, but they hadn't seen him since. Maybe the kidnappers had killed him. Or maybe he was working with them. Scott was the only one who knew him at all, and even Scott probably knew less than he thought.

"If we're lucky."

Gwen shook her head: *I don't understand.*

"It'll give the police a lead. Also he can reach out to James, make a deal. WorldCares can pay these guys off, get us back quietly."

As usual, Hailey was a step ahead of her.

"Think we're still in Kenya?"

"No idea. I hope so. Same reason."

"Me, too." Somalia seemed like a whirlpool, sucking down everything that came its way. "Are you scared?" As soon as Gwen said the words, she knew the question was the real reason she'd woken Hailey.

Who didn't hesitate. "Of course not. I'm counting my money from the book deal we're gonna get. Now, hush before you wake our buddy."

For the first time since they'd been taken, Gwen felt they might be all right. Then she heard a rustling. She opened her eyes to see Sunglasses standing. The guard turned the lantern all the way up and reached for his chair and slammed it against the floor until the cheap plastic split down the middle. He stepped close to Gwen and tore off his sunglasses and tugged on her chain until her arm twisted painfully behind her. A forest of red veins covered his eyes. No wonder he wore the wraparounds. Gwen hated and pitied and feared him all at once. She forced herself to hold his gaze.

He grabbed the lantern, stalked out of the hut. The darkness was absolute.

"Sorry," Gwen whispered. "I'm sorry." No one answered.

A few minutes later, Sunglasses returned with the Joker, who wore a loose white gown that looked like something her grandmother might wear. Gwen hoped they lived through this just so she could tell her family about this moment, about their captor, a three-hundred-pound man in a nightie and a Halloween mask. He knelt beside Gwen, squeezed her arm. His hand circled her skinny biceps easily. "Do you know why we don't feed you?"

Gwen shook her head.

"Answer me."

"To punish us, I guess."

"No."

"So we know what it's like to be hungry."

"Wrong again. Because if you're hungry and weak, you won't make trouble. If you fight, try to escape, I may have to hurt you. I don't want to do that. You're worth more undamaged. Understand?"

She nodded.

"I would have given you a decent meal tomorrow. Another day or two, I might have let you talk. You've spoiled that. You've broken the only rule I gave you. Woken me in the middle of the night." He shouted something in Swahili and Sunglasses walked in, holding the hoods.

He turned to Gwen. "Meshack here says that you spoke the most by far. So you must have a hood." He looked away from her, at the others. "But as for you three, you have a choice. Wear the hood. Or sit without one and watch her suffer."

Gwen held herself silent. She was sure that any objection would only anger him. He had chosen the penalty perfectly. The other three already blamed her for getting them in trouble. Now the Joker was forcing them to choose between their sight and their honor.

Hailey raised her hand first. After that, the other two had to follow. Gwen watched as the Joker pulled the black bags over their heads. Then her turn came. She bent her neck forward. The Joker pushed up her chin and stroked her face with his hand, and she bit her lip to keep from screaming. He grabbed her long blond hair and pulled it back. She closed her eyes.

When she opened them again, the world was dark.

4

Nairobi, Kenya

The Airbus 340 set down onto the tarmac and stopped so smoothly that it hardly seemed to have been moving at all. "On behalf of your Virgin Atlantic flight crew, I welcome you to Jomo Kenyatta International Airport. Local time is 9:30 a.m., three hours ahead of GMT." Nothing more. As if they'd flown four hundred miles instead of four thousand. English understatement hadn't entirely disappeared.

The layover at Heathrow had proved a blessing of sorts, giving Wells time to catch up on the kidnappings, the Kenyan response, and the broader refugee crisis. The Kenyan Interior Ministry was blocking Western journalists from Dadaab. Wells wondered whether the government in Nairobi wanted to hide how much it was doing to find the hostages — or how little.

Either way, the police had placed checkpoints around the camps and the roads that led to Dadaab. According to the media reports, the police were detaining any white person who didn't have permits from national police headquarters and the Kenyan Department of Refugee Affairs. As far as Wells could tell, the lockdown had succeeded. He'd seen no articles written directly from Dadaab.

Years before, Wells might have found a driver willing to hide him and race to Dadaab straight from the airport. But these days he made the police his enemy only if he had no other choice. Especially here, where he had no on-the-ground knowledge and couldn't blend in. Getting caught at a roadblock and returned to Nairobi for deportation would be anything but heroic. So Wells planned to spend the day persuading government officials to give him the permits he needed. By persuading, he meant bribing.

Wells looked out the jet's narrow window, shielding his eyes from the equatorial sun. He felt an unexpected anticipation. For all his years living outside the United States, he'd seen little of Africa. The closest he'd come was Cairo, which was two thousand miles north, and more Arab than African. And the simplicity of this mission pleased him. Get them out.

If getting them out meant making a deal . . . Wells would decide when the moment arrived. The United States government claimed it never negotiated with hostage-takers, that payoffs only led to more kidnappings in the future. But Wells wasn't working for the government. If he felt a ransom was the only way to save the lives of the hostages, he'd probably agree. Even so, he wasn't planning a payoff. The offer he expected to make went more along the lines of *Let them go. Or die.*

His diplomatic passport carried him quickly through immigration. He slipped on his Ray-Bans and stepped outside the terminal to find a sunny day, cooler and more pleasant than he'd expected. Nairobi was about a mile above sea level, a fact that had proved crucial to its fortunes. The city hadn't even existed before the late 1800s, when the British settled it as a depot for the railroad they were building from the Indian Ocean to Uganda. Its mild weather and lack of malaria-carrying mosquitoes appealed to Europeans and local tribesmen alike. Now Nairobi had four million residents and was the most important city in East Africa. But its deep poverty had made it one of the most violent and dangerous cities anywhere.

Expatriates called it Nai-robbery.

Still, the taxi line belied the city's fierce reputation. Cabs queued neatly at the curb. Wells slid into the front seat of the first. The driver was a skinny man who wore fingerless leather racing gloves, as if he were driving a Ferrari and not a gray four-cylinder Toyota.

"Where may I take you?" Because of the British occupation, Kenya's public schools taught English. Nearly everyone in the country spoke some. A break for Wells.

"Anywhere I can buy a local cell." Wells didn't think the agency had a problem with him being here. But if Duto or someone else at Langley decided otherwise, Wells wanted the option of disappearing. Prepaid local phones were tougher for NSA to track than American numbers. Though not impossible, as more than one al-Qaeda operative had realized too late.

"A cell?"

Wells had forgotten. Only Americans called them cells. "A mobile phone. Then downtown."

"To your hotel?"

"The Intercontinental," Wells said, picking a name at random. "Let's go."

"Very good. Be sure to look to your left in a minute, sir. The giraffes are visiting."

So even before the Toyota left the airport grounds, Wells saw his first African wildlife, a herd of giraffes munching contentedly on the open plains to the west. If he hadn't known better, he would have wondered if they were animatronic props for tourists: *Welcome to Kenya. Have you booked your safari?*

"How can they live so close to the city?"

"We have a national park that extends almost to the airport."

As Wells watched, one of the giraffes loped away. Its first steps were uncertain, but stride by stride it gained speed until it galloped over the plain. The others followed. Wells wondered if the animals had sensed a threat or were taking flight preemptively.

Fifteen minutes later, Wells was the proud owner of two new handsets. Basic models with inch-square screens and twelve-button keypads. Nothing fancy, nothing with a GPS locator for the boys at Fort Meade to trace. Plus four different SIM cards, two each from Safaricom and Airtel, the main Kenyan carriers. The driver glanced at Wells as he clicked cards into handsets. "You collect phones?"

"What's your name?" Wells liked the guy. The gloves hadn't lied. He drove with an edge.

"Martin."

"How much to hire you for the day, Martin?"

"Ten thousand shillings, sir. Plus petrol." About $120, in a country where most people lived on a few dollars a day. Martin sounded like he couldn't believe he was asking for it.

"Okay, ten thousand, good. Long as you drive fast. Get me where I'm going."

"I can do that, sir. Thank you."

"And call me John."

"Of course —"

But Wells was already making his first call. Before he went anywhere, he needed a fixer.

"New York Times," a woman said. "Nairobi bureau."

"Jeffrey Gettleman, please." Gettleman was the bureau chief. Wells had never met him, but he'd seen the byline for years.

"Who's this?"

"I have information about the aid workers, the kidnappings."

"He's not in. I can have him call you."

"Trust me, he'll want it now. If you can give me his mobile."

A pause, then the numbers. Wells dialed.

"This is Jeffrey."

"Mr. Gettleman. You don't know me, but my name's John Wells." Wells had thought about using a fake name but decided not to start with a lie. He might need Gettleman later. "I just landed in Nairobi and I'm reaching out because I've been hired to investigate the kidnapping."

"Hired by whom?"

"I have a favor to ask."

"That was quick."

"A small one. I need a fixer."

"You called me for a recommendation, Mr. Wells? Like I'm Zagat's?"

"Good enough for *The New York Times*, good enough for me. You help me, I promise I won't forget."

"Tell me who hired you, I'll hook you up with the best guy in town. He's connected everywhere. Smart. He can give you all the background you need on the camps. And the political situation, which is complicated."

"Nothing free with you guys. Always trading."

"You called me."

Wells couldn't argue the point. "You can't use this, not yet, but Gwen Murphy's family brought me in."

"From the U.S.?"

"Yes."

"Have they gotten a ransom demand?"

"No. The fixer, please."

"His name's Wilfred Wumbugu. I'll text you his number. Will I see you at the press conference tonight?"

"Anything's possible." Wells hung up, thinking, *Press conference?*

But first the permits. He called Wilfred, explained what he needed.

"It's not possible. Since the kidnapping, there's no access. Essential aid workers with existing permits only. No exceptions."

"I'll pay. Whatever it costs."

"We talk in person. At Simmers. Thirty minutes."

"Simmers."

"Your driver will know."

They were closing — slowly — on downtown Nairobi. To the northwest, office towers marked the central business district. Kenya remained desperately poor, but after decades of stagnation, its economy was reviving. New apartment buildings and office parks rose along the highway. Billboards advertised low-fare airlines connecting Nairobi with the rest of East Africa. And the traffic was horrendous, as the new middle class jammed dilapidated roads. Despite his frustration, Wells almost had to smile. Back in Montana, Evan probably imagined him with pistol in hand, cracking skulls. Instead he was stuck in traffic on his way to get a permit. The thrilling life of the secret operative.

Though Wells didn't doubt the skull-cracking would come.

Simmers was a restaurant and dance hall under a big tent in the midst of the office towers, smoky, almost shabby, with plastic chairs and tables and a barbecue grill. A cantina, really. Wells liked it immediately. A man at a corner table caught Wells's eye, waved him over.

"I'm Wilfred." He was a slim man in a crisp white shirt and wire-rimmed glasses. Back home Wells would have pegged him as a Web designer.

"How'd you guess it was me?" Wells was the only white person in the place.

Wilfred waved over a waiter. "You want something?"

"A Coke."

"Not a Tusker? The national beer."

"I try not to drink before noon."

"In here, time doesn't matter. Simmers never closes. Open twenty-four hours. We call them day-and-night clubs."

"Coke."

"Two Cokes," Wilfred said to the waiter. "Now tell me again what you want."

Wells did.

"You understand, these camps, all of eastern Kenya, it's dangerous now. Because of Shabaab. You know about them?"

"Yes." Al-Shabaab was a radical Muslim group that controlled much of Somalia and enforced strict sharia law in its territory. Women wore burqas. Thieves faced amputation. But the group also had a criminal side, smuggling sugar into Kenya and protecting the pirates who kidnapped sailors off the coast. The United States and United Nations had tried to destroy Shabaab for years. Lately they'd made progress. United Nations peacekeepers had pushed Shabaab's guerrillas out of Mogadishu, the Somali capital. And Kenya had briefly sent troops into Somalia from the west. Still, Shabaab remained a threat. The Kenyan government had publicly announced that the group was the prime suspect in the kidnapping.

"But doesn't the government or the UN try to screen Shabaab out of the refugee camps?"

"Wait until you see them. A half-million people. Almost ten percent of the population of Somalia. And you think they tell the truth about who they are? Oh, yes, I'm Shabaab, I shot three peacekeepers. They know the story to tell to get in. The UN doesn't even try to screen them anymore."

"Everyone gets in?"

"They call the policy prima facie. You're Somali, you get across the border, you're an automatic refugee. In the United States you would call them illegal aliens. But here CNN runs pictures of starving babies, so they're refugees. If you're a Kenyan living in Kenya you don't get free food and shelter, but if you're a Somali you do."

Wells saw what Gettleman meant about the complexity of the political situation. He hadn't considered how the Kenyans viewed the refugees. "Would that anger extend to the aid workers? Could a Kenyan gang have kidnapped them?"

"Possible. It wouldn't be political. Just for money. But I don't know how they would get paid without getting caught. In Somalia it's much easier. There's a whole setup."

"So you think it's Shabaab."

"That's the most likely. And the police say so. Though in Kenya the police say lots of things."

"Why I need to go up there myself. Today."

"You can't hide up there, mzungu" — the not-entirely-friendly Swahili term for a white person. "Everyone will know you're American."

"I'm not so sure," Wells said in Arabic.

"Arabic?"

"Get me the permits or I'll find a fixer who can," Wells said, still in Arabic.

Wilfred looked at Wells's coiled hands and broad shoulders. For the first time he seemed to understand who Wells was, *what* Wells was. "You have money? Not one, two hundred dollars. Real money."

Wells handed Wilfred a packet of hundreds from his backpack. "This enough to start?"

Wilfred riffed the bills. "Castle House first. If the Department of Refugee Affairs approves you, the police will follow. By the way, my rate is two hundred fifty a day in Nairobi. Whether I get these permits or not. If I go to Dadaab, five hundred."

Wells felt he had to protest, if only to prove he wasn't a total sucker. "Gettleman said your rate was a hundred."

"Gettleman didn't see how much money you have."

The refugee department was headquartered west of downtown. Martin slalomed through traffic on a broad avenue shaded by oak trees, then swung onto a rutted road hemmed by concrete-walled houses. The neighborhood's wealth reminded Wells of the fancier precincts of Los Angeles. The homes here had similar private guards, security cameras, and signs promising armed response. "There's money here."

"You want poor people?" Wilfred said. "We'll take you to Kibera. Over the hills just southeast. A few square kilometers, maybe a million people, no one really knows. No running water, no open space, no legal electricity. Shacks and shacks and shacks. After the elections in 2007, the politicians stirred them up and they rioted. Tribal warfare, the Kikuyu against everyone else. Five hundred died, maybe one thousand. The police waited for them to fight themselves out. Like animals."

"Nice."

"Don't let what you're seeing here fool you. This country, a few hundred thousand live well. Two, three million more have a decent job. Teachers, truck drivers. Everyone else feels hungry just looking at the price of sugar. You want to see, I promise you'll see. Now let me talk to the DRA so we can get this piece of paper." Wilfred reached for his phone.

Four calls later, he was shaking his head. "Everyone says the same. It's impossible."

"Wilfred Wumbugu, the great fixer. Fine. I'll go without a permit."

"I have one other contact. But I don't

trust her, she's strange."

Wells lifted his hands: What are you waiting for? Wilfred dialed, spoke for a bit. "She'll see us." Five minutes later, they stopped at a brick-walled compound protected by a guardhouse. Behind it was what looked like a fieldstone manor, straight out of the English countryside, with turrets and recessed windows. Beside the main entrance, a sign proclaimed "Castle House, Department of Refugee Affairs, Ministry for Immigration and Registration of Persons — Renovated in 2009 by the Government of Kenya with funding from the United Nations." "They never let us forget where the money comes from," Wilfred said.

The building's interior was disappointingly conventional, concrete floors and white-painted walls. Wilfred led Wells down a corridor lined with posters from the International Organization for Migration and knocked on an unmarked door. "Come," a woman said. Inside, a comfortable office. Satellite photographs of refugee camps hung from the walls. A heavyset forty-something woman sat at her desk, typing an email. Behind her a window looked out on a lushly planted garden.

"Wilfred. *Jambo.*" One of the few Swahili words that Wells knew. Literally, it meant

"Problems?" but was used in the sense of "Hey, how are you?"

"Sijambo." The usual response, meaning "No problems."

She finished typing, gave Wells a broad smile. "And you? *Jambo?*"

"*Sijambo.* I'm John. Nice to meet you."

"I'm Christina. Please, sit." Wells waited on the couch as Wilfred and Christina had a heated conversation. Wells hadn't felt so linguistically helpless in years. He hated needing translators, treasured his hard-earned proficiency in Arabic and Pashtun. Knowing those languages had saved his life more than once. Unfortunately, Swahili wasn't all that common in the North-West Frontier.

Finally, Christina took Wilfred's arm and pointed at the door.

"How much does she want?" Wells said.

"She didn't name a price. She says she wants to help you, she likes you, but —"

"Go," Christina said to Wilfred in English.

"I'll be outside." Wilfred left.

Christina came over, sat beside Wells. She had dark skin and wore a long green dress that clung to her breasts and hips. She was big all around. Pretty. "So you want to visit our refugees. Most tourists prefer a safari."

"I'm looking for the aid workers."

"Are you sure you're not a reporter?"

"I barely know how to read."

She grinned, touched his cheek with a long purple fingernail. "What are you, then? A soldier?"

"Used to be."

"And now?"

"You've seen guys like me before. We're all over the place."

"Not exactly like you, mzungu."

He couldn't tell if she was serious or playing, hoping to annoy him. "Is that a compliment or an insult?"

"Your eyes are dying."

No wonder Wilfred had said she was strange. "Now that's definitely an insult."

"What about me?" She leaned toward Wells.

He looked at her, really looked. "Your eyes aren't dying." It was true. They were big and black and glimmered with life.

Outside the windows, a cat meowed. "That's Njenga."

"What are her eyes like?"

"Are you joking, mzungu?"

Wells reminded himself that this woman, strange or not, was probably his last chance to get to Dadaab legitimately. "Do you like working with the refugees?"

"I've never been to Dadaab and I hope I

never go. Tell me, why do you care so much about these aid workers?"

"My son knows them. Asked me to help find them."

"And you came all the way from the United States. For them or your son?"

"Both."

"You must be a very good father."

She rested a warm hand on his arm and squeezed. Like she was a movie producer and Wells an aspiring actress. *There's some nude scenes in this film. Just need to know you're okay with that. Mind taking off your top?*

Fine. He'd play. He put his hand on top of hers. "I'm a terrible father. I missed my son's whole life."

"Are you a terrible husband, too?"

"I'm not married. But I have a girlfriend back home. Named Anne."

"I don't want to hear about her." She touched his chin, turned him toward her, leaned in. Her breast touched his arm. Her skin smelled sweet and buttery. Despite the insanity of the moment, he felt himself stir. "Your eyes."

"What about them?"

"They're coming back to life."

Wells didn't say a word. The permit was the prize.

"Dadaab is a waste. They might be anywhere. Mogadishu. Even here. What will you do that the police or the Army can't?"

"Only one way to find out."

She put her lips to his. She tasted of milk and tea, and her skin was so smooth and supple that it was almost oily. She cupped his hands around her face, pulled him close. He closed his eyes and didn't fight. *It's for the permit. For the mission.* But she kept kissing him until lightning struck. He opened his mouth to her and his excuses melted. He wrapped her close and ran his hands through her finely curled hair until finally she broke off, pulled away, leaned back against the couch.

She grinned at him. "I've never kissed a mzungu before."

The noise in his head resolved into Bruce Springsteen: *Everybody's wrecked on Main Street from drinking that holy blood . . .* The song was called "Lost in the Flood." It was nearly as old as he was. He hadn't thought of it in years.

"I've never kissed an African."

"Is it different?"

"Different and the same."

"I'm glad." She put a hand on his leg, smoothed her fingers toward his crotch, leaned over. He wondered how far she would push him, how far he would go. Then she pulled away, stood, smoothed her dress.

"You can have your permit. I'll say you're a doctor going to the camps. That should work."

"Thank you."

"Also, I need three thousand dollars."

His face must have betrayed his surprise.

"You think I'm joking? Because you're pretty? Anyway, three thousand is cheap."

"If you say so." Now Wells really felt like a starlet, toyed with and tossed. She'd proved to both of them that she could have her way with him and then proved that she didn't care.

Outside, a knock. "Everything all right?" Wilfred said.

"We have a deal," Christina said.

"What happened?" Wilfred said as they drove back downtown.

"She's strange. Like you said."

"You know, Kenyans, we believe in wizardry. That the spirit world has power here and certain sorcerers can reach it."

Did Wilfred really believe Christina was a witch? Wells didn't want to know. "Any woman can be a sorceress if she wants to be."

"So what happened? Truly."

Wells ignored the question. His lips still

burned with her. He wanted to remember every detail and at the same time forget. Aroused and ashamed. But soon enough only the shame would remain. How could he respect Anne so little? He loved her, cared for her, but in their three years together she'd never jolted him this way. Only Jennifer Exley, his ex-fiancée. But he'd lost Exley long ago and she wasn't coming back.

Fine. Forget Exley. Forget them all. Forget everything but the mission.

He'd done it before.

"What's next?"

"Now we have this permit, you don't have to come to the police."

"You can get it without me?"

"Yes. Go to your hotel. Take a nap." Wilfred grinned. "You look tired."

Wells chose to ignore this little dig. "And we leave tomorrow morning."

"Early as you like. The drive is maybe five hours."

"All right." Then Wells remembered. "Do you know anything about a press conference today? About the kidnapping?"

"Yes. The Hilton. Eight p.m." Wilfred's accent gave the word a pleasant sound, *Hill-ton.*

"The police are having a news conference

at a hotel?"

"Not the police. James Thompson."

"The man who runs the WorldCares charity."

"Of course."

"Isn't he in Dadaab?"

"He came to Nairobi this morning to speak to the police, the Interior Ministry. That's what the newspapers said."

"Has he said what he'll be talking about? Progress on the investigation, anything?"

"I don't think so."

Wells leaned forward. "Martin, forget the Intercontinental. I'll stay at the Hilton."

The Hilton was a twenty-story-tall cylinder in southeastern downtown, near Moi Avenue and the busy River Road neighborhood. Until 1998, the American embassy had been located nearby. Then al-Qaeda blew up the embassy, killing 258 people, mostly Kenyans, the first major attack in the terrorist campaign that culminated in September 11. A memorial garden now occupied the embassy's site. The new embassy was miles to the north, in a rich neighborhood called Gigiri that was also home to the presidential palace. Wells imagined the place was a fortress. He wondered if he'd see it this trip.

The Hilton had security, too. A metal gate blocked the driveway. Everyone entering the lobby passed through a metal detector. But Kenyan culture was naturally friendly. The checks felt halfhearted, nothing that would stop a determined bomber. Despite setting off the detector, Wells was waved through. Inside, the Hilton looked like Hiltons everywhere, bright and clean and friendly-efficient, the front desk attendants wearing bright red jackets. In five minutes, Wells had a room.

Upstairs he set a wake-up call for 7:30 p.m. He found the pocket-sized Quran he'd tucked into his backpack and lowered his head to the faded blue carpet. The midday prayer had ended hours before and the sunset call was still hours away, so he prayed free-form: *Help me, Allah. Help me to be a better person. Give me the peace that only you can grant . . .* Really, the prayer could have been the same to any God. But not the language. The language was Arabic, and Arabic took Wells back to the North-West Frontier, his purest years. He had lived in those mountains without the consolations of the flesh, without a warm house or a soft bed. And certainly without women. He had lived without killing, too. He had lived almost as a monk. Gaunt as that life had been, he missed it for its very emptiness. But he'd left the mountains behind. They were closed to him now. He had chosen the world and all its complications. He had chosen this mission. So he prayed for the strength and insight to find the kidnapped. Then he pulled the shades and slept.

The press conference was on the Hilton's mezzanine floor, in the Simba Room. Wells expected a reporter or two, maybe a guy with a digital video camera uploading to YouTube. But when he arrived at 7:45, a half-dozen camera crews were in place. He had known this was a big story, but he hadn't realized just how big. He understood now why Thompson was holding the conference so late in the day. Eight p.m. in Nairobi was noon in New York. From what Wells could see, CNN and Fox were setting up to carry it live.

Precisely on time, James Thompson walked to the lectern. He wore khaki pants and a plain white long-sleeved shirt and held a notepad. His face was lined and tired, like he hadn't slept much in the last week. "Is everybody ready? I have a short statement and then I'll take questions."

"Can you wait a few seconds, Mr. Thompson?" the Fox reporter said. "We're still in break back home."

"Say when."

The Fox reporter held up three fingers, two, one, then a big thumbs-up.

"Hello, everyone. My name is James Thompson and I'm the chief executive of WorldCares/ChildrenFirst. I'm speaking to you from Nairobi, Kenya. I know there's tremendous concern around the world for our kidnapped volunteers and the driver who was taken with them. I thank you for your thoughts and prayers. We've had so many questions, I'd like to fill everyone in on what's happening. Then I have a message for the kidnappers themselves. I'll finish by taking questions from the reporters here." He spoke slowly, as if the pressure of the worldwide audience had finally hit him.

"As many of you know, Hailey Barnes, Owen Broder, Gwen Murphy, and my nephew Scott Thompson disappeared one week ago. My staff and I are working with Kenyan authorities to bring them home. I regret to tell you that we still have no specific information on their location. As has been publicly reported, several days ago Kenyan police recovered the vehicle they were driving when they were taken. Police are interviewing villagers in that area. I'll leave it to them to update you on what they've found. I can only tell you that we have not received credible ransom demands or proof of life." On the last three words, Thompson's voice broke. He looked down, then squared his shoulders and faced the camera.

"While we wait for these kidnappers to come forward, thousands of you have already reached out to WorldCares/ChildrenFirst to ask how to help. You have our thanks. I hope that you'll take a few minutes to learn about the refugee crisis in Somalia. Hundreds of thousands of people in the region face grave dangers every day. Thousands of aid workers are trying to help them. That's why Gwen, Hailey, Owen, and Scott came here."

Thompson rested his hands on the lectern. "Now. I speak directly to the kidnappers. I beg you, please return these young men and women. I'm sure your lives have been more difficult than most people viewing this right now can imagine. But I ask you not to hurt these blameless volunteers. They came here with only one mission — helping the people in Dadaab. Set them free for their families. And for your own hearts."

Thompson was wiping tears from his eyes now. Wells didn't doubt that millions of people around the world were doing the same. Thompson coughed, wiped his mouth. "Thank you for listening," he finally said. "I'll take whatever questions you have."

The hands went up.

"Yes?"

"Erin Dudley from CNN. I know this is difficult, and we all appreciate your taking the time to talk to us. Can you fill us in on exactly how the United States government is helping the search?"

"They've asked me not to be too specific, but I'm sure you know that the United States Navy has a major presence off Somalia. I spoke to Ambassador Whalley today and he assured me that the United States stands ready to assist local authorities if called on."

"By assistance, do you mean surveillance? A military operation? Both? And could that take place in Somalia?"

"That's a question for the ambassador, not for me."

"Are any United States agencies involved in the search? Like the CIA or NSA?"

"I don't mean to be unhelpful, but again, that question should go to them. I can say that the FBI routinely consults on the kidnapping of Americans in foreign countries."

"John Sambuti from Fox. Is WorldCares

prepared to pay for the safe return of the volunteers?"

Thompson paused. "Ransom is sometimes paid in these cases. But as I mentioned, we haven't received a credible ransom demand, so considering that option is premature."

"Are you worried that all this attention may drive up the ransom price?"

"That's a good question. I hope not."

"One more, sir. Is there any evidence that the Somali Muslim terrorist group al-Shabaab is involved in this kidnapping? We know they've kidnapped Westerners before."

"I'm sure you know that the Kenyan police have named the Shabaab group the most likely suspect. They haven't shared specific evidence with me."

"Have they with the U.S. government?"

"I don't have the answer to that. But this is a very good moment for me to remind everyone that WorldCares/ChildrenFirst does not proselytize. Need crosses all faiths, and so do we. We help every child we can and we never ask about religion. Never. And we welcome volunteers of all religions, including Islam, of course."

In other words: Dear Shabaab, if you do have them, please don't cut off their heads to make a point.

"One more," Thompson said. A boyish-looking guy with long hair raised his hand.

"Jeffrey Gettleman, *New York Times.* Sir, since the kidnapping, the Kenyan government has restricted access to Dadaab, saying that the camps are too dangerous except for essential aid workers. Even journalists are barred. These volunteers had no experience in a high-risk zone. Do you think your organization bears responsibility for what's happened?"

Trust the *Times* guy to play hardball. Thompson's jaw tightened. "If you've been to Dadaab, you know the camps are very large. Some areas are safer than others. We operate in relatively safe zones, and we have our own security officers watching our compound. So far there's no evidence that anyone from the camps was involved."

"But especially as you get closer to Somalia —"

"I hope everyone will remember my nephew Scott is one of the kidnapped. I would never have let him travel to Lamu if I thought he was at risk. I hope that answers your question, sir." Sir, meaning asshole. "Thank you all for listening. Please pray for our brave volunteers."

As Thompson stepped away from the podium, reporters surrounded him. "I hate to put you off, but I have to talk to the police. If you have questions later, I'm in room 1401."

Four hours later, just past midnight, Wells rapped on the door of Thompson's room.

"Hello?" Thompson sounded exhausted. Good.

"My name's John Wells. We need to talk."

Heavy steps, then the door opened a fraction, the panic bar still in place. Thompson peered out. His face was blotchy and red. He wore boxers, nothing else. His chest was weirdly hairless, as if he waxed. He rubbed his eyes, tried to muster a smile. "Can we do this tomorrow or do you have a deadline back home to meet?"

"I'm not a reporter. I work for Gwen Murphy's family."

"I don't understand."

Wells handed over the email from Brandon Murphy.

"This doesn't look very official."

"The Murphys will be glad to confirm it."

"You're a private investigator? They're paying you?" With a slight emphasis on "paying."

"Let me in and I'll explain."

"In the morning."

"Now. Just pretend I'm a reporter. There's plenty around."

Thompson seemed to understand the implied threat that Wells might complain publicly if Thompson refused. "Let me dress." He shut the door. When it reopened, Thompson was wearing a T-shirt and a pair of khakis. Good. The day had been too long. Wells couldn't face that hairless chest.

Room 1401 turned out to be a suite, with a view southwest over the Kenyan parliament. The remains of a steak sat on a room-service tray, and an empty bottle of wine sat on the fridge. Wells found the room's luxury mildly irritating. He supposed that Thompson needed the space to meet reporters. He needed to eat, too. Didn't mean he was a bad guy. Thompson gestured at an overstuffed chair and Wells sat.

"You asked if the Murphys are paying me," Wells said. "The answer's no. My son knows them. They asked me to come, so I came. I used to work for the CIA, but I'm retired now." The abridged version of Wells's career.

"Have you worked in Africa before, Mr. Wells? You speak Swahili?"

"I've worked a lot of places."

"I guess that means no. So you don't speak the language, you have no experience here. What are you planning to do besides come to press conferences? Like that jerk from the *Times* said, Dadaab's shut."

"I have permits."

Thompson wrinkled his nose like he'd just smelled something unpleasant. Like he'd realized for the first time that Wells might be hard to shake. "Then you'll be in the way there instead of here."

Wells stood, looked out the window. Even at this hour, the downtown streets had plenty of traffic. "It's late. We're both tired. Let's try this again. Gwen's family wants my help. Whoever you're dealing with at the embassy, I guarantee you they'll know my name. Let's have a civil conversation about what happened up there, what you know. Maybe I can help."

Thompson tented his hands. "A civil conversation. Where do we start?"

Wells sat back down, pulled a pad from his jacket. "At the beginning. What was WorldCares doing at Dadaab? How'd you get involved?"

"We came in late. To be honest, we're not what you'd call a top-rank aid organization. Catholic Relief Services, CARE, those groups have been around a while, they have tremendous infrastructure. They were in Dadaab early. But they got stretched because the camps grew so much. They put out the call in the aid community, asked for help. Several groups stepped up, including us. We took over some food distribution at Haragesa, that's one of the older camps, so CARE could push forward. After we got settled, we started on our specialty, services for children, broadly defined. Clothes, vaccines, vitamins, books, high-calorie food, whatever we can source and bring in for pre-teen kids."

"Teaching?"

"That's under local control. We give English lessons where we can, on the theory that knowing English is never bad. But we don't promise it. Too expensive."

"And how big is WorldCares?"

"About nine hundred employees."

"Big."

"It sounds more impressive than it is. That's mostly local nationals in the countries where we work, Kenya, Haiti, the Philippines, a few other places. In terms of Americans, Westerners, about seventy. Mostly back home in Houston. Usually we have no more than two to five Westerners living in the countries where we operate. They're too expensive. A foreign employee in Kenya costs one hundred fifty to three hundred thousand dollars a year."

"Three hundred thousand? For an aid worker?"

"That includes housing allowances, six to eight weeks of vacation. These are tough jobs. People need a break. Insurance, medical and life. It adds up. The locals are a lot cheaper. Plus the United Nations encourages aid groups to hire locally."

"Build expertise."

"Correct." A phone buzzed in Thompson's pocket. He pulled it out, looked at it. "The Associated Press." He stuffed it away. "They can wait. You were saying?"

"So why bring over these volunteers?"

" 'Volunteers' being the magic word. The cost to us was close to zero. And when my nephew proposed it, I initially thought they'd be around six weeks or so. Not three months–plus."

"They get along with the full-time workers?"

"As far as I know, John. Look, you've seen the pictures. Who wouldn't want Gwen and Hailey around? Gwen tutored English, Hailey worked at the hospital, Owen and Scott helped with manual labor. All in all, I'd say they did a decent job. Better than I would have predicted."

"When did they decide to go to Lamu?"

"Maybe two weeks ago. Scott's idea."

"Any particular reason? They could have gone on safari or climbed Kilimanjaro or come to Nairobi for the weekend. Why Lamu?"

"I didn't ask, but I think Lamu has a certain cachet among aid workers, backpacker types. One of those places that only the cool people know about."

Odd that Thompson didn't put himself in the category of aid worker, Wells thought. But then, he was more of an executive, right down to his use of Wells's first name in the conversation. Always use the other person's name; it establishes a bond. Every management seminar on earth taught the trick.

"Ever been to Lamu yourself, James?"

"Truth is I haven't spent all that long in Kenya. I came just about five weeks ago. I'd heard that the situation was getting tougher and I wanted to see for myself. In fact, I was supposed to leave this week, be in Haiti right now."

"Before that, when was the last time you were here?"

"Maybe a year ago. I split my time between Houston and the country ops."

"So who's in charge on a day-to-day basis?"

"Her name's Moss Laughton. Irish. Her title is director of logistics."

"And she's up there now?"

"Better be."

"Okay. So this trip to Lamu, you didn't mind."

"My understanding before this happened was that parts of the camps were troubled, but eastern Kenya was mostly safe. Al-Shabaab has a few thousand men at most, and they've lost ground. They're in Dadaab because they're getting squeezed."

"But haven't there been kidnappings in Lamu?"

"That was before the Kenyans went into Somalia. Since then, no. The locals there know that tourists pay the bills." Thompson leaned forward, put his meaty hands on his knees, locked eyes with Wells. "John, I swear to you, I told Gettleman the truth. If I thought my nephew was in danger, I wouldn't have let him go."

He spoke with conviction. Whatever the truth, Wells didn't doubt he'd pass a poly. "Tell me about the driver. Suggs, right? He hasn't come up much. Are you keeping his name out of it on purpose? Could he have been involved?"

"Possibly, yes. We called him Suggs, but his real name was Kwasi. He was our best fixer and he'd worked for us since almost our first day here. We paid him one hundred twenty thousand shillings a month. Close to fifteen hundred dollars. The most by far of our Kenyan employees."

"But much less than the mzungus. He ever get upset about that?"

"Just FYI, John, the plural of 'mzungu' isn't 'mzungus.' It's 'wazungu.' " Letting Wells know exactly how much he didn't know. "And no, he never got upset. Local nationals know the score. As a rule, they're happy to have these jobs."

Wells wasn't so sure. "He have a family?"

"Married, two kids."

"They live in Dadaab."

"No. Nairobi, I'm not sure where. Suggs was Kenyan, not Somali. But he'd worked the camps long enough that he was connected inside."

"You met his wife?"

"Not yet. I should."

"And you've talked to the other fixers and Suggs's contacts in the camps?"

"Moss and our security guys have talked to everyone who works for us. Nobody will admit to knowing anything. As for the camps, that's harder. Our security guys don't have any authority. It's up to the police."

"And have the police had those interviews?"

"If they have they haven't told me."

"Doesn't that bug you? They've been

quick to put this on Shabaab."

"It disturbs me. It doesn't necessarily surprise me. Kenya's deeply corrupt and the police are what you'd expect. If not worse."

"They're not Sherlock Holmes."

"They're not even the Pink Panther."

"Okay, going back to the trip, your nephew specifically asked for Suggs to drive."

"That's right. A few days before."

"Did Scott say whether he'd suggested the trip to Suggs or the other way around?"

"It wasn't clear. I think he phrased it like, 'We want to go to Lamu next week. Suggs says he'll drive if that's cool with you.' That's how Scott talks. I said fine."

"Let me just detour for a second. Gwen and Hailey. They ever complain about problems with men in the camp, harassment, anything like that?"

"Not as far as I know."

"Okay. So, in the days leading up to the trip, anything unusual happen?"

"Not that I can think of. My publisher back home had sent me the final proofs for my book. I was spending time on those. And Paula, this reporter from Houston, was coming to visit, so I wanted to make sure everything was ready."

Wells barely stopped himself from saying

something like: Sounds like you were very involved in feeding hungry kids.

"I can guess what you're thinking," Thompson said. "But the *Chronicle* story was going to be important for fund-raising, and fund-raising matters. There's a lot of good causes in the world. We don't get our share of donations, we can't do the work we want. I was happy to have Paula come, see our work. Naturally this was before the kidnapping. She set up the trip a couple months ago."

Wells wondered if Thompson had come to Kenya to be here when the reporter showed up. A hands-on chief executive instead of a guy calling the shots two continents away. But so what? Up close Thompson came off as slicker than Wells would have liked, but the truth was that WorldCares was a business, with employees all over the world.

"Okay, the big day comes, they pile in the Land Cruiser, head out. You say good-bye?"

"No."

"You didn't say good-bye to your own nephew?"

For the first time, Thompson seemed slightly defensive. "I thought he'd be back by the end of the week."

"Then what happened?"

Thompson went to the window, looked

out into the Kenyan night. "They vanished. Into thin air, that's the cliché, right? And true in this case. No emergency calls, emails, nothing. Scott told me that they were planning to go north to Dadaab, then west to Garissa and down, but I guess the Kenyan police had blocked the road north that morning, so they went south instead."

"Was that typical, the roadblock?"

"Moss could tell you better, but I think so. Maybe once, twice a month. But the roadblocks don't usually last long. Anyway, I don't know why Suggs didn't wait, but instead he decided to take this one-lane dirt track that goes maybe a hundred miles south and eventually hits another little track that runs east-west. If they'd taken that second road west, they would have linked up eventually with the main road to Mokowe. But they never got there. The police found the Cruiser on the first road, about ninety miles south of Dadaab."

"In an abandoned village."

"Not exactly. When you get there, you'll see. Eastern Kenya is mostly scrubland and watering holes. The settlements are a few houses each, extended families. The photos show a single hut nearby. Crumbling. Maybe somebody started to dig for water there and thought they had something and then it dried up."

"Any reason they would have been taken there?"

"From what the cops showed me, the road turns in a way that makes it easy to block."

"And the car was just left there?"

"Taken off the road, next to the hut. The police found it when they drove down the next day."

"Is there phone service down there?"

"I think so. From what I've seen, even the most desolate parts of the scrub have at least some service."

"Did you know where they were staying?"

"They were planning to pick a hotel after they reached the island. So, that afternoon, I was talking to the reporter and then, I'll never forget, Jasper — our security guy — he came in, said he had to tell me something. Since then I just keep waiting for them to show up, like if I take a cold shower or chew off my tongue or something, they'll walk right in."

Again, the answer felt canned to Wells. Thompson didn't strike him as the type to fade into this-must-be-a-dream wish fulfillment. "I'm sorry. I know it's late and I have just a few more questions. Have you talked to my old friends from Langley?"

"At the embassy, after I was done talking

to the State guys, a man who said his name was Gerald came in. He didn't give me a card, just a phone number. I felt he was more or less telling me where he worked without saying it. He asked for numbers and email addresses for the volunteers and Suggs, too. He gave me an email address, told me to forward any ransom demands. Even if they didn't seem real. He said they checked the satellites, too, but they didn't have anything in the area that afternoon."

"Too bad. That would be the easiest way to track them. He get back to you?"

"Not yet. Which kind of upsets me."

"It sounds like they're running databases. They may not be able to do much more. I wouldn't count on them having too many sources inside Shabaab, and if it's a smaller group it's even less likely. One last thing. Tell me about the ransom demands."

"All junk. Someone emails from a Kenyan email account asking for a million dollars to an account in Dubai. I ask for proof, I get a Photoshopped picture from the paper."

Wells took a final look around the suite. Two laptops sat on the coffee table beside a black leather wallet. A map of Kenya lay on the bedside table, along with two phones, a Samsung touchscreen and a cheap local handset like the ones Wells had bought.

Then Wells realized. An international phone . . . a local handset . . . and at least one more mobile, the one in Thompson's pocket. Three phones, if not more. Wells carried multiple handsets so he'd be harder to trace. What about Thompson?

"You have a phone fetish," he said. "Like me."

Thompson followed Wells's gaze to the bedside table. "Local and international."

"Plus the one in your pocket."

"Oh yeah, I like to have two local carriers just in case."

"Sure. Can you give me all your numbers?"

"Of course. And my emails too, the private and the public." They traded numbers. Wells stuck out his hand. Thompson ignored it and enveloped him in a hug, his thick arms heavy on Wells's back, palms moist through Wells's shirt. "You think you can find them, John?"

"I'll do my best." Wells extricated himself. He'd never been the hugging type.

"And you'll go up there tomorrow?"

"Probably."

"I'm going to fly back in a couple days. I'll see you up there."

"Can't wait."

■ ■ ■ ■

Nearly three a.m. in Nairobi, seven p.m. in Langley. Back in his room, Wells called Shafer.

"No rest for the wicked."

For a heartbeat, Wells found himself back on the couch at Castle House, his mouth on Christina's.

"John? You there?"

"I have numbers and an email for the elves to trace." He gave Shafer everything he'd gotten from Thompson.

"And these belong to —"

"The CEO of WorldCares."

"Getting conspiratorial in your old age."

"I just spent an hour-plus talking to the guy. He answered every question I had."

"Then what's the problem?"

"I don't know. Probably nothing. He drinks."

"How much?"

"A bottle of wine for dinner." It didn't sound that bad when Wells said it out loud.

"Don't be such a Muslim neo-Puritan."

"Forget the wine. Tell me why he has two local phones."

"I'll do my best to find out. Maybe I'll do a little bit of research into WorldCares, too.

That press conference rated five hankies. I wanted to go over there my own self."

"You do, I'll feed you to the lions."

"How Old Testament. I'll call you after we run the numbers. Could be a day or two."

"Night, Ellis."

"An honest man's pillow is his peace of mind." *Click.*

5

Lower Juba Region, Somalia,
near the Kenya/Somalia Border

Little Wizard knew about the hostages. Four wazungu and a fat Kenyan. They were over the border in Ijara District, north and east of Ijara town. Of course Little Wizard knew. He knew everything that happened in the lawless zone where Somalia met Kenya.

Little Wizard was twenty years old. He'd been born Gutaale Muhammad, but no one called him that. Not since a firefight four years before in Mogadishu. Gutaale was at the point, leading a half-dozen other teenage soldiers. He was a scrap of a boy, wiry and strong, with light brown skin and tightly curled hair. They walked around a corner, past a burned-out building that had been a guesthouse for aid workers decades before, in happier times. Gutaale looked up to see a boy even younger than he was leaning out a second-floor window twenty meters away.

The boy swung an AK out the window, shooting wildly. Not a boy, then. An enemy soldier. Gutaale was about to fire back when all the air went out of him. Like he'd fallen from the top of a high tree. A killing shot. He doubled over, went to his hands and knees. Blood trickled from his stomach, just below his ribs. A wrecked pickup truck lay five meters away. He dragged himself to it and lay halfway under it in dust and mud.

He closed his eyes and listened to the pops of AK fire. Then the unmistakable whoosh of a rocket-propelled grenade. An explosion shook the truck above him, followed by a high-pitched scream. Waaberi, Gutaale's best friend, always carried an RPG. Gutaale's killer would die with him. The thought pleased him.

The shooting and shouting went on awhile. Gutaale didn't much care. He closed his eyes and listened. The noise seemed to be a long way off. Finally it stopped. His friends would surely come for him now.

"Move on," yelled Samatar, their nineteen-year-old commander.

"Gutaale," Waaberi said.

"We can't help him now. He's gone. On the way back."

Their feet crunched as they walked past the truck. They turned a corner and the shooting started again, single shots at first, then longer bursts. Gutaale lay in the dust and waited. No doctors or hospitals for him, not even the room at the back of the mosque that served as an infirmary for wounded fighters. A few minutes more passed. The shooting moved away. And Gutaale realized something strange. He felt stronger.

He crawled from under the truck, forced himself to his hands and knees. He raised his head over the side of the pickup. He was alone. Smoke billowed from the second-floor window where the boy who shot him had stood. Gutaale stumbled across the road and hid behind a pair of rusted oil drums. He breathed deep, feeling the burn in his belly. The bullet hole glowed pink in his brown-black skin. He reached down for it, pushed the tip of his finger inside. As gently as if he were touching a woman. Still too hard. The muscles around the wound pulled back and the pain spiraled inside him. Foolish. He reached behind his back, found the exit wound just above his hip, the skin around it slick and wet. He put his fingers to it, careful this time. He found a trickle of blood, nothing more. Like water from the dried-out wells in Bay Region. He wasn't sure how, but he sensed that the bullet had gone through him without hitting anything important. Not the heart or the lung or the other parts whose names he didn't know.

He would have to get the wounds stitched up. He would have to take the money hidden in his shoes to buy the special cream that kept them from getting infected. But he was sure he wouldn't die. When boys were dying, their eyes rolled up. They soiled themselves and screamed. They couldn't talk or stand. The fear settled into their eyes and then it left and then they died. Not everyone who died had all those things, but everyone had some. He had none. He was going to live.

The bullet had come and his body had rejected it, pushed it aside. Like he was metal and it was flesh instead of the other way around. Gutaale remembered a movie called *Terminator* about a man who was a robot. But he wasn't a robot. He was hungry and thirsty like other boys. He wanted women like other boys. So he was better than a robot, he was a man with a robot's strength. He was a wizard. He brought his fingers to his lips and kissed them and tasted his wizard blood.

A minute later, his friends came back around the corner, their heads hanging. Gutaale wondered if they were sad, sad he'd died. He ducked behind the oil drums and waited. They could have spotted him, but they were looking for a corpse, not a living boy. Not a wizard.

"Gutaale," Waaberi said.

"His own doing," Samatar said. "He danced around, dared them to shoot. Like no one could hurt him."

The wizard — for Gutaale already thought of himself that way — didn't remember dancing or daring anyone. No matter. Samatar was more right than he knew. *No one can hurt me.*

"He fought the best of all of us," Waaberi said.

Behind the drums, the wizard smiled. His truest friend. Waaberi would be his lieutenant, now and forever.

Waaberi squatted, looked under the pickup. "Here, wasn't it?" He waved the others over. "He's gone."

"It's not possible." Samatar knelt beside Waaberi. "Damn him. I wanted his shoes."

"See the blood. Someone took his body already."

The wizard stood from behind the oil drums. "I did, my brothers. I took my body." They turned to him, and he saw awe in their eyes. And fear. "I took it and gave it back to myself."

War and famine had killed most of Mogadishu's birds. Not the gulls. They went to the sea when the streets exploded. One was circling over the street. It offered its ugly cry, *caw-caw, caw-caw.* It circled down, landed on the drum beside the wizard. *Caw-caw! Caw-caw!*

One by one, the other boys came to him, touched his wounds like disciples. Samatar hung back. "You were lucky. Nothing more." He looked at the others. "He was lucky. Sometimes people are lucky." His voice trembled. "Or a djinn."

The wizard didn't argue. He looked at Waaberi, sure Waaberi would know what to do. "If you don't believe, then go," Waaberi said. "Leave us." He lifted his rifle. The others followed. And Samatar ran.

From then on, the men on that patrol called Gutaale Little Wizard. A month later, he and the others left Mogadishu for Lower Juba, the region in southwestern Somalia where he'd grown up. Only a line on a map split Lower Juba from Garissa and Ijara districts in Kenya. The region had two distinct climates. Near the coast, breezes from the Indian Ocean brought humidity and heavy seasonal rains. Creeks fed mangrove forests and swamps filled with giant black centipedes and snakes like the green mamba. The centipedes were ugly but harmless. The mamba was a skinny, beautiful creature whose fangs held venom that paralyzed in minutes and killed in hours. The swamps couldn't be farmed or ranched, and almost no one lived in them. Luckily, they didn't go on forever. Around forty kilometers inland, the ocean lost its influence. The wet breezes ended, and the creeks and swamps vanished.

But the dry region was only slightly more hospitable. Farming was nearly impossible, and even the deepest wells couldn't be trusted. Even before the drought and war, the region had been sparsely settled, with a handful of villages scattered across thousands of square miles. Now most of its inhabitants had fled for Dadaab. The rest had clustered into the few villages with reliable water. Little Wizard and his men faced no resistance when they moved into an abandoned village called Bora. At first they survived by smuggling sugar into Kenya. Kenyans loved sugar, but the Kenyan government taxed it heavily, creating an opening for smugglers. Wealthy Somalis bought sugar by the ton in Dubai and shipped it to Mogadishu and Kismaayo. From there, militias trucked it across Somalia and into

Kenya. Crossing was easy. For long stretches, the border wasn't even fenced. The Kenyan police rarely operated in the area. If they had to approach Somalia — if, say, a light plane crashed near the border and they were ordered to recover the pilot's body — they traveled in packs of a dozen or more officers from their headquarters on the coast. Otherwise, they avoided traveling within thirty kilometers of Somalia. They knew the militias outgunned them, and they feared being kidnapped.

Little Wizard used his sugar-smuggling profits to build a small but potent militia. On missions, his soldiers wore white T-shirts and kerchiefs to hide their faces. Villagers called them the White Men. Besides smuggling, they survived by charging aid convoys to pass through the region and collecting protection money from villages.

The White Men had about sixty-five soldiers. They could have had more. Every day, hungry men and boys trudged across the north part of Lower Juba on their way to the refugee centers in Kenya. More than a few had tried to join. But Little Wizard preferred a small force. His men could break camp in hours. They could live for months on food and water that a larger force would exhaust in weeks. Still, they had the firepower they needed to block humanitarian convoys and extract what Wizard called a toll, five percent of the food the trucks carried.

Little Wizard sometimes wondered whether the people sending the food understood that militias like his took most of it. Only a little reached the refugee camps in Bay Region. Even there the armed men who lived in the camps took most of the rest. Did these foreigners know that their plastic sacks of grain and sugar fed — literally — the war and the soldiers who fought it? If they knew, why did they keep sending the trucks?

When the Kenyan army invaded Somalia, Little Wizard knew he'd been wise to keep his force small. The Kenyans said they'd come for al-Shabaab, but they didn't care that groups like his didn't support Shabaab. Because Somalia had no central government, villages banded together to defend themselves. Some paid taxes to Shabaab. Others formed self-defense groups to keep raiders at bay. Villages too weak or too poor to protect themselves were overrun.

Shabaab flourished in the chaos, becoming the strongest and largest of the militias. But Shabaab didn't truly govern Somalia any more than anyone else. Outside its base towns, it had only provisional control. It lacked the firepower to stamp out groups like the White Men. And Little Wizard wanted nothing to do with Shabaab. He was Muslim, but not like them. As far as he was concerned, a man's prayers were his own business. The Shabaab fighters were fanatics who would have stoned Wizard to death as a heretic for his name alone.

But the Kenyans seemed to think that any armed group in Somalia was an ally of Shabaab. And they had tanks and planes, weapons the Somali irregulars couldn't match. Little Wizard didn't try to face the Kenyans. He ordered his men to pick up and melt south into the swamps, letting the soldiers roll past, into Shabaab's heartland. As far as he was concerned, every Shabaab fighter the Kenyans killed was one fewer for him to worry about.

The Kenyans had pulled out of Somalia a couple months before, after killing hundreds of Shabaab fighters. Shabaab still had plenty of men in other regions, but it basically no longer existed in Lower Juba. Wizard relaxed, figuring he'd escaped his biggest threat.

He knew now he'd made a mistake. Three weeks before, Awaale, the leader of a militia called the Dita Boys, asked him to meet. Little Wizard didn't want to go. He had nothing to say to Awaale. As far as he was concerned, the Dita Boys were undisciplined at best, vicious killers at worst.

On the surface, the Ditas and the White Men had a lot in common. Both would trash wells of villages that refused to pay protection. And, yes, the White Men killed villagers who fought them. But Little Wizard had strict rules for his men. A year before, he'd caught a new recruit raping a six-year-old girl. Wizard and Waaberi tied the rapist to a tree and beat him until his face looked like a melon that a truck had run over. Then Wizard ordered his men to come round.

"This is what we do to men who fuck children." Wizard pulled the knife strapped to his calf, a weapon made for murder with a black plastic handle and serrated blade. He sliced off the rapist's clothes and took the man's limp, blood-spattered penis in his left hand as he raised the knife with his right.

"Please," the rapist said, the words barely audible through his split lips. "Anything else."

"Your choice." Wizard plunged the knife into the man's stomach. The man's shoulders lifted in shock. For a moment, before the pain took over, his eyes widened and he raised his ruined face. Then he grunted, tried to scream. Wizard pulled the 9-millimeter pistol he carried in place of an AK, put it to the man's head, pulled the trigger. The man's brains moistened the tree behind him.

Wizard turned, faced his men.

"I have told you before. This one didn't understand. We don't rape. We don't steal. We take what we need, what I say we need, and no more. We are soldiers. We are an army. You want to be a beast, fight for someone else. Not for Wizard."

He pulled the knife from the rapist's belly, sliced open the rope, left the corpse on the ground with its guts hanging out. There were no more rapes.

The Dita Boys were different. Little Wizard knew what they did to refugees they caught crossing their territory. Especially women. He wished he could turn down the meeting. But he had to know what Awaale wanted. They agreed to meet in neutral territory, a watering hole on the edge of a village called Buscbusc, the strongest town left in all of Lower Juba. It had a sixty-man self-defense force. The militias left it alone.

Little Wizard arrived two hours early with

fifteen of his best men. They convoyed in two pickup trucks with .50-caliber machine guns mounted in their beds and two armored Range Rovers. The armed pickups, called "technicals," were the most common fighting vehicle in Somalia. The Rovers were more unusual, stolen from a UN lot in Mogadishu. They were Wizard's only indulgence. He'd spent $180,000 on them, half his profits of the last two years. They had run-flat tires, bulletproof windows, thick steel plates in the doors. They'd stop anything up to a machine gun round, maybe even a rocket-propelled grenade if it didn't hit a window. Wizard was unduly proud of them. When they needed repair, he brought in parts from Kenya. Being chosen to ride in a Rover was a mark of pride among the White Men.

The watering hole at Buscbusc consisted of four deep wells surrounded by a rock wall to keep animals or children from wandering in. Little Wizard put the pickups against the east wall, where their machine guns would have a clear field of fire. He put one Rover at the break in the wall that served as the watering hole's vehicle entrance. He stayed in the other Rover, next to the second well. He expected Awaale to bring more than fifteen men and he wanted to be ready.

The meeting was supposed to happen at eleven a.m. The Dita Boys arrived at noon, their pickup trucks blasting rap. When he heard them coming, Wizard stepped out of the Rover and stuffed a wad of miraa leaves — the stimulant that many Somali men chewed — in his mouth. His bodyguard, Ali, followed.

The faintly sour taste of the miraa filled Wizard's mouth. He felt the leaves lift him, sharpen his focus. His men hid their faces behind their white kerchiefs and tucked in their white T-shirts. Every boy who joined him got three kerchiefs and three T-shirts and had to be sure at least one was always perfectly clean. Wizard was the only fighter not in white. He wore a black shirt and black pants and no kerchief. The White Men might not be the biggest militia in Somalia, but they were the coolest. They didn't need Pit Bull or T-Pain to prove it.

The Dita pickups rolled up. Wizard counted eight, five with .50-calibers. Forty men, maybe more. Ali put a hand on his shoulder. Wizard brushed it off. He didn't fear these men. He walked to the Rover that blocked the gap in the wall, jumped on its hood. The diesel engine vibrated underneath his shoes. Three of his men tried to stand beside him. He waved them back, and they got low behind the hood, covering him with their AKs. Good.

His enemy had the numbers but not the tactical advantage. The Ditas were stupid, and they had stupidly lined their pickup trucks along the wall rather than clustering around the Rover. They were piling out of the trucks, but only the ones nearby had a clear shot. Wizard was less exposed than he seemed. But only a little, and not for long. He would have to control the moment.

"Awaale!"

Awaale stepped out of the nearest pickup. He was tall and broad and wore camouflage fatigues with the sleeves rolled up to show his big arms. The Dita Boys liked camo, but only a few had full uniforms. The rest made do with pants or T-shirts in mismatched patterns. Wizard had given his militia simple white shirts precisely to avoid this problem. Awaale's uniform had four silver stars on the shoulders. With his thick gold necklace and mirrored sunglasses, he could have passed for an old-school African dictator.

"You scared of me, Awaale." Wizard rested his hand on his 9-millimeter. Awaale raised his palms to the sky: *What, me worry?* Both playing to the fighters around them.

"You not scared, why you bring so many men?"

"Because I have so many. Don't know even what to do with them. And all them want to see you. The famous Little Chicken. Cluck cluck."

Wizard edged his pistol halfway from his holster. "Say it again."

He found himself looking at a forest of AKs. Awaale tapped his chest, his big arms glistening. "I say what I like."

"You called this parley. I came. You not scared —" Wizard pointed at the Rover. "We take a drive and talk, you and me only. Otherwise, let's get to it. Three seconds to choose."

"No need to count." Awaale raised his hands, gave Wizard two big thumbs-up. "Show me your fine Rover."

Wizard jumped off the Rover as Awaale stepped away from his men. They slid inside the SUV, Wizard driving.

"Nice," Awaale said. "Still smells new-like." He took a wad of miraa from his pocket. Wizard touched his arm. "Not inside. Leather seats and all that."

"Serious."

"Serious."

"I like this vehicle, Wizard. You know I do. But it just a car."

Wizard ignored this heresy. He drove west,

toward the border, on a dirt path that even the most optimistic mapmaker wouldn't have called a road. Both men still wore their sunglasses. One of Awaale's technicals trailed them. Wizard waited for Awaale to speak.

"You know we got to talk," Awaale finally said.

"Talk, then." Wizard hated the way Awaale said "you know" with every sentence.

"Shabaab, you know they're gone."

"Uh-huh."

"Juba open. Me and you come together, it's ours to take."

Awaale slipped off his glasses. Wizard followed. Down to it now.

"Plenty much room," Wizard said. "We do our business, you do yours."

"What I'm telling you, you know it can't be that way no more. With you, without you, I'm taking over. Bring your men in, you can be my number-one commander."

"You mean I give you my men and you tell me what to do?"

"I mean you my big lieutenant."

"Too much miraa, Awaale. Make you crazy."

"How many men you have? Sixty? Seventy? I have two hundred, and more every day."

Awaale was lying. He didn't have but 140 fighters, and they weren't nearly as good as Wizard's. But Wizard knew better than to argue. Arguing showed weakness. He contented himself with saying, "One of my men is worth five of yours."

"Two hundred. It's true. I got backing now."

"From who."

"People in Eastleigh. They see this chance. You don't believe me, come to my camp, count my men yourself."

Wizard stopped the Rover. "I come to your camp, I'll leave a hole in your head."

Awaale slipped on his sunglasses. "Then nothing else to say."

They didn't speak on the way back. Wizard wondered if Awaale might try to ambush him and his men when they returned. But he found that during the drive, Ali had moved the other Rover and the technicals outside the watering hole, making an attack impossible. Smart man. Wizard stopped the Rover beside Ali.

"Out."

"You won't drive me back to my men? Thought you were a wizard. No one touch you. Your men may believe that nonsense, but I don't, and I see you don't either."

"Out. Now."

Awaale offered Wizard a mock salute. "See you soon, Wizard."

Back at camp, Wizard told his men to be ready, that Awaale could attack at any time. But he knew that in Awaale's position, he'd wait. He'd add more fighters while letting the White Men exhaust themselves with overnight watches.

That night Wizard ordered a feast. He told his men the meal was a reward for their hard work. In fact, he wanted an excuse to slaughter the camp's animals. The herd wasn't much, a few bad-tempered goats and a dozen stringy hens. But if the White Men had to flee, they would leave the animals behind, and Wizard didn't plan to let the Dita Boys have them. A handful of younger boys protested. Wizard realized too late that they liked taking care of the goats and especially the chickens. He let them keep three hens and two goats. He wondered if he should put off the culling entirely, but reversing the order would seem strange to his men.

So they ate well that night, too well, and it was with a full belly that Wizard called Waaberi into his hut for a meeting. From the foot-locker by his bed, he unearthed the bottle of Johnny Walker Blue he had bought after his first successful smuggling run. Muslims weren't supposed to drink, but Wizard didn't much care. He poured them both a glass. Not too much. They needed clear heads tonight. Somewhere in the vast emptiness to the west, a hyena howled. A few seconds later, another answered. Then a third. The hyenas roamed all over East Africa, and they weren't afraid of war. They liked it. War left them meals.

"Take a drink and I tell you about the meet," Wizard said. He handed Waaberi a glass. Waaberi sipped carefully and listened. He knew his place. He didn't interrupt.

"You told him no," he said when Wizard finished.

"Of course no. Wants our men. We link with him, won't be a month before he slit my throat, and yours, too. You know he don't want a wizard around."

"You think he told true, about having two hundred? No brag?"

"I think. He had swagger, like he only needs one leg to walk. Told me to come by his camp if I didn't believe."

"Must have happened sudden or we would have heard."

"Said he getting money from Eastleigh. Someone fronting cash to pay new boys, give them guns, feed them. Even so, we can hold off two hundred. Those Dita Boys can't fight."

"But in three months, what if he have three hundred, four hundred?"

"What I'm thinking too, Waaberi. Plenty boys out there."

"So we bring in new boys, too."

"Could be." Wizard had enough extra weapons for another fifty men, and he could buy more. But recruiting might be tricky. Awaale's camp was closer to the main refugee routes, and Wizard guessed he was paying bonuses to anyone who joined. Plus adding men too fast had its own risks. Wizard knew the names of every one of his fighters. Every one of them had heard his story, seen his scars up close. They believed in him. He didn't want to risk that bond for a bunch of half-trained boys who might run if the Ditas attacked. "We can add ten or fifteen quick, but after that I don't know."

Again the hyenas howled, closer now. Wizard drank his Johnny Walker in one gulp and felt it glow inside him. He refilled his glass. He'd never had more than a single drink before.

"What about we talk to the villages? Everyone know we fairer than Awaale or anyone. They help us, we have plenty power."

Wizard wasn't so sure the villages would take sides. No doubt Awaale had spread the word that any village that supported the White Men would face payback after the Dita Boys won. The local elders didn't like Awaale. But they feared him even more.

"This my fault, Waaberi."

"Not so."

"Just so. Should have seen it, built us up. Should have known Shabaab gets weak, someone else going to try to get strong. How it is. Any weakness and the hyenas jump."

"You fix it, Wizard."

"I will. Always. Sentries posted?"

"You know it."

"In the morning, I'll talk to the villages."

But the elders put him off everywhere he went. They were polite. Some even friendly. They agreed when he told them they'd be sorry if Awaale took control. But not one would pledge support, not even weapons. Such important decisions had to be made carefully, they said. They had to talk over the situation. Like they ran provinces instead of villages with fifty families. Like they couldn't gather around and choose a side in five minutes. He knew what they were doing, but he couldn't argue.

The days ticked by. The sun rose at six a.m. and set at six p.m., as it always did on the fattest part of the globe. Twelve hours of day, twelve hours of night. The White Men added a few soldiers and buried their weapons reserve south of their main camp. Wizard knew he had to do more. The scouts he sent to the Dita Boys camp told him that Awaale was adding soldiers every day. In a month he'd have an overwhelming advantage. Then the White Men would have to run. Or die.

Yet Wizard felt paralyzed. He couldn't imagine crossing to the camps in Dadaab. Giving up his home and his Rovers and his men. For how would their faith in him survive such cowardice? He thought of attacking the Dita Boys, trying to catch them in the night. Spiking into their camp and killing Awaale and his top men. But the White Men would be hitting a force more than three times their size. They would need perfect surprise to win. And Wizard's scouts said that Awaale had his own sentries outside his camp. Wizard wished for the weapons the Americans had, their planes and helicopters. Even a few old Kenyan tanks. Instead he had his Rovers.

Then he heard about the hostages. An idea

crept on him, quiet and deadly as a mamba. He would be taking a big chance. The hostages were across the border. Wizard didn't know how many men held them. He couldn't be sure how he'd collect the ransom. He would make himself a target for the Americans. In normal times he would have dismissed the idea.

But these times weren't normal. He fell asleep every night wondering whether he'd wake to rap blasting from fifty Dita Boys technicals. He needed money. Money to make the villages choose his side. Money for seasoned fighters, not raw recruits. These hostages were young and American. They had to be worth millions of dollars. Enough money to change the balance of power in Lower Juba. Enough for him to destroy Awaale.

So, really, he had no choice. No choice but to hope his magic was even more powerful over the next days than it had been that morning in Mogadishu.

6

From Nairobi to Garissa, the A3 was freshly paved and lightly traveled. Martin drove flat out, slaloming past tanker trucks and matatus — brightly colored minibuses packed with travelers. As the Toyota descended from the central highlands, the giant baobab trees gave way to sisal plantations and open grassland. The morning sun poured in through the windshield, and Wells was glad for his Ray-Bans. Every few miles, troops of baboons ran along the road, cackling over jokes only they understood.

"I see why the settlers thought it was such a beautiful country," Wells said.

"The most," Martin said.

"It was settled long before the settlers," Wilfred said from the backseat. "Kikuyu and a dozen more tribes. Even after World War Two, the British didn't get the joke. Even then they made us fight for our country. After they put us to work to win their own freedom from Hitler."

Wells couldn't handle a lecture about colonialism on two hours' sleep. Besides, Wilfred was right. A pain in the ass, but right. "All I said was that it's beautiful. The British colonized America, too, and we fought them just like you did."

"We have so much in common." Wilfred put a skinny hand between the front seats. "Fist pump, my brother."

"I pay extra for the attitude, or is it included?"

"And on that couch yesterday you went digging for your roots."

"You chicken, Wilfred? Hoping I toss you out of the car so you can hitch your way home? Not happening. You're in it now. You want out, you quit. My brother."

"How can I be scared with the great white hunter protecting me?"

Wells supposed he'd just have to put up with the guy. Wilfred was smart enough, anyway. He'd shown up at the Hilton at six a.m. with a permit from the Interior Ministry: two pages, three signatures, and four stamps. "With this you can go anywhere the police do. After that, you're on your own."

They ran into their first roadblock at Mwingi, halfway to Garissa. A chicane of crude metal spikes forced Martin to pump the brakes. An officer in cheap mirrored sunglasses and a powder blue uniform stood by the road, waving cars through with a scarred wooden baton. When he saw Wells, he chopped the baton at the Toyota like a conductor demanding a surge from his orchestra. Martin pulled over, wheels on gravel. The officer strode up, ignoring the cars still passing through the chicane. Wells lowered his window, handed over the permit. The officer examined it through his shades.

"Passport."

The cop looked at that, too, shook his head in disgust. Wells expected questions, but the officer handed everything back, waved them on. Wells had questions of his own: Have you been told to look for any specific vehicle? Were you put here before the kidnapping or after? But the cop walked away before Wells could speak.

"If the papers are in order, why was he angry?"

"Because they are in order. And stamped by senior men. No bribe."

East of Mwingi, the land grew hot and dry. The grass thinned and patches of thorn bush appeared. The hills didn't disappear, but they shrank, as if the sun's rays had pounded them down. To the south, sheep nosed through the brush, watched over by unsmiling men with pistols on their hips, protection from lions and rustlers both.

The highway turned to gravel. The villages shrank to rows of concrete shacks along the road selling drinks and fruit and all manner of junk: choking-hazard toys, used batteries, donated clothes. "Tuck Parts," a sign above one shack proclaimed. Unrecognizable metal bits filled the shelves inside. At every village, the traffic pooled as truckers pulled over for food and less savory refreshment. Martin crept along as skinny men in mud-stained pants stood in the road holding mangoes. "Good, good, good," one said to Wells, his voice fast, desperate.

"I told you Kenya was poor," Wilfred said from the backseat.

"You should be a talk-show host. You never quit."

They hit another roadblock west of Garissa. Again the cop appeared more angry than happy to see Wells's papers. Garissa itself was a town of ten thousand or so with a slapped-together feel, new buildings with paint already peeling. Barbed wire and concrete barriers ringed the police headquarters. The stink of baked cow dung clotted the air. The place reminded Wells of the less attractive parts of the central Plains, right down to the name. Garissa, Nebraska. Class B football champs three years back.

"Big cattle market here," Wilfred said. "The herders bring cows and sheep from all over the province. Somalis mostly. Garissa is filled with Somalis."

"Refugees?"

"No. Kenyan Somalis. Even before the refugees, Kenya had Somalis. They live between here and the border. Also in Eastleigh. That's in Nairobi, near downtown."

"A slum?"

"Yes and no. Eastleigh's crowded, but not cheap to live in. The Somalis in Nairobi have money. Nobody knows where it's from. Probably they take the profits from kidnapping and smuggling and move it to the banks in Kenya. In the last few years, they bought up Eastleigh. You have an apartment worth one million shillings, they give you one million five hundred thousand for it. Then they move all their family in, twelve or fifteen or them. They stay together. They think they're better than Kenyans."

"They're Kenyan citizens?"

"Some yes, some no. Doesn't matter. They're all Somali. You can tell because they have round heads, small ears."

"Round heads and small ears?"

"Ugly little people." Wilfred tilted his head at the men walking on the street. "See, he's Somali, he's Somali, that whole bunch is Somali —"

Somalis did look different from the Kenyans, though Wells wasn't sure he'd call them ugly. Northern Somalia was a short boat ride from Yemen and the Arabian peninsula. The Arab influence was clear. Most obviously, Somalis had relatively light skin.

"You're quite the racial scholar, Wilfred. The National Socialists would be proud."

"National Socialists?"

"Nazis." Wells found himself irrationally pleased to have gotten one past the guy.

"Say what you want. Everyone knows the Somalis look different. And Garissa is a Somali town."

"I give you twenty bucks, will you stop talking until the next roadblock?"

"No."

An hour past Garissa, they hit another barricade. This one was serious, a five-ton truck blocking the road, a squad of guys in camouflage unis and AKs peering into vehicles.

"The army?" Wells said. "Will they take the permit?"

"They're General Services Unit. Specially

trained police. In America, you would call them paramilitary. They watch the camps."

"So they're in charge of investigating the kidnapping?"

"I think so, yes."

But paramilitary guys were usually door-kickers. Wells wondered if they'd have any interest in the detective work required to solve a kidnapping. Another reason why the Kenyan police investigation seemed to be moving so slowly.

Martin stopped near the pickup. Two officers walked over. Special training or no, their weapons discipline was unimpressive. One guy held his AK loosely by the barrel, like a hitter heading back to the dugout after a strikeout. Even Afghans took gun safety more seriously.

The first officer leaned into the car. "Turn around. No foreigners."

Wells handed over both permits and his passport. The officer barely looked at the papers before handing them back. He pointed down the road the way they'd come: *Go home.* Wells reached for the door, but Wilfred moved first. He snatched the permits from Wells and nearly jumped out of the backseat. He stepped up to the officer, yelling in Swahili. The commotion attracted the rest of the squad. The officers fanned out around Wilfred.

Wells stepped out, grabbed Wilfred by the arm, pulled him away, around the back of the Toyota. "I'm telling him, the permits are good, you're allowed —" Wilfred said.

"You're blowing this up on purpose —"

"It's my country. Let me."

The police had circled the Toyota now, rifles at their sides, muttering to each other. "He sends us back to Nairobi, you're riding in the trunk," Wells said. He let go of Wilfred, who walked back to the officer. The shouting match started again. Wilfred reached into his pocket and Wells heard the distinct click of a safety being dropped —

Before Wells could move, Wilfred came out with a phone. "Call Nairobi if you want, you donkey," Wilfred said in English to the officer. "Tell Commander Embu you're rejecting us. That or let us go. Enough."

The final miles to Dadaab passed quickly. The road was deserted aside from a slow-moving food convoy, a dozen trailers with a four-truck police escort. The land around them was inhospitable, arid plain patched with scrub. They reached the WorldCares compound around noon and found that James Thompson had kept his word. When Wells showed his passport, the guards waved the Toyota through. The compound immediately impressed Wells as simple and functional, not overly fancy. Residential trailers filled one corner, the food and supply warehouse another, the kitchen and headquarters a third, and parking and mechanicals like generators the fourth. A neatly tended rose garden outside the headquarters building provided the only color.

But the place seemed to be running at half-speed. Four Land Cruisers sat under a metal sunscreen, their windshields covered in red dust. A black cat with a white blaze emerged from the roses, meowed at Wells, strolled off. The place reminded Wells of a military base set to close: *Why bother?* was practically skywritten overhead. He imagined the kidnapping had stunned everyone. Still, he was surprised not to see Kenyan cops around.

"You and Martin go talk to the local staff and the guards," Wells told Wilfred. "Anyone you can find. Ask them about this guy Suggs. Who he knew in the camps, his relationship with the volunteers, if he had money problems —"

"It's Kenya. Everyone has money problems."

"Just do it. You hear anything I should know, find me."

"Yes, great white hunter."

As Wells walked toward the headquarters, one of the homeliest women he'd ever seen emerged. "Mr. Wells. I'm Moss Laughton." She led him to her office, a simple square room with white-painted concrete walls, their only decoration maps of Hagadera. She had short hair and black glasses and sat on her couch with her legs folded. She reached out a hand and offered Wells a snaggle-toothed smile.

"Thanks for having us."

"Jimmy's orders."

"People call him Jimmy?" James Thompson didn't strike Wells as a Jimmy.

"I call him Jimmy. Whenever possible. It irritates him, but he can't fire me, because he sure doesn't want to be in Dadaab eleven months a year. Anyway, I'm thinking about quitting, so I do what I like."

Thirty seconds in and this conversation was shaping up to be as odd as his encounter at Castle House. Wells wondered if Moss was trying to say *You'll get the truth from me if you ask the right questions* or if she was simply half crazy from the heat and dust.

"So what do you think happened?" Wells said.

"No idea. Gwen's family hired you?"

"Yes. I used to work for the CIA."

"Of course. I remembered your name, but it took me a bit of Googling to figure out why."

"That's me."

"And now you're here."

"Now I'm here."

"Any progress so far?"

Wells shook his head. "Do you remember when they planned the trip? James wasn't sure."

"I don't know exactly, but Gwen mentioned Lamu to me maybe three days before they went. She was nervous, poor thing, but the others convinced her."

"And off they went in a WorldCares Land Cruiser."

"Correct."

"Which had no sat phone."

She smiled. He saw she was pleased, that he'd passed a test he hadn't known he was taking. "We have seven Cruisers. Four have phones. Not this one. A coincidence, no doubt. Anyway, off they went. You know the rest."

"When did you report the kidnapping?"

"To the police? Or the embassy?"

"Either."

"I didn't report anything. I think Jasper —"

"The head of security —"

"Yes. He made the call. But it might have been Jimmy himself. In any case, it wasn't until the next morning. I wanted to do it right away, but Jimmy thought we should wait."

"Why?"

"He said the Kenyan police were useless and corrupt. He's right about that. He said that if the kids were okay, we'd hear in the morning and there was no need to panic everyone. If they weren't, there was nothing anyone could do until the sun came up, and we might as well wait."

"You didn't agree."

"I thought the risks were the other way. Let the cops throw up a roadblock, no harm. See if anybody in Nairobi would pay attention. I thought at the time he was worried about bad publicity. Although he's turned out to be wrong about that. From what the staff in Houston tell me, this has been pure gold. Millions of dollars in donations. Biggest week in WorldCares history."

"He didn't mention that last night."

"Of course, we're taking every dime. We have to —"

"Because your insurance company won't cover this. And the ransom could be several million dollars. That much he did tell me." Wells realized something else, a connection he wished he'd made before. "No insurance company paying —"

"Means no hostage negotiators on site and no pesky insurance investigation into what happened."

Moss Laughton was throwing out some big hints. "You don't trust your boss much."

"I don't know what you're talking about."

"Does Jasper feel the same?"

"You ought to ask him. Too bad you can't. He's in Nairobi with Jimmy."

"The head of security isn't here?"

" 'Head of security' is a fancy way to describe him. Basically he makes the schedules, makes sure we have guards out front. Nobody says it, but we like having one white guy with a gun around. So we call him head of security."

"Whatever you call him, I'm surprised he's not here."

"He doesn't speak Swahili, so I'm not sure what he'd do."

"How about the police? They must have come by."

"The GSU, sure. They poked through the trailer that Gwen and Hailey shared. I think they were more interested in Gwen's underwear than anything else. If they found anything, they didn't tell me."

"Where's the Land Cruiser?"

"They towed it to their headquarters in Garissa. I doubt there was any forensic evidence to find, but if there was, I can guarantee it's gone. They've talked to everybody here, I wouldn't call them interviews, more like, tell us what you know or we'll take you out back, give you a working-over. Truncheon in hand."

Truncheon. A good Irish word. "Anyone give them anything? Here or in the camps?"

"Not that I know of. They're not good at sharing, the GSU."

"Any Americans been here?"

"Four nice men with short haircuts showed up three days ago. Two had business cards saying they were from the embassy. The other two didn't tell me their names. They wanted to take the laptops that the kids used. I said no, but I did let them do what they wanted to them here."

So the agency and NSA were doing what they did best, chasing electronic intel. No doubt they had mirrored the hard drives. "What about phones?" Wells said.

"They asked about mobiles too, but I told them the truth, those kids couldn't be separated from their handsets."

"They look at anyone else's computers?"

"Like mine or Jimmy's? Now, why would they do a thing like that?" She pulled two water bottles from the minifridge beside the couch. "My one luxury. Have to have cold water."

She passed him one. He drank gratefully. His thirst had come up quietly. The sun here baked out moisture in a way that was almost pleasant. Until it wasn't.

"So, just to be clear. They didn't look at your computer, or Jimmy's."

"No. Anyway, it wouldn't have mattered. Jimmy practically chains his laptop to his wrist. Very concerned about computer security, my boss."

"Any reason in particular?"

"Not that I'd know of." Moss showed him her crooked teeth again. "I'm trying to stick to the facts here, you see. What I know firsthand."

"That's admirable. How about this, then? What did you think of the volunteers? Were they in the way?"

"The truth is that on a daily basis this isn't rocket science. We provide food, water, basic medical care. The Kenyans police the camps. The refugees govern themselves. We're not supposed to get involved with their politics. We can advocate for them, but our power is limited. That's not just World-Cares, by the way. It's everybody, even the big groups. What I'm saying is reading to the kids like Gwen did, working at the hospital like Hailey, it's as useful as anything anybody here is doing once you get past the basic provision of services."

A long not-quite-answer. Wells tried again. "You got along with them?"

"I had a funny moment with Gwen her first day. She came out of her trailer wearing a T-shirt that hardly covered her chest. I told her that wasn't how we did things here. To her credit, she was more appropriate after that. Made the effort. Hailey and Owen worked hard, and even Scott. Though I didn't like him much. Spent his time either insulting or screwing Gwen, from what I could see. Why she put up with it, I don't know."

"And how well did you know Suggs?"

"Suggs. Anybody ever tell you about the chairs?"

Wells shook his head.

"No reason they would have. A couple years back, the Kenyan members of parliament decided they needed new seats on which to rest their royal asses. They found these chairs that cost, I think, twenty-five hundred dollars each. The Kenyan parliament has more than two hundred members, so they'd be spending half a million dollars on these chairs. In a country where the average income is about two dollars a day. Naturally, the newspapers found out and made a stink."

"And the MPs backed off."

"They went right ahead. What I'm trying to say is that the Kenyans, they're very friendly people. And they aren't all crooks. Plenty of them are honest. But, blame it on poverty or loyalty to tribe or whatever you like, the me-first attitude runs deep. Suggs was one of those guys, we paid him well, he helped us, but I never trusted him. He looked like a gangster. That was intentional. He liked everybody to know he could work both sides. I don't know if he set this up, but I wouldn't be shocked."

"But when you talk to staff —"

"If they know, they aren't telling. And I've talked to them all."

"Did Suggs suggest the Lamu trip to Scott Thompson?"

"Don't know. But a couple weeks ago, Suggs and Scott Thompson drove off together. They said they were going to another camp to see if they could start deliveries there. It didn't make sense then and it makes even less now."

"You think Suggs set him up somehow?"

"I'm telling you what I saw. I can't guess what it means."

"Suggs was from Nairobi, right?"

"No, Mwingi, west of here. His family lived in Nairobi."

"In Eastleigh."

"No. He wasn't Somali."

"But he'd worked at Dadaab awhile."

"That's right. He was connected in the camps. But let me tell you something you might not want to hear, Mr. Wells. I don't care what you've done over the years, how tough you think you are, you are not going to be able to go into Hagadera or any of these camps and crack skulls and get answers —" The last five words were delivered in a parody of a tough Mickey Spillane voice. "These people can see you coming a hundred kilometers away. And what will you threaten them with? You can't send them back to Somalia, you can't arrest them, you don't know anything about them, you have no leverage. All you are is another mzungu poking at them."

"Guess I'll have to use my charm, then."

"Good luck with that. And before you ask, I don't have any great ideas for you. But I thought you should know."

The warning didn't come as a surprise, but it was depressing anyway. Wells took another glance around. No photos or personal items of any kind, just the desk, the fridge, and the battered furniture. "Tell me about yourself."

"What do you want to know?"

"I've seen prison cells are better decorated than this."

"Sentiment's a luxury, as I suspect you understand."

"How long have you worked for WorldCares?"

"Three years. I was at the Red Cross, but they stopped promoting me and Jimmy came looking, told me he wanted to professionalize WorldCares. He'd gotten dinged for spending too much money on fundraising and overhead, not enough on projects on the ground. He said he wanted to do a better job."

"And."

"And he did. In Haiti and here. The year before I came, WorldCares raised five million dollars and only a million-two hit the ground. Last year it got up to sixteen, seventeen million dollars and maybe six million went to programs. About half in Dadaab. Do the math, we were spending twenty-four percent on programs. Now it's thirty-seven percent."

"So that's good."

"Yes, but if you look at it the other way, overhead's gone from four million to ten million in three years. Jimmy makes eight hundred thousand a year, plus benefits. Which are big. He lives rent-free in a nice house in Houston, gets a new Lexus every year, flies first-class. Really, he's paying himself over a million. Look at the way he lives, you'd think he worked for Exxon. Not a charity serving the poorest people in the world. I mean, he's a right smart fund-raiser, you saw it in Nairobi. Puts a tear in your eye and a lump in your throat."

"You're reaching for your checkbook and your credit card at the same time," Wells said.

"Exactly. But I always thought the idea was to raise money to do good work. I fear Jimmy has that equation reversed."

Wells nodded.

"I've done all right, too. He started me at three hundred thousand. Now I'm at three-fifty and he's offered to bump me to four 'cause he's worried I'm serious about quitting. Which is a lot for these jobs, believe me. Truth is I just put it in the bank anyway. I don't have kids, I spend eleven months a year here, and you see my fashion sense. But I'm starting to feel like he's buying me. Which I can't abide."

"You've told him this."

"And he tells me fund-raising is part of

the game, it takes money to make money. And look, we spend three million dollars a year here, we do some good. My big project for next year, before this happened, was supposed to be getting glasses and dental work to the kids here. Those maybe sound like luxuries, but they're not. You can't see, you don't have much chance in a place like this. Your teeth hurt all the time, it's misery. That's the upside of working with a guy like Jimmy. Places like the Red Cross, they're in love with their own bureaucracies. Anything new takes years to approve. Jimmy lets me do what I want, long as I send back pictures he can use for fund-raising."

"Were you surprised when he came over for so long?"

Moss sipped her water. "Smart boy. Yes. I thought it was for the reporter from Houston. His hometown paper and he wanted to look hands-on, and if that meant putting in a few weeks here, he would."

"Now you're not so sure."

She shook her head. "I can't figure it. I know I mentioned the insurance. But the fact is I can't see Jimmy risking those kids. He may be greedy but I've never seen him as a psychopath. And I can't believe the four of them, or five if you count Suggs, are hiding in a hut somewhere, watching the world go crazy. Maybe Scott would think it was a lark, but not the others. Gwen wouldn't put her family through that worry for all the money in the world. I'm sure. Beyond that, anything's possible."

Anything's possible. The world's epitaph. "I come up with anything else —"

"I'm here. Not much to do right now. I wasn't sure about you, thought you might be a cowboy, but now I see you're serious, I'm happy to give you the run of the place. You can stay in Hailey and Gwen's trailer. It's empty. Not counting the beauty products Gwen left behind."

"Further proof she was planning to come back."

Moss laughed, the sound surprisingly sweet. "That is the truth."

The trailer was cluttered with what Wells would always think of as girl stuff, nail files, shampoo bottles, and panties. He assumed the Kenyan police had left the mess. Still, he found himself glad to be in his forties, too old even to imagine being with women so certain that their looks would carry them through life. He poked around half-heartedly, but the search depressed him. He hoped he didn't find anything too intimate, not just topless photos or love letters, but the private stumblings that everyone had at home, expired vitamins and half-finished doodles and unread Christmas cards.

After a few minutes he felt foolish for his modesty. The girls would trade loss of privacy for freedom in a heartbeat. So he stripped the beds and looked under the mattresses. He turned out Gwen's backpack and the twin chests of drawers and even looked through her magazines, hoping for a scrawled phone number or email address.

By the time he finished, the sun was down and Wells could hear the compound's electric lights droning outside. He straightened up the place and walked over to Owen and Scott's trailer to repeat the search. Wilfred intercepted him.

"Bossman. Superbossman. Great mzungu. A guard, Ashon, he told me, two, three weeks ago, he saw Suggs with all these papers, brochures for houses in Johannesburg. Like he wanted to jet" — Wilfred raised his hand like a plane taking off — "out of Kenya."

"People have fantasies."

"Suggs hid the papers when Ashon saw them."

"People don't always want to share their fantasies. Did Ashon tell the GSU?"

"He tried, but they told him to shut up.

Like you, man. They don't listen. Ashon said Shabaab, Shabaab, Shabaab is all they talk about."

The fact that Suggs had been checking out real estate didn't interest Wells nearly as much as the fact that the police didn't care. They seemed intent on ignoring any lead that didn't point to Somalia.

"Nice job, Wilfred. You get anything else, you tell me."

Wells spent the next couple hours searching Owen and Scott's trailer, which was littered with brochures for safari camps in the Tsavo game parks. Those were two hundred miles southwest of Dadaab, nearly as close to Dadaab as Lamu. The parks would have been a natural choice for a vacation, one that Owen and Scott seemed to have considered. Then they'd decided to go to Lamu instead, with Suggs encouraging them. Suggs. Wells wondered if he shouldn't have stayed in Nairobi, tried to find Suggs's wife.

He was leaving the trailer when his phone buzzed. Shafer.

"How's it going?"

"I'm in Dadaab."

"Finding anything?"

"Bits. Suggs, the fixer, I think he was probably involved, but it's just my gut so far. And the Kenyan police seem obsessed with proving Shabaab's behind this. From what I can see, they've hardly looked at him. They're not even here. You get anything from Fort Meade?"

"You think I'm calling just to hear your voice? They ran all three numbers. The international is clean. Incoming calls from the families, press, WorldCares in Houston. One of the locals is the same. Thompson used it for calls to other Kenyan numbers, and we've found almost all of them. The police, other aid agencies, other local WorldCares employees."

"And the third number?"

"That one's a problem. The problem is it doesn't exist. It's not a working number in Kenya or anywhere else. Never has been. You sure you wrote it down right?"

Wells eyed his phone like a baseball player checking out his glove after an error: *I blame you.* "Yes. He gave it to me twice."

"Did you call it when you were in the room with him, hear it ring?"

"No."

"You know, four years ago the Texas attorney general investigated the charities in the state that spent the most money on fund-raising and the least on programs. WorldCares was high on the list. Thompson wasn't indicted or anything like that, but the report isn't pretty."

"The woman in charge here told me something similar." Wells explained what Moss had said. "But she also said they've come back strong. Tripled fund-raising and spending more on programs. Why blow everything up?"

"Think like a grifter, John. When things are going good, that's when you press your luck. Double down."

"If you're right, why would he let me come here and give me the run of the place? He didn't have to. Could have said it was too dangerous for me."

"Maybe he thinks you're too dumb to find anything."

"Thank you, Ellis."

"Another fun fact. You know Thompson's got that new book coming out. It's not even being published for two months, but since that press conference it's number one on Amazon."

"You think he'd let his nephew get kidnapped for a book?"

"I think you better get that third phone of his so the smart boys can trace it."

"Unfortunately, he's in Nairobi."

"Then get him to Dadaab." Shafer hung up.

■ ■ ■ ■

"Couldn't stay away?" Moss said when he walked into her office.

"How many phones does James have?"

"Two, I think." She scrolled through her own phone. "I have two numbers for him. One local, one U.S."

"Could he have had a second local handset?"

"Don't know why. We all use Safaricom here and it works fine."

"Can you get him back here?"

"That's up to him. He's the boss, remember?"

"Okay, say I can convince him to come back. Can he charter a plane tonight?"

"Nobody sane will fly to Dadaab at night. Tomorrow morning is the best you can do. But you'll need a good reason."

"I'll think of one."

"He has another phone?"

"I saw it. Last night in the hotel. And he lied to me about it."

"So what will you tell him?"

Wells paused. "What about, I think I've found the volunteers, that they're here, and I want to saddle up tomorrow and go in and get them. I'll tell him I'm gung-ho and locked and loaded. And if he asks you, you tell him that you think I'm dumb enough to do it."

"But what if you're right and he knows they're not here?"

"Then he has to come. To stop me from causing a riot or worse. Whatever he's got planned, that's not part of the program."

"Okay, say it works. You get him on a plane. But there's one thing I don't see. What are you going to do with him when he lands?"

7

Langley

Age brought wisdom. So Shafer had heard. He disagreed.

He was closing in on seventy, old enough to know the truth. His friends and neighbors and college classmates hadn't grown wiser over the years. They'd just grown more like themselves, become more of whatever they were when they were young. The introverts faded into oblivion. The lazy divided their time between television and naps. The business guys played golf every day, shooting ninety-five with fifteen mulligans. The drinkers . . . they drank. Until they died.

Shafer didn't understand any of them. So few winks left on this mortal coil, and they wanted to *golf*? He tried not to spend time with anyone his age, though all too often he had no choice. Only his wife understood how he felt. His friends didn't want to hear about their mortality, and nobody under fifty had a clue what he meant. They thought they did, but they didn't. They couldn't help but find him ridiculous. Young people always found their elders ridiculous. Just you wait, sonny . . .

So Shafer worked. A few months ago, he'd admitted the truth. No more talk of retirement. He would come to Langley until the guards locked his office and dragged him out. He guessed he'd become more like himself, too. He was sharper and more impatient and more cynical than he'd been when he joined the agency almost forty years before. And he'd been plenty cynical then. Working in Africa in the 1970s had wiped away any and all his illusions about human nature. Sometimes he thought that Idi and Mobutu and the rest of the Big Men were running their own private game to see who could be most brutal, most decadent, most flat-out evil. I'll see your gold-plated electric testicle clamps and raise you a soup bowl made of a human skull. First prize was eternity in hell. Second prize was eternity minus a day. But young Ellis Shafer didn't protest. No one from the agency did. Human rights had been even lower on Langley's priority list back then.

Now Africa had come back to him. Thanks to Wells. Poor Wells. Odd to think of the man that way when he'd killed more guys over the years than a plane crash, but Shafer knew as much as anyone the price Wells paid for what he did. Especially the last couple years, as the wars dragged on and the missions got messy. Wells was still big, but the pictures were small.

This one had looked different at first. Simple. Clean. A way for Wells to rebuild his relationship with his son. Shafer wanted Wells to have that chance.

Then James Thompson gave Wells that fake number.

Even before the NSA told Shafer about the phone, he wondered about Thompson. Everything about him seemed a little too slick. Pictures of him were all over the WorldCares website. One page highlighted Thompson's availability for speeches. "Let the head of one of America's fastest-growing charities share his inspiring secrets with you! Mr. Thompson donates all speaking fees from corporations or for-profit organizations to WorldCares," the page explained. But when Shafer checked Thompson's schedule, he found that the guy spoke mostly to non-profit groups like colleges and think tanks. The website was silent on what happened to those fees.

Then there was the Texas attorney general's report: "WorldCares's board has been overly deferential to Thompson . . . Thompson's pay is in the top one percent nationally for all charities of WorldCares's size . . . Thompson regularly charged meals at some of Houston's most expensive restaurants to his WorldCares expense account . . ."

Since then, Thompson had run WorldCares more carefully. The group had increased spending on overseas programs. But Shafer wondered if he was doing the minimum so WorldCares wouldn't get dinged again.

After he hung up with Wells, Shafer scoured Thompson's life for signs of distress, financial or otherwise. He found nothing. No liens, no lawsuits in state or federal court, no drunk-driving charges or even jaywalking tickets. Thompson attended an inordinate number of galas in Houston, if the *Chronicle*'s society page was to be believed, but going to fancy parties wasn't a crime. He'd never been married, but being a bachelor — or gay — wasn't a crime either. By 7:30 p.m., Shafer's eyes ached from all the reading. He wanted to go home, but he knew he ought to stay, look over the classified briefings Nairobi station had produced in the last two days. Then the phone trilled —

"Ellis." His master's voice. The one and only Vinny Duto.

"Director."

"I'd like to offer you a ride home this evening."

"Need a partner to carpool? Sides of beef up front don't count?"

"Something like that."

"Don't you usually make the proles stand aside with your emergency lights?"

"See you in five." Click.

Shafer had trouble believing the kidnapping of four volunteer aid workers had turned into a seventh-floor problem. On the other hand, the story was everywhere. #freethefour was the top hashtag on Twitter. CNN and Fox were still running clips from Thompson's tearful press conference.

Duto's convoy was idling when Shafer got downstairs. Three Crown Vics and two Suburbans. The showiness of these official details infuriated Shafer. They sent the message that citizens existed to serve the government, instead of vice versa. A generation ago, CIA directors had made do with a couple of bodyguards. Now even one-star generals who specialized in procurement were given armored cars.

"Evening, Vinny. Shouldn't you be kissing ass for campaign donations? Instead of riding around like a Russian plutocrat?"

"Your dentures are clicking, Ellis."

They rolled out the main Langley gate onto 123. The evening traffic was hardly moving, but the convoy wasn't running its flashers. Shafer figured that Duto expected the conversation to last awhile.

"What's Wells doing in Dadaab?" Duto said without preamble.

"You care about the Fab Four?"

"What's Wells doing in Dadaab?" As if Shafer hadn't spoken at all.

"Ask him."

"I'm asking you."

"You know what he's doing. Looking for them."

"And you're helping. Asking our friends in Maryland to run numbers for him."

"They're not our friends. They're more like our geeky half brother, the one we made fun of all through high school. Then out of nowhere he invented Google and now he's a billionaire."

"I don't think you answered my question, Ellis."

"In my cleverness I've forgotten it."

"Cleverness or old age?"

"I can't remember."

"Let me ask again. Why are you asking NSA to run Kenyan phone numbers?"

"John asked me to."

"You know what the Kenyans want? What their ambassador told the President last night?"

Shafer had plenty of answers to that question, from *More visas* to *A new pony,* but years of trial and error had taught him that these conversations had a rhythm. Annoying Duto too hard for too long put him in lockdown. And Duto seemed to have something important to say. Shafer held his tongue.

"They want us to help them out with al-Shabaab," Duto said. "And by 'help out,' I mean invade."

"They must know we're not going anywhere near Somalia. They've seen *Black Hawk Down* like everybody else."

"That was twenty years ago. This is now. Nick Kristof writes about South Sudan so much it's like he's running tours to the place. And guess what, people listen. They want to know why we and our trillion-dollar military don't do something about it."

"But South Sudan is a thousand miles from Somalia."

"Out there" — Duto pointed vaguely at the cars on 123 — "it's just Africa. And

Africa is hot again. Right now we the people, in our infinite wisdom, for reasons neither you nor I can divine, take our minds off the economy, whatever, we have decided to give a rat's ass. Conflict minerals, Joseph Kony, Congo, it's all bad. And we need to fix it. Shoot the Children and Save the Warlords, or maybe the other way round."

"You're on a roll, Vinny. Please continue."

"Which is to say these four nitwits picked either a really good time or a really bad time to get kidnapped. The Kenyans, they see everybody's paying attention. And, back to where this started, they want us to finish off Shabaab. Go over the border into Somalia and wipe them out."

Shafer understood. "Why they keep fingering Shabaab for the kidnapping. The next step, they start pushing us, first in private, and then in public, to go into Somalia to get the volunteers."

"Correct. And there are folks in Stuttgart more than happy to do that."

"Stuttgart?"

Duto smiled. His teeth were white and perfect. They hadn't always been. "I'm disappointed in you, Ellis. You don't know that Stuttgart, Germany, is the home of Africom, especially created by the Pentagon in 2007 to oversee military operations in

Africa. And General Ham, commander of Africom, knows very well that his pride and joy is A-one on the chopping block with budget cuts coming."

"His name's really Ham, Vinny? That's unfortunate. On several levels."

"Carter Ham, yes. Point is that he's looking for something to do. You can assume that colonels in Germany are working up PowerPoint presentations as we speak."

"And you're sharing all this with me because you're not in favor."

"Enough is enough. Time to give the frontline guys a break. Even if this is only ten, fifteen thousand soldiers, you know what everybody who just got home from Afghanistan is gonna think? Here we go again. Now we're attacking Africa? Guys are gonna snap. But our lifers by the airport" — the Pentagon was just across 395 from Reagan National — "you know how they are. Best way to get promoted is to plan a war that actually happens."

"You think we could send fifteen thousand men? For four hostages?"

"We sent more than that to Mogadishu twenty years ago."

"That was a famine, Vinny."

"It's Somalia. There's always a famine. Not saying it's a lock. Just that everything's lining up. The media's going crazy, the Kenyans are whispering sweet nothings, Africom's gung-ho, and it looks like an easy win. White House loves those. So we figure we'll go in with a battalion, and before we know it we have three brigades committed. Mission creep."

Shafer enjoyed hating Duto. Not just because Duto was arrogant or a bully or a liar, though he was all those. Duto was the system made flesh, the physical embodiment of the agency's worst traits, its self-protective bureaucracy and endless craving for more. More meaning more money, more operatives, and more authority to fly unmanned drones in a worldwide covert war. The drone program galled Shafer. The agency killed scores of suspected terrorists each year without ever telling the public — much less the targets — how it chose them.

Killing top-level targets like Ayman al-Zawahiri made sense. But Shafer believed that Duto had allowed the agency to rely too heavily on missile attacks. The endless assassinations damaged America's moral standing. They would inevitably create a new generation of terrorists desperate to revenge themselves on American soil. Even the names that the Air Force and General

Atomics had given the drones annoyed Shafer: The MQ-1 Predator. The MQ-9 Reaper. What, The FU-69 Awesome Flying Killing Machine That'll Blow Your Terrorist Ass to Shreds would have been too subtle?

But as far as Shafer could tell, Duto didn't worry about long-term blowback. To him, the drones were the best kind of program, one that provided easily measurable evidence of its effectiveness. Every quarter, Duto could offer PowerPoint shows to the congressional intelligence committees detailing how many missiles the agency had fired, how many targets it had killed. Even better, the strikes happened in unpleasant places like central Yemen. Independent journalists and aid groups had little chance to discover who had really been killed. The congressional committees were happy to take Duto's assurances. No one wanted to ask too many specifics and mess up a program that seemed to be disrupting terrorist activity at little risk to Americans.

Truly, Duto had won. On his watch, the CIA had helped find Osama bin Laden and set back the Iranian nuclear weapons program. Within the alphabet soup of agencies that made up the American intelligence community, no one doubted that Duto was more powerful than the Director of National

Intelligence, his nominal boss.

Now he'd decided to get involved with these hostages. Shafer suspected Duto couldn't care less about the morale of the soldiers who might be sent to Somalia. Most likely he wanted one final triumph before riding off into his Senate campaign. If the CIA found the hostages, it would make sure that the reporters who covered the agency gave it — and its director — full credit.

But Shafer knew he had no choice but to rise to Duto's bait. He couldn't stand by as the United States skidded toward another military adventure. In his own way, Duto was brilliant. He was profoundly amoral, but he knew how to use morality's tug to mold Shafer and Wells to his own ends. He knew they would grit their teeth and let him use them. He didn't even have to lie, at least not today.

Duto turned toward Shafer now, his body broadcasting his eagerness to win Shafer's agreement. "You're about as subtle as a car salesman," Shafer said.

"Another war. You want that?"

No. I don't. Especially not if this kidnapping is some game James Thompson is playing.

"What's John doing, Ellis?" Duto pressing his advantage.

"He's at the WorldCares compound, that's

really all I know."

"Why'd he get involved at all?"

"His son asked." Shafer explained Evan's connection. "Anyway, he talked to Thompson last night after the press conference. Asked me to run Thompson's phone numbers through NSA."

"And one came back blank?"

Fortunately, at that moment the Suburban stopped short and Shafer had a chance to hide his surprise. He wondered if he'd ever stop underestimating Duto. Just because the guy had stubby fingers and eyelids like Nixon's didn't mean he was stupid. He'd obviously spent the last twenty-four peeking over Shafer's shoulder. Now that Shafer had come up with evidence that maybe the case was more than a simple Shabaab kidnapping, he'd stepped up.

"Yeah. One was blank. We don't know what it means. Could be a mistake."

"Does Wells think he's involved?"

"If he does, he hasn't told me. What does the station think?"

"The last few years they've focused on the relationship with the Kenyan police and Interior Ministry."

"Meaning they don't run any decent agents on their own in Kenya and are stuck with what the Kenyan government tells them."

Duto didn't disagree.

"And the Kenyans are saying privately what they're saying publicly? That they're sure it's Shabaab."

"Yeah. But when we ask them for details, to tell us where they think the hostages are so we can put a rescue plan together, they say they don't know yet, they're still working. And by the way, so far they've made clear that they don't want us to run our own investigation. More or less insisted we stay in Nairobi. I'm starting to think we may have to go around them."

As always, Duto had figured out how to play both sides. By using Wells as a back-channel investigator instead of the agency's officers in Nairobi, he would avoid any blowback in case the Kenyans were telling the truth and Shabaab was holding the hostages. In that case, the Kenyans would be furious if the CIA interfered. They'd complain to the White House, and Duto would leave Langley on a less than triumphant note. Using Wells would let Duto skip that trap. He'd look like a hero if the Kenyans were wrong about Shabaab, and lose nothing if they were right.

"What do you want from me, Vinny?"

"Wells gets a lead, you let me know ASAP. Whether it's Shabaab or not."

"And you'll put something together to save the hostages. Something that doesn't involve SEAL Team Six."

"That'll be a White House decision. They want to use Special Forces, no problem. But realistically, it'll depend on the size of the opposing force and on timing."

"Long as you get full credit for finding them."

"It's not about credit, Ellis." Duto almost sounded sincere. "Point is, Wells needs our help —"

"How's that again?"

"He wanted NSA to run those numbers, didn't he? He wants our help, he's got to give to get. And if he understands the stakes, he's more likely to agree. So make sure he understands them."

"This mythical invasion."

"You don't believe me, call your friends in the five-sided building."

But Shafer knew what they'd say. The story rang true. He could already imagine the Chairman of the Joint Chiefs beating the drums on the weekend's talk shows, the Secretary of State's op-ed in the *Post* this Sunday. *Sending soldiers to war is never an easy decision. But the United States has no choice but to intervene in Somalia. Let me be clear. We are not invading merely to rescue these four aid workers, though their kidnapping has thrown a spotlight on the collapse of the Somali state . . .*

Finding the hostages quickly was the only way to make certain a war wouldn't happen.

"What if Shabaab has them, Vinny? You know that's possible."

"Then I guess we'll go to war. But at least we'll know what we're doing."

"Fine. I'll tell him." Duto had steered him as effortlessly as a jockey on the homestretch. "But you know no matter what I say, he'll do what he thinks is right."

"I'm counting on it." Duto sat back in his seat, reached for his phone. Then he reconsidered. "You know, Ellis, don't you think it's time for you to admit you belong to the agency as much as me? Maybe more. I'm the one who's leaving. Your little idiosyncrasies, the ugly clothes, all the rest, they're just part of the shtick."

"I speak truth to power, Vinny. I don't kiss its ass."

"Sure you do." Duto's voice was smooth. Soothing. He sounded like an oncologist delivering bad news. *You're going to need to come in for some more tests . . .* "Every big company has somebody like you. Somebody to wave his tiny fists in the air so we can all pretend to listen before we go do whatever it is we were going to do anyway."

"You know, Vinny, towards the end of the thing in Kabul" — Wells's last mission, where he'd gone to Afghanistan to look for a traitor inside the CIA station — "I thought you might be human after all. Humbled by what had happened. It made you harder to hate. I should have known it wasn't real. And, I have to admit the truth, I'm glad it wasn't. I'm glad you're back, Vinny."

"I sleep fine."

The convoy rolled up to Shafer's house, clogging his gentle street.

"I know it. Try not to choke on a pig in a blanket at your fund-raising fellatio tonight."

"That's sweet, but you know I can't fund-raise yet, Ellis. Call John."

Shafer popped open the armored door with his bony old man's shoulder like he was escaping a four-wheeled tomb. "Aye aye, captain." He saluted, slammed the door hard as he could, and watched the Suburban roll away with his mouth twisted into a powerless scowl.

8

Near the Kenya/Somalia border

Gwen crawled across the dusty African plain, trying to ignore the thorns digging into her belly, the big black caterpillars teasing her legs. She didn't need to look back to know the man in the Joker's mask was chasing her. Ahead she saw Dadaab and the acacia tree where she read to the boys. Safety. But as she crawled closer, she realized she wasn't in Kenya. The refugees wore threadbare striped uniforms. They had mouse heads and human bodies and they waved merrily to her. *Join us! Join us!* She tried to turn, crawl away. But she couldn't, something was holding her, chafing her —

She woke in the darkness.

Fortunately, she was no longer hooded. The Joker had punished them for only a day before removing their hoods. He didn't bother with another warning. He'd made his point. For the next two days not much happened, but they did get more food. Canned fruit for breakfast, boiled eggs for dinner. Not a great long-term diet, but it satisfied their basic caloric needs, and the food could be prepared easily. Even the eggs could be boiled over a hot plate, no open flame required.

Gwen was convinced now that Suggs had set them up. Otherwise, how could the kidnappers have known they'd be on that road? Either they'd been trailed as soon as they left Dadaab, or someone from World-Cares had given them a heads-up. And Suggs was the one who'd changed their route. He was probably hiding in a hut nearby, working out a deal with James Thompson. Gwen wondered if being forced to sit in silence was good for her. Without YouTube or Netflix or texts from her girl-friends to distract her, she was relying on her own mind for the first time in years. Maybe ever.

Not that she planned to thank the Joker.

Late on the eighth night of captivity, the Joker returned. He held a camera in one hand and a page of *The Nation,* an English-language Kenyan daily, in the other. "From today's paper," he said. "Each of you holds it while I take your picture. It's called proof of life. Your families will be glad to see it."

Gwen wanted as much as she'd ever wanted anything to walk up to the Joker, put her hand on his arm, lock eyes with him, smile. Then knee him in the balls hard enough to make him piss blood. She'd done it before, to a Sigma Chi who'd raped one of her sorority sisters.

When the Joker gave her the paper, she held it beside her face with her free left hand and glared at the camera. She raised her middle finger a fraction of an inch, silently cursing the Joker, his proof of life, his ransom demands, and most of all his mask. "Smile," the Joker said.

She lifted her finger another fraction. He didn't seem to care, or even notice.

"Good. Very pretty." He took back the paper, turned to Hailey —

And gunfire punctured the night. A man shouted and another took up the cry and then the shooting and shouting came from everywhere at once. Gwen felt rounds slam the hut as if someone were kicking its brick walls. Then an explosion. A man screamed. The Joker yelled to their guard and they both ran outside.

Outside, a man yelled in Swahili, high pleading tones, until a fusillade cut him off.

"I wonder if it's the cops," Owen said.

"That doesn't sound like the cops," Gwen said. For the first time since their capture, she thought they might die.

"We'll know soon enough," Hailey said.

The firing slowed. The men outside no longer shouted. They spoke in measured tones. Their feet crunched on the dirt. They were close.

Four men walked in. They were all black. Three carried AKs and wore white kerchiefs over their mouths and white T-shirts. The fourth was lean and wiry and wore a black T-shirt, no kerchief, and a pistol on his hip. He carried a key ring that until very recently had been the property of the Joker.

"Who are you?" Scott said.

"You can call me Wizard."

Joker, Wizard. All these guys thought they belonged in comic books. The man knelt beside Gwen and riffled through the key ring. Up close his face was smooth and unlined. Gwen realized he was even younger than she was.

"Will you behave?" he said in English. "I have fifteen men outside."

Gwen nodded. He opened the lock and she stood. "Put your hands behind your back." She did, and he cuffed her.

"Are you with Suggs?" Scott said.

"I don't know anyone named Suggs."

"Then who are you and what are you doing here?"

"You speak to me this way."

"I speak to you how I like. You're smart, you'll run back to whatever hole you crawled out of before the United States Army smokes your ass —"

The man crossed the hut and stood before Scott. "Be careful now." He made a gun with his index finger and pointed at Scott's chest. "Three times. Twice in the heart and once in the head. Then I leave you for the hyenas." He spoke unemotionally, as if he were threatening to send a spoiled child to his room.

"You think you scare me?"

"Scott —" Gwen said.

"He's not killing me, dummy. He can shoot all the Africans he wants. He knows the score. How's he going to ransom a corpse?" Scott leaned forward and with his free left hand reached out and patted the cheek of the man who called himself Wizard. "Make nice and I'll make sure you get paid."

The man put a hand on the butt of his pistol. Then he shook his head and gathered himself, his effort at self-control obvious to Gwen.

He balled his fists, stepped away from Scott.

"That's right," Scott said. "Walk away, little man."

He nodded at Gwen. "Told you."

The man turned back, pulled his pistol. No hesitation now. The gun was as black as everything else he wore. "All right," he said, and Scott must have realized he'd gone too far. His mouth came open and he pulled himself away from the man.

"Hey," he said. "Hey now —"

The last words that Scott Thompson ever spoke, *Hey now,* because Wizard pulled the trigger twice. The shots broke thunder-loud inside the hut. Scott slumped backward against the wall and raised his free arm like he meant to pull out the bullets. His hand became a claw and he touched his chest with his fingertips. Then his arm dropped away. He gurgled a mouthful of blood and slid to the floor.

Hailey put her hand to her mouth and the tip of her tongue poked through her fingers. Gwen screamed once, once only. She watched death leave the hut through the ceiling and knew that she and Hailey and Owen would live tonight. She felt strangely serene.

The Wizard pointed his pistol at Scott's

head for a finishing shot. "Don't," Gwen said. "You already killed him."

He tilted his head to her. She saw he was surprised that she'd spoken. So was she. He didn't answer. But he holstered the pistol. He unlocked Hailey and Owen and handcuffed them beside Gwen and his men led them outside, where more men in white kerchiefs waited. The Wizard spoke in a language Gwen had never heard before and his men melted into the night, back to Somalia or wherever.

For the first time Gwen saw the compound where they'd been kept. It wasn't much. Three mud-brick huts stood a distance from theirs. Three bodies lay in the center of the compound, and two more beside a hut. Suggs and the Joker. They lay side by side. She'd been right. Suggs had been here all along. He hadn't been a hostage. He'd died defending this place. He'd set them up for sure. But why had Scott kept asking for him?

Had he been in on the kidnapping from the beginning? But he'd suffered along with Gwen and Hailey and Owen. He'd been chained up, too. And why? Were he and Suggs planning to split the ransom? Gwen didn't get it.

But she understood this much: Even if she

and Owen and Hailey were still in Kenya now, they wouldn't be much longer. The guards in white shirts ushered them out of the compound along a dry stream-bed. After a week-plus of disuse, Gwen's legs felt rubbery. Still, she was glad to be out of the stink and desperation of the hut. The air felt humid but clean, with a slight breeze. Half the sky was covered with thick clouds. Gwen sensed rain was coming.

Aside from the compound, the plains and low hills around them were empty. Not a house or car or streetlamp in sight. The stars shone even more brightly than they did in Montana. No one spoke. Five minutes later, they reached a pair of Range Rovers, glowing white and beautiful under the night sky. The man in black turned to them.

"You understand," he said. "Those Kenyan fools don't have you anymore. You're mine now."

Part Two

9

Dadaab

Wells didn't like what he was about to do. It felt sneaky and cheap and — for lack of a more politically correct word — unmanly. With a few days and help from the bright boys at the National Security Agency, he might have found a high-tech way to locate James Thompson's missing phone. But Wells couldn't wait. He was stuck with Plan B.

He hoped Thompson liked coffee.

The night before, Thompson had been predictably unhappy when Wells explained that he was certain the hostages were in the Ifo 2 camp and that he planned to raid it as soon as possible.

"You haven't even explained why you think they're there."

"That goes to sources and methods, Mr. Thompson." A rare bit of agency jargon that Wells liked. Especially in this case.

"You've been in Dadaab twelve hours. What sources could you possibly have?"

A logical objection, one Wells ignored. "I have a very specific location."

"That's my nephew, my volunteers. Your sources and methods are wrong. If they even exist. I'm telling you they're not in Ifo 2. The police would find them."

"You said yourself Kenyan cops aren't exactly brilliant."

"So you're planning to what? Drag them out. Without the police backing you up. You think the Somalis are going to stand by and watch while you shoot up the place?"

"I'm not going to shoot up the place. Mr. Thompson, I'm happy to talk this over with you face-to-face. Show you the intel, sat photos, forensic work, et cetera. You're not convinced, I'll reconsider. But it has to be tomorrow morning. My men and I are going in at noon."

"Your men? Where'd they come from?"

"Sources and methods."

"Please stop saying that. It's meaningless. Anyway, what kind of commando attacks in broad daylight?"

Another point for Thompson. "Why they'll never expect it."

"What if I told you that I've just received a credible ransom demand and I'm sure the hostages are nowhere near that camp?"

"I'd say the timing's awfully convenient. And I've got to trust my own intel."

"Give me Moss."

Wells handed over the phone. "I told him he was being rash . . . I'm not the one who said he could come, Jim. You did . . . I can tell you he's not listening to me . . ." She gave the phone back to Wells.

"I want to talk you out of this foolishness, I have to come to Dadaab tomorrow morning," Thompson said.

"Correct."

"I'll take the first plane I can. And I'll expect you to be on it with me when I go back to Nairobi. And then you're going home. I don't care who you are."

"Moss and I will pick you up."

"Promise me you won't do anything before then."

"Agreed. Over and out."

The next morning, Wells had just finished his dawn prayers when his phone rang. "You still serious about this?" Thompson said without preamble.

"Yes."

"I'll be in the air in five minutes. Should be in Dadaab around seven a.m."

"We'll be there. With a thermos of hot coffee, plenty of milk and sugar."

"First smart thing you've said since we met."

Dadaab's airport was a fenced strip of pockmarked runway, with a one-room concrete building for a terminal. A wind sock at the far end served in place of a control tower. North of the runway, an old Dash-8 listed over its front wheels, paint peeling. Wells doubted it could taxi, much less get airborne. A GSU officer smoked in front of the terminal, his AK tossed over his shoulder.

"No flights today."

"We have a charter. A friend coming in a few minutes," Moss said.

"He has permits?"

"Of course."

"No permits, he can't stay."

Wells wondered again why the GSU seemed so much more interested in keeping people out of Dadaab than finding the volunteers. But this officer wasn't the man to ask. Instead Wells followed Moss around the building as a plane rumbled in the distance. "Right on time," Moss said.

A boy of six or so ran from a cluster of huts south of the fence. He ducked through a hole in the wire and ran to them, his arms outstretched like wings.

"De plane, boss, de plane," he yelled when he got close.

"Our very own Tattoo," Wells said.

"I don't know who taught him that, but he does it whenever a plane comes in," Moss said. "Hey, Freddy," she yelled.

"Hey, hot mama." The boy wore a blue T-shirt imprinted with the words *San Diego Yacht Club.* He ran to Wells and said, "My name is Prince Charles, what is your name? My name is Prince Charles, de plane, boss, de plane —" The speech was delivered so fast it was almost a rap. He gave Wells a desperate grin that reminded Wells of the puppies at the North Conway animal shelter, the ones that still believed in human kindness. "Fifty shillings, boss."

"No fifty shillings, Freddy."

"Ten shillings, boss."

"Go on. Back to San Diego." Wells was surprised to see Moss dig into her pocket, hand the boy a coin. She said something in Swahili. The boy ran off with his arms spread. Moss nodded at the huts. "Have to give him something or whoever's watching over there will take a stick to him when he gets back."

"What about when five kids show up? Or five hundred?"

"I know. Solve one problem, create dependency and a bigger one. You have a better solution?"

"My first instinct would be to beat the stuffing out of whoever's hurting that boy."

"Then you leave, and he gets paid back tenfold."

Wells had no good answer. They watched as the plane came in low and slow, a stubby-winged four-seat Cessna 172, the Toyota Corolla of aviation. Simple, cheap, reliable.

"So how's this going to work, John? You tell Jimmy you want his phone and the truth? And he confesses everything because you've asked the question just so."

"That would be the elegant alternative."

"I sense you're not the elegant type. You want to tell me, then?"

"Better if you don't know."

The Cessna touched down, bumped over the potholed runway, taxied to a halt fifty feet away. The passenger door swung open. Thompson stepped down, his laptop bag strung over his shoulder. He closed the door, walked toward them. His face was tight and angry. "Let's go," he said. "Get this over with."

Wells sat in the back of the Land Cruiser and poured himself a mug of coffee.

"I get one?" Thompson said. "Been up

since four." Wells poured another mug and handed it forward. Thompson took a long swallow. "Hits the spot. Best thing about this country, the coffee." He drank again. "You use something artificial as a sweetener, John?"

"Just sugar."

"Because it has kind of a funny aftertaste."

"I'm not getting that."

"Strange. Guess I'm tired." Thompson licked his lips, drank for the third time. "I feel, I don't feel —" He looked over his shoulder at Wells. "You."

Thompson's mouth hung open. His eyes drooped closed. His head hung down and his body slumped forward, deadweight against his seat belt. The mug tipped from his nerveless hands and coffee rushed onto his khakis.

Moss pulled over. "What in the name of all that's holy just happened?"

"Your Irish comes out when you're stressed."

"This was your plan? Tell me you didn't poison him."

"He'll be fine. Sleep twelve hours, maybe a little more, wake up with a headache." Unless he drank too much. Then he might die.

"What is it?"

“Rohypnol.” Wells had packed the pills in his bag of tricks from New Hampshire. He’d ground up twelve, mixed them into the thermos. Coffee and milk masked their bitter taste. “It’s a sedative, like Valium. Puts you to sleep. Just faster.”

“Don’t piss on my leg and tell me it’s raining, John. You carry that stuff around? Isn’t that the date-rape drug?”

“I don’t plan to rape him. Though you’re welcome to.”

“I thought you were going to talk to him.”

“I am, eventually.” Wells lowered the window, dumped out the thermos. “Let’s go.”

“I hope to God you’re right about this.” Moss slipped the Land Cruiser back into gear and they drove in silence for a while. “What are you going to tell him when he wakes up?”

“By then we should know more.”

“But if you don’t.”

“That he passed out suddenly, that we have no idea why. What’s he going to do, ask for a tox screen at the MSF hospital?”

“He’ll know you’re lying.”

“He won’t be able to prove it, and he can’t touch me anyway. If Shabaab really does have these kids deep in Somalia, there’s not much I can do. I’ll switch passports and disappear. And if something else is going on, if he's involved somehow, I'll be the least of his problems."

"I can't see you as the least of anyone's problems."

Wells and Wilfred carried Thompson inside Gwen's trailer. He was bigger than Wells had realized, two hundred pounds of deadweight. They laid him on his back on Gwen's bed.

"What happened?" Wilfred said.

"Tell you later."

"You hit him with mzungu magic." Wilfred mimed beating drums. "A curse from the ancestral spirits."

"A curse from Roche." Wells put two fingers to Thompson's carotid, picked up a slow, steady pulse, fifty beats a minute. He rummaged through Thompson's windbreaker, found his passport and international phone. In his pants, a wallet and a local phone. Wells recognized the number taped to the back. This was the legitimate phone.

Wells couldn't believe Thompson had left the third phone in Nairobi. He'd want it close by. In the laptop bag, he found a computer and a half-dozen Cadbury wrappers. So far the only secret he'd discovered was Thompson's sweet tooth.

He patted Thompson's legs down. The man didn't stir. Wells had the unsettling feeling that he was robbing a corpse. He found nothing. He double-checked the windbreaker —

And finally found a tiny Samsung handset zippered into an inside compartment just above the waistband. No number taped to the back. Wells booted it up, but it demanded a four-digit password. Wells tried 1-1-1-1. No good. Hopefully, Moss would have some ideas. Wells pocketed the phone, turned Thompson on his side so that if he threw up he wouldn't choke on his vomit.

"Watch him," Wells told Wilfred. "Call me if he wakes up."

"And if he stops breathing?"

"Call me then, too."

Back in Moss's office, Wells booted up Thompson's laptop. It was password-protected and the obvious choices failed. The NSA could break it, but Wells couldn't. He switched on the phone. It demanded a combination, four digits. Wells tried 1-2-3-4, then 4-3-2-1. No good.

"What's his social?"

"His what?"

"The last four digits of his Social Security number."

"How would I know?"

"It's got to be on a record somewhere," Wells said. She reached for her laptop, but he put a hand on her shoulder. "Forget it. Let's try his birthday first. Egomaniacs love to use their birthdays for passwords."

"That's March 19, I think." Moss flipped through an old-fashioned planner. "Yes."

Wells keyed in 0-3-1-9 and the phone unlocked. He scrolled through the menus until he found the phone's number. It was almost the same as the number Thompson gave Wells, but two digits were transposed. If Wells asked, Thompson could say he'd made a legitimate mistake.

The call registry showed that Thompson had used the phone sparingly, making just a handful of calls to three numbers in the last week, all with Kenyan prefixes. Most calls ran less than two minutes. In the hours after Wells demanded that Thompson come back to Dadaab, Thompson made several late-night calls, none of which were answered.

"Recognize these? Suggs, anyone?"

"No."

"Let's call them."

Moss reached for her phone.

"Use Skype so they can't trace the call," Wells said.

Moss pulled up Skype on her laptop. Her

first call went to a voice mail without a greeting. So did the second. The third rang three times before it went to voice mail. A man offered a greeting in Swahili and then said in English, "Joka-joka-joka call back-back-back."

"Is Joka-joka-joka Kenyan slang?"

"Not that I know of. What he says in the Swahili part of the greeting is standard, leave a message and I'll call back."

"Is that Suggs?"

"Not sure. Let me hear it again." She redialed. This time the call went straight to voice mail. "I'm about ninety-five percent sure it's not Suggs." She redialed one more time. This time a man answered. He said something, laughed, hung up.

"What'd he say?" Wells said.

"I don't know. He was speaking Somali. Not Swahili."

"But the voice mail message was Swahili?"

"Yes."

"So either the greeting is intentionally misleading or the phone has been taken by someone who speaks Somali."

"Correct."

Wells tried to come up with a happy explanation for that particular fact pattern. He couldn't. He called Shafer. "I got Thompson's third phone."

"Want to tell me how?"

"I roofied him and took it."

"You what-ted him?"

"You heard me. I gave him a cup of coffee with some special sweetener."

"This is why I love you, John. You're insane. You're telling me you drugged James Thompson so you could steal his phone."

"We both know I've done worse."

"He's going to want your head when he wakes up."

"That's why I'd like you to run the number, Ellis. And three more. All Kenyan country codes, but they're either in Kenya or Somalia."

"It's almost midnight here, John. But I'll try. Give them to me."

Wells did. "Names would be nice, but what I really need is an approximate location for the receiving handsets. Anything new on your end?"

"The level of interest here is extreme."

"Because of the press conference."

"Because they're oh so pretty. Because of the wall-to-wall coverage on every network. This thing's picking up speed. We could wind up invading Somalia."

"Hard to imagine."

"Not really. The Kenyans want it. They think we can solve their problem with Shabaab once and for all. Then they'll say Somalia's been pacified, close the camps, send the refugees home. They're talking to the White House."

Now Wells understood why the Kenyan police weren't trying to find the volunteers. "But Duto —"

"Would rather you find them yourself. Even better, tell me where they are so he can send in a SOG team, play the hero. A nice liftoff for his campaign. He's watching. You want help from us or Fort Meade, I can't hide it from him."

"Including these phone numbers I just passed along."

"If it turns out some Somali gang has your friends, you might be glad for the help."

"Doubtful."

"I'll let you know as soon as I hear." Shafer hung up.

"The United States government can track those phones?" Moss said. "Even if they were inside Kenya the whole time?"

"In a country like this, one where we more or less don't care about the diplomatic consequences if we get caught, we have tracking software on every mobile network. Manufacturers install it or we sneak it in later. Don't ask me how it works, because I don't know. But it does work. I can tell you firsthand. Hopefully, they'll have something for us before Sleeping Beauty wakes up."

"But if Jimmy and Suggs faked this kidnapping, why did Jimmy make such a fuss that first day when the reporter from Houston said she was going to write? Wouldn't he have wanted the media to know?"

"I think he did. He knew she was going to write something even if he told her not to. He figures he holds a press conference, raises a few million bucks, and then in a couple weeks gives everyone the good news. The hostages escaped. Or WorldCares paid the ransom. Or, best of all, the kidnappers heard his appeal to their humanity and let these poor aid workers go. The publicity will be huge. He'll sell a million copies of his book. The hostages will probably all get paid too, books and movies and who knows what else. Best part is that once the volunteers get home, it's not like the Kenyan police will keep looking for the kidnappers. Everyone will be happy to drop it. Like you said yesterday, there's not even an insurance company to care."

"But he didn't understand how big this would get, and how soon," Moss said.

"I think that's right. He figured he could control it, but now it's running away from him. Maybe that's why a Somali answered that phone call we just made. Maybe Suggs decided he wants more money, so he's moving the hostages someplace where Thompson can't get them so easily. Like Somalia."

Moss looked unconvinced. "Suggs is Kenyan, and Kenyans prefer this side of the border. So are you going to hit Jimmy with this theory that has absolutely no factual support?"

"Not just yet. For now I'm leaving your boss to you. I decided after you told me to forget the camps that I should see the kidnapping site for myself. Meantime, NSA will run the numbers. With any luck between us we'll come up with enough to put some heat on James by the time he wakes up."

"And if you don't?"

"I'll burn that bridge when I come to it. Meantime, I do have one more favor."

"You never quit, do you?"

"I don't think Martin's car can handle these roads. Can I borrow a Land Cruiser, preferably one without WorldCares's name on the side? No offense."

"None taken. I might have another present for you, too —" Moss led Wells to a closet beside Thompson's office. Inside, a padlocked case held a Glock .40-caliber pistol and a 12-gauge Mossberg shotgun with a matte blue barrel, a mean-looking weapon. Boxes of ammunition were heaped on the floor.

"Aid workers aren't supposed to need guns. But Jimmy wanted them."

"Sure you don't mind giving them up?"

"I never liked them."

Wells didn't like shotguns much either. They were overkill up close, useless at a distance. They were heavy, clumsy, and hard to hide. But for sheer intimidation, they couldn't be matched. A Mossberg could stop a riot. Wells pulled it from the case, checked to be sure it wasn't loaded, then put his nose to the barrel. It smelled of oil, not powder. It had been fired only a few times. The Glock was similarly new. Anne would be pleased. Wells tucked the pistol into his waistband and reached for the ammunition boxes.

Thirty minutes later, the WorldCares gates swung open. Wilfred was driving, Wells beside him. Wells had insisted Martin stay and watch Thompson. An excuse. Martin had a wife and three kids. Wells didn't want to subject him to the risks they were about to take.

The camp stretched for miles, with only an occasional acacia tree to break the monotony. Women wearing long black abbayas clustered around a pumping station, pails in hand. A group of kids waved. But after the Land Cruiser passed, one grabbed a clump of dirt and flung it at the SUV. It hit the rear window, leaving a red-brown smear.

A GSU checkpoint marked the intersection of the camp track and the road that connected Dadaab with Ijara District. "To Dadaab?" an officer said.

"No. South." Following the path of Suggs and the volunteers.

"I don't advise anyone to go that way. The situation is unstable."

"Then we'll fit in fine."

Even with the Cruiser's four-wheel drive and big tires, Wilfred rarely got out of second gear. The land seemed set on rewind, endless miles of scrub and red dirt. Twice they passed flocks of sheep and goats watched over by armed herders. About an hour out of Dadaab, Wilfred made his way around a caravan of five camels, the tall humped beasts loaded with sacks of grain and charcoal.

After ninety bone-jarring minutes, the Cruiser reached Bakafi. Wells's map showed it as the only village of any size on the road.

Though size was relative. A handful of stores sold food and charcoal. A green-domed mosque marked the middle of town, followed by a police outpost and a school whose red paint had faded to a weak pink in the sun. Barefoot kids shouted as they passed.

Near the south end of town, a sign in English and Arabic marked a plain white building as "King Fahad Muslim Infirmary. Gift from the Kingdom of Saudi Arabia." Even in this flyspeck town, the Saudis spread charity and Islamist teachings. A hundred meters farther down, a tall concrete building stood alone. Four men stood outside, smoking. The place was painted a striking canary yellow. A torn plastic banner hanging from the roof proclaimed: "Broadway Hoteli/Best in the District/Live Premier League Football/Tusker TOO!"

"A hotel? Here?"

Wilfred pulled over. " 'Hoteli' is our word for a restaurant. Serves fried potatoes, mutton, all those things. A whole meal one hundred fifty, two hundred shillings. Usually it's okay, but when they use the grease too long —" He rubbed his stomach.

"And this one serves beer? In a Muslim town?"

"Bakafi must not be all Muslim. Kenyan

and Somali, Christian and Muslim. So the alcohol is okay."

The place was the Kenyan equivalent of a Montana roadhouse, Wells thought, a way to keep drinking and trouble outside the middle of town, but close enough for the police to step in if a fight got out of control. Past the hoteli Wells saw a man on a motorbike. He fit the Somali stereotype, small head, coffee-colored skin. He held a cell phone at arm's length, like he was taking a picture with it. A picture of the Toyota, maybe. The motorcycle between his legs was a dirt bike, stubby tires and thick shocks. As they moved closer, the guy tucked away the phone, kicked the bike into gear, rode south.

Wells wondered if he should have Wilfred follow. But if they got close, the guy could go off road, find a patch of soft ground that would trap the SUV. Plus Wells couldn't imagine that the volunteers were being kept in a town where the Kenyan cops had a presence. No. If they were still in Kenya, they'd be at Dadaab, or in a cluster of huts that wasn't on a map. Probably close to the Somali border. If the police had cared, they could have made the same calculation, hit every settlement within fifty miles of the border. But either they truly believed Shabaab was behind the kidnapping, or they had received instructions from Nairobi not to look.

"Let's find where they were taken," Wells said.

Wilfred lowered his window, shouted to the men across the street. One walked over and had what seemed like an endless conversation with Wilfred before finally wandering back to his buddies.

"It's around twenty kilometers south," Wilfred said. "The road takes a turn. A few kilometers before the intersection."

"That's all he said."

"These men, it takes them an hour to answer a question. Country people. Not like Nairobi."

Wells understood. He'd grown up in the seventies in Montana's Bitterroot Valley, a little town called Hamilton, south of Missoula. Back then the houses on the edge of town still had shared phones — party lines, they were called. The ranchers could make a conversation about the weather last an hour. Why not? The cattle weren't going anywhere.

South of Bakafi the land turned hilly, a blanket on an unmade bed. The road faded until it was little more than potholes in the scrub, and Wells's legs ached as the Cruiser thumped along. They drove about forty minutes before the road came over a hill and swung hard left. Wilfred stopped and pointed at a mess of cigarettes and water bottles in the road ahead.

The kidnappers had chosen wisely. Wells figured they'd blocked the road with one or two of their own SUVs. A driver coming over the hill would have only seconds of warning. If he tried to swerve past the roadblock, he would risk getting stuck in the hill's soft dirt or flipping over. But once he stopped, he'd be trapped. Gunmen would have positioned themselves behind the WorldCares SUV, pinning it down.

Wilfred eased past the kidnapping site, stopping a hundred feet away. Wells tucked the Glock into his waistband and walked back under the hammering noontime sun. On all sides, the land was surpassingly quiet. No railroad tracks or cell towers. To the west and southwest, he saw scattered huts, but nothing that qualified as a village, much less a town. East, toward Somalia, the land appeared entirely empty. Southeast, maybe five miles away, Wells saw a few black smudges coasting through the sky. Smoke, maybe. He checked through his binoculars. He couldn't be sure, but they looked like birds. Big ones. A bunch of them, widely spaced, but all moving southeast.

Rich tourists came to Africa under the illusion they would see the untouched world. But mostly they stuck to national parks or private game reserves as closely managed as zoos. They should have come here instead. Wells squatted down, pored over the road, the land around it. But the police had destroyed whatever evidence the kidnappers might have left. The soft red dirt held at least a half-dozen different tire tracks, dozens of footprints. Maybe the guys from CSI could tell the tracks left by the kidnappers from those left by the cops. Wells couldn't. Pretending otherwise would only waste time.

Still, this trip strengthened his certainty that Suggs was involved. First, the kidnappers must have known the route the volunteers were taking. Why else wait here, on a road used by only a few vehicles a day? On the flip side, Wells couldn't imagine why the volunteers would have chosen this route unless Suggs had suggested it. The road barely appeared on the map, and it was terribly slow. They'd covered a little more than 150 kilometers — not even 100 miles — in three hours. Going to Garissa and then south on the gravel road to the coast would surely have been faster, even with roadblocks.

"What do you think?" Wilfred said.

"I think Kenyan cops smoke a lot. Any of these brands unusual? Somali?"

"No, all Kenyan."

Then Wells realized what he hadn't seen. No spent rounds, no brass casings. No evidence of a firefight. He double-checked to be sure. Yes. Another sign that the kidnapping had gone off without a hitch. He took one last look around, walked back toward the Cruiser.

"That's it?" Wilfred said. "We came all this way for that?"

"Sometimes you have to see a place with your own eyes."

"Now we go back to Bakafi, see if anyone talks?"

"No. South." Wells felt strongly that the kidnappers had gone away from Dadaab. If they had planned to hide in the camps, they would have taken the volunteers much closer to Dadaab.

"And you think these people around here want to talk to you?"

"Never know unless you ask."

"I can tell you they aren't much interested in talking to outsiders. Maybe you tell them you're an Arab and you want to buy the girls for slaves. Like a vulture coming in after the kill."

Like a vulture . . .

Wells raised his binoculars and looked at the black smudges on the horizon. They were still heading southeast. They'd shrunk to specks now. But even as he watched, another entered his field of view. This one was closer, close enough for him to see its wings, big and black and jagged, like they'd been sewn on the cheap and could unravel easy as tugging a string. The bird rode a thermal, rising hundreds of feet in seconds, then flicked its wings and circled southeast, same as the others.

"That way." Wells pointed toward the vulture.

The track south ended a half hour later at a T-junction with another, equally unimpressive road. Twenty or so huts lay a kilometer west. Wilfred turned left, east. Toward Somalia, which was no more than thirty barren kilometers away. Wells racked the slide on the Glock, making sure it was loaded. The pistol felt strange in his hand, heavier and bigger than the Makarov he had carried for so many years. But Anne was right. He should have retired the Mak long ago. Now he had an excuse, a new pistol that fate, in the form of a plug-ugly Irishwoman, had pressed on him.

The smudges in the sky were as good as a GPS. They'd all heard the same announcement: Delicious carrion in aisle two. They might be headed for a cow or a sheep or even a camel. But Wells didn't think so. After another twenty minutes in the Cruiser, Wells could see the birds slowing, organizing themselves into a ragged circle. They were almost directly to the south, maybe five kilometers. Three swung lower, disappearing behind a hill. Soon they popped up again. Wells imagined they'd tried to feed and been chased out by stronger predators, jackals or hyenas or even lions. The big Kenyan national park called Tsavo East lay about 150 kilometers southwest of here. No doubt lions sometimes ranged this far from its boundaries.

The birds rose, riding on thermals, black spurs against the empty blue sky. Wilfred pointed to a faint pair of ruts marked by a cairn of a half-dozen stones. He started to turn into the track, but Wells put a hand on his forearm.

"Go straight. Park over the next rise. Then we leave this and walk."

"It will take forever. And snakes. There are snakes."

"We go on foot, no one knows we're coming."

"Better to have this." Wilfred patted the dashboard like a horse's flank.

"We walk. You don't like it, stay in the car."

They trudged south through the ugly low scrub. The dirt was soft, almost spongy, swallowing their steps. The refugees walked through hundreds of miles of this to reach Dadaab. No wonder they were starving when they arrived. Wells carried the essentials in his pack: water, a first-aid kit, binoculars, a sat phone and GPS. He'd strapped on a climber's headlamp, goofy-looking but essential for keeping his hands free if he found himself in a dark hut. The shotgun was slung across his chest, the Glock tucked into his waistband. He'd given Wilfred the Makarov.

"You don't shoot unless I shoot."

"Okay, yes."

The Land Cruiser's clock had read 14:20 when they left. Wells figured they'd need close to an hour to reach the area directly beneath the vultures. That didn't give them much time on target if they were going to return to the Cruiser before dark. They walked in silence, Wells a few feet ahead, scanning for smoke, huts, any sign of human habitation.

A high-pitched cackle, an ugly gasping

sound, half laugh, half choke, erupted somewhere in front of them. Wells stopped with one foot in the air like Wile E. Coyote. "Hyenas?"

"That's their song."

"Pretty."

"The devil rides them through hell."

"Save the folk tales for the anthropology professors."

Wilfred shook his head in perplexity.

"Come on. Unless you want to be out here in the dark."

Twice more they heard the cackling, and once an answering call behind them. Neither man mentioned it. The vultures floated high overhead, using the thermals, barely flapping their wings.

A half hour later, Wells came over a hill and saw the huts. Four in all. Three small and close to each other. The last larger, maybe fifty meters away from the third. They were mud-brick, hand-built, like a thousand other huts that Wells had seen that day. The big one had a tin roof, angled slightly so the rain would pour off. The other three had traditional branch roofs. No walls or barbed wire separated them from the land around. Hidden in plain sight. No vehicles either. They were gone, or hidden.

Wells dropped to a knee, scanned the

compound through his binoculars. In the middle of the compound, he saw a man, or more accurately what was left of him. His arms and legs were chewed to stumps, his belly torn open. Intestines glistened against black skin like stuffing pulled loose from a cheap toy. Two more bodies lay in front of the second hut, similarly dismembered.

"See them?" Wilfred muttered.

He wasn't talking about the corpses.

The hyenas lay in the shade of the huts, lazing, their bellies swollen. Beards of blood coated their muzzles. Wells counted ten. As he watched, one stood and waddled over to a corpse. The hyena poked and snuffled the body and then clamped its jaws around an arm. It put its paws on the dead man's chest and lifted its head and grunted and strained, its body shaking, until the arm tore from the shoulder with a gunshot-loud snap. Over the years, Wells had seen human beings destroyed in almost every conceivable way. Even so, the violence done to these corpses tightened his throat.

Wells stood, unslung the shotgun. No need for stealth. Whoever had killed these people had left the camp to the hyenas. "Time to restore our place at the top of the food chain."

"You want to go down there."

"When they learn how to shoot, I'll worry." Wells strode down the hill. After a few seconds, he heard Wilfred follow. When he reached the base of the hill, fifty yards from the nearest corpse, the animals stood and looked at him. They were motley creatures, with big cupped ears that made him think of fly-eating flowers. Their brown fur was marked with dark spots like an old man's hands. Their tails angled downward, toward the earth. When dogs put their tails at that angle, they were showing submission. Wells figured hyenas behaved similiarly, but he wasn't sure. He didn't know much about them. He'd have to remember to read up before his next trip searching for volunteer aid workers.

A breeze ruffled the hyenas' fur and brought Wells the sour stench of the torn, bloated corpses. Over millennia, humans had invented rituals to hide the monstrousness of postmortem decay. But here was death in its truest form, destroying not just the spirit but the body itself.

Wells lifted the shotgun high and shouted, "Go! Git! Go on, now!"

The hyenas were less than impressed. One yawned, its pink tongue flopping out. Another scratched furiously at the dirt like a drag racer spinning his wheels before the flag dropped. The one closest to Wells went back to tugging on a corpse.

"Get lost! Hubba-hubba!" Wells cocked the shotgun and strode closer. Most of the pack padded away. But four stood their ground. The hyena nearest Wells seemed to be the leader. It raised its tail, bared its teeth, growled low in its throat. Wells felt his adrenaline rise. The creature might not be pointing a pistol at him, but its intent was more than clear. It stared at him with unblinking black eyes. It was enormous, three feet tall. As big as a Great Dane but sturdier. It had to be almost two hundred pounds. It had a thick neck and teeth that looked like they could tear steel.

Wells put the shotgun to his shoulder, angled the muzzle skyward. "GO!" The hyena merely licked its lips. "I thought you were cowards." He squeezed the trigger. The Mossberg bucked against his shoulder and its blast rattled through his skull. He pumped the shotgun, fired again.

Finally, the hyena stepped away from the corpse and turned aside. It looked over its shoulder at Wells and loped off, its tail between its legs. *You don't scare me.* The other three holdouts followed, forming a single-file line as they disappeared into the scrub. They moved with an odd precision.

The stink of the corpses would lure them back by nightfall, Wells thought. Another reason not to tarry.

Wells topped up the Mossberg with two more shells, slung it over his chest, and turned to the bodies. They looked worse up close, rotting meat covered with quilts of flies. Wells wished for a kerchief to shield his mouth, or even better, some Vicks Vapo-Rub to hide the stench. He squeezed his nose, forced himself to ignore the flies and the stink and look close at the corpses. Their faces had been chewed into unrecognizability, but in their flesh he saw neat punctures. GSWs, as trauma surgeons said. Gunshot wounds.

He didn't see any rifles or pistols, but brass casings glinted in the red dirt around the bodies. Wells picked up a handful. 7.62-millimeter jackets. AK rounds.

Beside the third hut he saw two more bodies. A piece of torn rubber lay between them. It looked like it had been chewed and then spit out, as if even the hyenas wouldn't bother with it. A mask. A Joker mask.

Joka-joka-joka call back-back-back.

Wells had heard plenty of lies over the years, and told his share. But he couldn't remember anyone who lied with as much conviction — as much flat-out style — as James Thompson. The man had been close to tears at the press conference in Nairobi. Wells wondered what explanation Thompson would offer for having the Joker's number programmed into his phone. No doubt it would be a beaut. Wells grabbed the mask, threw it as high and far as he could. Let the vultures have it, if the hyenas wouldn't.

The first hut held supplies, mostly canned food and water. Cases of peanut butter and jam. Whoever had been here had wanted to be sure he wouldn't need a fire to cook. At the back, two hot plates with electrical cords and a half-dozen plastic jerricans of gasoline. No generator. Wells wondered if the raiders had taken it.

In the next hut, six cots, their mattresses thin, stained, and lumpy. The dank sour smell of a locker room that hadn't been cleaned all season. T-shirts and jeans and sneakers and Tusker bottles strewn across the floor. Against the wall, an empty AK magazine, no rifle in sight. Wells imagined the chaos of a surprise night attack, men scrambling for weapons and running outside to die. He rousted the room for notebooks or phones, didn't find any.

The third hut had only two cots. Wells

guessed the leaders had lived here. A wooden chest held shoes and clothes, including a bright yellow polo shirt, size XXL. Wells put it in his pack. Maybe Moss could identify it as belonging to Suggs. Between the cots, a cardboard box held two oversized bottles of off-brand scotch. Nothing else. The whole camp felt temporary to Wells, as though the men who'd lived here hadn't planned on staying long — evidence for the theory that Thompson and Suggs planned to end the kidnapping quickly, once the media attention peaked.

One hut left, the big one. Process of elimination said it was the place where Gwen and the others had been kept. Up close, Wells heard grunting and snuffling and scratching, horror-movie sounds. He reached for his pistol, flicked on his headlamp, stepped inside —

The room was airless and dark and painfully hot. In the headlamp's stark white light, Wells saw a hyena tugging at a corpse against the far wall. The animal turned to Wells and screeched and Wells stepped backward. He knew instantly he'd made a mistake. The hyena bared its teeth and raised its tail like a battle standard and charged, pouncing across the hut, angling toward Wells. Wells raised the Glock, a classic shooter's two-handed stance, and pulled the trigger. The Glock had more kick than the Makarov, more than Wells expected. The pistol pulled sideways and the round caught the hyena in its hindquarters. The hyena screamed now, but kept moving. Wells pulled the trigger again —

This second shot caught the beast farther up. Wells expected the hyena to go down. Still it came. Ten feet away now. It opened its jaw wide, its teeth white and vicious under the headlamp's single eye. Wells knew he had time for only one last shot. He raised the Glock high and, as the hyena leapt, he pointed the pistol into the beast's open maw and pulled the trigger —

The hyena's head exploded and its body convulsed sideways. It flopped against the hut's dirt floor. When it stopped moving, Wells poked it gingerly with his foot. He knew he had killed it well and truly. Yet he half expected it to rise. The devil's pet indeed. Those fierce slavering jaws. And the stink. A stomach filled with carrion, the meat twice dead now. Wells found himself murmuring the Shahada, the Muslim creed, *La ilaha illa Allah . . . There is no God but Allah, and Muhammad is his messenger.*

"Holy shit," Wilfred said behind him. "Score one for the great white hunter."

The stench of decaying tissue clotted Wells's throat. He pressed his forearm against his nose and forced himself to walk deeper into the hut. And realized something about the body at the far end. It was white. The face was still largely intact. A man. His mouth open, and his eyes. Wells had never met him, but from photos he knew the frat-boy chin. Gwen's sometime boyfriend. James's nephew.

Scott Thompson. Resting in nothing like peace. Wells would have to leave him here. Before he did, he leaned close, examined the body. Two shots in the chest, close range. They didn't look like AK rounds to Wells, though he couldn't be sure. He looked away, saw a glint in the wall. A metal ring. A chain hung from it.

He clamped down on the acid rising in his throat and checked the rest of the hut. Three more empty rings in the walls. The other hostages, gone. Why had Scott been killed and left? Had he fought the kidnappers? Was his death a message to James Thompson? Wells wished he had a forensic team helping him. Instead he had a head-lamp and Wilfred. Who called to him now, urgently.

"John."

Wells stepped outside. The sun hit him,

and before he could stop himself his stomach clenched viciously. Bile coursed through his throat and into his mouth, and he vomited a thin brown muck that the dirt swallowed instantly.

He groped in his pack for a bottle of water. He gulped until his cheeks were full, swished, spat. And again. Rinse and repeat. Anything to hide the angry sour taste. He poured a second bottle over his face and hands, hoping the lukewarm liquid would wash away the stink. As he tilted up his head, he couldn't help but see the vultures dirtying the sky. Death and its minions were everywhere in this camp.

"Listen," Wilfred said.

In the distance, to the north: The hive-of-bees buzz of a dirt bike engine revving high. And a second, meshing with the first.

"Coming this way," Wilfred said. "If we had the Cruiser —"

"We don't."

"What then?"

"We kill them."

"Mzungu. That some sickness. Don't even know them, what they want —"

"We kill them. Unless you'd rather they kill us."

10

Southwestern Somalia

After the man in the black T-shirt made his three-word speech — *You're mine now* — Gwen and Hailey and Owen were led into the Range Rover and blindfolded and driven through the silent African night. Gwen felt like she was in a plane that had suddenly spiraled into a dive. She was terrified, but also helpless, and that helplessness distanced her from the insanity that her reality had become. She felt almost as if she were starring in a movie of her life: *Taken 2: Africa*. Or would that be *Taken 2 Africa*? Anyway, she wished someone could tell her whether it would have a Lifetime-style happy ending or be more of a downer.

It had been a downer for Scott, for sure. She didn't want to believe he'd been in on the kidnapping. Maybe he'd had another reason to ask about Suggs. Maybe he was confused, or scared to have a gun pointed at him.

But he hadn't sounded scared to Gwen. He'd sounded pissed.

Then he'd died.

Gwen had never seen anyone die before. She'd hardly been to any funerals even. Her parents and grandparents were still alive. Two of her mom's friends had died of cancer, which seemed nasty. You looked bad, then you looked better and everybody got excited and took you out to dinner. Then it came back and your hair fell out and you went into the hospital and turned yellow and died. That was two funerals. And one of her high school classmates had died in a drunk-driving accident. So Gwen wasn't unfamiliar with the *concept* of mortality. But she had always had a difficult time believing that death would ever come to her or her immediate family. Especially not since her sister pulled through that car accident. Death was something that happened to other people. People who weren't as lucky or beautiful or American as she was.

She wanted to believe Scott would be waiting at the next hut. But she couldn't escape the reality of what she'd seen, the *You shot me* shock in Scott's eyes before they glazed over like a shower door closing. No, Scott wouldn't be apologizing. He had seen his plan, whatever it was, going bad, and he had lost his temper and spouted off. Just like he had a hundred times at frat parties and football games and wherever else he thought he was cool enough to get away with being a jerk. Which was everywhere. Only this time he hadn't gotten a beer poured over his head. He hadn't gotten into a slappy sloppy fight that stopped before anybody got hurt. He'd gotten himself killed. He'd learned the hard way that in Africa death wasn't shy around the young. It didn't just hang out at nursing homes. It slipped the bouncer a twenty and came to dance at the club.

Yep, Scott was finally the tough guy he'd always pretended to be. Part of Gwen wanted to congratulate him. And ask, by the way, what have you gotten us into? But he wouldn't be around to answer that question either.

They drove awhile. At least an hour. At one point, a prop plane passed overhead. The Range Rover abruptly stopped. They waited in silence for several minutes, then drove on. No explanation.

When they stopped again, Gwen heard men nearby. Her door opened. She was shouldered out of the truck and guided along a rough path. She was still blindfolded and cuffed, and once she stumbled and nearly fell, but a firm hand held her. The path flattened. For a few seconds, Gwen caught the rank odor of raw sewage. Then the stink was gone. Not much later she felt a squeeze on her shoulder. She stopped walking and someone uncuffed her hands and lifted off her blindfold. She found herself with Hailey and Owen in the center of a bush settlement, fifteen or twenty mud-brick huts. No lights. If the place had a generator, it wasn't running.

Wizard and another man led them to a hut nearby, shined a flashlight inside. Three blankets lay on the ground, along with two pairs of sweat suits. No chains or handcuffs.

"A guard will be outside," Wizard said. "You need the toilet, you tell him. You go one at a time. You two" — he waved the flashlight at Gwen and Hailey — "wear those" — he pointed at the sweat suits — "when you're outside. My men are Muslim, and some will be happier if you stay covered. As for food, whatever we eat you'll eat."

"We're not locked in?" Owen said.

"This is Somalia. Believe me, you're safer with me than anywhere else. We'll protect you."

Like you protected Scott, Gwen wanted to

say. But she couldn't see any upside in making this man mad.

"Sir?" Hailey said. "Mr. Wizard? Can we ask you one more question?"

"If it's not trouble."

"Are you from the Shabaab?"

Wizard said something to the man with him and they both laughed. "You would like me to be Shabaab? You would feel better?"

"I meant no disrespect."

"I'm not al-Shabaab. I took you for money. I want to get it and send you back where you belong. But I could sell you to them if you wish. Lots of people want to meet you. Maybe you see all of Somalia. Would you like that?"

"No, sir."

"Tomorrow morning we take pictures. And email addresses and phone numbers to reach your families." He handed Owen the flashlight, closed the door, a tin sheet with a half-dozen holes punched for air. They sat in silence as his footsteps faded.

Hailey spoke first. "It makes sense now, the last place."

Gwen couldn't see how anything made sense. She lay down and closed her eyes and exhaled softly, all the sadness in the world in that puff of air. Hailey seemed to understand. She took Gwen's hand in her own.

Her palm was warm and sweaty and sweet.

"How do you mean?" Owen said.

"I mean, the Joker's mask, getting chained up, it felt like overkill. You know, the hoods were awful. But why didn't they just beat us? It was all this other stuff instead. Like they knew they couldn't hurt us physically, so they were looking for other ways to scare us. They knew they were going to set us free and they wanted to impress us."

Gwen hadn't felt that way at the time, but she saw the truth of what Hailey said. "Scott wanted us to have a crazy story to tell when we got back to Dadaab," she said.

"Whereas this guy is the real thing," Owen said. "Doesn't waste time on making threats. Doesn't need to. We just watched him kill our friend. Somebody he thinks was our friend, anyway."

"Our ex-friend," Hailey said. Gwen felt the jittery laughter rising in her and didn't fight it, because what better way to describe Scott? Ex-friend, ex-boyfriend, ex-human. Hailey squeezed her hand and the giggles passed.

"Bet he thought it was a big prank," Hailey said.

"A dumb hazing stunt that went too far," Owen said.

Then Gwen put the last piece together.

"But it wasn't his idea. James."

"What about James?" Owen said.

"He did this."

"You think the CEO of WorldCares set us up to get kidnapped?"

"She's right," Hailey said. "Think it through. Scott wouldn't have given himself to Suggs without a guarantee he could get out. He wasn't that crazy. And doesn't James have that book coming out? We disappear for a couple weeks, come back, we're all telling this story."

"We got kidnapped for his *book*?" Gwen said.

They lay in silence, contemplating James Thompson.

"Before, we were protected, even if we didn't know it," Owen said a few minutes later. "No more."

"Maybe James set this up, too," Hailey said.

"And got his nephew killed? No, they were going to end it. Bring us back to Dadaab. Until this Wizard guy heard about us."

"How? If the Kenyan police didn't?"

"I'll bet he knows what's going on around here better than the cops. Yeah, they heard, came for us, took out Suggs and the Joker, now we're here."

"Now we're here," Hailey said.

"What I'm wondering, he said lots of people are looking for us."

"No," Gwen said. "He said lots of people want to meet us."

"You're right," Owen said, drawing out the word like he couldn't believe it. "What I'm wondering, what did he mean by that?"

"Hopefully, some SEALs who will helicopter in, come get us," Gwen said. She could almost see them, wraparound sunglasses and tight T-shirts. "That would be ideal. I'd be glad to thank them. However they liked."

"Try not to go back to being idiot Gwen," Hailey said.

Gwen felt a flush spread up her neck. She was amazed that she had the energy in this place to care about a casual insult. But she did. She didn't want to go back to being idiot Gwen.

"Maybe," Owen said. "Maybe our families have made so much noise that the Army, the CIA, they're on the hunt. I don't know how fast that could happen. What I'm worried about is, these guys took us out of Kenya. What if somebody grabs us from them, brings us another hundred miles into Somalia? And what if the next group is Shabaab, and they don't want to ransom us, they want to hold us forever for the publicity?"

"That Wizard guy looks like he can handle himself," Hailey said.

"Suggs and the Joker thought so, too."

"We can't do anything about it anyway," Gwen said.

"Maybe."

"You think —"

"I think even if there's a real risk, we see a chance to grab one of those Range Rovers we've got to go for it."

"Try to escape? From an armed camp in Somalia?"

"If we see a chance. That's all I'm saying. Doing nothing isn't always the safest."

"We don't know the roads," Gwen said. "We don't know if there *are* any roads. These guys will shoot us if we make trouble. Wizard already proved it."

"I'll bet we're no more than fifty miles from Kenya. Less. We weren't in the cars that long." Owen turned the flashlight on both of them and then on himself. He looked tired, worn, his skin stretched tight over his face. Gwen wondered how much weight they'd all lost. "Say I'm wrong, there's no chance that anyone else is going to take us. We're still stuck here. We got kidnapped barely a week ago and none of us is holding up that great. You want this to go a month? Six months?"

"Our families —"

"They can spend every dime they have, every dime these guys ask for, and there's no guarantees anybody's going to let us go. Some of these kidnappings go on for years. Promise me this. When they let us go to the toilet, get food, whatever, we'll all do some recon."

"Recon."

"Figure out where they keep their weapons —"

"I know what it *means,* Owen."

"If phones work here, Kenyan or Somali. Do they have dogs? Motorbikes? Stuff like that."

Gwen couldn't listen anymore. Like they could possibly get out of here on their own. She couldn't bear the thought of being held for years, either. She closed her eyes, squeezed Hailey's hand, tried to dream of soldiers in helicopters flying low over the dusty red plains.

She woke to find Wizard nudging her foot with his own. This morning he wore sunglasses to go with his black T-shirt and boots. "Picture time." He was so young, yet he spoke with absolute command. She propped herself against the wall. He produced a cell phone and snapped pictures of her and Hailey and Owen. They gave him their email addresses and parents' phone numbers and he left.

"You think there's an Internet connection around here?" Hailey said.

"Let's hope," Owen said. "He emails from this camp, I'll bet the CIA can trace it in about ten seconds."

"He's too smart for that," Gwen said.

"He's a kid playing at being a soldier. Probably can't even read."

"Scott talked down to him, too," Hailey said. Owen had no answer for that.

Gwen's bladder was uncomfortably full. She didn't want to leave the hut, but she pulled on the sweat suit. It was cheap and scratchy. She would have sold her soul for a hot shower and a pair of brand-new undies and Lulu yoga pants.

The guard slumped on the chair outside was maybe seventeen. "Toilet," Gwen said. "Latrine." He pointed left. Gwen shielded her eyes, walked into the rising sun. The sky was mostly blue but the air heavy and moist, an unsettling combination. The camp felt dingy and temporary. Gwen didn't see anyone older than twenty-five. Maybe Owen was right. If the Shabaab attacked, how could these guys defend them?

Something else bugged her, too. Women. There weren't any. Maybe they were hiding somewhere, but Gwen didn't see any high walls and all the huts looked the same. Maybe the ones with wives had sent them to Dadaab. Maybe they raided the local villages when they wanted women. Or maybe they just did without. And got horny. A couple soldiers stared at her like she was walking around in a bikini, not a sweat suit. Not that they said a word, but she didn't feel great about being one of two women in a camp filled with armed men. Nothing to do with the fact that they were African, either. At least, she didn't think so. Black, white, whatever, groups of guys this age could get ugly, sometimes without much warning.

She wondered again if Owen was right. At least she ought to try to work out the camp layout, like he'd suggested. Recon. It sounded good. A serious word. A professional word. She left the main camp area, walked to the latrines, three sheds of trash wood and burlap.

Up close, the smell overwhelmed her, sunbaked excrement and urine, eye-burning, throat-gagging. She recognized the odor from the night before. So they'd brought her along this path. Gwen decided to go past the sheds, see if she could find where the vehicles were kept. If anyone caught her, she would say she'd decided not to use the toilets, the smell had been too much. She double-checked to be sure no one was watching her and trotted past the sheds, away from the main camp. The path narrowed and curved around a low hill. A hundred yards on, a man sat on a lawn chair at the top of the hill. A floppy hat protected him from the sun. A rifle and binoculars were slung over the chair. As she watched, the man stood, shielded his eyes, took the binoculars and carefully surveyed the horizon from north to south.

Gwen guessed the Range Rovers were on the other side of the hill. But she decided not to try to see them. She'd pushed her luck far enough. The sentry wouldn't let her by, and she'd be in trouble if he spotted her. She'd already stayed longer than she'd intended. She turned back, walked quickly to the latrines. She realized something else, too. Owen's instinct that the camp faced a serious threat of attack seemed right. Why else post a sentry facing east — toward Somalia, not Kenya?

She didn't notice the man beside the shed until she was a step away. He wore a torn

T-shirt and green cargo pants with a big oil stain down one leg. Gwen hoped it was an oil stain, anyway. He was broad-shouldered, narrow-waisted, with meaty hands and thick shoulders. All the weight training in the world couldn't build muscles like his, but half the men in Africa seemed to have been born with them.

He raised a hand in a gesture that obviously meant stop. Gwen stopped, wished she hadn't. She waved her hand in front of her nose like she was a nineteenth-century heroine with the vapors. "I couldn't take the smell, you know, it's so stinky —" She was jabbering now, hoping to drown him in a stream of English he didn't understand. "I should probably get back to my hut, I have decorating to do —"

She stepped past him. He reached for her arm, pulled her close. She couldn't help herself, she screamed —

Ten minutes later, she sat cross-legged in a half-built hut on the western edge of the compound. Today's life lesson: She wasn't cut out to be a secret agent. Her scream had brought men running. After some shouting and pointing, they'd led her back to the camp and the hut she shared with Owen and Hailey. Then they'd dragged her out again without explanation and dumped her here. This side of the camp was even more run-down than the eastern half. Two scrawny goats nosed at a pile of trash outside her hut. The hut next to this one seemed to have been converted into a repair shop for the dirt bikes these guys liked. At least two bikes were in the hut, and she'd seen a scrawny boy on his back, tinkering with an exhaust pipe. Now an engine turned over, came briefly to life, and stalled out. Even without knowing Swahili, she understood the curses that followed.

The man who'd dragged her here stepped into the hut. He was chewing that stuff the Somalis liked. Khat, or miraa, whatever they called it. It looked like parsley to Gwen, but they couldn't get enough of it.

"Where's Wizard? Is Wizard coming?" She knew she sounded pathetic. Begging for him like a first-grader asking for her dad. If her dad were a Somali bandit and murderer. She didn't know why she was putting so much trust in the guy. Probably because he was in charge. At this moment she feared chaos more than anything. Maybe she just liked saying Wizard, like the word itself was magic.

The Somali twirled his finger. Gwen wasn't sure whether the motion meant *he's not in camp* or *he's busy* or something else. She leaned against the wall, closed her eyes. A few minutes later, she felt her foot being nudged. Somali men seemed to like foot-nudging as a way to avoid more substantial contact with women.

Gwen opened her eyes. Her captor pulled a rubber-banded packet of leaves and stems from his pants. He removed the bands, stuffed his mouth full of leaves. "Miraa."

"Everybody loves miraa."

"Miraa." He pointed at her, then mimed putting a handful of stems in his mouth.

"You want me to try some." She pointed at her own mouth. He nodded. "That's very generous, I always wanted to chew grass out of someone's pants pocket, but I think I'll pass —"

He selected a chunk of leaves.

"No, see, I'm saying nada —"

He squatted beside her, smiled. His cheeks bulged like a chipmunk's. And Gwen decided, screw it. What was she worried about? That she'd wind up hooked? It was a leaf. Not exactly meth. And at this point she'd be happy if she lived long enough to get addicted.

She stuffed the leaves in her mouth between her cheek and her jaw. Back home she'd had a reputation for being a bit of a germophobe. Maybe more than a bit. Once, after she refused to eat at a barbecue at his frat, Scott had told her she had OCD. She hadn't even known what the letters meant. She looked it up later. Obsessive-compulsive disorder. Maybe a little. The joke was on him, though. He was dead, and she was sitting with a mouthful of addictive parsley, her head buzzing like she'd just had ten cups of the world's strongest coffee —

"Hey. It works."

"Miraa."

"Dah-duh-duh-dah-dah." The McDonald's theme song. "I'm loving it." She was, too. Uppers were her drugs of choice. Booze and pot bored her. She didn't see the point of sitting on a couch giggling like an idiot, or getting drunk and weepy and ending the night with the spins. She wanted to stay out all night dancing, see the world in hypercolor. Every few weeks she bought pills from her friends with ADD, which everyone knew was just an excuse to get Ritalin prescriptions. This miraa was a nice solid stimulant, north of nicotine but south of coke. She felt focused, awake, without the crawly feeling Ritalin gave her.

The best part was that the stuff made time hurry by. For an hour, maybe more, she did nothing but track the movements of the tiny lizards running along the creases of the hut. They were fascinating.

When Wizard showed up, she felt she was seeing an old friend. He sat beside her. "You like the miraa? Mostly Somali women don't do this."

"Mostly I don't wear sweats when it's a hundred degrees."

He handed her a water bottle. "Drink. Easy to forget when you're chewing." She realized as he said the words that she was insufferably hot, her face flushed and sweaty. She drank deep, finished the bottle. He gave her another. "What your name?"

"Gwen. Gwen Murphy. Of the Missoula Murphys." She spat. "Are you actually a wizard?"

"They call me that because no one can kill me. I was in Mogadishu and they shot me in the belly, and I made the bullet escape without hurting me. Only a little blood." He lifted his shirt to show her the scar.

"Now you think you can't die?"

"My men think I can't die."

"Cool."

"I'll take you back to your friends, but first I must ask, what were you doing out there?"

"Lost. I'm not very smart."

"I don't believe you."

"Ask anyone who knows me."

"Let me tell you again. If I want to punish you, I let you leave. You don't have to fear anyone here. My men do what I say."

"Always?"

"Always." That confidence. "They'll never touch you. But outside here, if they find you —"

"Okay. I believe." She did, too. She wanted to ask him about the sentry, Owen's theory about the threat to the camp, but she couldn't figure out how.

"Your family wants you to give personal information for them. Something secret, to prove the photo is you."

My family. He's emailed them. They know I'm alive. "Like what?"

"Anything. As long as it's a secret between you and them."

"Tell them, tell them when I was little I had a cat named Oscar."

"Oscar?"

"O-S-C-A-R. He was black and white."

Wizard grabbed his phone, pecked away on the keypad. "Oscar. Black and white." Gwen wondered if he was sending a text or just making a note. When he was done, he scrolled through menus, handed her the phone. The screen showed a photo of a white SUV, blurry, like it had been taken with another cell phone.

"Do you know this vehicle?"

"It's one of WorldCares's, a Land Cruiser." She didn't feel like lying. Anyway, Wizard probably knew already. She noticed that the signal strength showed a single bar, weak but maybe enough for texts. There must be a cell tower somewhere.

Wizard scrolled to another photo of the Land Cruiser, this one closer. A black man sat in the driver's seat, a white man beside him. The black guy was young, skinny, high-cheekboned, and sly. The white guy was rough, in a good way. Close-cropped hair, strong chin, big shoulders, Ray-Bans. He looked like a soldier. Nice. Maybe a tiny bit old, but Gwen had no problem imagining him coming for her.

"You know them?"

"Never seen 'em before."

"Tell the truth."

"I am. No idea who they are. Neither of them." The time stamp on the photo showed it was taken only a couple hours before.

Wizard stood, extended a hand, pulled her up. Her head went light and the world spun. She braced herself against the mud wall and he held on to her. For a small guy, he was stronger than he looked.

"Too much miraa," he said. "Any reason

they might be looking for you?"

"I told you. I don't know them. Are they? Looking for us?"

Wizard looked west, like he could see the men and what was about to happen to them. "If they are, they won't be much longer."

11

Ijara District,
near the Kenya/Somalia border

Through his binoculars Wells saw the motorcycles pounding along the track, big tires churning up rivulets of red dirt. Two men on each bike. White handkerchiefs hid their faces, but not the AKs strapped to their chests. Wells watched them from the compound's third hut. Even if the riders were looking directly at him, the shadows would hide him.

The track dipped and they disappeared. Wells figured they were maybe two minutes out. Most likely they would stay on the bikes the whole way in. Untrained fighters habitually underestimated the importance of moving quietly, especially in open country like this. These men were making a particularly obvious approach. Maybe they had a strategy Wells hadn't figured. More likely they were young and high on miraa and fearless, certain that they could deal with whatever they came across.

Wells assumed these men were part of the raiding party that had attacked the camp and grabbed the hostages. He hoped to capture at least one alive, find out where the hostages were now, why Scott Thompson had been killed. But facing four men with AKs, Wells would settle for survival. His and Wilfred's. He'd come up with a simple plan. He didn't want to run for the Land Cruiser, or hide in the scrub and wait for darkness. He preferred to use the raiders' overconfidence against them. He had explained his plan to Wilfred as they stood in the center of the compound, the stinking corpses around them a reminder of the stakes.

"Wait in the first hut. Step out as the first bike passes. Make sure they know you're there. They'll stop when they see you. That's what we want. Even before they stop, yell to them. Doesn't matter what you say, as long as it gets their attention. Once you start talking, don't stop. I'm going to give you the shotgun. Carry it by the barrel in one hand so it's clearly no threat. Don't point it at them under any circumstances. Don't give them reason to shoot. The first thing they'll do is tell you, Put it down. Don't argue with them. Do what they say."

"Why do I carry it at all, then?"

"If they disarm you, they've dealt with you. You're no threat. Now, if they ask about me, where I am, who, tell them I work with WorldCares. But say you're alone, you dropped me off before you got here. I was afraid to come so near Somalia. If they ask why you're here, tell them that you found this place by accident."

"They won't believe me."

"Doesn't matter. Point is to confuse them, slow them down."

"Then what?"

"Take another step or two towards them. The closer you can get, the better. They have AKs and we have pistols. We get in close, we shave their edge. Keep your hands in the air. I'll be in the third hut, but don't look for me. Not for any reason. Focus on them, keep them focused on you. Talk. I know you're good at that. When you hear me shoot, you do the same."

"But I already put the gun down —"

"Not the shotgun. With the Makarov. It'll be tucked into your waist at the back, where they can't see it. When I come out of the hut, I'm going to come out shooting. No warning. When I do, they'll turn towards me."

"You can't be sure."

"It's instinct to focus on the active threat. And all this is going to happen fast. At most twenty seconds after you first come out of the hut. They'll be sitting on the bikes, looking at you. When they hear me step out, they'll twist towards me. That's when I'll shoot them. I'll take out the two on the bike closer to me. You focus on the bike nearer you. Understand?"

"What if they shoot me as soon as they see me?"

"Most men can't kill someone that fast. Not unless they've already met you, know you're the enemy. They have to ask questions, get themselves ready. Decide."

"But that's not what you're going to do. You're just going to kill them."

"Why I'm still alive, Wilfred. Now we practice."

They did, twice, before the motorcycles got loud and Wilfred ran for the first hut. Now Wells heard the motorcycles slow, drop to idle. Seconds passed. Then one bike moved again. The other stayed where it was. They'd split up to approach the compound from both ends. So much for Wells's plan.

■ ■ ■ ■

Guy Raviv, Wells's favorite instructor at the Farm, liked to say, *Never forget. The enemy gets a vote, too. No matter how great your strategy looks on paper, when the battle starts, nothing works exactly how you drew it up.*

Raviv reminded Wells of the best noncoms he'd known during Ranger school. Ranger training was famously tough, nine weeks of runs and marches with hundred-pound packs — on four hours' sleep. The NCOs helped the guys on the bubble while pushing the toughest soldiers even harder. "Everybody suffers," a master sergeant named Jim Grant said to Wells. "Don't let me see you smile. I'll hurt you more." By the end, Wells understood the strategy. Ultimately, the instructors were sending the message *Don't worry about anyone else's limits. Find your own. Then beat them. Because no matter how good you are, when you wind up in combat, you'll discover that the hell we've put you through is nothing at all.*

Raviv treated Wells the same way, a harshness born of respect. The night before the paramilitary survival exercise that the CIA put all its trainees through, he called Wells.

"You awake? Not worried about tomorrow?"

"Should I be?"

"I'll swing by around ten."

Wells figured Raviv wanted to run one last countersurveillance exercise. Instead, as midnight approached, Wells found himself in the overheated basement of a backstreet bar in Norfolk playing poker with a table of middle-aged men he'd never seen before. Raviv, who was famously cheap, bought beers for him all night. The game didn't break until four a.m. Then Raviv insisted on stopping at a Waffle House for breakfast. By the time they reached Camp Peary, the sun was up. So was Wells's hangover. He reeked of Raviv's secondhand smoke. He wanted nothing more than to sack out, but he knew he wouldn't have the chance.

"You did this on purpose."

"Whining doesn't suit you. How much did you lose, eighty?"

"I guess." Actually, Wells had lost a hundred and fifty. He couldn't figure out how. The game was only quarter-ante. But he wasn't much of a poker player. After all those Budweisers, the cards and chips floated away like balloons at a state fair. Up and up and gone.

"You gonna be a covert operative, you

can't even play poker?"

"I'm not going to be that kind of operative."

Raviv pulled to the side of the access road that led to the Farm's main campus. "You're a fool."

Wells felt like he'd stumbled into someone else's life. "What are we talking about, Guy?"

"Why'd I bring you to that game?"

"I don't know, so I'd have trouble with the exercise?"

"Idiot. It's glorified Capture the Flag. Nobody fails. You're a Ranger. I could cut off your legs, you'd still make it. I made you play poker because I wanted to watch you play poker. And let me clue you in. You have the worst tells I've ever seen."

"Tells."

"You give away your hands. Raise your eyebrows when you have a winner. Always look left when you're bluffing."

"Guy. Gotta be honest. Maybe I'm still drunk, but I'm not getting it."

Raviv twisted toward Wells in the seat and — a moment Wells knew he'd never forget — slapped Wells across the cheek. Wells suddenly knew that Raviv loved him. Not sexually, maybe, but the desperate feeling here was love all the same.

"You don't get to pick what kind of operative you are," Raviv said. "It picks you. You want to go non-official, you're going to have to lie so deep it's in your bones. No tells. I promise you one day someone's going to ask you to do something that's going to destroy you. Something you can't even imagine right now, in this pretty place. With its nice high fences so nobody gets hurt. Farm? It ought to be called a nursery. It's like you're in strollers in here. And when it happens, that thing, whatever it is, you're going to have to nod and say, yes, like it was your idea all along. Or you're going to die. And maybe get some agents killed, too. All this training" — he spat the word like a curse — "they never say a word about that. You understand me? You copy? Over?"

"Yes."

"No, you don't. But you will." Raviv reached across Wells, opened the door. "Get out."

"Guy —"

"I said out."

Wells stood in the cool early-morning Virginia air trying to understand what had just happened, what he'd done wrong. Raviv drove off without saying good-bye. Wells didn't see him for the rest of training. In fact, Wells never saw Raviv again. He died of lung cancer while Wells was living as a jihadi in Pakistan's North-West Frontier, the deepest cover of all. Wells found out only after he returned to the United States.

But he never forgot that speech. He learned its ugly truth even earlier than Raviv might have expected, in the miserable civil war in the Russian province of Chechnya. The conflict attracted a few hundred Afghan fighters, the true crazies, guys who hadn't killed enough Russians in the 1980s. Wells joined up, figuring a few months in Chechnya would be the fastest way to prove his devotion to the cause.

The first few weeks were quiet. Wells lived with sixty Afghan and Chechen fighters in the mountains outside Grozny, the Chechen capital. The Russians fired artillery at them, but the shells never did much more than send rock slides down the slopes around their camp. Wells was almost ready to discount the stories he'd heard about the war's brutality. Then the fighters heard of a Russian convoy that had the bad luck to be traveling at night without helicopter support. They trapped the Russians on a hairpin curve a few kilometers from camp and blew up four BTRs, Russian armored personnel carriers. Wells's first battle. Everything happened at once. Waves of heat from the carriers as their ammunition and fuel exploded. Desperate Russian soldiers jumping from the hatches, falling down, picking themselves up, running for the forests beside the road as the guerrillas opened up on them. The seven surviving BTRs firing blindly left and right. Wells knew that he ought to be afraid. Yet he was exhilarated. Time slowed to quarter-speed. The relativity of war.

The real hell started when the battle ended. The jihadis took five Russians alive. Back at camp, the rebel leader — a pouch-faced unsmiling Chechen who called himself Abu Khalifa — decided to kill the prisoners. The murders would be taped, the videos sent to television stations in Moscow and Grozny, a warning to every Russian soldier in Chechnya: Don't expect to be held for ransom if we catch you. Or traded home in a prisoner swap. Expect to die.

Abu Khalifa gave five fighters the honor of slitting Russian throats. He chose Wells to be fifth. Wells wasn't sure whether he'd been picked at random or as a test because he was American. He only knew he couldn't refuse. Backing out wouldn't save the Russian's life, but it would end Wells's own. Yet how could he kill an unarmed prisoner? Wells cursed Abu Khalifa and Raviv both. Somehow he felt that if Raviv hadn't warned him, this choice wouldn't have been forced on him.

The prisoners were lined up, the camera set. Like the other executioners, Wells pulled on gloves and a mask. A faceless killer. Abu Khalifa made a long speech that Wells didn't understand. Then the slaughter began. Wells waited for the fighters to turn away in disgust. Instead a hum went through the men around him. They edged closer so they wouldn't miss the show. Wells was glad for his hood. *Not supposed to go like this,* he thought. Cavalry's over the hill. They'll be here any minute.

When his turn came, he took the knife — a scimitar, really, a curved steel blade with an edge sharper than any razor. The oaken handle was wet under his fingers, slick with the blood and gristle of the soldier who'd just been slaughtered. Wells dried the knife on a piece of cloth and took his place behind the sacrifice chosen for him. Two men flanked him, grappling the Russian's arms, holding him steady.

No angel appeared with horn or ram. No cavalry, either. Wells knelt, wrapped his hand around the Russian's forehead. And heard a single word whispered —

Don't.

Wells wondered if the soldier was speaking. But the Russian wouldn't know English, and anyway his mouth was gagged tight.

Don't don't don't. Louder now. His conscience. His soul, pleading its case. Let this crime belong to someone else. You don't even know his name. But his name didn't matter. Whoever this Russian was, he would die tonight for the crime of surrendering to an enemy that took no prisoners. Nothing could save him. Not Wells or anyone else.

"Ready?" Abu Khalifa said.

Wells felt the blade heavy and full in his hand as he pulled the man's head back. The first four soldiers had accepted their fate. This one moaned under the gag, fought the rope that held him, twisted his head under Wells's gloved fingers. If he hoped for mercy, he was mistaken. His fear fed the bloodlust. The jihadis jeered in four languages, the angry shouts tumbling over one another. A rock gashed the soldier's cheek. Cutting his throat would be a mercy, Wells saw. Else he'd be stoned, stomped, torn limb from limb. Wells dug the tip of the scythe into the man's throat and twisted the curved blade deep and sliced. As his blood gushed, the soldier screamed. The moan tore at Wells, maddened him. To stop it, he tore at the soldier's neck until finally the man was quiet. Even then Wells didn't stop cutting, not until blood sopped his hands and the soldier's head flopped loose on its neck. The other jihadis gathered around him and cheered. Abu Khalifa himself took Wells by the wrist and raised his arm high like Wells had just won a prizefight. The blood dripped down from the knife. Wells thought he might go mad.

"Allahu Akbar," Wells said. Though he had never felt more distant from God. The jihadis never did put out the video of that killing — upon further review it was too messy even for them — but Wells saw it. Once. He couldn't believe how little time the whole episode had taken. Nine seconds. Nine seconds to make a living man dead. Nine seconds and a knife.

The Russian was the first man Wells had killed. An unarmed prisoner. Wells tried to forget what he'd done. He'd never told anyone about it, not Anne, not Shafer, not even Exley. He thought he'd buried it. And for years he had. But in the last few months the memory had crept up on him, distracted him at crucial moments. Like this one.

The thrum of the motorcycles brought him to reality. Think: He and Wilfred faced split targets who could cover each other at a distance they couldn't match. Nor could

Wells change the plan he'd already set. No more than a hundred feet separated him and Wilfred, but they didn't have phones or radios. Their only advantage was surprise, and if they shouted they'd lose it. Wells would have to hope Wilfred decided to follow what was left of the plan. In other words, take out the two guys closer to them. Hope the two at the other end of the camp weren't great shots even with the advantage of AKs.

Wells flattened himself against the wall of the hut, a step from the doorway. He pulled the Glock from his waistband, made sure he had a round chambered. Outside, one bike drew close. The other circled around the compound.

Suddenly, Wilfred shouted in Swahili. The bike stopped and someone yelled back. Wilfred yelled, in English, "Okay! I put it down!" Smart. Letting Wells know. The second bike sounded like it was at the far end of the compound, by the fourth hut. But were its riders dismounted? How quickly would they answer when Wells opened up?

More shouting from the first bike. A word leapt at Wells. *Mzungu.*

Time to move.

■ ■ ■ ■

Wells slide-stepped to the edge of the doorway, peeked out. He saw Wilfred, on his knees, hands raised, a half-dozen steps from the first hut. The shotgun's black barrel glinted on the dirt behind him. The bike was eight meters from Wilfred, fifteen from Wells. Its riders wore jeans and white T-shirts and those white handkerchiefs. A kind of uniform, Wells supposed. The rider looked awkwardly over his shoulder at Wilfred. The passenger sat crossways, both legs on the near side of the bike. Now he was yelling something, bringing his AK around —

Wells stepped into the doorway, raised the pistol, fired. No warning, no hesitation. Two shots. Aiming center mass. Nothing fancy. Wells was ready for the Glock's kick this time. The shots caught the kid high in the chest, pushed him backward. He sprawled off the back of the bike and thudded to the earth, already dead. The rider reached for his AK, tried to unstrap it, but then seemed to realize he wouldn't have time and let go of the gun and grabbed for the handlebars —

Wells pulled the trigger of the Glock three

more times. The pistol jerked. Blood painted the rider's shirt. He sagged forward over the handlebars. His head sank and his hands reached down like he was trying to make peace with the earth. For a second the bike stayed upright, the kid's weight balanced fifty-fifty even in death. Then his left leg sagged and the bike tipped with him —

Wells knew he was no longer a threat, forgot him, turned for the second bike. Hoping that the men on it would make the fatal mistake of riding forward to help their buddies. Or just take off for reinforcement. He'd settle for that. He and Wilfred could grab the first bike, ride back to the Land Cruiser. Instead the men at the other end had jumped off their bike. They hoisted their AKs, their faces half hidden under their kerchiefs, their rifles swinging toward Wells —

Wells spun away, knowing he had no time to return fire, that he could only go to ground, get inside the hut. Though he wasn't sure if these mud bricks would do much against AK rounds.

Then he heard the Makarov behind him, three quick shots, its bark lovely and familiar even if Wells wasn't pulling the trigger. Wilfred joining the action, coming up with his hidden pistol. On the far side of the compound, someone yelped in pain. Wells turned back toward the door and fired two quick shots, not aiming for anything, just trying to get the enemy fighters wavering between him and Wilfred instead of focusing on a single target and unloading with the AKs. Two and three and two. Seven shots fired now, plus the three at the hyena. Wells was thankful for the Glock's nineteen rounds. With the Makarov, he'd be reloading right now.

He peeked through the doorway. The fighter on the right had taken a bullet to the right shoulder, his gun arm. His AK dangled low. As Wells watched, he jammed his right elbow into his stomach to brace the rifle and fired a wild burst aimed half at Wells and half at Wilfred. Lottery shooting. A round slapped the corner of the hut behind Wilfred, but nothing more.

The fighter on the left was more dangerous. He dropped to one knee and focused on Wilfred, his left elbow propped on his left knee, the butt of the rifle hard against his right shoulder, his head tilted as he squinted over the AK's crude but effective sight. The classic shooter's position. He was looking into the sun, which made the shot tougher. But less than a football field separated him and Wilfred. Trained shoot-ers were plenty accurate with an AK at that range. Wells saw all this in a fraction of a second, those years of close combat experience, knew Wilfred was in trouble —

"Down —" he yelled. Spent cartridges flared from the AK, glinting in the sun. Wilfred grunted in Swahili. Even without looking at him, Wells knew he'd been hit. Bad. Wells took his own shooter's stance, knowing that if he didn't take the guy down, he and Wilfred were done. Wilfred would be wounded on open ground, Wells pinned in the hut. The two bandits would kill Wilfred without too much trouble, then focus on Wells. So, really, now or never. Wells reminded himself that the Glock would kick harder than the Makarov and —

From behind the huts came a low growl that grew until it split the air, a wall of sound as overwhelming as a jet engine. Only one animal dared announce its presence in so lordly a fashion. The hyenas knew, too, the enemy they hated even more than man had come to steal their feast. As the roar wound down, Wells heard them gobbling and cackling in dismay —

But Wells forced the lion and the hyenas out of his mind, made himself focus on the man with the rifle. *When they learn to shoot, I'll worry about them. Hurry, but slowly.* He squinted over the Glock like a pool player looking for just the right angle on a tricky bank shot. Pulled the trigger, controlled the recoil, pulled it again. And missed. Two jets of red dirt spurted up left of the shooter. Who had also been distracted by the lion. Now he shifted his eyes back to Wells, fired a burst —

That drilled bricks two feet to Wells's right. Wells didn't duck or dive. No point. He had as clear a chance as he could hope. He would make good with this pistol at long-gun range or die trying. Arms steady. Don't overgrip. Let the weapon do the work. He moved the Glock a fraction of an inch to the right, fired. Didn't wait to see whether the shot was true but fired again —

The fighter must have fired back just as he was hit. An AK round swept over Wells's right shoulder close enough for him to feel the punctured air it left behind. Another tore through the mud brick beside the doorway. Across the field Wells saw the Somali stumble, hands fumbling over his belly like if he just pressed down hard enough he'd straighten himself out, put the skin and muscle back together —

But now the other shooter, the one Wilfred had hit in the shoulder, was running at Wells, legs pumping, AK on auto, locked and closing. Wells had no choice but to dive out of the doorway, hope the kid shot himself out of bullets before he got too close.

He rolled down onto the hard-packed dirt inside the hut and twisted himself against the wall as AK rounds gashed through the rough bricks. Then Wilfred's Makarov popped three times and a body thumped down.

Wells stood, walked out. The fourth shooter was face-planted in the dirt, his AK sprawled over his head. Wells didn't know where Wilfred's shots had caught him, but they'd done the trick.

"Saved you," Wilfred said, his voice fluttery. He lay on his back, unmoving. No wonder the fourth shooter had ignored Wilfred. From across the compound he probably looked dead. Wells ran for him. His jeans were two different shades now, light blue for his left leg, blue-black for the right. Wells knelt beside Wilfred's right leg, found the denim soaked through with blood.

"I got you here and I'm getting you home."

Wilfred cleared his throat.

"Yes." Wells had a sat phone, but calling the agency wouldn't do any good. Even if

Shafer got through to Nairobi right away and convinced the station chief to spend thousands of dollars to medevac a Kenyan it didn't know, the station wouldn't have a chopper ready to go. It would have to find one willing to fly at night to the Somali border. Plus they were more than three hundred miles east of Nairobi, which meant the helicopter would have to refuel at least once on the way out, twice more on the return. It wouldn't get Wilfred back to Nairobi for close to twelve hours, long past midnight.

Better to get to the Land Cruiser and then drive for the Saudi-financed infirmary in Bakafi, the village they had passed on the way down. With luck, the clinic would have a bush doctor who could stabilize Wilfred enough to keep him alive overnight. If not, they'd have to drive for the hospital that Médecins Sans Frontières ran in Dadaab.

From behind the huts, the lion bellowed again. Wells scrambled for the shotgun. He didn't think the lion would attack, not until it scattered the hyenas, but the thing sounded like it was six feet tall. Wells had been on bloodier battlefields, but nowhere closer to a true state of nature. No reinforcements were coming for either side, no medevacs, no police, not even any curious locals. Only the lion and the hyenas, pacing and watching and waiting for darkness.

"He wants fresh meat," Wilfred said. "That's me."

"With a side of fries." Wells laid down the shotgun and ran for the third hut, where he had stowed his pack before the shooting started. On his way back, he detoured for four bottles of water from the first hut. He handed one to Wilfred.

"Drink." Wilfred dropped the bottle, trying to unscrew the cap. Wells picked it up, opened it, shoved it back into his hand. He clasped his fingers around Wilfred's and lifted the bottle to Wilfred's mouth. Most of the water went down Wilfred's chin, but he swallowed a few sips.

"Good." Wells reached for the scissors in the first-aid kit, snipped off Wilfred's jeans high on the thigh. The bullet hole was four inches above the knee. Blood was seeping out, not a gusher but heavy and steady. Wells thought the round had cracked the femur and nicked the popliteal artery, the main artery down the leg. He'd seen a man die from a similar wound years before in Afghanistan.

Wells raised Wilfred's leg as gently as he could to feel for an exit wound. Nothing.

"Listen to me. I have to do things you won't like." Wells tapped Wilfred's cheek to make him focus. "Get a tourniquet on your leg, tie it off so you don't lose more blood. That's going to hurt bad, because the bullet probably broke a bone in there. Then we have to get to the Cruiser. Either I leave you or we ride. I don't want to leave you. I'm afraid you'll pass out. Even though the lion might like it."

Wilfred sipped his water, nodded. He was relaxed now, no wasted motion, no panic. "We ride."

"That's right. You on the back with that broken leg. I'll tie you to me and you hold on and we'll get there. But I promise you it'll hurt more than anything in your life."

"One question, mzungu."

Wells hoped that Wilfred wouldn't ask if he was going to lose the leg. Wells didn't know, didn't want to guess.

"I get a bonus for this?"

This kid. Cooler than the other side of the pillow. Wells squeezed his big hand around Wilfred's skinny arm. "Five bucks. Only if you live."

The bare-bones first-aid kit had rubber tubing that might have worked for Wilfred's forearm. Not his thigh. A T-shirt or pant leg wouldn't do the trick either. Wells thought of the hot plates in the first hut. He cut loose their electrical cords, twin four-foot lengths of thick black plastic. He grabbed a whiskey bottle from the second hut, a crude way to sterilize the wound, an even cruder painkiller. Not the ideal choice, since alcohol slowed clotting, but Wilfred needed a distraction. "Take a drink. Not a big one —"

Wilfred nearly gagged but choked down a sip.

Wells pulled off his T-shirt, balled it up. "Put this in your mouth and bite down, hard as you can."

Wilfred stuffed the shirt in his mouth. It stuck out like a limp flag. Wells raised the cord.

"I'm going to tie this around your leg. It's going to hurt. The shirt's in your mouth so you don't bite off your tongue. Ready?"

Wilfred nodded. Wells chose a spot two inches above the bullet hole, wrapped the cord around Wilfred's leg. He crossed the ends and pulled, tight as he could and then tighter. Wilfred keened, a high strangled sound the hyenas might have recognized. He banged his hands against the earth and his eyes bulged wide. But he didn't move his leg. Not an inch. Wells pulled until the cord dug into the meat of Wilfred's thigh and then knotted the plastic.

He wiped away Wilfred's leg with his shirt, watched the bullet hole for fresh blood. It still leaked, a trickle but steady, too much. Wells grabbed the second cord. This time he pulled until he thought the plastic might break. Silent tears lit Wilfred's eyes as Wells tied off the cord. Wells wiped away the hole again and watched as the trickle slowed to a dribble. It would have to do. Wells poured whiskey over Wilfred's leg and wiped off the wound with the little tube of antibiotic from the first-aid kit and taped gauze over his thigh. He pulled the T-shirt from Wilfred's mouth, offered him a water bottle. Wilfred sipped a few drops and let it drop. He wiped the spit from his lips, the tears from his cheeks.

"That all you got. Too easy."

"Easy." Now Wells needed a way to keep Wilfred on the bike. A rope. He hadn't seen any ropes. But he had seen chains. In the fourth hut. He picked up the shotgun and walked the hundred-meter battlefield, stopping beside the men Wilfred had killed, turning out their pockets. He found no identification, but one man did have a cell phone. Wells grabbed it.

Outside the hut he took a lungful of air,

like a man trying to see how long he could stay underwater. He stepped into the stinking swollen darkness, Scott Thompson's eternal home. He walked over the hyena — it had stayed dead, at least — and found a chain. A reminder that three hostages were still missing, probably alive, with any luck close to here. Wells needed to bring Wilfred to safety so he could return to finding them. He put the tip of the shotgun to the post in the wall and pulled the trigger. The chain clanked down to the floor, a strangely playful sound. Wells liberated a second chain and jogged out, still holding his breath. He wondered whether any Scott Thompson would be left by the time the Kenyan police found this place. Probably not. Though maybe the hyenas and the lion would be so busy outside that they wouldn't bother with the hut for a while.

Wilfred lay on his side, his eyes closed. Wells picked up the bike, put it in neutral, dropped the kickstand, sparked it. Wilfred opened his eyes, tracked the chains. "Mzungu. You dirty man."

"I'll cinch them around us. You hold me and I'll hold you."

"Sound like a song."

Wells knelt behind Wilfred, reached under

his arms, pulled him up. Wilfred grunted and his body shook, but he didn't complain. He leaned against Wells and held his bad leg off the ground. Wells half-threw him over the bike and wrapped the chains around his back and slid in front of him. Wilfred put his arms around Wells's waist, but he had no strength. Without the chains supporting him, he couldn't stay on the bike. Wells needed his right hand for the throttle, which meant he would have to hold the chains in his left hand. But he couldn't get the bike going unless he pulled in the clutch, put the bike in gear — a move that required that same left hand. He tried twice. Both times he lost his grip on the clutch handle and stalled the engine as he struggled to hold the chains. After the second try, he sat in silence and listened to the hyenas gibbering. The animals had moved closer. It wouldn't be long before the bold one, the big one, returned.

"Let me," Wilfred said.

"You know how?"

"Come on."

Wells leaned forward until his chest nearly touched the bike's gas tank. He pulled the chains tight to keep Wilfred close. Wilfred snaked his left arm under Wells's shoulder and pulled in the clutch. Wells twisted the throttle a fraction, giving the engine a taste of gas. Twenty-plus years of riding had made these moves as intuitive as inhaling and exhaling. But today he was on a respirator, trusting Wilfred to help. Wells tapped down his left foot, put the bike into first. "Let go —"

Wilfred eased off the clutch and Wells rolled his right hand a half inch on the throttle. Dirt bikes were twitchier than street bikes, and the bike jumped ahead. Wells thought Wilfred would drop the clutch too quickly and stall them. But he let the handle out smoothly. Wells added gas and then they were moving, bouncing along. Wilfred jabbered in Swahili, no doubt cursing Wells for this mess, but Wells held the chain tight, and with every turn of the tires, they left the corpses and vultures and hyenas behind and rode toward the Cruiser. And life.

12

Langley

In his golden years — oh, my, how he hated that phrase — Shafer had unaccountably developed a liking for sugar cereal. He had a boy's taste buds and an old man's colon. So it was that he sat down to a lunchtime bowl of Frosted Flakes and Lactaid as he watched a White House press conference livestreaming on CNN.com.

The question-and-answer period had started a few minutes before, with every question so far about the hostages. Now Josh Galper, the White House spokesman, pointed at a dark-haired woman in the front row. Galper wasn't afraid to smack down dumb questions. Shafer appreciated him. The reporters didn't.

"Emily. I'm sure *The Wall Street Journal* has a question on the budget? Taxes, maybe?"

"Can you tell us if the President has been

in touch with the families of the missing volunteers?"

"The President has spoken privately to family members to express his concern."

"Can you tell us what he said?"

"Last time I checked, that wasn't what 'privately' meant." Galper pointed to a black guy in the second row. "Brett?"

"Brett Ward, *Washington Post.* Would the United States consider the use of force to rescue the hostages if and when their location is confirmed?"

"We're ready for any eventuality."

"Including an invasion of Somalia?"

"All options remain on the table."

"Including military action?"

"I'll say this as clearly as I can. It would be premature to discuss an invasion at this time. That said, I think the American people should understand al-Shabaab is a terrorist threat both within and outside Somalia. For many years, the United States and United Nations have been concerned about the situation. That's the context here."

"So this would be a full-scale invasion, not just a rescue mission."

"I didn't say that. Please don't say that I did."

"Would the President ask for congressional approval before an invasion?"

"You've gone way past what I've said, Brett. However, in the theoretical event of a theoretical invasion, the President would inform senior congressional leaders —"

"That's not what I asked —"

"Brett, you know I love dancing with you, but I need to let some other reporters cut in."

Shafer had seen enough. The war drums were a-beating, as Duto had predicted. He muted the conference and dug into his Frosted Flakes before they could get soggy. But he managed only two spoonfuls before his cell phone rang. Wells. Who was probably in Mogadishu by now, hanging out with clan leaders as he pretended to be a Saudi royal with a hankering for blondes from Montana. Say what you wanted about the man, he wasn't boring.

"John. Roofied anyone lately?"

"I found the camp where they were being held."

"That's great —"

"Not so much."

"Are they dead?"

"Scott Thompson was. The others, gone. It's possible they were killed and I didn't find them, but my best guess is some Somali bandit group got wind of them and came after them and whoever was holding them."

"When?"

"Probably last night. The bodies were still fresh."

"By bodies, you mean Thompson."

"And a bunch of Kenyans."

"Did it look like a real kidnapping? Like they were prisoners? Or hiding out, waiting to come in?"

"Prisoners. There was a hut where they were chained up. Where I found Thompson."

"This was Somalia?"

"Kenya. Near the border, but Kenya."

"You have a lead on the others?"

"Not yet. My fixer took a bullet. I'm getting him to a hospital." Wells told Shafer how the bandits had attacked him and Wilfred at the compound, how Wilfred had been wounded.

"And you think the ones who attacked you were Somali?"

"Yeah. The Somalis look different than ethnic Kenyans. Plus I took a cell phone off one. The numbers in the register have the Somali country code, 252, not the Kenyan."

"Where are you now?"

"Outside this village called Bakafi, ninety miles south of Dadaab. There's an infirmary here. I'm hoping they can stabilize Wilfred.

But he'll need a helicopter to medevac him to Nairobi tomorrow morning. Otherwise, he'll lose the leg."

"I'll see what I can do."

"No ifs. Promise me, Ellis."

"All right."

"Now. Please tell me the grown-ups have put a stop to this invasion nonsense —"

"I'd say we're up to at least fifty-fifty."

"To attack Somalia?"

"There's momentum. And when people hear Scott Thompson's been killed —"

"But he was killed in Kenya. After being kidnapped by Kenyans."

"The Kenyan police will tell a different story. And I'll bet by the time they get to that compound, there's nothing left but bones. Can you tell a Somali femur from a Kenyan? Because I can't. And there's something else. Even if the Kenyans were wrong about what happened before, they're not anymore. You said it yourself. The other three are probably in Somalia now."

Wells was silent.

"John, I have to give Vinny a heads-up about the camp. Can't leave that kid's body rotting. And he's going to have to tell the families and James Thompson. It's going to leak, and the hysteria's going to hit a whole new level."

"You can't tell Thompson. I've got proof he was in on it." Wells told Shafer about the Joker's mask he'd found, the corpse that had to be Suggs. "What must have happened, Thompson figured Suggs could hold the hostages a couple weeks while he got publicity and money for WorldCares. He didn't count on it getting this big. Or these Somalis catching wind of it."

"A mask? That's your evidence?"

"What was James doing with that third cell phone? Why was he calling the kidnappers?"

"He had every reason to talk to the kidnappers, John. He'll say he was trying to put together a back-channel deal to free the volunteers quietly."

"But he knew Suggs —"

"Exactly. He knew Suggs. So Suggs set this up with some Somalis and then came to him and said, 'I kidnapped your nephew and his friends, now pay me, and by the way, if you tell anyone anything, I'll kill them all.' And Thompson agreed. Who's going to say he's lying? Not Suggs. Suggs is dead. Which limits his ability to offer a contradictory narrative."

"You can't seriously believe that."

"I'm just saying, don't assume he's going to go away quietly. He's got cards to play, and remember the Kenyans want to pin this on Shabaab as much as Thompson does. They won't be happy you've been playing vigilante."

"I thought I was killing the Somali bandits they hated."

"The beauty of life, John. All kinds of ways to look at things. So many different perspectives."

"Like you think you're witty and clever, and I think ninety percent of what comes out of your mouth is nonsense."

"All I'm saying is, you want to be sure Thompson can't get to you, find the hostages."

"Noted. Has NSA gotten back to you on the numbers from Thompson's third phone? Locations or anything?"

"Not yet."

"Ellis —"

"Truly beyond my control. But give me those Somali numbers and I'll put them on the list, too."

Wells did.

"Any other good news?" Shafer said.

"Walk through one last set of what-ifs with me. Suppose I find the other three, and the White House and Duto already know that Scott Thompson was killed. We'd go in with a special ops team, yes? We'd have to assume their lives are at risk."

"Sounds right."

"And then it gets messy, the hostages get killed. What happens next?"

Shafer saw where Wells was headed. "The public pressure, we'd have to invade. Teach them a lesson."

"Because from what I saw today, these guys, they're young, but they're real soldiers —"

"You took out four by yourself."

"It was close. I'm not saying they could stop a commando team for long. But long enough to kill the hostages. Wasn't there something like that in Nigeria?"

"Last year. The British sent in a team to rescue two hostages. They didn't get there in time."

"Let me chase this, Ellis."

"I have to tell Duto what you found. You want this kid Wilfred choppered out, he's going to insist on knowing what happened. And you know I'm right about that body. It needs to come home. Not fair to the family."

"Give me the night. One night."

"Best I can do, if the delay with the numbers from Thompson's phone is my guide, NSA will need at least twenty-four hours to get anything on the Somali mobile numbers. So I'll call over on those, and I'll tell Duto what you found. But I forgot to ask you exactly where the camp is. Oops. He'll make me call you back, but I can't make you answer —"

"Thank you, Ellis."

"Not finished. By the time Duto wakes up tomorrow, I won't be able to put him off any longer. And he wakes up early. Which means within twenty hours, give or take, early afternoon tomorrow your time, dawn here, we'll have a team on the way to the camp to pick up what's left of Scott Thompson. And the families are going to know. After that, you better figure things will happen fast. Not to mention whatever James Thompson tells the Kenyan police."

A long sigh from the other side of the world. "I get it. Can I go now?"

After all he'd done, Wells still acted every so often like the high school football star he'd once been. The coolest kid in town. Shafer relished those offhand moments. He hoped they revealed that Wells's sunny Montana boyhood hadn't entirely fled his soul.

"Try not to get in too much trouble."

"Call me if NSA comes through." Click.

Shafer returned his attention to the bowl on

his desk. Unfortunately, the life expectancy of Frosted Flakes was measured in minutes. They sagged in the Lactaid like an overage starlet's arms. Even so, Shafer shoveled them into his mouth, hoping the sugar rush would give him a kick start as he imagined how to spin this call to Duto.

He'd just finished when the phone on his desk trilled. This time the caller ID showed Duto's office.

"I saw the press conference. You were right."

"Not why I'm calling. Can you come up? There's something you need to see."

Duto's personal assistant, a bright-eyed thirty-something who would surely join Duto in his quest for the Senate, led Shafer into the director's giant seventh-floor office. Shafer had been introduced to the assistant at least twice but refused to remember his name. Duto raised a single finger, the universal *Give me a minute* sign, and went back to pecking at his keyboard.

Over the years, Duto's office had filled with the gifts that men like him received for the work of their subordinates. The items ranged from kitschy to extraordinary. Tucked on a bookshelf, on a cream-colored card an eighth-inch thick, a personal note from Prince William. In tightly scrawled blue ink, the prince elliptically thanked Duto for disrupting a terrorist plot against Kate Middleton on a trip the princess had taken to Turkey. Hanging on the room's far wall, a fifteenth-century Katana samurai sword, three feet of sleek and vicious steel. The sword arrived after the agency intercepted four North Korean operatives plotting to bomb Tokyo's subways. On Duto's desk, the depth gauge from a miniature submarine that a Mexican drug gang had used to move tons of cocaine. The Drug Enforcement Administration offered up the gauge to commemorate the agency's help in disrupting the cartel.

The sheer number of tokens in the office testified both to Duto's longevity as director and the CIA's reach. The agency went wherever the United States had interests, and the United States had interests everywhere. Even eastern Kenya. Shafer wondered what trinket Duto would receive if the agency rescued the hostages. Probably nothing. He'd settle for a Senate seat.

Shafer grabbed the Katana off the wall. The sword's blade was narrow and angled and polished so closely that it seemed to glow. Shafer took a practice swipe. Duto ignored him and kept typing. The assistant raised a hand.

"I don't think you should be doing that."

"Avast, Handy Smurf —"

"Handy Smurf?"

"Out!" Shafer sliced at him. The blade nearly sliced off the tip of the assistant's tie. He fled. Shafer raised the Katana high in victory.

Duto stopped typing. "Unnecessary."

"I get bored, I act out."

"Put it back before you hurt yourself."

Shafer sat, resting the blade on his lap. "Think they'll let you keep it?"

"Sadly, no. I didn't know when I got it, but it came straight out of the Tokyo Museum. Been appraised at six hundred thousand."

"A little over the gift limit."

Duto turned his laptop around so Shafer could see the screen. "Recognize her?"

The woman's face filled nearly the entire screen, with slivers of a mud wall visible behind her. She had circles under her eyes and a scared puckered mouth. But she was still beautiful. Still Gwen Murphy.

"This was emailed to Brandon Murphy's personal account six hours ago." Duto pulled up two more photos, Hailey and Owen. "These two went to the Barnes and Broder families."

"Not Scott Thompson's parents?" Shafer said. Though he knew that Thompson's parents hadn't gotten a photo and never would. A half-eaten corpse would be tough to ransom.

"Nothing yet. They're freaking out, which is understandable."

"Do we know where they came from?"

"Nairobi. NSA has tracked the IP address to a few square blocks of downtown. They claim they'll have an exact location in the next two hours. But we're all assuming it's a public space, an Internet café or unlocked hotspot. They'll look for surveillance, but Nairobi's not DC. Very few cameras, even downtown."

"Have we told the Kenyans?"

"Not yet. The feeling is this thing's too hot already. You can imagine, the parents went crazy when they got these. The FBI is trying to talk them down, asking them to stay calm, not go public. The families emailed back, asked for proof of life. Nobody's heard back yet, but we're assuming the photos are real. Our experts say they look real."

"They look real to me. Any guesses on location?"

"The background doesn't give much to go on. The images are poor quality, like they were shot on a cell phone and then sent to another phone."

"Can NSA —"

"Trace the number and location of the first phone? They say it's unlikely. There's some specific technical reason, data compression and whatnot, but don't ask me to explain."

"Was there a ransom demand? A note, anything?"

"Just the pictures. Put that big brain to work and tell me what it means, Ellis. Why now? Is all the noise we're making about an invasion getting to them?"

Shafer busied himself putting the sword back on the wall, buying a few seconds before he had to answer Duto. He didn't see any alternative to the truth, didn't see how lying would help.

"Wells found a camp where they were being held, but they're gone now. He thinks that James Thompson set them up and that last night some Somali bandits found them and hit the camp and took them."

Duto grabbed the submarine depth gauge, a piece of steel the size of a soup bowl, and in one quick motion fired it at the oak door to his office. The glass face of the gauge shattered, scattering shards over the carpet. Shafer hadn't seen Duto erupt this way in years. Though Shafer understood. Like all executives, Duto hated surprises. Surprises threatened the authority he'd spent his life cultivating.

"Is everything all right?" Handy Smurf said through the door.

"Go away," Duto said. To Shafer: "When exactly were you planning to tell me?"

"I had just hung up with Wells when you called."

"Waste my time, dance with that sword like a mushy-headed freak —"

"You want to hear what happened or you want to yell at me?"

Duto looked away from Shafer, out the window. Shafer could almost hear him reciting whatever mantra his life coach had taught him. When he looked back again, he was calm. "I want to hear."

Shafer told him.

"So it was a fake kidnapping —"

"Not exactly. It probably felt real to the hostages. A setup by James Thompson and this fixer, this guy Suggs."

"Thompson let his nephew get kidnapped and then the kid wound up getting killed?"

"That's how it looks to Wells."

"Muy frio." Lousy Spanish, but Shafer understood.

"Ay, caramba."

"Okay, so the volunteers wind up at this camp, then these Somalis hear about it, attack it, kill the nephew, snatch the others. Which explains the pictures landing today. These guys want money and they want it now."

"That sounds about right."

"And where was the first camp? Kenya or Somalia?"

"Kenya, but Wells didn't tell me where exactly."

"You two are so clever. Either of you consider he might need help?"

Shafer didn't plan to confess to Duto that he'd told Wells exactly that. "He's afraid that when the word about Scott Thompson gets out, the pressure for war will be unstoppable."

Duto rose, picked up the depth gauge, carefully wound a thumb around its shattered face before plunking it back on his desk. "He might be right."

"You ought to know by now, this is what you get with Wells. He's never going to ask for help unless he has to have it. He wants control." Shafer resisted the urge to add *Just like you.*

"So what's his plan?"

"He didn't tell me that either." *Probably because he doesn't have one.* "Yesterday you said you might bring in an ops team."

"I gave the order soon as I saw the photos," Duto said. "They're coming from Dubai to Mombasa." Mombasa was the second-largest city in Kenya, a run-down port in the country's southeastern corner, closer to Somalia than Nairobi. "Unfortunately, they don't arrive until around seven a.m. tomorrow local time. Best they could do even on a chartered jet."

"So you can't move on Thompson's body until tomorrow morning anyway."

Duto nodded.

"Then let's give Wells the night, see what he finds. I promise that after the team lands, I'll get the exact address of the camp and you can send them in."

"I still have to handle the White House."

"Tell them the truth. You have an unconfirmed report that Scott Thompson is dead, no location, and you're following up. We don't have to tell the families that Wells thinks he found the camp yet either. Same thing. Nothing confirmed, so why mention it."

"You think your boy can solve this overnight."

"If he can't, by the morning I'll bet he'll link up with your team." Especially since James Thompson will be screaming to the

Kenyan cops for his head. But Shafer saw no reason to mention that particular complication. "And maybe Nairobi station finds out who sent those emails. Or NSA traces those Somali phones. Lot of shots on goal here."

"Turning into an optimist in your old age, Ellis."

"I've learned not to bet against John. Anything else, Vinny?"

"Not at the moment."

"Then I'll be leaving."

Duto pointed at the door. "Don't let it hit you on the ass, et cetera."

"I'm glad we have the kind of frank, honest relationship where you don't feel the need to be polite."

13

Bakafi, Kenya

The King Fahad Infirmary was better than nothing. But not by much.

It had six narrow beds draped with mosquito nets stretched thinner than a drag queen's panty hose. It had three almost expired bottles of doxycycline. It had one patient, a woman, her cheeks sunken, belly swollen, breathing a slow unsteady rattle. And it had a doctor, or at least a man in a grimy white coat, napping in a chair when Wells carried Wilfred inside.

Wells laid Wilfred on the bed farthest from the dying woman as the doctor walked over with no great urgency. He extracted thick plastic glasses from his pocket and wiped them cleanish on the hem of his coat. He rustled in his pocket for latex gloves, pulled them on, laid a finger against the bloody gauze taped to Wilfred's thigh.

"You have AIDS?"

"No."

"Sure?"

"No HIV, no AIDS."

The doctor pulled off the gauze. The ride had loosened the tourniquets and blood trickled from the bullet hole. "What happened?"

"Shot myself."

"Shot yourself?"

"When bad things happen to good people," Wells muttered.

"What time?"

"Three, four hours ago."

The doctor laid two fingers against Wilfred's neck to take his pulse. "You feel cold?"

"Little bit."

The doctor looked at Wells. "How long did he bleed before you put these on?"

"A few minutes. His jeans were soaked."

"I can try to take out the bullet, but I don't recommend it. My best advice, I stabilize him tonight. Clean the wound, give him antibiotic so it doesn't infect, fluid for the blood loss, elevate the leg, put pressure on. You take him to a hospital tomorrow."

More or less what Wells had expected.

"But I have to stay here tonight to watch him. Stay up all night. It cost fifteen thousand shillings" — almost two hundred dollars.

"Supposed to be free," Wilfred said.

"Can't stay awake on this government salary. Can't buy coffee."

"Fifteen thousand's fine." Wells reached into his pocket, peeled off the shillings. The doctor opened his mouth like a frog after a fly as he stared at the roll of bills. Wells realized too late that he should have kept the money hidden.

"I give him medicine for the pain, five thousand shillings more."

"No more for this hustler," Wilfred said. "I take the pain."

Wells peeled off five thousand more and then stuffed the rest of the money away. "What about her?" He nodded at the woman.

"She got cancer. Liver, kidney, who knows. She gets big like that because the fluid builds up in her, she can't get rid of it. Tumors under her skin. Lumps like stones. Whole body shutting down. Even mzungu medicine can't save her now. She have a better chance with the witches. I tell her family, take her back, but she crying all the time. Stinks. They don't want her in the hut."

Wells handed the doctor the shillings.

"Give her what she needs." If he couldn't save this nameless woman's life, at least he could ease her death. "You understand."

The doctor nodded. Wells squeezed Wilfred's hand. "I'm going over to the hoteli, see if anybody knows about our friends on the bikes."

"Remember. Don't eat the mutton."

"Or the ladies," the doctor said.

On the way to the hoteli, the phone that Wells had taken at the camp buzzed. The incoming number started with a 254 country code: Somalia. The same number had come up as Wells was driving to Bakafi. Someone was worried. Wells decided to leave him guessing. Wells would make a direct approach only if he couldn't find the bandits another way.

The hoteli was ramshackle, crowded, loud. A good time. Bars lined two walls. The deep sour smell of marijuana smoke was heavy in the air. Rick Ross pumped from tall speakers, *Every day I'm hustling, hustling, hustling,* as a band set up against the far wall. The women huddled at two circular tables in the center. They wore low-cut dresses and neon lipstick and wide smiles. They were big and pillowy. If they weren't prostitutes, they were doing a good job of pretending. But the men weren't paying them much attention. They were focused on Arsenal and Man U., live, nil-nil in the first half. The reach of English Premier League football always impressed Wells.

His entrance created a pebble-in-a-pond stir. Men slid their eyes over, then did their best to ignore him. Wells suspected he would have drawn a stronger response if the game weren't playing. The women were his best bet. They would make it their business to keep an eye on outsiders, potential new clients. Wells could find out what they knew for a few hundred shillings.

As he closed in on the center table, a woman in a bright yellow dress patted the empty chair beside her. "Come here, baby. You look lost."

"Maybe." Wells sat.

"You been found, then. I'm Julia. What's your name?" Everything about her was oversized, from her hoop earrings to her breasts to her voice.

"John." He reached out a hand. She held it as she ran her other hand up his arm, squeezed his biceps.

"Nice muscles on this one," she said to the table. She leaned in, smiled. Up close, Wells could see the desperation under the glamour, the maze of blood vessels in her eyes, the bruise along her jaw, the sweet liquor on her breath.

"You come down from Dadaab, John."

Her English was good enough for the conversation he wanted. "I'm looking for someone."

"And here I am."

"A man."

She leaned back, wagged her finger at him.

"He rides a motorcycle, a dirt bike. Hangs out around here. Somali. You know him?"

"What you want this man for?"

Wells put his face to her ear. "Let's go outside, talk in private."

"It cost."

"Doesn't everything in this world?" Wells draped an arm around her smooth shoulder. "One thousand shillings to go outside. One thousand more, you tell me anything."

"Two thousand and two thousand."

Wells nodded. She grazed his cheek with her warm sticky lips. "Naughty boy." She stood with a grace that belied her size, led him through the men clustered around the televisions. The back side of the building was plain brick. Why paint what no one would see? About thirty meters away was a tin-roofed hut. Wells glimpsed a mattress inside. No doubt the women took clients there.

"Two thousand."

Wells handed over the bills, careful this time to hide the rest of his cash. She tucked them in her pocketbook, cheap shiny black vinyl, and came out with a pack of Embassy cigarettes and a lighter. She handed the lighter to Wells and he sparked her up.

"A gentleman."

"Been called a lot of things, never that. You know this Somali?" Wells felt the night slipping past. He had to find these bandits, or at least get close to their camp, before Langley and the Pentagon and White House took over. He had twelve hours, fifteen at most.

"Lots of Somalis in Bakafi. You have picture?"

"No. But I can tell you he rides a dirt bike. Wears a white T-shirt. This would be the last few days."

"Yeah, some of them hanging around. Three, four boys. They in a gang we call the White Men. Always wearing white shirts like you say. They do business with me one time. Quick boys." She touched his arm. "You quick, Mr. John?"

"They Shabaab?"

She inhaled deeply on her cigarette, shook her head.

"No, no. We don't see Shabaab here for

three, four months. Plus they have rules. They want to sex, they make big fuss before, pretend we getting married. Then afterwards get divorced. It all nonsense. Take too much time."

Temporary marriage was one of Islam's cruder aspects, designed more or less explicitly to coat prostitution with a gloss of respectability. It was common among Shia. Sunnis like Shabaab usually rejected the practice, but maybe Shabaab's leaders had decided to allow it to relieve the libidos of their teenage fighters.

"So these White Men, they're Somali but not Shabaab."

"What I say. They mostly bringing in sugar when they come. Sometimes other food, too, sacks of maize."

"It's a big gang?"

"Don't know."

"They have guns?"

She laughed. "What you think this place is?"

"They rob people on this side of the border? Shoot them?"

"They okay. Don't make trouble. Come and sell they sugar and go on back to Somalia."

They made trouble last night. "Did you talk to them this time?"

"No chance. They stand around, watch the road. Nobody bother them and they don't bother nobody." She finished her cigarette, threw it down, stamped it out with a gaudy pink heel. "These stupid questions, mzungu. Missing out on business. Give me 'nother thousand now."

Wells handed over another thousand shillings. She put the bill to her lips, kissed it. She was drunker than he'd thought.

"You too rich. Think too much about money, not enough about women." She put a fresh cigarette in between her lips and he lit it.

"Do you know who's their leader?"

"What leader?"

"The White Men."

"Back on that again? Name Wizard. Some these boys, they say he's magic. Put up his hand to stop bullets. Nothing kills him. One time he dead, brought himself back to life."

"Neat trick. Ever seen him?"

"Not sure."

"You have any idea where in Somalia they live?"

"You think they drawing me a map?"

"A town, anything."

"Never been to Somalia. Never been and never will. What else?"

Wells wondered if the other women might

have more information. Or maybe the shopkeeper who bought the smuggled sugar. But before he could say anything else, the back door of the hoteli popped open and a man came out with a pistol loose in his hand, a dumb sideways grip.

"Police."

The guy wore a short-sleeved shirt and jeans. But Wells had seen firsthand that Kenyan cops didn't always wear uniforms. Anyway, the pistol was real enough. Wells had left his weapons in the Cruiser. He thought about disarming the guy. Then heard a second man approaching from behind, the back corner of the hoteli. This one held an AK.

Wells raised his hands. "These real police?" he murmured to Julia.

She ignored him, walked to the man in the jeans, kissed him full on the mouth. He looped his left hand around her ass, squeezed through the dress. When he let go, she walked inside without as much as a wave to Wells. "I thought we were friends," he said.

"Hands on the wall," the guy in jeans said.

Wells did as he was told. He wondered if James Thompson had come to and convinced the Kenyan police to arrest him. But Thompson didn't know where he was. More likely the cops had simply heard he was at the hoteli, decided to check him out.

"I'm sorry, sir. Is something wrong?"

"Name."

"John Wells. I have the right permits, if you're wondering." Though Wells had a feeling those papers wouldn't do much good here.

"Did you leave your driver Mr. Wilfred Wumbugu at the King Fahad Infirmary?"

"Yes."

"Tell us what happened to him."

"He shot himself. An accident. I taped him up to stop the bleeding and brought him in."

The officer stepped close, raised his arm. A moment later, the pistol crashed into Wells's ribs. A silver spur of pain ran up his right side. His knees buckled. He steadied himself, controlled his breathing.

"The truth this time."

"I'm telling the truth."

This time Wells relaxed as the pistol hit, twisted away a fraction. Still the cop made solid contact and Wells felt his ribs waggle under the blow.

"The clinic doctor says that Mr. Wumbugu couldn't have shot himself. Admit you shot him."

The accusation didn't make sense. If Wells

had shot Wilfred, why would he take him to the hospital? Or pay the doctor fifteen thousand —

Then Wells thought of the naked greed that had flashed through the doctor's eyes when Wells pulled out his roll of cash. The doctor had told the cops about the money, and they were shaking him down. He couldn't even blame them. To them, he was another foolish mzungu carrying more cash than he or anyone needed. Fine. They wanted money, they could have it. As long as they'd let him go.

"I'm sure we can work this out. What does Wilfred say?"

"Doctor say that Mr. Wumbugu can't talk. He in too much pain. Meantime, we gon' hold you."

Wells couldn't lose the night to these two. He wondered if he should tell them what had really happened this afternoon at the camp. But the Kenyan police were invested in the story that Shabaab was behind the kidnapping. The cops would accuse him of lying, lock him up until someone senior told them what to do.

Wells chanced a quick look over his shoulder. He thought he could take the pistol off the cop behind him. But the other had him covered with the AK.

The cop leaned close enough for Wells to smell the Tusker on his breath. He ran his hands up Wells's legs, around his waist. The money was in the right front pocket of Wells's jeans, so if the cop wanted it now he would have to get intimate —

"What's this?"

"Money."

"How much?"

"Funny question for a felony investigation, isn't it?" Wells braced himself for another smack, but the cop was too focused on the money to notice.

"Take it out, give it to me."

Wells handed it over.

"Put your hands behind your back."

The steel cuffs snapped tight around his wrists.

The men in front of the hoteli chattered to him in Swahili as the cops frog-marched him along. Wells guessed they weren't wishing him luck. Fortunately, the Land Cruiser still had half a tank of gas and two five-gallon jerricans in the back. Wilfred had insisted on the extra fuel, and Wells was glad for it now. If he could get to the Toyota, he could get a long way from here. But first he had to shuck these cops. He didn't want to kill them, either. They were in the way and corrupt, but those weren't capital crimes.

The station's main room had two steel desks back-to-back and tatty maps of the region taped over concrete walls. An anticorruption poster featured a smiling female officer in a fresh blue uniform: *Asking for money for police services is illegal in Kenya; if your rights have been violated, dial* — But the number to call had been torn away.

The cops marched Wells to a corner and cuffed his right arm to a chain dangling from the wall. He had two pieces of furniture: a scuffed wooden stool for sitting, and a plastic bucket for a toilet. Wells realized that his mouth was dry, his belly empty. He hadn't eaten since he'd thrown up this afternoon. The hyenas and the firefight seemed to belong to another world. The cop with the AK disappeared through a door at the back of the room. The other parked himself at a desk and counted the money he'd taken, taking his time, snapping off each bill, smoothing it flat against the desktop. Either he didn't care that Wells was watching this blatant theft, or he wanted Wells to see.

Finally, he tucked it into a plastic bag. "Evidence."

"Take it," Wells said. "I don't care."

The cop reached under his desk and came

up with two big bottles of Tusker. He popped the tops and flicked them at Wells and walked into the back room, humming to himself, leaving Wells alone, locked in a corner, staring at the clock mounted high on the wall above the torn poster. Every tick mocked his uselessness.

14

Lower Juba Region,
Southwestern Somalia

Little Wizard wondered what hidden devils these wazungu had brought to his camp.

In his mind the plan had seemed simple enough. Hide them away, arrange a ransom. Use his half brother Bahdoon as a go-between to contact their families. Wizard didn't want to email the pictures himself. Lower Juba had only a few Internet connections, and he knew the Americans could track these things. Bahdoon lived in East-leigh, the giant Somali slum in Nairobi. He got by as a small-time miraa dealer. Wizard imagined he'd be glad to make a thousand dollars passing along a few messages. Wizard had decided to ask for one million for each hostage. Waaberi, his lieutenant, had suggested five million dollars, but Wizard didn't want to be greedy.

The ransom wouldn't take long to arrange. Once he and the Americans agreed on a price, he would tell them to deliver the money to Abukar, his old clan leader in Mogadishu, a tall man, thin as a stick, with one eye and three wives. Wizard had never been part of a kidnapping before, but he knew how they worked. Everyone in Somalia knew. The payment came in cash, bundles of twenty- and hundred-dollar bills. Sometimes the wazungu brought the money to shore in Mogadishu on boats thick with guns. Sometimes they flew it in on the charter jets that the United Nations ran. Once it arrived, a clan leader took it, and with it the duty of ensuring the hostages would be freed unharmed.

In exchange the leader kept one-third of the money. Of course, everyone involved had to operate on faith. But Wizard trusted Abukar. He'd worked as a middleman before, and anyway, two of Wizard's cousins still fought for him. After Wizard received his share from Abukar, he would leave the hostages at the border with a phone and a few liters of water. They could figure the rest out themselves. Then he would break his camp, tell his soldiers to head to Dadaab in small groups that wouldn't arouse suspicion. In a month, everyone would forget the kidnapping and they could come back to

Lower Juba. He'd have plenty of money to take on the Dita Boys.

Swarming the camp in Kenya had been easy. The men there were amateurs. They'd come running into the open as Wizard's soldiers crashed down on them from three sides. Not one White Man had been killed or wounded.

But then Wizard found the wazungu. And the devil found him. That stupid white boy spoke to him like he was nothing, nothing at all. Even at the time, Wizard told himself to control his temper. Killing whites caused trouble. But he couldn't tolerate the boy's sneer, his disrespect. He gave his pistol its freedom.

The other three came quietly after that. But Wizard knew the Americans would be angry when they learned what had happened. More than angry. They might refuse to pay.

Back in the camp that night, Wizard lay in his cot and traced a finger over the scar in his stomach. He closed his eyes, but he couldn't sleep. He was awake at dawn when Waaberi came in to tell him that a sentry named Hussein, a runt of a boy, had missed two radio checks. Wizard ordered a search, but his men found nothing, not a body or a scrap of clothing.

"Was the Ditas," Waaberi said. "Telling us, they know we're here, can come for us whenever."

Wizard hated to think that the Ditas had snatched one of his men. He hated even more the possibility that Hussein had defected on his own. Hussein knew how many fighters and weapons the White Men had, what routes their sentries walked, where they'd hidden fighting posts. And he knew about the wazungu. Awaale wouldn't pass up a chance at that prize. He'd come after the White Men double-quick.

"We going to move the sentries about. And put out the word. Everybody be ready. This serious now."

"Done."

"Done and done." Their lingo for an order given and received.

When Waaberi left, Wizard turned to the next step in his plan, calling Bahdoon. But Bahdoon didn't bite.

"One thousand U.S. to send a few emails and you saying no?"

"You not here. You don't see. The Kenyans making much much noise on these hostages. Every minute on the radio and TV. GSU in Eastleigh. Patrolling up and down. Asking, anybody know anything. Saying if they catch a man who knows and didn't tell, they take him and beat him until his legs and arms is broke. Then leave him in Kibera for the poor ones to do in."

"Words only, man. GSU don't know nothing. Never heard of the Wizard. You don't tell them, then they never know. They have no juju on me, Bahdoon."

"You have such magic, how come you in the desert eating snakes? Get someone else. Leave Bahdoon alone."

"I tell you what. I give you ten thousand U.S. when the money come. Not one. Ten."

"How I going to get away with this?"

"You know how. Find a place with nobody watching, make a new account, send the emails, get ten thousand dollars. Double-safe."

"I do it for fifty."

"My brother."

"Americans promising one hundred thousand if somebody help them out, tell them where the hostages are."

"One hundred thousand shillings?"

"One hundred thousand dollars. You didn't hear?"

Wizard hadn't heard. He wondered what else he hadn't heard. "They lying."

"I want fifty from you. You asking one million each. Fifty is nothing."

Wizard didn't have a choice. Bahdoon was the only one he could trust to do this job, who wouldn't take the pictures to the Americans and give him up for a reward. "Fifty, then. You rascal."

"Too easy, Wizard. I should have said one hundred. Send me them snaps."

So Wizard woke up the wazungu, took their pictures, sent them mobile-to-mobile. Back into his hut, he closed his eyes, tried to catch a few minutes of the sleep he'd missed. Maybe he could dream the devil away.

His phone woke him. It was Muhammad, a good soldier and one he trusted. Days before, when Wizard heard where the hostages were, he'd sent Muhammad and three others to watch the road from Dadaab to Ijara for police or anyone who might make trouble. They slept in the bush, hung around Bakafi during the day.

But the road stayed quiet. The Kenyan police had an outpost, but they left it only to drink Tusker and pick up whores at the hoteli. Wizard didn't know why the Kenyans weren't looking harder. Whatever the reason, their laziness was one reason he'd decided attacking the camp was a safe bet.

Now someone must have showed up. Muhammad wouldn't call in daytime otherwise.

"Muhammad."

"Wizard. A mzungu and his driver come through."

"American?"

"Don't know."

"What kind of car?"

"Cruiser."

"Just one?"

"Yah. They stop, talk awhile. Now they driving again."

"Back to Dadaab."

"No, man. South. Toward the camp."

"You got pics."

"Yah."

"Send them."

"You want me to watch them?"

Wizard figured the man was driving to the spot where the Americans had first been taken. No way could he find the camp the White Men had hit. It was just four buildings, and hidden in a little valley miles from any road. But if he did find it somehow, he couldn't be allowed to tell anyone.

"Give them space. Lest they find the camp. Then get them."

"Kill them?"

"Catch them, kill them, either one."

"Done and done."

■ ■ ■ ■

Finally, Bahdoon called with good news. "Cousin. They hit me back. All three. They say, please let them go, don't hurt them, don't shoot them, they didn't do nothing, they good wazungu, came to Africa to help, please please, all that."

The appeals might have meant more to Wizard if his own mother and father hadn't been killed by a stray shell fired by African Union peacekeepers in Mogadishu when he was ten. "All that. What about paying?"

"They want proof the pictures real. The wazungu got to give you a secret. Like, what they favorite color? What they favorite food to eat?"

"Favorite *food*?"

"It what they want."

So Wizard asked the three for a secret and sent the answers to Bahdoon. Next email he'd tell about the one million dollars. He knew he ought to make sure Abukar would take the ransom for him first. But Wizard wasn't ready to make that call, not until he felt his luck changing, caught the devil looking the other way.

Meantime he waited for Muhammad. But the call didn't come. At first Wizard wasn't worried. Maybe Muhammad's phone had died. He and his men wouldn't have trouble with one mzungu. But the afternoon stretched on and finally the sun disappeared. Wizard's hopes sank as the sky darkened. He wanted to send more men into Kenya to find out what had happened, but he couldn't risk losing them. Not with the Ditas lurking. He was down five soldiers already today. Too many.

He wondered if he should pull up camp, take his men south into the mangrove swamps. They could live with the crocodiles and snakes while they waited out the Ditas. But the swamps had no phone service. Wizard would have to leave to arrange the ransom. Anyway, he hated the place. The ground itself was rotten. A man who stepped the wrong way found the earth kissing his feet, caressing his legs, pulling him under with a lover's embrace. The mosquitoes never stopped biting, and they came with malaria that could kill a man in a week. The swamps were the last resort. Had to be.

Ali stepped into his hut. "You want dinner, Wizard?"

He joined the line outside the hut where two of his youngest soldiers stirred pots of rice and meal over a low smoky fire. No meat, of course. Wizard still regretted slaughtering his herd on the night he met Awaale. But they had the hostages now and the hostages would pay for all the goats in Somalia. "Smells good tonight," he said to Ali, loudly, so the men around him heard. They stood straighter when they saw him. The soldiers at the front of the line waved him forward. But Wizard shook his head, stayed where he was. A good leader ate last.

Then, from the northeast, guns popped. A round, another, then a yell and a long, rattling burst of AK fire. The line dissolved as men ran for their weapons. But the shots stopped as abruptly as they'd started. Waaberi's walkie-talkie crackled. He put it to his ear, listened, strode to Wizard. "Omar say they killed one, caught two more."

"Ditas?"

"He don't know."

"Bring them here."

The boys were small and ragged and bleeding into their camouflage T-shirts. Wizard's men had tied their hands behind their backs. One couldn't walk without help, but the other one seemed okay. Wizard waved them into his hut and ordered his men out, all but Ali and Waaberi and Omar, the sentry who'd spotted them.

Wizard looked them over. One had a scar

across his forehead big as a squashed bug. The other, the weaker of the two, had only one eye. The left socket was empty, not even a patch, just a sunken space where his eye should have been. They were thirteen, fourteen at most. They barely looked big enough to hold AKs. Wizard would have rejected them if they'd tried to join the White Men. Told them to go to Dadaab where they belonged. He didn't understand why Awaale had sent them to him to be slaughtered. He wanted to put a knife to Awaale's thick neck and make him tell.

"Which way they come?" he said to Omar.

"Down from the road that go to Giara El. They walk straight straight toward the old post." The sentry position that Wizard had ordered abandoned after Hussein defected.

"Have AKs?"

Omar held up three little pistols that looked like .22s to Wizard. "These pop-guns."

"They just walk to you."

"Yeah, we saw them, got ready, made sure they was the only ones, when they got close we blasted them. Kill one there, hit these two."

"No others."

"None we saw."

The boy with one eye was bleeding from

his stomach. Hard. Wizard lifted the boy's shirt, saw two neat holes. "No good for this one. Get me water. Too fast." He knelt beside the boy, pulled his knife. The boy shirked away, but Wizard twisted him around, cut the plastic cord binding his hands. "What your name?"

"Yusuf, sir." His voice was a whisper.

"This my land. Why you come to my land?"

"Awaale say —" The words faded into a cough. The boy was losing his way. In another minute, he would be past speaking. Wizard pinched his ear. "He tell you you going to die?"

Ali returned with a cup of water, and Wizard took it and tipped it to Yusuf's throat. The boy drank a little and then the water came back out of his mouth and he grunted and tipped sideways and he was dead. "No magic for this one," Wizard said. He looked at Ali. Ali picked up the body, swung it over his shoulder like a sack of rice, walked out. They'd put the corpse in an empty hut and come morning bury it a few hundred meters away, hope to dig a hole deep enough that the hyenas didn't get it. All they could do.

"Other two dead. You the last one left," Wizard said to the third boy, the one with the scar. "Tell me why you come here like this." This one had been shot in his left shoulder, but he wasn't whimpering. He looked cold and straight at Wizard.

"Awaale send us. Tell us to give you a message."

"Give it, then."

"He want the wazungu. He say you have one night to give them over or he coming here to put all your magic and all your blood in the dirt. He say you better give him the answer 'fore the sun comes up. He say the time to play is over."

Wizard saw that Awaale had sent two messages. The words, and the boys themselves. *I have so many men that I can throw away these three. Toss them to you.* The only reason the Ditas hadn't attacked already was that Awaale was worried that the hostages might be killed in the confusion. He knew their worth.

"Anything else?"

The boy shook his head. Wizard didn't want to kill him. Two useless dead boys was enough for the night. But the White Men couldn't keep him either. Wizard stood, pulled the boy up by his bad shoulder, punishment for his sass.

"You going back to Awaale. You tell him, he wants the wazungu, it cost him three million U.S. That the price. He don't want to pay, he can come get them his own self. You understand?"

The boy nodded.

"Tell me so I know you heard."

The boy repeated Wizard's words.

"Good. And tell him his other boys best fight better than you. Elseways we gonna have too many bodies for the hyenas to eat." Wizard shoved the kid away, sent him stumbling. "Put him on the road back," he said to Omar.

Then he and Waaberi were alone. "It coming," Wizard said. "Soon enough."

"Let it come. Long as Awaale keep sending 'em that way, it no problem."

"Two down. Three hundred to go."

15

Bakafi

Wells wasn't sure that he'd been formally arrested, much less what charges he faced or what rights he had. Not that it mattered. Most Americans thought of police officers as honest and reliable, and cops generally repaid that trust. Anne would take a bullet before she took a bribe. But in Kenya, like many places where Wells plied his trade, the police were best avoided at all costs.

The cuff squeezing his wrist was a simple mechanism, a few links of chain connecting two adjustable steel rings. A trained thief could pop a handcuff with a paper clip in seconds. But if there were any paper clips in this room, Wells couldn't reach them. He spent a few unpleasant minutes squeezing his thumb against his palm and sliding his wrist against the steel to see if he could slip his hand through, but the cop had cuffed him tight and he was no escape artist. He chafed his skin until it bled, but the cuff stayed in place.

Next he went for brute force. Wells faced the wall and wrapped his left hand high around the chain and twisted his right hand so it, too, held the links. He raised his foot to the wall and shoved his boot against it and tugged until the muscles in his arms felt like Silly Putty. But the metal plate holding the chain to the wall didn't give a fraction of an inch.

The only item within arm's reach was a stack of paper on the desk. Though the cop had taken Wells's phones, he'd missed the lighter that Julia had given Wells. But even if Wells managed to start a fire, he'd still be stuck to the wall. At best, the cops would douse the flames and beat him up for causing trouble. At worst, they'd leave the station and let him roast, a mzungu barbecue. Even so, the lighter might come in handy. Wells extracted it from the front right pocket of his jeans and slid it into his back pocket, where he could reach it even with his hands cuffed behind him.

Two hours passed. Wells found himself fighting an ache that slashed across his back to his hips. His body had been wounded by bullets and batons, fists and feet. Aside from lots of Advil, Wells dealt with the damage by ignoring it. But tonight his muscles and joints and bones all sang the same sad song, *You're too old for this nonsense.* The clock on the wall magnified his discomfort, seeming to measure not seconds but weeks with each tick. As if whole worlds were dying while he sat in this room. The relativity of arrest.

Finally, the back door opened. The cop walked out, looked Wells over. His eyes were bloodshot and his belly slipped from his shirt over his jeans.

"You work at Dadaab," the cop said.

"I'm an aid worker." Using a loose definition of *aid.* "May I ask your name, sir?" A little deference never hurt.

"Mark." Though the cop's Anglo-Kenyan patois made the name sound like *Maahk.* "What you doing here?"

"Wilfred and I drove to see the place where the volunteers were taken."

"Don't you know it's dangerous? Shabaab kidnapping wazungu."

Suddenly, Mark the cop was his best friend. "We thought we'd be okay. Wilfred had a pistol. But he tripped and it went off, hit him in the thigh. I bandaged him up, brought him back. I'd seen the infirmary when we drove though." The story didn't make much sense. Not that Mark cared, Wells thought. He had his own lies to keep straight.

Mark pretended to smile. "Tomorrow we talk to Mr. Wumbugu, sort this out. Let you go to Dadaab, where you belong. You don't bother with Bakafi anymore. Of course, we keep the evidence."

"Of course." A scheme occurred to Wells. He'd need to be careful setting the hook. Not too much at once. "I see why you have to investigate. We come to the hospital, my driver's been shot, I have nineteen, twenty thousand dollars."

"Twenty thousand?"

"Whatever I was carrying."

The cop stepped close. Wells could have reached out with his free left hand, throttled him. But Wells would still be locked to the wall.

"You said twenty thousand. You carrying five thousand."

"I don't know. Whatever I had."

The cop squeezed Wells's handcuffed arm, like a manager sending a pitcher to the showers, a friendly warning. "Big mistake to lie to police. Even for a mzungu. Where is it, the rest?"

"I think there's been a misunderstanding."

The cop stepped away, reached under his

desk, came up with a black metal tube the size of a flashlight. He pushed a button on the side and the cylinder quadrupled in length. An expandable baton. American cops loved them, and apparently they weren't alone.

The cop stood before Wells. He raised his right hand high, waggled the baton like a tour guide, brought it down on Wells's left biceps.

"Come on," Wells said. As an answer Mark raised the baton again.

"In the Cruiser. In the Cruiser, okay?"

The cop laid the baton against the desk where Wells couldn't reach it, then walked out the front door. Ten minutes later, he returned, carrying the Mossberg and the Glock. Wells didn't know where the Makarov had gone.

"These in your car. No money. What kind of aid worker you are?"

"You said yourself, it's dangerous."

"Where's the money?"

"It's in a trap compartment in the back, hard to find."

"You show me."

"You promise to let me go tomorrow."

"Yes. But this a secret, between you and me. Not —" He pointed at the back door.

Just as Wells had hoped. The cop didn't

want to share this new windfall with anyone. Not even his partner.

"We go get the money, come back. Try to run, I shoot you. Understand?" Wells nodded. Mark unlocked him, cuffed his hands behind his back, marched him out the door and into the night. Only the hoteli, the police station, and the infirmary had generators. The rest of Bakafi was dark, families huddled for the night. The Cruiser was parked where Wells had left it outside the infirmary. Not a great spot for his purposes. He'd have to disable Mark fast, before the guy shouted for help.

At the Cruiser, Wells expected Mark to uncuff him. Instead the cop swung the back gate open. The bulb inside threw dim light on the toolbox and two-by-fours and plastic jerricans in the back compartment. "Where is it?"

"Easier for me to show you."

"You think I'm stupid? Keep them handcuffs on, tell me where." He leaned forward, legs spread, and reached inside. With his arms free, Wells would have had plenty of options. Now he was down to one.

"Right there, next to the toolbox —"

Wells sidestepped until he was directly behind the cop. He leaned slightly forward and pulled his arms off his back for balance. He swung his right leg back, then drove it forward, like a field-goal kicker, aiming for a spot just below Mark's butt. He swung through and felt the soft center of Mark's crotch collapse beneath his boot. Mark moaned, a sound that under other circumstances could have been mistaken for ecstasy. His knees buckled and he sagged against a jerrican.

Wells turned so that his back was to the Cruiser. He tucked his hands into the waistband of Mark's jeans and slung him to the ground. The cop was panting now like a dog that had run too long, his tongue looping meaningless circles over his lips. He would be frozen for a minute or more. With his cuffed hands, Wells grabbed a fuel jerrican, flipped it on its side, edged his fingers around the cap, and twisted. Gasoline slopped out. Wells steered the can so the fuel sloshed onto Mark's shirt.

When Mark was soaked, Wells flipped the jerrican upright. Mark feebly edged his arm toward the pistol holstered at his waist. Wells pulled the lighter from his back pocket. He squatted on Mark's chest, facing Mark's legs, so the cop was looking at his back. Wells splayed his own legs, stamped his boots down on Mark's forearms. The cop's breath came fast. He smelled like a charcoal grill about to be lit. Wells lifted his cuffed hands. The lighter was simple and plastic, the Kenyan equivalent of a Bic. Wells flicked its flint. "Do as I say or burn. Understand?"

"Yes."

A light popped on inside the infirmary. The doctor yelled, *"Jambo!"*

"Tell him, no jambo. Keep him inside."

Mark coughed, shouted back in Swahili. His voice was halting, but whatever he said seemed to work. The light flicked off.

"Where are the handcuff keys?"

"Right pocket."

Wells lifted his boot from Mark's right forearm. "Get them. Slowly." Mark inched his right hand forward, plucked the keys from his pocket. "Uncuff me."

"Man —"

Again Wells flicked the flint.

"Okay." Mark reached his hand higher until it was behind Wells, a dangerous moment. If Mark went for the lighter, Wells had already decided that he would toss it aside. He wasn't setting this man on fire. He just had to hope Mark wouldn't take the chance.

The key scraped into the hole with the faint click of metal on metal. Then Mark turned the key, and the steel bracelet came loose from Wells's wrist. Freedom. Wells lifted his right elbow, reversed it into the cop's temple, getting his shoulder into the strike. The elbow was underrated as a weapon. Wells couldn't see what he'd done, but he felt the shiver of contact run up his arm. Mark's head snapped sideways and a tiny wheeze escaped his throat. Wells grabbed Mark's pistol, rolled forward into the dirt. He came up and turned around, the pistol in his right hand in case Mark tried to come back at him. But the cop stayed flat on his back. He twisted sideways and vomited a stew of beer and rice.

Wells grabbed the handcuff key, unlocked the left cuff so the handcuffs came free. He tucked Mark's pistol into the back of his waistband. Mark tried to sit, but Wells flipped him onto his stomach, put a knee in his back, cuffed him tight.

"You no aid worker."

"You're not much of a cop."

He pulled Mark up as someone shouted from down the road. Wells saw a man outside the hoteli. Time to go. Wells grabbed the pistol by the butt and swung it against Mark's head. The cop went limp.

The man from the hoteli was walking toward him now. Wells wondered if he had time to go back to the police station, get his guns and his phones. He decided he had no choice. He could make do with Mark's Makarov, proof that fate had a sense of humor. But without the phones he'd have no way to reach Shafer or anyone else. He grabbed the Cruiser's keys from Mark's pocket and threw his unconscious body in the back of the Cruiser. He slammed the gate shut, ran for the driver's door. Two more men had come out from the hoteli now and were walking up the road. Wells drove to the police station. Inside, the front room was empty. He shoved the phones in his pockets, scooped up the shotgun. As he did, the handle of the back door twisted. He pointed the Mossberg at the anticorruption poster, fired. The devil's thunder echoed off the concrete walls and the poster turned into confetti. So much for a quiet exit. Wells ran outside, fired the Glock wildly at the police pickup truck outside the station. The front left tire burst open. He wasn't sure how much other damage he'd done, but the tire alone ought to buy him a few minutes.

He slid back in the Cruiser and rolled off. A dozen men stood in the road. Wells clicked on his brights, hunched low in his seat, floored the gas. The Cruiser's engine roared. It accelerated madly down the street, bouncing over ruts like an ATV on steroids. Wells saw two bullet holes appear in the windshield and then the hoteli flashed past and he was clear of Bakafi.

He wasn't expecting a warm welcome if he came through town again.

16

Lower Juba Region,
Southwestern Somalia

Gwen wanted more miraa.

She and Owen and Hailey were waiting for dinner when the shots echoed in the night and the camp dissolved into chaos. Three of Wizard's men dragged them back to their one-room prison. With the door closed, the room was black. Gwen clicked on the flashlight and she and Hailey sat side by side against the wall. Owen stood by the door, peeking out through the ventilation holes punched in the tin. Gwen chewed the inside of her lip, pressing her teeth into her own tender flesh, as she waited for the firefight to start, for grenades exploding and soldiers shouting in a language she couldn't understand. Then the shots stopped and the night was quiet.

Seconds later, she heard a low sob, almost a moan. She was almost surprised to realize that she hadn't made the sound. Hailey seemed to be having a full-on panic attack. She was curled against the wall, arms wrapped around her knees.

"It's gonna be okay —"

"I wish they'd just shoot us —"

"Don't say that, Heartbreaker." Gwen hugged Hailey, the only comfort she could offer. Hailey tried to break free but she held on. "It's okay, it's okay, it's okay." After a few seconds, Hailey's sobs dissolved into something like laughter and she stopped rocking.

"Don't take this the wrong way, Gwen, I'm sure I'm exactly the same, but you smell terrible. I mean —" Hailey waved her hand in front of her nose.

The sudden mood shift didn't surprise Gwen. She'd taken the same roller-coaster ride herself dozens of times. "You know what I'd like more than anything? A long, hot bath. Bubble bath." Gwen could almost feel herself sliding into the tub until she couldn't even see her body, shedding dirt, sweat, smoke, fear, emerging clean and new.

"You know what I'd like? To be alone for a few minutes. Totally alone."

"Hailey —"

"Shh —" Owen hissed. "I hate to break this pity party up, but something big is going on." His tone silenced them. After a few minutes, Owen stepped away from the door, sat next to them. "We have to get out of here. Tonight. I just watched them bring in two kids, when I say kids I mean like twelve years old. Arms tied behind their backs. To Wizard's hut. Then, a few minutes later, the big guy who's always with Wizard, he came out with one boy slung over his shoulder. He was dead. I'd bet on it."

"Doesn't mean they killed him —" Gwen said.

"No? Just now they brought the other one out. And they're slinging their AKs around and a couple of them are carrying these big long tubes that I think are rocket launchers. They are loaded for bear, and I know you think Wizard's your best friend, Gwen —"

"That's —"

"But that kid was alive when he went into that hut and dead when they brought him out. These guys aren't nice. And the worst part is, I'm telling you, they are scared right now. Maybe 'scared' is the wrong word, maybe they don't get scared, but they are on edge. Amped. Strutting around, swinging their guns. I'm surprised nobody's gotten shot by accident."

"They're protecting us. That's what Wizard told me, he told me his men wouldn't hurt me, us, that we were safe here —"

"Gwen, if they wanted to let us go, they had their chance," Hailey said. "Last night. After they killed Suggs and the Joker, they could have left us there. Even driven us back to Dadaab."

Gwen wanted to argue, but Hailey was right. "Fine. You win. They're just waiting for the right moment to heat up the pot, make mzungu stew. What do you want us to do about it? Hope our guard falls asleep tonight so we can run for it?"

"My thought is, everything that's happened so far came from the east. Whoever's out there, Shabaab, I assume, they're totally focused on it. We get out of camp, head west, maybe they won't realize for a while."

"They won't realize? Please, Owen, imagine what you'd think if I just said that —"

"She's right," Hailey said. "How can we outrun them? They have those Range Rovers and who knows what else."

Gwen hated to bring up the motorcycles, but the other two deserved to know. "When they put me in that hut this morning, I saw two motorcycles, dirt bikes, in the hut next to it. I'm not sure they work, but someone was in there trying to fix them."

"I can ride," Owen said. "Can either of you?"

"I can," Gwen said.

"You can?" Hailey couldn't have sounded more surprised if Gwen had said she was a virgin.

"My high school boyfriend showed me. He always had this plan that we'd ride cross-country together. But I shouldn't have even brought it up. There's no way this is gonna work. What, Owen? You think we run to the hut, spark the bikes, take off, and nobody notices?"

"In a few hours, two or three a.m., it's gonna look different out there. If we don't get attacked tonight, these guys'll have to get some sleep. Half of them were up late last night attacking the Joker's camp. And the sentries they post will be on the edges of camp, not the middle. We can get to that hut, grab a bike, take off, catch them facing the wrong way."

"We don't know what's out there," Gwen said. "We don't even know where we are. And what about the guard?"

Owen pressed his palms together. "I'm not going to try it alone, okay? I'll stay with you to the end. But here's how I see it. We sit here, wait, nothing good is gonna happen. I think best case, Wizard decides he can't stay alive long enough to get paid by our families. So he sells us to Shabaab and God only knows what they'll do with us. Another possibility, this place gets attacked straight up and we either get taken, kidnapped again, or maybe get shot in the cross fire. If we run, hopefully we make it. If not, they're not going to hurt us. They need us. Wizard said this wasn't about some holy war for him, and I believe him. He wants money. If we're dead, he doesn't get any. Worst case, they catch us, smack us around, lock us up. We're no worse off than we are right now."

"Unless Wizard gets mad and shoots us like he shot Scott," Gwen said.

"Thought he was your buddy."

"Let's vote," Hailey said. "All those in favor of Owen's plan, trying to get to the bikes, raise your hands."

"Is that even a plan?" Gwen said.

"All those in favor of doing nothing, keep them down," Owen said.

Owen raised his hand. Gwen kept hers in her lap. They both looked at Hailey.

Hailey slowly lifted her hand. "Sorry, Gwennie."

They spent a while whispering over ideas. In the dark, because Owen insisted that they turn off the flashlight to save the batteries. The camp outside slowly quieted, seemingly going back to normal, whatever that meant here. Finally, the guard brought them three plates of rice and three bottles of water. The rice was mushy and lukewarm, but they ate every bite, a silent acknowledgment that they might be lost in the scrub for days with nothing to eat or drink.

When they were done eating, they talked a little more, worked through the plan. Even Owen admitted that once they escaped, if they escaped, they would just have to ride west and hope.

The conversation ran down. Gwen wasn't sure of the hour. Her body and mind were spent. But sleep wouldn't be an option tonight. She needed to stay awake. She needed more miraa. Lucky for her, getting some was part of the scheme.

She opened the door, stepped out. Their guard sat against the hut's outside wall, his legs splayed loosely, working a mouthful of stems. The sight made her own mouth water. For the first time, he was armed, an AK strapped across his chest. Gwen hadn't calculated on the rifle, but she decided it didn't matter. If their scheme worked, they could take the AK. If not, the guard wouldn't shoot them without asking Wizard's permission. Probably.

The guard looked up idly. She pointed at

her belly and then at the latrines. He raised a hand, three fingers spread, a gesture she took to mean three minutes. Owen's guess that the camp would settle down for the night had been right. Most soldiers had disappeared. Still, two men were hanging around outside Wizard's hut, two more near the cook hut. Not her problem, at least for now. She hurried to the latrine, held her nose as she did her business, hustled back.

Now the hard part. She squatted beside the guard. "Miraa." She pointed at herself. He reached into his pocket, but she pointed at the hut. "Not just me. Owen, too." She opened the tin door. "Owen —"

On cue, Owen stepped into the doorway. Now the guard stood, waved Owen back into the hut with the AK. Owen backed away. Gwen stood in the doorway, holding the door open. Still the guard hesitated. Gwen hadn't expected the language barrier to cause so much trouble. Plus, back home she could rely on a move as simple as touching a guy's arm to get what she wanted. She couldn't take that chance here. Injecting sex into the situation could blow it up.

She could still use her voice, though. "Didn't mean to freak you out." She kept her tone low and smoky. "Miraa, we just want some miraa. Whyn't you come in and show us?" She gave him a come-hither wave with her fingers.

He pointed at the flashlight, which was next to the door. She handed it over. She stepped inside and waited by the door as he waved the beam around, seemingly checking for a trap. Finally, he walked in. He sat next to her and handed over the miraa. She took a handful. He waved his finger at her, apparently saying, *too much, too much,* and she put a few sprigs back and stuffed the rest in her mouth and handed the packet to Owen, who put a bunch in his mouth and coughed and gagged. The guard laughed, physical comedy apparently playing as well in the Somali bush as it did everywhere else. Then Hailey stood.

"I have to pee." She pointed at herself as Gwen had, and the guard nodded and held up three fingers as he had for Gwen. Hailey walked out. And Gwen felt her blood surge, not just the miraa kicking in, but Hailey's clean exit, the point of the entire exercise.

Nobody said much until Hailey returned, sat back beside Owen. "Much better," she said. The guard nodded and stood and left.

"So?" Owen said.

Hailey hadn't gone to the bathroom. She'd checked out the hut with the dirt bikes. They'd needed the guard inside the hut so he wouldn't see where she was headed. None of them had any idea how to hotwire a motorcycle. Even Owen admitted that they needed the keys to have any chance of success. He said the keys would be close by the bikes. But Gwen had insisted they find out for certain before they did anything irreversible.

"Good news and bad news. And a bonus. Good news is there's two bikes and they don't look messed up, I mean, I didn't see any parts on the ground. And Owen was right, the keys are there. On nails hammered into the wall."

"What's the bad news?" Gwen said.

"Bad news is somebody's sleeping in there. He didn't see me, he was out cold, but there's no way he's going to sleep through an engine starting up."

"And the bonus?" Owen said.

Hailey reached into her sweatpants and pulled out a wrench. "I knew I was taking a chance, but I figured we'd be glad to have it."

The wrench was greasy, rusted, about a foot long. Owen's whole body came to attention as he looked at it. He reminded Gwen of a dog that had just found a sixteen-ounce sirloin unwatched on the dinner table. His eyes had a liquid shine. Gwen realized he saw this situation very differently than she did. She couldn't help herself. She thought of their captors as kids. They were mostly younger than she was. And they didn't seem like bad guys. She felt sorry for them, playing at being soldiers in the scrub. Maybe her experience reading to Joseph and the boys in Dadaab had affected her more than she realized.

But Owen was angry. Furious. He didn't care why these Somalis had ended up here. To him they were the enemy, kidnappers and murderers. If he had to kill them all to escape, he would. Every last one. Probably he was right. Probably she was being soft and stupid. These soldiers might be boys, but boys could kill and these boys had. Wizard had shot Scott for no real reason. She ought to take comfort in Owen's coiled wrath. But she couldn't. His eyes frightened her as much as anything that had happened so far.

Owen reached for the wrench. "We can do something with this," he said. "Oh yes, we can."

Part Three

17

Garissa District, Kenya

The Cruiser thudded along the dirt track like a carnival ride gone wrong, slapping Wells against his seat belt. Its wheels spun up a dust cloud that rolled with it, making it a vehicular version of Charlie Brown's buddy Pig-Pen. Still, Wells had the windows down. He preferred the acrid taste of dust to the sweet stink of gasoline rising from Mark the cop.

The track dipped over a dry streambed and the Cruiser bottomed out its shocks. Wells laid off the gas, but only for a moment. He knew he risked blowing a tire, or worse, but he had no choice. Five minutes outside Bakafi, he'd seen light in the darkness behind him. No doubt the other cop had found a ride, and the concerned citizens of Bakafi had joined in the fun.

Wells didn't think they could catch him. But he didn't think he could outrun them either. They could track his taillights as easily as he saw their headlights. He'd tried to run with his beams off, but flicked them on again a few seconds later. The road was impossible in the dark. He did have a night-vision scope that he'd brought from New Hampshire, standard infantry gear. It strapped over one eye and lit up the night with an eerie green glow. But he didn't want to use the scope for driving. On patrols or in fixed positions, night vision offered an enormous advantage. But the scopes also provided a strangely flattened perspective. To compensate, most soldiers now used gear that covered one eye and left the other uncovered. Putting the two views together took practice, especially at driving speed on a road as bumpy as this one. So his scope stayed in his pack, and the Cruiser's lights stayed on. Thus his pursuers could track him no matter how far ahead he pulled. Wells thought he might have a way to use that fact to his advantage, though the trick he had in mind would leave him exposed if it failed. He had a few minutes to decide.

He reached down through the dust for his phone, called Shafer. "Our friends have a location?"

"Not your lucky day, John. It's gonna be a while."

"I even want to ask?"

"In the bush, the signals are carried by low-power microwave repeaters before they get to real cell towers. In the U.S., we only use them a few places, like to keep calls from dropping in underwater tunnels. But where you are, they're a cheap way to get coverage to places where there isn't enough demand for full service."

"So NSA can narrow the phone to a single tower —"

"But that still leaves a huge area to cover. They're not sure there's any solution, and if there is, it's gonna take time. Days at least."

The NSA was so good at solving these puzzles that Wells had hardly considered it might not be able to find the phone in time. He wanted to be angry, but he knew the truth. Like everyone else in the field, he had grown too dependent on the magicians back home.

"Shame. Things are getting messy." He told Shafer about Bakafi.

"You beat up a cop and broke out of jail."

"Let's just say I released myself on my own recognizance."

"You stole that line, and don't think I don't know it. Cop gonna live?"

Wells looked back at Mark and was rewarded with a curse and a cough. "Long as he doesn't go near any open flames."

"Even so, you've reached your sell-by date. Forget Shabaab. When the sun comes up tomorrow, you're public enemy number one. And you don't fit in so good. In case you haven't noticed."

"Still leaves tonight."

"If I were you, my number-one goal would be getting somewhere safe. Though I'm not sure where that might be. Maybe you should beg the UN for help."

"Funny."

"I'm serious."

"I've got a line on the Somali militia that took the hostages. The locals in Bakafi know them, call them the White Men because they wear these white T-shirts and bandannas."

"How creative."

"They smuggle sugar into Kenya, so they have to be close to the border. Leader's a guy called Little Wizard. He's got a reputation as magic. Can't be killed."

"How conveeeenient." This in the voice of the *Saturday Night Live* Church Lady.

"I ever find him, I'm going to ask him the secret."

Wells heard Shafer typing. "You won't be surprised to hear that neither the White Men nor Little Wizard are anywhere to be found in our Somali database."

"If I can pin them down, I don't suppose there's a SOG team ready to roll?"

"I believe I just heard you ask for help. This must be even worse than it sounds."

Wells offered Shafer an Arabic curse that roughly translated into *May your mother ride a dead camel,* with particular emphasis on *ride.*

"Duto ordered a team to Mombasa, but they don't land until tomorrow morning. It'll be too late for them to do anything but get you out of there. It'll be something of a miracle anyway. We're going to have to beg the Kenyans to look the other way. That means me begging Duto, and you know how I feel about that."

"I think I can find them. Tonight."

"John. You cannot go into Somalia on your own. Suicide. And even if you could, even assuming you're right and these White Men are based near the border, that's, what, a zone sixty miles long, forty deep, twenty-four hundred square miles of scrub. How will you narrow that down?"

Wells explained, waited for Shafer to respond. And waited.

"Ellis?"

"I'm thinking. What if your new friend loses it when he realizes what you've done, shoots you and the volunteers?"

"Why would he do that?"

"You're asking for rationality from a Somali warlord named Wizard?"

"He wants a deal. He took them last night, and he's already looking for ransom."

"This is beyond foolish, John. Way too many variables. The only reason we're still talking about it is that you're so far out on the ledge already. I'm not sure the Kenyan police will let you surrender under any circumstances. No doubt they're thinking dead or alive."

The headlights behind Wells were creeping closer. He edged down the gas pedal and the Cruiser surged. Meanwhile, Shafer had gone quiet again. Wells could almost see Shafer in his office, pulling on the last wisps of his hair, the Sideshow Bob tufts that stretched over his ears. He'd be scanning a map across his desk, looking for answers, not finding them.

"I have to ask Duto," Shafer said. "I can't promise what he'll say. Even if he goes for it, I'm not sure how fast we can get operational. And you're going to have to get this guy to bite. You really think you can do that?"

Almost too late, Wells saw a foot-high rock about to lance his left front tire. He braked, twisted the steering wheel right. The Cruiser skittered sideways like a two-ton puppy just learning how to run. Its right front tire slid into a rut and the ugly screech of metal on rock filled the night and the Cruiser tipped, its left back wheel coming off the ground. The jerricans and spare tire and Mark all banged around the cargo compartment. Wells kept both hands on the wheel and feathered the brake and the Cruiser leveled out, though it now had an odd clicking coming from the right front tire like the bearings were damaged. Wells edged it back onto the track. The steering felt loose, but after a few seconds the clicking stopped and the Toyota kept moving.

"Didn't sound good," Shafer said.

"Work your end and let me make my call."

"Talk soon. *Adiós, amigo.*"

Wells drove in silence, rehearsing his lines. Then he reached for the phone he'd taken from the dead White Man at the camp. He found the missed-calls register and the most recent incoming number. Odds were it belonged to Wizard. He called Wizard's number from his own Kenyan phone. Two rings later, someone answered in a language he didn't understand.

"Do you speak Arabic?" Wells said. In Arabic. The phone went dead. Wells called back, repeated himself. *"Aribiya,"* the man on the other end said.

"Nam." Yes. Even if Wizard didn't speak Arabic, some of his men must. Wells heard shouting, then a new voice.

"You speak Somali?" the man said in Arabic.

"Only Arabic. Is this Wizard?"

"How did you get this number?"

"I have an offer for him. Him only."

"You'll have to tell me. Wizard doesn't speak Arabic. What's your name?"

"Jalal. From Syria."

"What do you want?"

"The hostages."

Wells heard a conversation in what must have been Somali. Then: "What hostages?"

"Tell Wizard I know who he is, I know he has them. I want them. I'll pay for them."

Another off-line conversation before the man returned. "You come to us?"

"Yes, *inshallah.*"

"How much will you pay?"

"One million U.S."

"One million each."

"Too much."

"That's the price."

Wells reminded himself not to seem too eager. "One million for all three. I have it with me. You get it tonight."

Whispering. "Wizard wants to know, what will you do with them?"

Wells hadn't expected that question. He hesitated, wondering what answer the man wanted. "That's my business," he finally said.

"Wizard says they belong to him, and he must know."

Wells tried to put himself in the tattered shoes of this Somali warlord who had killed Scott Thompson. He was poor. He was Muslim. He wasn't part of Shabaab, but he probably didn't have much love for these rich Americans. "I'm sure he can imagine what I'll do with them. I won't treat them like kings, I can promise him that."

"You are al-Qaeda?"

"I don't say yes or no."

More whispering. "Wizard says you can't have them."

What? Wells was so surprised that he almost said the word in English before catching himself. "We've agreed," he said in Arabic.

"He wants one million for each."

"I can't give him all of that tonight, but he'll have it."

Another pause. "It doesn't matter. You can't have them for any price. They're not for you."

"Is this a joke?"

"He wants to sell to their families."

"If he doesn't give them to me, then my men and I will come to your camp and take them. And I promise, you fools will wish you'd taken my money."

"Wizard says, come and get them, then, Arab whore."

The line went dead.

For a minute that stretched to five, Wells replayed the conversation in his mind. He was sure he had understood. His Arabic was as good as ever, and the connection had been clear enough. *You can't have them for any price. They're not for you.* Was it possible Wizard's conscience was bothering him? Then why hadn't he freed the hostages? After everything he'd seen, Wells mistrusted any explanation that relied too heavily on the milk of human kindness. More likely Wizard just didn't trust an Arab who'd called him out of nowhere to pay him a million dollars.

Whatever the man's logic, Wells faced a more immediate problem. He'd hoped the offer would convince Wizard to give up the location of his camp. Now Wells needed a fresh lure. He wondered what Wizard would make of a second unexpected call in just a few minutes. At least this time he'd recognize the number. Anyway, Wells was low on options. At the end of this road, he'd have to turn east toward Somalia or west, back into Kenya. In that case he'd try for the United Nations compound at Garissa, hoping to win shelter until the SOG team extracted him. But he had no guarantees that the UN would take him in, and anyway, he wasn't sure the Cruiser could reach Garissa, which was at least two hours more of hard driving. The front right wheel was clicking again, and Wells thought that under the gasoline and dust he smelled the acrid burn of plastic overheating.

Again Wells found the missed-calls registry in the dead Somali's phone. He punched the call button. "Muhammad?"

"Muhammad's dead, Wizard," Wells said in English. "Gone to the other side. And I don't mean Kenya."

"Who this?"

"Fantastic. You speak English. I'm the American, the mzungu in the Land Cruiser. I came through Bakafi this afternoon. Muhammad sent you my photo before I shot him and those other half-trained scraggle boys you call soldiers. Bang bang, they're dead. You give them AKs, but that doesn't make them fighters. And I'll let you in on a secret. Those white shirts are big fat targets." Wells wanted to infuriate Wizard into making a mistake.

"I *don'* believe you."

"You think Muhammad gave me his phone because I talked nice to him? Him and the others, they're rotting back at that camp where you took the hostages. You *don'* believe, go see for yourself. But I warn you the hyenas already have. They're having a hyena feast tonight."

The man spat at him in Somali.

"Yeah, yeah, yeah. I want the hostages back, the three who are still alive. I know you killed one, left him at the camp."

"Them wazungu popular tonight. Americans, Arabs, Ditas, everybody want them."

"In Bakafi they told me you think you can't die. African nonsense. I'll put a bullet in your head and you'll die like everyone else. You understand?"

"The last man who spoke to me this way was the other American. The one at the camp."

Wells didn't want to anger Wizard so thoroughly that he'd refuse to speak. "I called you to make a deal."

"Who you work for?"

At least Wells knew the right answer to that question. "Their families."

"The price for them, three million U.S."

"The price is fifty thousand dollars and I let you and your soldiers live."

"You killed four my men already."

"You killed Scott Thompson. Call it even."

Wells knew Wizard had every reason to believe that Wells was trying to trap him. But he thought Wizard would have to respond, if only to see whether he could somehow turn whatever snare Wells was setting.

"Fifty thousand not enough. One hundred fifty."

"Gonna take me a little while to put that money together, but okay." Wells was happy to agree, though he knew that Wizard would never hand over the hostages for one hundred fifty thousand dollars. Wizard probably knew that Wells knew. The whole conversation was what the ranchers in Hamilton back in the day called ten pounds of bull in a five-pound bag.

"Where you wan to meet?"

"Your camp."

"Tell me where you are, I come get you."

"Try again. You know the road that runs north of the camp you raided last night?"

"I know every road in Ijara, mzungu."

"Congratulations. Let's meet at the border on that road. I'll have your money."

"What time?"

The clock on the Cruiser's dashboard read 11:45. Wells wanted Wizard to believe he had time to put his own trap in place. Plus Shafer would need as much time as Wells could give him. "I need to get the money from my people. Two-thirty a.m. Two hours, forty-five minutes from now."

"Two-thirty a.m."

"Be there or be square."

18

Langley

For the second time this day, Shafer faced the dubious honor of a trip to the seventh floor. Getting Duto's help would require face-to-face pleading. Especially after the hiccup earlier.

He found the director sitting at his desk, hands folded, lips furled. The expression was no doubt meant to look serious-yet-sensitive. It came off as constipated to Shafer. On the couch beneath the Katana sword, a fiftyish man with a drinker's bulbous nose sketched in charcoal on an oversize pad. The man's name eluded Shafer, but his face was familiar. It belonged to a New York artist known for tasteful portraits of the powerful. Evidently, Duto had decided that his tenure as director merited a higher-caliber artist than the usual D.C. portraitists. Normally, Shafer would have happily skewered this vanity. With Wells's life at stake, he contented himself with a mild cough. The painter scurried off.

"Affairs of state," Shafer said.

"You get three minutes. Wouldn't even sit down if I were you."

"Can we get a Reaper over southwestern Somalia in the next hour?"

Now Duto grinned, the leer that was his version of a real smile. Shafer wished the painter were here to see it, though no doubt it would send him through another fifth of scotch.

"Thought you were against unmanned aerial vehicles in no uncertain terms, Ellis. Thought we abused them, the poor terrorist on the other side has every right to an attorney, should he be unable to afford an attorney we'll provide him with one, preferably a nice Jewish boy whose head said terrorist can cut off at his leisure, et cetera."

Ouch. Of course Duto remembered Shafer's complaints about drones. "A place for everything and everything in its place. Anyway, most likely we'd only use it for surveillance."

"So the Hellfires are just for show?"

"More or less." Shafer explained Wells's plan to free the hostages. He glided over the fact that Wells was still trying to set the meeting with Little Wizard.

"So Wells gets there and then what? He talks this guy into letting them go?"

"Even if he's wrong, he's doing us a huge favor by finding them. NSA's shooting blanks."

"I know. I told them to tell me if they locked it down. Before they told you."

Duto's way of making sure Shafer knew where he and Wells stood. "So Wells finds 'em, worst case, you know where they are. You can chopper that SOG team in tomorrow. Avoid a war. That's what you want, right?"

"Assuming Wizard doesn't kill the hostages as soon as Wells gets there."

"He's not killing them. He wants to sell them. Why else go to the families as soon as he caught them?"

"Ellis. The three-minute rule is off. Take a breath. Sit." Duto pointed at the couch.

Shafer sat.

"Just so I have this right. Wells is putting together a meet with some Somali warlord none of us have ever heard of who's probably ready to unload a magazine in him just because. I know he likes to run his own shows, but this feels more like a death wish. And you want me to put up a drone for the only backup he'll have."

Shafer feared Duto might be right. But

being honest with Duto rarely paid. As in never. "Death wish has nothing to do with it. Sometimes I think he's half Jack Russell. Once he starts a mission, he can't stop. Makes him crazy. And this time it's for his son."

"We don't put up the drone, he's still going in, isn't he? Try to find them on his own somehow and bang his way out."

"He's never lacked for confidence."

Duto turned away from Shafer, looked out the window. Shafer could almost hear him working through risk and benefit. Finding the hostages would be huge in his run for the Senate, especially since Wells would never try to take credit. But if they died after Duto put up the Reaper, would he be blamed? Did Wells have any chance of pulling off this stunt? Wells's own life was a tertiary consideration. At most.

Thirty seconds passed in silence before Duto spun back to Shafer and flipped up his laptop. "I'll call Djibouti."

The CIA operated Reapers out of bases in Ethiopia and Djibouti, near the tip of the Horn of Africa, halfway between Yemen and Somalia. Drones were built for stealth, not speed. The Reaper topped out at about two hundred sixty knots, just under three hundred miles an hour. On the other hand, it didn't need many preflight checks. The techs could put one in the air in four minutes.

Duto picked up his secure phone, consulted his laptop, punched in a number. "Hello. Hello? This is Vinny Duto." He grinned at Shafer. "No, I'm serious. It's okay. You're not in trouble. Turn the music down and we'll run the codes and I'll tell you what I want."

Five minutes later, Duto cradled the phone, gave Shafer a thumbs-up.

"So your boy's luck is improving. They've got a Reaper over Mog right now, and they graciously enough are going to switch the link and let us run it from downstairs." Pilots guided drones from a half-dozen bases worldwide, but Langley had its own link so that senior CIA officials could oversee the highest-priority, highest-risk missions in person.

"It's good to be king," Shafer said.

"You'd better get down there, tell the pilot what to look for. And Wells needs to understand that I'm looking over your shoulder on this. My first and only priority is saving those hostages. He's not an employee, he's not a contractor, as far as I'm concerned he's a random armed civilian on site."

"Not sure I understand what you're saying, Vinny." Though Shafer did. He'd understood before Duto even wasted his breath giving the speech.

"What I'm saying is we didn't get him in there and it's not our job to get him out —"

"Thanks for your help, Vinny." Shafer offered the Director of Central Intelligence his twin middle fingers and walked out.

19

Ijara District

Wells reached the T junction that marked the end of the road from Bakafi in good spirits. Despite the ominously loud rattling from the Cruiser's right front wheel, he'd lengthened his lead over the Kenyans. And Shafer had just assured him that a Reaper would be in position within an hour. Shafer didn't tell Wells what he'd promised Duto in return for this benediction, and Wells didn't ask. Some questions were best posed after the close of business.

At the junction Wells turned the Cruiser right, so it faced west, into Kenya. He stopped, grabbed the Mossberg, got out. The night was overcast. A humid breeze weighted the air from the southeast. Rain was coming, and soon. Wells held open the driver's door and jammed the tip of the shotgun's barrel against the driver's seat, its butt against the gas pedal.

Wells planned to send the Cruiser west while he ran east to the dirt bike he and Wilfred had left. He hoped the Kenyans would chase the Cruiser's taillights the wrong way. He'd pulled a similar stunt years before in the Bekaa Valley. But this time the Cruiser would have a passenger. Even in handcuffs, Mark could pull the shotgun off the gas pedal. Wells needed to knock him out.

Mark was curled up in the cargo hold between the plastic jerricans. Dust coated his gasoline-soaked clothes. Wells had the bizarre thought that he looked like a giant piece of chicken-fried steak. He kicked at Wells, splaying his legs as wildly as an angry four-year-old. Wells grabbed his right calf, flipped him, tugged him closer, reached for the tire iron wedged under a jerrican. Mark spasmed his leg free, twisted into a corner, balled up his knees, shouted in Swahili. Wells didn't know if the cop was cursing or praying. Yet for all the noise he was making, his eyes were profoundly disconnected. As though he believed that nothing he said or did could reach Wells, since Wells wasn't human enough to be reached.

Wells had seen that combination of panic and hopelessness before. Not in the jihadis. They seemed as willing to die as to kill.

Some truly couldn't wait to ascend to the heaven they were sure awaited them. Others viewed death almost dispassionately. Any man who'd fought in close combat knew that death came sooner or later. Kill or die was a myth. The truth was kill and die. And, whatever waited on the other side, death came with one unquenchable blessing. It ended the fear of death. Wells hoped he'd remember that truth when his moment came.

But civilians rarely viewed the void so calmly. Mark might be venal and corrupt, but he wasn't a killer. His panic proved it. A killer wouldn't panic this way. Wells found he couldn't lacerate the cop's body and soul further this night. He dropped the tire iron, grabbed his backpack. He fished in it until he found the hood that he'd carried from New Hampshire. "I'm not going to kill you. But I have to put this on you. Now."

Mark sputtered beneath the hood as Wells turned the Cruiser around and drove east. He glimpsed the headlights of his pursuers to the north. Much closer now. His attack of conscience had cost him half his lead. Or maybe it had saved him. Maybe the Cruiser would have run into a ditch right away and the Kenyans would have caught him before he got to the dirt bike. At least this way he knew he'd reach it, if the wheel didn't give out first. He had time for one last call. He found his phone, punched in a Montana number.

"Hello." His son's cool, assured voice. In the background: basketballs bouncing, sneakers squeaking on hardwood, a coach yelling, *"Hands up! Up!"*

"Evan. It's John."

"Let me get outside —" The noise faded. "We got these emails, pictures of Gwen."

"I'm close, Evan."

"You *are*?"

"You can't tell the Murphys."

"Why?"

"Promise you won't. Not yet."

"Okay. I promise. Is it the Shabaab who have them?"

"No. Which is good. I can't tell you much, but I'm hopeful. It's nighttime here, past midnight, and I'm hoping to get a look at them tonight. They're in Somalia."

"Like a raid?"

"Not exactly. I'm going in light —" An epic understatement. "Light and fast."

"But you have backup —"

Wells smiled. Backup wasn't exactly top-secret jargon, but he still enjoyed hearing the word from his peacenik son. "All the backup I need. Langley knows what I'm doing. They're good with having me here. If I can't get them out tonight, the agency and the FBI will probably reach out to the kidnappers to make a deal. Or they may bring the big guns for a rescue. Either way, at that point the Murphys and the other families will be told." Wells was keeping Scott Thompson's death to himself. Evan didn't need to know about it yet.

"But right now, tonight, you're going in alone? I mean, no other Americans with you? Not even the Kenyans?"

That's my boy. Evan had focused on the very fact that Wells was trying to obscure. Wells wished he could explain that he had a member of the Kenyan constabulary with him, hooded and handcuffed and ready to broil.

"I'll have eyes on me." Or, technically speaking, optics. "It'll be fine."

"But it might not be, right? That's why you called? In case it's not. To say goodbye. Tell me again you're sorry you were gone all those years. Give me a chance to say I'm sorry, too, for frosting you how I did. Oh Dad, I'm so glad we got to talk. Me too, son. Don't get killed, Dad. I won't, son. But if I do, I promise you'll be the last thing I think of. A single tear rolls down both our cheeks. Cut."

Wells didn't know whether the irony was real or faux, a cover for deeper feelings that Evan couldn't talk about yet. He did know that his son had just guaranteed that the word *love* would be found nowhere in the rest of this conversation. Yet Wells couldn't blame him. They were strangers to each other. Wells couldn't make them father and son in a few days, no matter what he did.

"I called to give you a heads-up. Good news coming. And work on that jumper. Your release has a hitch. You can get away with that in high school, not college." In truth, the kid's shot had looked smooth as silk the one and only time Wells had seen it.

"Thought you didn't know anything about basketball."

"As much as you know about special ops. I'll talk to you tomorrow."

"A conquering hero."

"I see a beautiful friendship coming. I'll give the Langley tour. Non-classified areas only, of course."

"I get it, okay. That you're only over there because I asked."

"Wrong again, Evan. I'm not here for you. Or even the volunteers."

"Why, then?"

"What Hillary said about Everest. Because

it's there." *Because this is all I do. Or ever will. Because if you take more than a few steps, you can never turn back. That's what they don't tell you at the Farm. Maybe they know it wouldn't matter, that anyone ready to walk this path wouldn't listen. Or maybe they don't want you to know.*

He'd have that conversation with Evan another day. Or never.

"And I'm not saying that so you won't blame yourself if something happens to me. I'm saying it because it's the truth. All right?"

"All right."

Wells saw the dirt bike ahead. "Gotta go, Evan."

"One last thing. Serious now."

"What's that?"

"I don't understand you. Don't understand the Muslim thing. Or a lot of what you've done. But it's time for me to stop pretending that I don't want to hear about it."

"When I get home. We'll have time."

"I'd like that. Don't get killed, John."

A gift Wells hadn't expected.

He pulled up beside the bike. He closed his eyes and let himself feel nothing but the clean happiness in his heart. It might not sound like much, this irony-laden call. But after what had happened the year before in Missoula, it was a Hallmark card. He had a chance for a relationship with his son.

First he had to stay alive. And bring home the hostages. Evan's goodwill would be fleeting if he survived and they didn't. He imagined that conversation: *Trust me, son, it happens. Best intentions and all that. Ever heard of the Bay of Pigs? Anyway, still hoping for a chat . . .*

No. He could die tonight if he got them out safely, but never the reverse. He strapped the shotgun to his chest, his pack to his back. He grabbed a jerrican and slopped gas into the bike's tank. These dirt bikes held four gallons at most. Even on pavement their full-tank range was under two hundred miles. In this trackless wild, Wells would be lucky to get one-fifty. Which would have to be enough.

With the tank full, Wells heaved the jerrican into the scrub. He grabbed the second can and circled the Cruiser at a radius of about eight feet, pouring out gasoline. When the can grew light in his hand, he poured the last of the gas into a puddle, stepped back, and flicked his lighter to the rainbow pool. A lustrous circle of flames swept into the night as Wells ran for the bike.

The blaze was a diversion, a gaudy trick. It would stop his pursuers temporarily as they focused on the Cruiser and the man inside. Under his hood Mark was shouting now, no doubt panicked by the heat. Wells heard him even through the Toyota's closed windows. The worst night of the cop's life. But he'd live.

Wells heard an engine rumbling behind the hill to the west. At least one vehicle had passed the T junction. Fortunately, the hill kept Wells hidden for now. He mounted the bike, started up. The engine rumbled to life. Wells turned away from the road and double-toed the bike into third gear to keep the noise down. He bumped along the faint track that followed a dry streambed south to the camp.

He planned to ride to the camp and steal an AK and all the magazines he could carry. Then he'd hole up. If he heard the Kenyans getting close, he'd take off again, dare them to chase him through the scrub into Somalia. Otherwise, he'd sit tight. Silence was his ultimate ally. The camp was only three miles from the road, but without the vultures as signposts it was invisible to anyone who wasn't on top of it.

With the Somali border so close, Wells

hoped the cop and his other pursuers might give up the chase when they got to Mark, bring him back to Bakafi instead. The Kenyan police didn't have the equipment to track him at night. The closest major GSU station was in Garissa, well over a hundred miles away. Instead of trying to catch a crazy mzungu in the dark, the cops could bring reinforcements in the morning to sweep the area. They might even ask the army for help.

Wells had landed at Jomo Kenyatta International in Nairobi less than three days before. He couldn't remember a mission turning upside down as quickly as this one. But if he rescued the hostages, no one would care about the trouble he'd caused. He hadn't killed Mark, and he'd uncovered enough evidence against James Thompson that Thompson's own problems would trump any revenge he might want. The story would have a happy ending, Scott Thompson's demise notwithstanding. And everyone loved happy endings, Duto most of all.

As the late and unlamented Al Davis liked to say, *Just win, baby.*

Five minutes later, Wells reached the little rise that overlooked the camp. He didn't know why he was surprised to see the hyenas. He'd been so focused on escaping the Kenyans, he'd forgotten them somehow.

They hadn't forgotten him, though. They were awake. Maybe they were nocturnal as a rule. Maybe the bike had roused them. They looked at him with their heads cocked. Wells felt almost that they were annoyed with him, like he was a delivery guy who'd accidentally shown up at the wrong house, crashed a party. He knew he was projecting, but he couldn't help himself. A half-dozen of the beasts lay beside the third hut. Another group rested near the fourth hut, at the far end of the camp. The big one, the two-hundred-pound alpha, stood in the center of the camp, where he'd been when Wells had arrived that afternoon. The corpse he'd been eating at the time was almost gone. A long white bone, probably a femur, lay beside his front paws. A few feet away was a half-eaten rib cage, crunched like chicken wings at a sports bar. The bodies of the White Men whom Wells and Wilfred had shot had been pawed at and torn open. Their AKs, the reason Wells had come, lay atop the corpses. The hyenas had torn the rifles' straps but left the AKs themselves alone. Wells felt a sort of shame for the corpses, for what would happen when the hyenas grew hungry again. Even from a hundred meters away, the stench seeped over him.

The lion was nowhere in sight. Wells figured the hyenas had run him off. Whatever their reputation as weaklings, they seemed firmly in control tonight. He wanted to put the bike into gear, ride a hundred miles from this mess. But he needed an AK and a couple hundred rounds to have any chance against Little Wizard. The Glock was useless past thirty or forty meters. With an assault rifle that could give him a couple hundred meters of space and the right firing hole and plenty of ammo, and with the Reaper watching his back, he could play one-against-fifty long enough to make Wizard pay attention. A lot of ifs, but he'd have the advantage of surprise. And drone strikes unnerved even the boldest fighters.

"Tell you what, boys," Wells yelled down the hill. "I'll take what I need and go. Toodeloo and all that. Won't even know I was here. What do you say?"

As an answer, the big guy spread his jaws wide, picked up the femur. He crunched it in half as casually as Wells breaking a stick over his knee. He chewed noisily for a few seconds, tilted his big ugly head, dropped what was left of the bone from his mouth. Pieces of femur fell out. He bent his head and ran his tongue over the biggest shred like a kid licking an ice cream cone. Wells understood now why Africans hated these beasts. They seemed almost intentionally disrespectful.

Wells feared giving away his position to the Kenyans up the track, but he had to try to rattle the hyenas. He revved the dirt bike's engine for a few seconds. The alpha male took a half-step back, but no more. Two others stood up. Wells wondered if they would be bold enough to attack the bike. Animals naturally feared objects they didn't know. And even in packs, smaller predators rarely attacked larger beasts. They knew instinctively that the bigger animal would kill several of them even if they succeeded in taking him down.

But Wells wasn't sure these hyenas were thinking of him as predator anymore. In their minds, they'd driven him off once already. They'd spent the day developing a taste for human flesh that under normal circumstances they never would have known. They'd learned that these strange two-legged creatures were filled with delicious meat and marrow like every other animal. They were holding off only because they weren't sure how much damage he could do to them. If they decided he wasn't a threat, they would come at him. Wells wasn't at all sure that he could ride fast enough in the dark to escape them.

Two more hyenas stood.

"Tried to play nice. You wouldn't listen. Some hyenas you just can't reach." Wells spread his arms wide and howled at the black clouds above with the gusto of a D-list actor desperate for the role of Werewolf #2. Without waiting to see how the hyenas reacted, he grabbed the handlebars and poured on the gas as he came down the hill.

The hyenas stood now. They chirped and cackled at one another, curious, almost alien sounds that grew more intense as Wells closed in. The alpha stood apart from the rest, his tail unfurled straight behind him, his eyes on this legless man-beast coming at him. The ground was hard-packed dirt, and Wells rode confidently. He twisted his handlebars and came straight at the big guy. Who tilted his head high and opened his bloody muzzle and screamed — no other word would do — screamed his frustration at the dark heavens above. He loped sideways toward the third hut, the rest of the pack, tracking Wells with his eyes. *This isn't over, and don't think it is . . .* For a creature that couldn't speak, the hyena communicated clearly enough.

Wells stopped beside one of the White Men he'd killed that afternoon. Up close the corpse was deeply compromised, pink grooves carved into its black skin, one eye gone, its guts open and stinking of ordure and covered with flies. Another hyena took up the alpha's cry now, and another. *Step away. That meat is ours . . .* Wells closed his mouth against the flies, leaned over, reached down, wishing for gloves and a kerchief, wishing for a Biosafety Level IV protective suit. He pulled the rifle away from the corpse —

The alpha's keening scream rose another octave and he lowered his head and charged —

Wells raised the AK, slipped his left hand under the barrel, found the trigger guard, slid his right index finger inside —

The hyena bounded at him, a low black streak in the night. Another followed, and another —

Wells tucked in his elbow to brace the rifle and squeezed the trigger, knowing that the safety had to be off, he'd seen the kid about to fire this afternoon. He was in a terrible firing position, bent over the bike, aiming with his off hand, no time to set himself. The rifle danced in his hands, but Wells kept his finger on the trigger and the hyena was so close that he almost couldn't miss. The hyena staggered and kept coming, and then the whole top of its head exploded and it took one more step and collapsed. Wells laid off the trigger just long enough to make sure the AK didn't jam and shifted to the next hyena, this one smaller but coming faster. He missed, shooting behind the animal. The hyena was only three steps away now, its mouth open, lips drawn back, ready to pounce. Wells twisted the rifle to the right, kept shooting. Chunks of flesh spurted out of the beast's belly, eruptions of blood and sinew and muscle. The animal took another half-step and tumbled and lay on its side gasping and dying. Wells was already focused on the next hyena. He was catching up with their speed. This one he took out twenty feet away, blowing open its jaw so it flopped down onto its back in agony. Wells shot it until it stopped moving. No mercy in these rounds, hate only. Two more hyenas moved toward him but turned away when they saw what had happened to their betters. They ran now, howling in fear. The rest of the pack followed, disappearing into the darkness.

Wells would have killed them all if he could, shot them down nobly or not. These corpse-devouring beasts filled him with an ugly fury. But they would be dangerous to men no more. They would skulk the scrub in fear and leave the two-legged animals to invent their own terrors. Now Wells, too, had to flee. The shots and screams had surely reached the road. He didn't know if the Kenyans would chase him, but he couldn't chance staying here. He liberated the corpses of their ammunition, trying not to hear the laughing voice in his head calling *hyenaman hyenaman,* and rode over the trackless scrub. East. To Somalia.

20

Lower Juba Region

Wizard wished for quiet tonight, time to think. But quiet was hard to find. Everyone in the world wanted these hostages. After the Dita Boys came the phone calls. When Waaberi hung up with the Arab, he pushed the phone at Wizard like it was cursed.

"He offer us three million dollars, Wizard. One, two, three million."

"Don't believe he has such money."

"Find out, then. Make him drop one million. Send some boy to pick it up. Some boy you know to trust."

"They ours now. Not for Arabs to cut up. You know these Arabs hate us, look down on us. They say we all pray to the same Allah, but any Somali who works in Saudi, they treat him worse than a donkey. Beat him and such."

"Gutaale" — the first time in the years since Mogadishu that Waaberi had called him by his former name — "you know what that way." Waaberi tilted his head east. "And you know what the other way. They coming for us, Kenyans, Americans, what-all. To the south the swamp and to the north nothing at all. You going to buy us an airplane and fly us out of here, Wizard? Maybe we swim to China or I don't know where? We need money, Wizard, and this man say he give it to us. He beat Somalis like donkeys, what you care? He the devil himself, what you care? What you owe these wazungu? Last night you kill one. Now you 'tecting them."

"You 'fraid, Beri? Fancy to leave me now? Go on, then. Take anyone who want to follow. Take them all. I don't stop you." Wizard came out with a key from his pocket. "Even give you a Rover." He pressed the key on Waaberi, but Waaberi crossed his arms over his chest, tucked his hands under his armpits.

"Don't disrespect. Not leaving, Wizard. Not now, not ever. I asking, what is the plan? We just waiting for them Boys to come? Then tell me so. I make sure my RP ready. Put a hole in some Ditas."

"Only sent the emails twelve hours ago. Put in for the money tomorrow. I don't want to hear about them Ditas no more. They talk talk. Man threaten once, he serious. Threaten twice, he scared. Trying to do with words what he can't with bullets." Wizard wasn't sure he was right, but the idea pleased him more than the alternative. "If they come, they gon' wish they didn't. Meantime, these wazungu belong to me. I decide what to do with them. No one but me."

Wizard couldn't fully explain, even to himself, why he wouldn't sell the hostages to the Arab. Something to do with seeing the girl, Gwen, chewing the miraa, her blue eyes all bright and hopeful when she saw him. Like she was scared but not scared of him. Like she trusted him even after what he'd done to the other one. That plug in her mouth like she was born to it. And all afraid of rape, too. He couldn't sell her to some Arab who would hurt her that way.

"That the plan, then. Hope this money comes from the sky, the Americans drop it down in a parachute."

"The families gon' pay, Beri. I know it. Go on and sleep. And tell the Donkeys and the rest, they sleep too. No miraa tonight."

"You know that not happening, Wizard."

"Yah. Tell them, go inside, keep the AKs close, but we got to rest while we can."

Waaberi saluted, a quick, sloppy finger-to-forehead dance that meant *I'll do what you say, but I think you're crazy,* and disappeared.

Wizard found his tools in his pack. He laid a thready brown blanket on the dirt and reached for the AK that hung from the wall on a crude wooden peg. He folded his legs under him and set to field-stripping the rifle. He preferred pistols as a rule. Commanders carried pistols. But if the Ditas attacked, they'd all be soldiers. Also, the AK was a simple clean weapon and working with it soothed his fingers. But he'd only just removed the bolt carrier when his phone rang.

Wizard wondered if the Arab was calling again. Instead the screen showed Muhammad's number. Finally, good news.

Only it wasn't.

When the call was done, Wizard wanted to slice up this American, cut out his evil tongue, end his boasts. Wizard knew better than to think the man was lying. Muhammad wouldn't give up his phone if he was alive. The American had killed him. Wizard still couldn't figure if the man was a soldier or something else. In the pictures Muhammad sent him, the American and his driver were by themselves in the Land Cruiser. No other vehicles, no more men. Yet they'd somehow killed four of Wizard's own. And the man was wrong about Muhammad. He knew how to survive. He'd fought in Mog for years.

Then the man told Wizard to give back the hostages. For fifty thousand dollars. Did he imagine that Wizard didn't know what these wazungu were worth? If he worked for the families, why didn't he offer a fair ransom? But Wizard didn't ask those questions. He held his anger and told the American one hundred fifty thousand. Too low a price, but he didn't care. Anything to lure the man to the border, where Wizard could gain his revenge. Of course, the American might have his own treachery set. But Wizard wouldn't back away from this man who'd killed his soldiers.

Soon as he got off the phone, he decided to send soldiers to the border, two solid men. Riding there would take thirty or forty minutes in the rain that had just begun. They'd arrive well before the meeting. Wizard didn't know why the mzungu had proposed that particular spot to meet. Wizard sensed that he didn't know the area well. White people rarely stayed long in this region. Wizard would have heard about this one if he'd been here for more than a few days.

He'd tell his men to hide themselves in the scrub north of the road. A little hill there gave cover. Let them watch the Kenyan side of the border, see if anyone tried to set a trap before the meeting. If they didn't sound an alarm, Wizard would send three more men in a technical an hour later. No, a pickup. No machine gun. No weapons visible. Two men up front in the cab, one hiding in the bed with an AK. Five men total. They ought to be able to deal with one mzungu. Anyway, Wizard couldn't spare more. Not tonight.

When the American arrived, they'd see if he had anyone with him, the Kenyan police, whoever. If he was foolish enough to come alone, Wizard's men would bring him back here. Wizard would open him from belly to chin and let him bleed, let the beasts of the scrub feed on him —

No. Better. He'd sell this one to Shabaab, the Arabs, whoever offered the highest price. Let them do what they liked with him.

If the American did have an army of his own, Wizard would tell his men to retreat, but northeast toward the Dita camp instead of here. When they got close to the camp they could start shooting. The Ditas would believe they were under attack and return fire. Then the Americans would attack the Ditas.

Wizard knew the plan had holes. What if

the American killed these five men just as he'd killed Muhammad and the others? But Wizard couldn't invite the American to his base until he was sure that he didn't have a hundred soldiers with him. At the same time, he couldn't send just one or two men to the border. The American was too dangerous to risk meeting one-on-one.

No, this choice was best. Wizard would put Shiny Khalid — one of the four Khalids in camp — in charge. The other Khalids were Tiny, Thirty Centimeter, and Big-Head. Wizard didn't know how they had earned their nicknames. A smart commander let his men have a few secrets. Anyway, Shiny Khalid was one of Wizard's smartest soldiers. He'd nose out a trap if the American was setting one. Plus, he knew where the Ditas were camped. Only problem with Shiny was his fearful streak. He wouldn't relish setting up a cross fire between the Ditas and the Americans.

So Wizard would team him with one of the Donkeys, the dumb brave boys who truly believed that Wizard couldn't die and that they couldn't either. They were proud of their fearlessness. They embraced their nickname. Donkey Gudud would be best. If he had to, he'd ride straight for the Dita camp, whatever Shiny Khalid said.

Wizard felt his confidence coming back. He knew his men, knew how to make them more than they were. They would kill this American and a thousand Ditas, too, if the moment came. Wizard striped his fingers over the rumpled skin on his belly and back, the only trace of the AK round he'd taken that day in Mog. He'd beaten that bullet. He had no fear.

He was so focused on putting together his plan that he didn't even realize that he had finished stripping and reassembling the AK. Only its magazine remained. His hands had done their work himself. He believed in signs, and this was a truespoke sign. The American would be his tonight. Wizard clapped the magazine into the stock and hung up the rifle. He felt five meters tall as he walked out of his hut to find Khalid.

He was pleased to see that his men had followed his order sending them back to their huts. Or maybe the rain had done the trick. Aside from Samatar, who was guarding the wazungu, the center of camp was deserted. Good. He had seven sentries posted tonight, and he was sending five more soldiers to the border. Everyone else needed to rest. Even miraa couldn't keep men awake forever.

■ ■ ■ ■

Fifteen minutes later, back in his hut, Wizard heard Khalid and the Donkey ride off toward the border. He'd have at least forty-five minutes before Khalid checked in, time for a nap. He switched off his lantern, lay flat on his blanket. He set his phone alarm and stretched out with his fingers locked behind his head. He closed his eyes and saw a bright precious city with buildings that stretched to the sky. He bent his neck until he was looking straight up, but still he couldn't see where they ended. Winged cars floated between the towers. An Arab with a thick beard came to him and told him the city would be his if he would give up the wazungu. No, Wizard said. In the distance, an engine kicked up and sputtered and died. What's happening, he asked the Arab, but the man only shook his head. Then Wizard heard more shouting and all around him the buildings shook and —

"Wizard!"

The city vanished as he opened his eyes. An upside-down Waaberi stood in the doorway of his hut. "The wazungu —"

"What —"

"They tried to escape."

Wizard pushed himself up.

"Samatar stop them."

Waaberi's face twitched, an expression that meant: *Bad news.* "See for yourself."

Wizard rubbed the sleep from his eyes, picked up his phone. The alarm was still fifteen minutes from ringing. He'd been asleep for only — he needed a second to make the numbers work, he was so tired — thirty minutes. No matter. Waaberi's hard eyes told him: *You won't sleep again this night.* Wizard grabbed a plug of miraa and chewed until his mouth filled with juice and the leaf cleared away the rubble from his city of dreams.

21

Nobody talked much after Hailey came back with the wrench. Gwen wasn't sure what the other two were thinking. But the plan seemed more real to her now, and more frightening. She couldn't get her head around the idea that they were going to try to kill their guard. The guy hadn't done anything to them. They didn't even know his name.

She didn't argue, though. She knew what Owen would say. That she'd gone soft. That these men were not her friends. That even if she didn't agree, they'd voted and they had to stick to their decision. Worse than the words would be the look, the eyes-narrowed-chin-tilted look that meant *If you were smarter, we wouldn't be talking about this, you'd get it.*

Before they were taken, Gwen would have said that Owen loved her, or at least that he had the world's worst crush on her. He lit up when he saw her, like a dog when the treat drawer came open. No more. Since the night that the Joker had hooded them to punish her for talking, Owen had dealt with her like a problem he had to manage.

She wondered whether Owen's love for her had ever been real. Like so many guys she'd known, maybe he wanted the *idea* of her instead of actually wanting her. Maybe he wanted the ego boost that came from walking into a room with a beautiful woman, the feeling that everyone wondered how he'd won her. Was he rich, famous, a great storyteller, a demon lover? One point in Scott's favor, maybe the biggest, maybe the only reason Gwen had put up with him: Scott didn't need that boost. Scott genuinely believed that Gwen was lucky to have him, not the other way around. His feelings for her couldn't have been simpler. He thought she was hot and a good lay. Which was pretty much what she thought of him. He'd been surprisingly good in bed, too. He had plenty of experience and zero performance anxiety.

Thinking about sex with Scott made her almost miss him.

She wondered what he would have made of their half-assed plan. Probably he'd have sneered at it. *Chill,* he would have said.

Nobody's gonna hurt us. We're worth more alive than dead. Way more than all these Somalis combined.

But what had Scott known about Kenya or Somalia? What had he known about this continent? What did any of them know? Gwen felt more grown up than she ever had before, and more childish too. There was a word for that, but she couldn't remember it. She'd come here thinking these Africans were simple and stupid. That they couldn't even feed themselves. She knew better now. They might be poor, but they weren't stupid and they sure weren't simple. The worst part was she hadn't even realized she was looking down on them. At least she was starting to see how little she saw.

She remembered. The word was *paradox.*

The camp quieted as the soldiers settled in for the night. Soldiers. Bandits. Gwen didn't know what to call these armed boy-men. She listened for trouble, shots or screams, heard nothing. She drifted for a while, half asleep. A dirt bike took off and disappeared. Gwen expected more to follow, but none did. The faint voices from the other huts melded into a sort of song, all the world's languages together. The minutes were as long as hours and as short as days, and she could float on the sea forever —

Owen nudged her awake. "It's time." He edged around the hut until he stood two steps from the door. He held the wrench flat against his leg. Even in the dark, Gwen saw how his body coiled. He'd played tennis in high school.

"Gwen." He wagged two fingers toward her in a come-hither motion. Again she thought of Scott, who'd given her the same peremptory wave more than once. She wanted to tell Owen to drop the wrench, sit down. But Hailey put a hand on her arm and squeezed. She couldn't delay any longer. She walked to the doorway, looked outside. The clouds were low and heavy. A steady rain soaked the earth. The wet season had come at last. Only their guard was outside. He wore an AK across his chest and squatted on an inflatable gray plastic ball that belonged in a yoga class. Gwen hadn't seen it before and couldn't imagine how it had arrived here. But she'd seen this in Dadaab, too, objects that didn't seem to belong anywhere in Africa.

Enough. If she waited any longer, she'd lose her nerve. She stepped out, squatted beside their sentry. He looked at her and then away and finally he settled for staring at her feet. "What's your name?" She pointed at herself. "Gwen. *Mi nombre es Gwennie.* You?"

"Samatar."

"Samatar. Come in where it's dry, have some miraa."

"Miraa."

"Miraa. Exactly."

He reached into his pocket. The bundle of leaves had shrunk. She could see he didn't want to share. He held it slightly away from her, like a frat boy with a flask that had only two good pulls left: *Sure you want this?*

"Keep it, then. No problemo. But come on in. No need for you to get wet." She stood, pointed at the doorway. *We're all friends here.*

He looked around. Gwen guessed that he'd been warned not to come inside the hut. But they both knew that he'd already broken that rule tonight and nothing bad had happened. He stood — then shook his head and squatted down. Gwen felt mostly relief. She'd tried, Owen and Hailey would have to admit she'd tried. She turned away.

And the rain picked up. Samatar raised his hand to the sky, stood. "Miraa."

"I know, miraa —"

He stepped toward the hut. She couldn't stop him, not without out-and-out betraying her friends. She walked inside. He followed. As he entered, Owen lunged, whipping his arm like he was hitting a topspin forehand, bringing the wrench into the side of Samatar's head with a terrible crunch. Samatar choked out a gasp and his head lashed forward and his body turned to string. He fell sideways without even lifting a hand. A bone broke as he hit, the arm or the shoulder, Gwen wasn't sure. He moaned just enough to prove he was alive.

Owen stooped, unbuckled Samatar's AK, tugged at it. The rifle's strap was caught between Samatar's body and the ground. "Help." Owen put his hands under Samatar and lifted. After a moment's hesitation, Hailey pulled out the rifle.

A thin foam bubbled from Samatar's mouth. His left arm twitched and his eyes rolled back until they were as white as hospital sheets. Gwen leaned toward Samatar and Owen grabbed her arm, pulled her back roughly. He looked at her like she was speaking a language he'd never heard. "He was holding us prisoner." He took the AK from Hailey, buckled it across his chest. "Come on." And he was gone. Hailey stepped toward the door, turned, looked at Gwen. "Give me a sec."

"Don't stay here, Gwennie." Then Hailey was gone, too.

Gwen knelt beside Samatar, kissed her fingers, touched them to his cheek. She wanted to do something more, but she couldn't think of anything. So she ran.

The rain was falling. The camp was quiet. Owen and Hailey were out of sight, running behind the huts, the path they'd decided would give them the best chance of reaching the bikes unseen. Gwen followed. She slipped on a patch of mud, caught herself. She reached the hut with the dirt bikes, ducked through the doorway.

Inside, the bikes stood side by side. Between them, tools and parts jumbled on a burlap sack. The mechanic lay in the corner, eyes closed. Even by the standards of these underfed soldiers, he was tiny. He slept with his legs splayed like he was trying to occupy as much space as he could. A motorcycle poster was pinned above him, a gleaming red sport bike that must have stood for something like paradise to him.

"We'll get out of here, you'll feel better," Owen whisper-hissed. "It's called Stockholm syndrome."

"It's called go fuck yourself," Gwen hissed right back.

"I'll ride with Hailey. Make sure we're ready before you hit the starter. The whole camp's going to hear when we start up."

"I get it."

"Once we're out, just follow us west."

Gwen wanted to punch him. Instead she nodded. The kid grumbled in his sleep. Hailey handed Gwen a key. She mounted the bike nearer the door, slipped the key into the ignition. It fit. Owen hopped onto the second bike. Hailey slid on behind him and wrapped her arms around him as he gave Gwen a thumbs-up. Gwen squeezed the clutch, made sure the bike was in neutral, jabbed the starter. The engine rumbled to life. She kicked the bike into gear, let out the clutch. The bike jumped forward —

And the engine coughed and all its power was gone. Gwen felt it going limp underneath her. She laid off the throttle and put the bike in neutral to try to save the stall, but she couldn't. She hadn't even had time to get her feet on the pegs.

"Gwen! You said —"

"I do. Hold on." She'd told the truth. She knew how to ride. She hadn't done anything wrong, she was sure. The engine had dropped. She hit the starter again and the bike rumbled to life. She offered it gas, careful this time to keep the clutch tucked tight, making sure the engine wouldn't stall —

But it did. As soon as she gave it more than a hint of gas. She knew that on cold days, some motorcycles, especially old ones that had carbs instead of fuel injectors, needed a tight choke and a few minutes at high-rev idle to get warmed up enough to move. But this bike was new, and anyway, it was plenty warm. She was no expert, but she figured the fuel line or the injectors were clogged.

She tried again, knowing this was her last shot. The engine gave up even faster this time, not even fully starting before it slid into a clicking half-stall like the battery was giving out. She laid off the starter. In the silence she heard a man yelling. She dropped the kickstand, stepped off the bike, peeked out the doorway —

Behind them the mechanic shouted. Owen raised the AK and fired a burst at the top of the motorcycle poster, shredding it, kicking a ragged line of holes into the wall. The mechanic dropped to his knees and raised his hands. Owen stepped toward him. As he did, he un-slung the AK and shifted his hands to hold the rifle's barrel like a bat —

"Owen —"

"No —"

Owen gave no sign he'd heard them. He chopped the butt of the rifle across the mechanic's temple. The Somali's skin tore like paper and blood gushed. He put one hand to his forehead to stanch the flow and scrambled back against the wall.

"You stay there," Owen said. Like he was talking to a dog. Gwen didn't know what had happened to him, where this violence was coming from, but she wanted it to stop now.

Outside, the voices increased. Gwen peeked out of the hut. A soldier walked toward them, holding an AK. "They're coming," she said.

"How many? Are they armed?"

"How many? Are you joking?"

"It's over," Hailey said.

Owen grabbed Gwen's shoulder, squeezed hard enough to hurt. "You go out there. With your hands up. Big smile. Tell them you want your boyfriend."

"Then what, Owen? Then what?"

Owen grinned like he was about to let her in on the best joke ever told, the secret of the universe. "What else? Tell Wizard we have a hostage."

She wanted to scream at him for his foolishness and sudden cruelty and this disaster he'd brought. But the soldiers were close, and she was scared he might start shooting, get them killed. She walked into the rain with her arms held high. More men had come out. They moved in groups of two and three, slumped and half asleep and spreading out vaguely around the hut. In the dark they looked like zombies, zombies with guns.

Two men pointed their rifles at her. She went to her knees in the muddy ground. The men walked toward her, clucking at each other in Somali. Inside the hut, Owen sang Katy Perry, *You change your mind like a girl changes clothes . . .* Gwen wondered if she was hallucinating. Maybe Scott had spiked her orange juice back at Dadaab. Maybe she'd been tripping since last week and never stopped. Merrily merrily merrily merrily life is but a dream. But no, the rain was cool and dear on her arms. Behind her Owen kept right on singing . . . *You're hot and you're cold . . .* the pitch just right.

The men stopped a foot stride from her.

"I need to see Wizard. Please, Wizard."

A yell from the middle of the camp, one word coming through clearly, Samatar. The clamor grew. Gwen didn't have to ask. She knew he'd died. The man nearest her stepped forward and raised an open hand. As he swung his arm down, she didn't flinch. She raised her chin and let his five fingers catch her across the cheek. No one had hit her like that before, no one had ever hit her at all. The slap knocked her head sideways and tears sprang to her eyes, but she didn't raise a hand to stop him —

Thank you, sir, may I have another —

As they pulled her up and dragged her away.

She sat on the ground inside Wizard's hut, legs crossed in a parody of a yoga pose, the skin of her cheek red and bruised, a separate mark for each finger. They were alone. A plug of miraa big as Gwen's fist filled Wizard's mouth, but his eyes were half closed in exhaustion. "What happened?"

She told him. Outside, the rain drummed on the hut's straw roof.

"You did this? Why didn't you listen to me?"

"You could have let us go last night, Wizard. You want me to think we're friends?" She was furious, these men playing in the dirt like boys in a sandbox, but the guns and bullets real. At least Wizard had an excuse.

"Your friend, what does he want?" His voice was barely louder than a whisper.

"Let us go."

"Where."

"I don't know. Back to Dadaab."

"After he killed my man."

"Well, you killed Scott."

"The mzungu."

"He had a name. Scott."

"He killed one and I killed one," Wizard said.

"He'll kill the one in the hut, too. The mechanic?"

"Yusuf? Then he'll have no hostage."

"He'll have me and Hailey. He'll shoot us and then himself. Leave you with nothing." Gwen wasn't sure that Wizard believed Owen would hurt her. She wasn't sure she believed it either. But she was out of cards to play.

"You think your friend will kill you."

"Why not? He's desperate."

Wizard closed his eyes. When he reopened them, he seemed calm. "How old are you, Gwen?"

The question was so unexpected that she needed a few seconds to remember. "I just turned twenty-three. Couple weeks ago."

"Older than me. But I know something you don't."

"You know lots I don't."

"People want to live. Do anything to live. Walk across a desert with no shoes, no food or water. Leave behind their sons and daughters, fathers and mothers. Crawl when they can't walk any longer. Crawl on their hands and knees and blind. You and your friend and the other girl, you might get free tomorrow. You tell me you desperate."

"We're not desperate enough for you, Wizard?"

He didn't seem to recognize the sarcasm. "No. You know what I should do to you?" He leaned down and pulled the knife strapped to his leg. He held it up so she could see the way the weak lantern light pooled on the serrated blade. He twisted it back and forth like a snake dancing.

Gwen shook her head, *no no no.*

"Should cut your clothes off, tell your friends that unless they come out right now I'm going to let every one of my men take a turn with you. Show them what desperate means."

"Please."

On the wall of the hut the knife's shadow loomed oversized, cartoonishly large. "You know that not even three hours ago, someone, an Arab, he offered a million dollars for you. Cash. Said he would pay tonight." He nodded at her as if daring her to disbelieve him.

"So are we going with this man? This Arab?"

"I said no. Man gon' hurt you. Make a vid of you." Wizard swiped the blade sideways, lazily, a neck-cutting motion. "I told him I send you back to America, back to your families."

"Why?"

He jabbed the knife at her and she fumbled backward, screaming, shrieking, "No, please —"

He tucked the blade into its sheath, sat back. Her crotch was warm and soaked, and she realized she'd peed herself. Shame on shame.

"You think I hurt you? I never hurt you. That's for letting my man die. Not telling me so I could stop it. Making me a fool. Now you have a choice. Stay here or go back to your friends."

She thought of staying. Then was ashamed she'd even considered. "Back."

"Back, then. Long as you like. You try to escape, we'll kill you. But not while you stay inside."

"What about Yusuf?"

Wizard shook his head. "I can't send more men after him. Lost too many already."

"I won't let Owen —"

"If you say so. When your friend gets tired, he puts down his rifle and the three of you walk out."

"That's it. No other punishment."

Wizard's skin was smooth, but his eyes were heavy, careworn. Old. "Don't you see. I need money for you, yes. Have to have it. But I want you gone as much as you want to be free."

22

Lower Juba Province, Somalia

Wells rested against a sloppy mud wall, his face kissed with rain. He was as alone as Adam without Eve. Though he was sure that the Garden of Eden was nowhere close.

He'd crossed the border more than an hour before. No fence marked it, but a few minutes after riding out of camp, he'd noticed rusted lengths of barbed wire that must once have sectioned the land, must once have meant the edge of something. The Kenyans had given up the chase. Wells hadn't seen their lights since leaving camp. He was happy to have lost them, though he hoped they didn't take out their anger on Wilfred.

The rain started as he left camp. At first Wells welcomed it. The day had filthied him with dirt and gasoline and blood from two species. He smelled worse than Tolkien's foulest troll, looked like a refugee from the end of the world. Even in Afghanistan, after weeks without a bath, he'd never reeked so badly. The storm came as a relief.

But the rain kept coming, soaking his shirt and jeans, dripping down his chest. He could hardly see. The parched earth turned to mud that sucked at his tires and forced him to creep in second gear. The good news was that the low clouds muffled the engine.

A half hour after crossing the border, Wells spotted three dim lights on a hill to the northeast, the first evidence of human habitation he'd seen in Somalia. He was too far off to hear voices or generators. He cut the engine, waited. But the lights didn't move or flicker and after five minutes he rode on, doglegging southeast. After another half hour, he checked his GPS. It showed him about twenty miles east of the border, and farther south than he'd expected. The ground was softening under his tires, and not just from the rain. Wells feared he had nearly come to the swamps that stretched from the Indian Ocean. He had only the vaguest idea of this land. His GPS was civilian rather than military, so it had almost no data on Somalia, just the broad outlines of Mogadishu and the other coast cities. Swamps weren't his favorite topography. Mountains had their dangers, but they were cold and clean, no snakes or gators or quicksand.

Wells saw a wide puddle ahead, rain splashing into open water, and decided to turn northeast and look for a place to call Shafer. After a couple minutes, he saw an L-shaped section of cracked mud wall, the remnants of an abandoned hut. He stopped, reached for his phone. Two-fifteen a.m. He was supposed to see Little Wizard's men at the border in fifteen minutes. He'd never intended to make the meeting. He'd set it because he wanted Wizard to send men to a place where the drone could find them. When he failed to show, they would return to their camp. The Reaper would follow them. He'd follow it. Simple as bread crumbs. The weather didn't matter. The Reaper's thermal-imaging systems and radar could see through walls.

"John."

"Ellis."

"Location."

Wells gave it.

"Awful far south."

"I'm aware. What are you seeing?"

"Five men. Two on their bellies, covering from a hill to the north. They were there when we got on station. Fifteen minutes ago, a pickup drove up, parked fifty meters east of the border. Two guys in the cab, a third lying down in the bed. Simple setup, but professional under the circumstances. Nobody's moving too much."

"Weapons?"

"The cloud cover's got us stuck on radar and therms, not optics. It's tough to tell for sure, but we think AKs only. I'd say they have orders to bring you in. Not shoot you."

"Anyone come from the Kenyan side?"

"No. We did pick up three vehicles maybe five km west of the border. Not moving. You clean?"

"Think so."

"It would be best if the Kenyans didn't get more involved."

"If they were going to get more involved, they would have already. You'll let me know when Wizard's guys go home?"

"I'll call you. But if I were you, I would start heading north. They're north. You a hundred percent sure you want to do it this way? That SOG team will be in Mombasa in a few hours. And the SEALs would be glad to join the fun."

"You gave me tonight, Ellis."

"Ever consider that getting our friends in uniform involved would tie Vinny down?"

Shafer had a point. Duto was oddly bipolar on these high-risk ops. Sometimes he liked belt-and-suspenders protection, presidential findings, memos from the Office of Legal Counsel. But every so often he liked to run off the books, in the dark, do what he thought best with nobody watching. What was best for him might not be best for Wells.

"I have the advantage of being here."

"Don't forget he gets to be most of the way there, too. Without getting killed if something goes wrong."

"Fear the Reaper, you're saying."

"I bet myself you'd say that."

"Glad you won. Vinny watching now?"

"No. But he wants to come down, I can't stop him. His house, his rules."

"Call me when you have that location, Ellis." Wells hung up without saying goodbye. He was tired of Shafer's wisdom.

He leaned back against the wall and thought of Anne. He wanted to hear her voice. They hadn't talked since he landed in Nairobi. But he had to move, and anyway, he still felt guilty for what had happened at Castle House. He didn't deserve to hear her tell him everything would be okay.

He mounted up and rode north. He wondered if the hostages had any idea that tens of millions of people were hoping they'd be saved. Probably not. Wells hoped they were being held together. At least they wouldn't be lonely.

His phone buzzed forty minutes later. "It worked," Shafer said. "They went back to camp."

"Where?"

"Where are you?"

Wells pulled his GPS, gave his location. "You closed the gap but they're still about eighteen, nineteen kilometers north-northeast. Shouldn't have gone so far south."

"Nothing I love more than twenty-twenty hindsight. What's the setup?"

"Big camp. My guy estimates sixty to one hundred soldiers. Until the clouds break enough for us to use optics, it'll be hard to know for sure. And unfortunately, the weather guys say the storm is stuck for at least two, three hours."

"Weather guys?"

"Got drones, got to have weather guys. Anyway, the camp runs basically east-west. Uncultivated land all around. Probably living off what they steal from convoys. There's a hill east of the huts and past that several vehicles, pickups and technicals mostly, behind a high wall. Well designed, tough to spot except from above."

"They have generators?"

"If they do, they're not running them. We're picking up very little noise. Lot of guys awake, though. Plus sentries —"

"How many?"

"We count seven. One west, one south, the others north and east. The whole camp is oriented to the east. There's also a cluster of men and vehicles several kilometers northeast. Not sure who they are or if they're connected with the camp."

"Define 'cluster.' "

"Maybe forty. And growing."

"No lights, lots of guys awake, sentries, another group massing nearby. Sounds like they're on combat footing."

"How it looks to us, too."

"Fantastic." Though Wells couldn't pretend to be surprised.

"Any guess where the hostages are?"

"It'd be normal in this situation to keep them in the center of camp, near HQ."

"Right."

"If you're going to do this, your best bet is to come from the southwest. Easier to hide. East, there's that ridge above the vehicles. A guy's posted there and he's going to see you coming. But whichever way, you've got to get in quick. You have less than three hours of darkness left."

"And there's only one sentry to the south?"

"Correct. Looks like he's in a static post because of the rain, maybe six hundred meters south of the western edge of the camp. I checked the topo and there's a route along a streambed that'll take you within two hundred meters before he sees you. I'll give you the waypoints. Get to him, take him out, you can get nice and close before anyone sees you, one hundred meters from camp."

Not for the first time, Wells found himself awed by American war-fighting technology. The United States spent almost as much on its military as the rest of the world combined, but it got what it paid for. No wonder the Taliban had been forced to depend on suicide bombs. How else could anyone fight an enemy that had the advantage of an extra dimension?

"Give me the waypoints, the coordinates for the camp and sentry posts. Also that cluster of guys to the northeast." Wells entered the figures into his GPS and saw a cluster of white dots north of his current position, which was marked in blue. He hadn't been sure how best to use the Reaper's firepower. He didn't want to panic the Somalis into hurting the hostages. But as he visualized the camp's layout he had an idea.

"The garage is east, yes?"

"Yes, but forget about stealing a pickup and taking off with the hostages. It's too well guarded."

"Not what I'm thinking." Wells explained.

"That might work. At least it'll get them moving the wrong way. Keep the body count down, too."

"You're not arguing? We must really be short on time."

"Two hours and fifty minutes to daylight."

"The Reaper okay for gas?"

"You mean, how long can it stay on station?" Shafer passed along the question. "Seven hours. Plenty of time for you to be a hero."

Wells didn't have to ask if Shafer was being sarcastic. They both knew what Shafer thought of this plan. If Wells was still in Somalia in seven hours he'd most likely be a prisoner. Or a corpse.

"Good news is it has a full payload," Shafer said. "Four Hellfires, two laser-guided bombs, five-hundred-pounders. Blast radius on those is at least fifty feet, by the way. Within twenty-five they're lethal."

"Then I hope you won't drop them if I'm within twenty-five."

"We'll do our best."

"I'll call you when I'm ready."

"Good luck."

"Forget luck. Just keep circling."

Shafer's route sent Wells along a two-foot-deep streambed. At midnight it had been dry. Now it was full of muddy water topped with a roiling white scrim. Despite the time pressure, Wells kept the engine nice and quiet as he closed, no more than twenty-five hundred revs per minute. Wells had set the GPS to warn him when he reached a kilometer of the sentry post. With no way to check until he was on top of it, he had no choice but to assume that Shafer had given him the right position. When the alert came, he ditched the bike, dug his hands into the earth, closed his eyes, and sopped mud across his face. Poor man's camouflage. He strapped his night-vision monocle over his right eye and clicked it on. He took a few tentative steps to make sure he was seeing properly, putting together the flat green panel in front of his right eye with the three-dimensional world before his left. When he was sure he was ready, he loosened the strap on his AK, moved north, the mud tugging at his boots. He acutely felt the pressure of encroaching daylight. Once the sun rose, the Reaper's advantages would be neutralized. Wells wouldn't be the all-powerful commander with an invisible army and the gift of night vision. He'd be a crazy mzungu with a dirty face and a beat-up AK.

Wells followed the streambed as long as he could, hoping it might loop around the hill and the sentry completely. The cover here was better than he'd expected, thicker scrub than on the Kenyan side of the border, probably because there were so few sheep or goats grazing it away. After a few minutes, he came over a rise and ducked low. He spotted two poles two hundred meters away with a piece of tarp strung between them. The sentry's cover, such as it was. Where the hill flattened to the right, he saw a single faint light. All right. He'd found the camp. He'd found Gwen and Hailey and Owen. They were so close he could almost yell to them. So close that when the sun rose, he might be able to see them. But he and they needed to be gone before then.

Wells had figured he'd kill the sentry and push to the edge of camp before he called Wizard. But he didn't have a silencer, so he'd have to use a knife on the guy. Which meant crawling to hand-to-hand range. Even with the goggles he'd need at least fifteen minutes. He needed a faster move. He needed a distraction.

He pushed himself down into the mud, reached for his phone.

"I'm here. Can you hit the target we talked about in five minutes?"

"Hellfire or bomb?" Shafer said.

"Bomb."

"That's one five-hundred-pound GBU special delivery. Your order will be ready in five minutes," Shafer said.

"Roger that."

"Over and out."

23

Another new number on the screen of Wizard's mobile, the longest he'd ever seen. He let the call go. He couldn't talk to anyone else. Too many men wanted these wazungu. He couldn't fight them all. He'd pushed his juju too far. He'd forgotten his name. *Little* Wizard.

Yet he knew, too, that he couldn't let the wazungu go, not without getting something for them. He would die with them first. Not only because he needed the ransom money to fight the Ditas. Not only because giving them up would cost him the White Men. Because they belonged together. Magic or fate or Allah had brought them here. Wizard was captive as much as captor. And his hostages had a hostage of their own.

He didn't want to die. He didn't want his men to die. He didn't even want the wazungu to die. If he could find a way out, he would. But he wasn't letting these three leave for nothing while he waited for the Ditas to attack. They were all in it now.

The phone rang again. Muhammad's number. Which meant the American. Wizard wondered what excuse the man might offer for missing the meeting. He half expected the man to lie, say he'd been there.

"Where were you?"

"English, please," the man said. "You forget I don't speak your language."

"Of course you don't," Wizard said in English. "Where were you? I sent men for you."

"Decided to come to you instead. Service with a smile."

"I told you last time, I don' tell you where I live."

"You don't have to. I found you."

"Lying."

"You know where you keep all those pickups and technicals?"

"Talking nonsense."

"Past the hill where you have the sentry."

How could this man know the camp's layout? Not just the trucks, but the watchman, too.

Wizard didn't reply, waited for what the mzungu would say next.

"Ever heard the term 'collateral damage,'

Wizard? Make sure nobody's standing too close to those technicals. You understand?"

"Crazy."

"You may feel differently in a minute." The man hung up.

Wizard stepped out of his hut, waved Waaberi over.

"Nothing new," Waaberi said. "Yusuf groaning in there like he hurt. Some boys mad about Samatar, saying we should go in there and get them wazungu. Say it past time to kill the one and take the others."

Wizard didn't have to ask which one they wanted to kill, or what Waaberi meant by "take." "That don't happen, Beri. They get hurt, they no good for ransom. Anybody touches them answers to me."

"You say so."

Waaberi spoke out of the corner of his mouth, sullen. They both knew he'd told Wizard that the hostages ought to be locked up, or at least handcuffed. Wizard wondered how many more mistakes Waaberi would let him make.

"Omar or anyone walkie-talkie from out east, Beri?"

"Last check an hour ago. They all clicked in fine. Since then, nothing. You think the Ditas moving?"

"Could be." Wizard turned to look for

Shiny Khalid, ask him if anyone could have followed him back from the border —

To the east, an explosion busted open the night. The earth shook. A gust of flame spurted above the hill at the edge of camp. It bloomed high and flared out in the rain. The camp was silent for a second, shocked, the only noise the fire chafing behind the hill. Then a windmill of motion. Boys ran from their huts in underclothes and socks, yelling: *The Ditas coming . . . Shabaab found us . . . Got to be the Americans. Saying we terrorists. Gon' kill us all . . .*

Wizard saw his men were close to melting down, disappearing into the scrub. How could they keep their courage when they didn't even know what they faced? Until tonight Wizard had convinced them to think of themselves as an elite fighting force. His truest magic. That illusion was fading at the worst possible moment.

"Listen! Now!" Wizard raised his hands. First the Donkeys and then the rest formed a loose half-circle. Even now, twenty or more wore white T-shirts that stuck to their skinny bodies in the rain. The sight gave Wizard hope. "You all listening?"

"We listening," they grumbled.

"Then listen. Thunder and lightning don't scare White Men."

"That no thunder and lightning —" Shiny Khalid said. "That a missile."

Coward. "Whatever it is, we take care of it together. Like always. Ali and me, we going to check this out. Waaberi, watch the wazungu. Everyone else, weapons ready, but into your huts. Nobody goes anywhere until I say. Whether it five minutes, ten minutes, an hour, nobody. Been much much noise tonight, and it stops now. Done?"

"Done and done," they said. Some more loudly than others.

Wizard didn't run. He wanted his men to feel his confidence. He walked. Past the latrines and up the hill. He found disaster. Three of his four technicals were destroyed, blown apart, fires greasing their steel bodies. The stench of burning gasoline hung over the hill. The flames were cooking machine-gun rounds, sending them sizzling and popping into the night. The Rovers were parked apart from the other vehicles and hadn't been damaged. Yet Wizard hardly cared. He loved the Rovers, sure, but his men couldn't fight the Ditas without the technicals and their heavy machine guns.

He turned to the sentry on the hill, Donkey Junior. "Anybody hurt?"

"No. All out there." He pointed east, beyond the flames.

"What you see?"

"Didn't see nothing. No rocket trail. Just a —" Junior whistled. "Then boom, and the technicals go sideways." Junior grinned. He was young enough and dumb enough to think of this attack as cool.

"Only one whistle? One explosion?"

"Only one. A big one. Whole hill shake."

So a bomb, not a missile. A missile could come from anywhere. Even Shabaab had a few. But a bomb had to be dropped from a plane. Which meant the Americans had a drone or a jet overhead. Probably a drone. Wizard would have heard a jet. He could no longer doubt that the Americans had found him. He wondered how. Maybe all the phone calls.

As if the American could read his mind, his phone rang again. This devil. Wizard stepped away from Junior and Ali. He knew the drone might be watching, ready to blast him. He answered anyway.

"You see."

"I'll kill you. Coward."

"You're hurting my feelings, Wizard."

"Hiding in Kenya. Come here, I show you how to fight. Cut you up."

"I told you I'm here."

"I don' believe you."

"Then get yourself to the other side of the

camp. The southwest corner. Sentry there will tell you different."

The man hung up, leaving Wizard cursing. He snapped his phone away. "Come on. Going to Two-Finger Hussein."

Ali turned to walk back down the hill toward camp.

"No." Wizard couldn't face more questions from Waaberi. The best alternative to walking through was a footpath three-quarters of a kilometer south that paralleled the camp for its entire length.

"Ditas out there, Wizard."

"Now, Ali." Wizard tapped Donkey Junior's shoulder.

"Me, too?"

"You got nothing left to watch."

They marched single-file through low scrub, Wizard leading, moving as fast as he could without running. The rain had picked up again and his feet sank into the mud. Water sopped through Wizard's T-shirt and khakis and even snuck into his black leather boots. He'd bought them in a market in Garissa months before after a successful smuggling run, winding up with a packet of thousand-shilling notes too thick to fit in his pocket. Everything had seemed easy that day. Now he was slogging through a storm, his technicals burning. He couldn't even imagine what he'd find ahead. He kept his hand on the butt of his pistol.

He had a flashlight but he didn't bother to use it. He knew each twist of this path. He'd walked the land around here too many times to count. He wondered if the drone was tracking him. He wanted to believe it had dropped its bomb and flown off. But most likely it was circling in the clouds, waiting and watching. Donkey Junior might think that Wizard's juju could stop a bomb big enough to blow up three technicals at once. Wizard knew better.

Ten minutes. The path rose. Wizard saw the tops of the two poles, the ragged tarp between them. But Hussein, the sentry, was gone. He raised a palm, stopped. He squatted low and crab-walked ahead a few meters and whistled, a single short note. No answer. Again. He heard rustling and grunting from under the tarp. He stepped forward and saw a man who might have been Hussein. The sentry's body twisted side to side. His arms were tied behind his back, his legs pulled together, his head cut off —

Head cut off? No. Yet Wizard saw it for himself, a body with no head and still moving. No wonder the man had killed Muhammad and the other three so easily. He was a true-born devil. He'd made a zombie of Hussein. Wizard went to his knees, drew his pistol, gripped it in both hands to hide the shaking.

Ali came beside him and Wizard pointed his pistol at the zombie. Ali fell to his knees and mumbled the Shahada, the Muslim creed: *There is no God but Allah, and Muhammad is his messenger . . .* About the only Arabic that Wizard knew. He joined with Ali, for all the good the words might do.

Donkey Junior stepped forward. "What you doing?"

"Hush."

"How come we don't get him? Get that hood off him."

Soon as Wizard heard the word, he knew Junior was right. The American had cuffed Hussein's arms and legs together, thrown a hood on his head, which was on top of his neck where it belonged. Wizard's imagination had tricked him. Too much had happened this night.

"What you think, he don't have a head?" Junior said. "How he goin' move like that with no head?"

"Shut your mouth. You two stay here. Donkey, you cover me. Ali, you watch down the hill."

He stood, walked to Hussein straight and

true. If the American was close enough to pop, Wizard would take his chances. He died, maybe Ali or Donkey Junior would revenge him. Anything would be better than feeling so foolish. This man killing his soldiers, bombing his technicals, now showing up here, playing with him. Had to stop.

Hussein's wrists and ankles were cuffed with thin strips of plastic. His AK lay beside him, the magazine gone. Wizard sliced Hussein's legs free, flipped him onto his back, sat him up, pulled off his hood, not too gently. Hussein's eyes bulged. "Wizard." His voice was raspy and soft, like it hurt him to talk. *"Hamdulillah"* — thanks be to God — "it's you, this man come from nowhere and choke me, I wake up with a hood on me, can't hardly breathe —"

Wizard squeezed Hussein's cheeks to shut him up. "Some sentry. Can't see a white man in the middle of the night."

"I hear the explosion, look back a second —"

"A second —"

"His hands around my neck and I can't do nothing. He bigger than Ali, strong, move quick —"

Wizard wanted to pull his pistol, shoot the sky from frustration. He'd only be wasting rounds. He grabbed Hussein's arms, pulled him up, cut his hands free. "Go on back to camp. Tell Waaberi we over here, we back soon." He shoved Hussein toward the huts, turned, looked out into the night. The mzungu was out there. Close. Wizard scanned down the hill to the south, left to right, east to west, looking for motion, white skin, anything. He turned, looked back to camp. The mzungu would need big courage to hide there, so close to the enemy. But this American seemed to do what he liked.

Wizard didn't see him. The rain was too hard, the night too dark.

He wasn't even surprised when his phone chimed.

"You see me, Wizard? 'Cause I see you."

Wizard would have blown the whole hill up, and himself with it, to make this voice in his ear go away.

"I gon' find you."

"Holding your pistol, wearing that black T-shirt. How come you wear black and all your men wear white? That a racial thing?"

"Say all you like, mzungu. Don' change I got something you want."

"Let them go. Get back to smuggling sugar, whatever. This is too big for you."

"You joking. I let them go, that bird drop an egg and no more Wizard."

"Let them walk, you can disappear. Your men, too. I promise."

Wizard raised a hand to the sky. "Mzungu promises worth not even one drop of rain."

"I could have put that bomb in the middle of your camp. I could have killed that sentry. I could open up on you right now. I'm keeping the body count down."

"Should have, then."

"I know you want to get them to their families, Wizard. I know they're not for sale to the highest bidder."

"How you know that?"

"Doesn't matter. What matters is that I'm your best chance. In twelve hours, this will be nothing but rubble. I can save you, but you have to let them go."

"You can't save me, mzungu. You think you see, but you don't see nothing. They killed one my men."

Pause. "Who killed who? And how?"

"Tried to run tonight, attacked they guard."

"You would have done the same."

"My soldiers see it different."

"Who's in charge? You or them?"

Wizard couldn't figure what to make of this man. "Talking peace now. After you killed four my men?"

"Self-defense."

"This talk talk talk. I need money. Ransom. No more talk. I want to see you now. Or else I go back to my hut, wait for you to attack. Everybody got to die sometime."

"If I come out. You won't shoot me."

Wizard felt his lips spread into a smile. "Gon' have to take that chance, mzungu."

24

Wells lay prone eighty meters from the sentry post, covered in dirt soft and sticky as toffee. Through his night-vision monocle, he saw Wizard peering down the hill. Wells wasn't worried. Even with a scope, seeing him through the rain and the scrub would be tough. Without it, Wizard had no chance, not as long as Wells stayed still.

His plan had worked. He had judged Wizard as a young, reckless commander who would want to see what had happened to his sentry firsthand instead of staying in camp. Wizard had obliged. And for whatever reason, he'd brought only two men with him. Now, even downslope, Wells had a huge tactical edge. Thanks to the scope, he could take out the three Somalis while they shot blindly into the dark. The men in camp would hear the firefight. But before they could respond, Wells would retrace his steps to the dirt bike a few hundred meters south.

In the darkness and confusion, he could easily outflank his pursuers, enter the camp from the northwest.

A perfect plan. Just one problem with it. By the time Wells reached the camp, Gwen and Hailey and Owen would be dead. A few minutes before, after the Reaper dropped its bomb and Wells choked out the sentry, Wells called Shafer for an update. Neither man needed to comment on the irony of the fact that Shafer, halfway across the world, had the better view of the camp and the technicals.

"At first it looked like panic, guys running everywhere. Then they clustered up. I'm guessing your man gave a pep talk. A bomb would have taken most of them out. My pilot figured three-quarters KIA or seriously wounded."

"Leaving the other quarter to skin Gwen alive."

"Why we gave peace a chance. What's your next move?"

"Hunker down, get him to come to me. He'll see that I'm here, what the Reaper's done. Now that he knows what he's up against, he should want a deal."

"And if not?"

"And if not, I'll take him out."

■ ■ ■ ■

Wells had been half right. Wizard found the sentry right on schedule. But he wasn't ready to bargain. Not at all. And Wells feared that the camp was close to anarchy. The attempted escape had changed the mood of Wizard's men. They were furious that these wazungu had killed one of their own. If Wells killed Wizard, they might tear the hostages apart.

Wells saw only one option. To give up his ideal tactical position. To come to his feet, throw down his weapon, and put himself in the tender hands of a Somali warlord whom he'd been taunting most of the night. Shafer and Anne would tell him he was mad to surrender voluntarily. They'd tell him to back off, wait for the Deltas or Duto's team to show.

But Wells didn't think he could afford to wait. The situation was too unstable. Plus Wizard had already demonstrated a kind of good faith. He'd refused to sell the hostages to the Arab, made sure his men didn't punish them for killing their guard. Now he sounded under his bluster like a man looking for a way out. A face-to-face meeting might convince him. Wells hit redial on his phone. Through the scope he saw Wizard shake his head, a *what now* gesture. Wells thought he might not answer. Then he did.

"I'm downhill from you. Almost straight south. Less than a hundred meters."

Wells saw Wizard's head tilt as he tried to see in the dark.

"I'm going to stand and put my hands in the air. Do me a favor, don't shoot me."

Wells clicked off, reached out to push himself up. Then stopped.

In his night-vision viewfinder, a stick was twisting across the hill above him, maybe seventy feet up. It hadn't been there a few seconds before. It pulled itself into an S-curved shape, turned toward Wells.

Not a stick. A snake.

Wells kept still as it slithered his way, expecting that it would turn, change course. He couldn't tell if it had any idea he was there, if it smelled him or sensed the heat of his body or saw him with its beady little eyes, but it headed directly for him, sliding under the bushes and along the muddy earth, long and sinuous and moving faster than he expected. When it was about twenty feet away, Wells saw it with his uncovered eye. Six feet long, not much thicker than a rope, with a narrow head and brilliant bright green scales, nearly neon in their intensity. Wells didn't understand the coloring, it seemed impractical, but he had bigger problems at the moment. He knew nothing about African snakes, had no idea whether this one was poisonous. Best to assume it was.

His phone buzzed. Wizard. No doubt wondering why Wells hadn't stood. Wells didn't want to answer, but he feared if he didn't, Wizard would shoot blindly down the hill and upset the snake. Wells brought the phone to his ear an inch at a time. The snake seemed to sense the motion. It stopped, shifted its green head side to side. It was no more than ten feet from Wells now, close enough for him to see that scales on its belly were lighter, a washed-out greenish white.

"No more tricks, mzungu. Get up."

"There's a snake." Wells barely breathing the words. Before him, the snake spread its jaws, displaying two stubby fangs.

"Snake?"

"Bright green."

Wizard said something in Swahili. Then, in English: "That a mamba. Bad poison. Don' move, man." He hung up.

Wells held himself just so, willing his breath to slow. The mamba lowered its head and slithered toward Wells, so close now that he could hear it rustling over the mud. It moved with a surprising elegance, a single sleek motion, no wasted energy from arms and legs. Wells seemed to remember that snakes were naturally frightened of humans and preferred smaller prey. But what if it saw him too late, or rubbed against him, and felt threatened?

He closed his eyes, hoping the darkness might relax him, quiet his breathing. It didn't. He needed to see where the mamba was going, what it was doing. When he opened his eyes, it was hardly a foot from him, a green jewel in the night, so close he could make out each scale on its head. Its forked black tongue slid from the tight slit of its mouth and flicked up and down, like a judge about to pronounce a guilty verdict.

Wells's pulse thudded through his neck. Yet some part of him couldn't help but be impressed with this unfathomable, beautiful creature. Such a tiny brain, and yet it survived. A purely instinctual beast. It felt hunger, thirst, pain. Possibly fear. But no pity or anger, no joy or love. What could it make of him? It had to know he was here. This close it would sense the warmth of his body.

The mamba flicked its tongue one last time and zipped to his left, under his arm.

Wells thought it might touch him, brush his cheek. He feared his control would break if it rubbed his face. But it slithered by —

Then turned and slid across his back, over his shirt, a living rope pulsing over him, only his thin wet cotton shirt between its scales and his skin. He imagined a bad gangster movie: *Nobody moves, nobody gets hurt.* What if the snake decided it liked the warmth of his body and coiled up on his back? The ultimate nightmare. Instead the snake slid off, rustled into the night.

Wells waited a few seconds and then turned himself carefully onto his left side and watched the mamba slither away through the viewfinder. When it disappeared, he pushed himself up, pulled on his pack. He unstrapped his AK and held it over his head as he walked up the hill. He tried not to wonder whether the mamba had friends in the vicinity.

Above him, Wizard yelled in Somali. The other two men stood and put their rifles on him as Wizard walked to meet him. "Put the AK down in the mud, we got plenty more."

Wells did. Wizard stopped a few steps away. He was short, with wary eyes and the lithe muscles of a gymnast. He had a pistol strapped to his hip, a knife sheathed to his calf.

"The pack, too. Take it off, I carry it." Again Wells complied. "You the American."

"Name's John. You're Wizard."

"That is so. Little Wizard."

"Came a long way to see you, Little Wizard."

"Almost didn't make it. You one lucky mzungu. Them green mambas put a bite in you, you get all swelled up, can't breathe." Wizard bent his head forward, snapped his jaws together.

"Can we stop talking about the mamba?"

"Pretty, though. What is it you want from me?"

A tickle ran across Wells's calf. He looked down, half expecting the snake to be curled around his legs. "Any chance we can get inside?"

They trudged toward camp, and Wells felt the full weight of the last three days. Even at forty a man could rise to his youthful heights in bursts — forty-year-old point guards and quarterbacks played in the pros — but Wells was past forty now. He was in great shape, but every mission left him more deeply spent. He walked carefully, conserving his strength for this last phase.

As they neared camp, Wells drew on his last reserves to make himself stand up taller, walk faster. He wanted Wizard's men to think of an emissary from the outside world, here to give them the choice of freedom or death. Not their captive.

He saw dozens of soldiers standing in the rain, waiting around the western huts. They had AKs and RPGs, and most wore their white T-shirts. Wells couldn't guess what they made of him, though one tall man pointed and laughed. "What's he saying?"

"That you almost as black as me."

Wells scraped a line of mud from his face. He was caked in it. His forearms itched, too, thanks to a dozen mosquito bites. The rain had brought them out and he'd been a perfect target lying in the mud.

At the edge of camp, several men watched a hut. "Mind if I say hi to Gwen?" Wells turned toward the men. Wizard grabbed his elbow, marched him along. Wells didn't argue. He'd found out what he needed to know. The hostages were inside.

Wizard's hut was clean and spare and most of all dry, with a cot and a wooden chest. Wizard turned on an electric lantern. A man brought in two rough-hewn wooden stools and a plastic bag filled with leaves. Wizard took the bag, offered it to Wells.

"Miraa."

"No, thanks."

"The girl with the white hair, she takes miraa." Wizard stuffed his lip with leaves.

"Gwen?"

"Yes. Gwen." Wizard smiled. He liked her, Wells saw. Was that why he'd refused to sell the hostages to the Arab?

"Is she all right?"

"All three of them, sure, 'til they kill my man. Now we got them pinned up with one more my men."

"They have a hostage?" No wonder the camp felt so unsettled.

"They not going anywhere unless I say. How you find me, mzungu?"

"The drone tracked your men from the border."

"Tricky. Then it bomb my trucks."

"That's right."

"It still here?"

"Yes. One for now. More coming."

"But you alone."

"The CIA, the Army, they know I'm here. In a few hours, they'll have helicopters here." Wells wasn't sure whether he was lying or not. Duto and Shafer knew, but whether Duto had told anyone outside Langley depended on calculations that Wells didn't presume to understand.

"And soldiers."

"Special Forces. Only thing that will stop them is if they're afraid you'll kill the hostages. That's the only reason I didn't kill you on the hill."

"Lying, mzungu. Couldn't even see me."

Wells handed over the night-vision monocle. "You couldn't see me, but I saw you."

Wizard looked through it. "Turn off the lantern," Wells said.

Wizard flicked it off and the hut was dark. "Neat toy. Mzungu magic." He flicked the lantern back on, gave the monocle to Wells, pretending he wasn't impressed.

"I promise you that right now, satellites are photographing this place, analysts are figuring out where the hostages are, planners are thinking up ways to hit you so hard it'll be over in thirty seconds. Plus, every SEAL and Delta within a thousand miles is raising his hand and begging to get in on this like a kid who doesn't want to be last pick at recess —"

Wizard spat a long stream into the dirt. "Don' know what you talking about."

"What I'm talking about, Wizard, is that this is over. However you expected to get paid, Nairobi, Mogadishu, no one will touch you. Maybe if you had a thousand fighters, big weapons, shoulder-fired missiles, the Pentagon and White House would take you seriously. If you were in Mog and had a million civilians on all sides, you'd have some leverage. But not here. Not this. Every man here is a legitimate target, and the United States will kill them all. In fact, that's probably the number-one option — hit quick, hit hard, so that you'll be too busy trying to save your own skin to shoot those three in the hut. It's what I'd do."

"Let them try. They don' scare Wizard."

Wells coughed, a wet phlegmy rumble that started low in his stomach and took too long to stop. He'd come to a land of drought and wound up drenched and sick. He wanted nothing more than to lie on the dirt, close his eyes. He knew that he'd wake burning from the inside out, skin stretched over his bones, eyes worn dry, throat clotted and chafed, and still he ached to sleep.

"Listen to me. We both know that you can yell out to your men to shoot me and I can't stop you. Maybe I take a few soldiers out, but not a whole camp. I gave up my chance to escape when I told you where I was."

"What the point."

"Point is" — another cough rose in Wells and he fought it down — "point is that if I tried to shoot my way out of here, it would be suicide. Not bravery. You try to fight the Americans, it'll be the same. Let Gwen and Hailey and Owen go. Keep me if you like — they won't send an army for me and you can ransom me back in a month when nobody's paying attention, but let them go. I know you want to get them back to their families anyway —"

"Second time you said that. How you know?"

"I was the Arab who called you," Wells said in Arabic, then in English.

Wizard grinned. And pulled a half-empty bottle of Johnny Walker Blue from his chest, the amber liquid glowing in the low lantern light.

"Plenty tricks in you, mzungu."

"I'll take that as a compliment."

Wizard handed Wells a glass.

"Are we toasting agreement?" Wells said. "You'll listen."

Wizard raised his glass. "This to thank you for letting somebody else kill me. You know I can't let them go."

At that they both drank. The scotch blistered Wells's throat and his head swam. Something deeper and darker than fatigue had come for him this night. The bites on his arms itched madly. But he hadn't been in Kenya nearly long enough for malaria or sleeping sickness to incubate. He wondered if he'd been unlucky enough to be infected with something more obscure, West Nile virus or Rift Valley fever. Whatever it was, he faced more dangerous threats in the next few hours. He forced the headache aside, focused on Wizard.

"You can trust me," Wells said.

Wizard smirked. "How many times you lie to me already? Kill my men. Now telling me, do what you say. Now, what if I foolish enough to believe you, give up these wazungu? Out there, not ten kilometers away, creeping close and close, Awaale got three hundred Ditas —"

"Ditas? Is that what you call Shabaab?"

Wizard shook his head like he couldn't believe Wells didn't know. "Not Shabaab. Dita Boys. Fighters."

"A local militia."

"Yeah, militia. Awaale tells me I don't give over the wazungu by sunrise he gon' attack me. I got not even seventy soldiers and now one technical left. If Awaale come, half my men go to him straight straight. The rest of us, he slit our throats and leave the bones for the hyenas. He want this land for *himself.* You say I got to be frightened of these Americans, but they not here. Maybe I take all you wazungu and hide away —"

"You think you can hide from the drones."

"No. You right. We gon' stay right here. Die like men. All of us." Wizard poured himself a fresh finger of Johnny Walker Blue and reached for Wells's glass. Wells covered it.

"Keep me. Gwen and Hailey and Owen didn't ask for this."

"Anyone ever ask to die, mzungu?"

Wizard's eyes glinted from the scotch, but his voice was steady and Wells knew better than to argue anymore. He wondered if he could overcome Wizard despite his fever, make a play for the hut with the hostages, but the Somali rested his hand lightly on his pistol.

"Been friends 'til now. Keep it that way."

Even if he disarmed Wizard, he'd die before he got to the hostages, and they would, too. So close and yet so far. Maybe the SEALs would arrive in time and hit the camp perfectly and they'd all live. But Wells didn't think so.

"You want something done right, you've got to do it yourself," Wells said.

"What that?"

"I said I'm going to learn plumbing when I get home. The basics, anyway. Expecting Anne to clear the drains is ridiculous. Can I have some water? There's some in my pack."

Wizard handed him a bottle. Wells forced himself to sip. He'd find a way through this night yet. He wondered how many hours he'd spent in rooms like this, huts and cells and airless apartments in the places anyone with a choice left behind. Such a strange way to spend a life, and yet he'd picked it freely.

"You Muslim, Wizard?"

"Little bit."

"That sounds about right. Me, too."

"Ditas, too, but they shoot us all anyway. They don' care what Allah think. Hey, mzungu, how come you didn't shoot me on the hill?"

"I didn't come here for you. I came here for them."

"But I tol' you on the phone no way."

"I thought I could change your mind."

"You wrong."

"Figured that out my own self." Wells leaned back against the wall of the hut, closed his eyes. He didn't expect to think of anything except the pounding in his head, but when he opened them he had a plan. He forced himself to stand, took a deep breath to clear his head. "Wizard. What if I can get rid of Awaale? Kill him. Will you let me have the wazungu?"

"No more Dita Boys?"

"I can't promise that, but with your help I can kill Awaale at least."

"And pay ransom?"

"Ransom, too. That's ambitious."

"They kill Samatar —"

"The guard."

"Yah. I need something to show my men."

And yourself. But Wells didn't argue. "There's forty thousand in the pack. In a bag at the bottom. That's all I have."

"Forty thousand shillings."

"Forty thousand dollars, give or take. Not too bad for one day's work. And I'll throw in my lifesaving idea for free."

Wizard sorted through the pack until he found the money, bundled up and dry in a Ziploc bag. "Okay. What your idea, mzungu?"

"First things first. You have a way to reach Awaale?"

25

Langley

The drone pilot was no taller than Shafer, muscled up the way short guys so often were. Like he thought he was fighting for real instead of with a keyboard. He had slick black hair combed straight back. His name was Augustine Tomaso. Shafer couldn't believe anyone outside the Old Country went for names like that anymore. He wanted to ask Tomaso, *Was there a recent wave of Sicilian immigration that I missed? Was it for a favorite uncle? Some kind of retro hipster thing? Come on, man, I have to know. And, by the way,* what's *with the hair*? He kept his mouth shut. Tomaso might look like a *Sopranos* extra, but he'd been invaluable so far.

The actual flying was the easiest part of piloting a drone. Unlike fighter jets, unmanned aerial vehicles were underpowered and designed to fly slowly and smoothly.

The Reaper's long wings gave it plenty of lift. Its onboard software rejected commands that might make it stall or spin out. Overriding the software was possible but rarely necessary. CIA and Army drones could even take off and land on their own — and they had a better safety record than Air Force drones, which pilots controlled during takeoff and landing. The gap didn't give Shafer much confidence in humanity's future.

But the pilot wasn't entirely useless. His real job was making sense of the flood of information from the drone's cameras, heat sensors, and radar. Both the drone and the computers that controlled it from the ground had software filters to process the data. But the software couldn't tell a kid holding a stick from a guerrilla pointing an AK, or a wedding party from a terrorist meeting. When three pickups filled with armed men broke off in three directions, the computers couldn't decide which was the most important to follow. Not yet, anyway. And tonight, when Wells asked for the Reaper to annihilate a row of technicals, the software didn't know that the right move after the bomb hit would be a pivot back to the center of camp to see how the White Men reacted.

"They're going crazy out there," Tomaso said. "See?"

Shafer didn't. Worse, he wasn't sure where Tomaso wanted him to look. The pilot's workstation was straight out of a Wall Street trading floor, a half-dozen computer monitors offering different feeds. The smallest screen, on the far right, replicated the altitude, speed, and heading of the drone's flight against a plain blue background. *The dummy shot,* Tomaso said when Shafer asked. *In case I get confused.* The Reaper's thermal cam fed another monitor with a smorgasbord of red and blue streaks that reminded Shafer of the worst acid trip of his life. Forty-five years ago, and his mouth still went dry to remember.

"What am I looking for?"

"They're huddling up." Tomaso pointed to a cluster of reddish shapes on the thermal cam. "If we wanted mass casualties, this would be the time. Put a bomb in there, it's seventy-five percent KIA, WIA." Tomaso knew the outlines of the mission, that the hostages were probably in the camp and an American operative was nearby, but no details.

"Not on the agenda." Not yet, anyway.

"Looks like this guy's talking." A red splotch that Shafer now recognized as a man stood in the center of the thermal cam, surrounded by dozens of similar streaks. Tomaso clicked on the man, surrounding him with a white border.

"Now, he moves anywhere, we'll go with him. It's a long shot. Let me see if I can get anything from the optical cam. Be nice to see his face." Tomaso pulled up yet another menu on another screen and ran through a series of commands. "Clouds still too thick."

The red figure grew taller. "What's that?" Shafer said.

"Raising his arms. Rousing the troops, maybe."

Shafer wondered what this man who called himself Wizard was telling his soldiers. Probably trying to calm them after the shock of the explosion. Whatever he said didn't take long. The clot of men broke up, and the white-bordered figure marched toward the site of the explosion.

"Checking out what we did to his trucks," Tomaso said. "Want me to go with him?"

"Yes."

Tomaso pulled up a menu. "I'm dialing down the therms so they don't fry the screen when we go back over there. There's an autofilter that comes on when you play Whac-A-Mole with the Hellfires or the GBUs, but I took it off when we went to the center of camp."

"You don't have to explain."

"Nah, man, I like it, it's thinking out loud. Plus I've found that above a certain age, this isn't that intuitive for people."

"What age would that be? Eleven?"

"No offense. It's easier if you've grown up with video games."

"None taken, Augustine."

Tomaso raised an eyebrow: *You're old enough to be my grandpa and you're making fun of my name? Classy.*

The Reaper's cameras turned far faster than the aircraft, so the drone flew away from the men on its screens for nearly a minute. The change in perspective made Shafer vaguely seasick. Tomaso didn't seem to mind, or even to notice. Shafer had never felt so obsolete. *Those old Mustangs were great. Pretty as anything. But they'd hardly get off the line today.*

"Okay, now they've met this third guy —"

Shafer's phone rang. Wells. Who wasn't showroom clean but still had a few years of useful life. Shafer hoped.

"You hit the trucks."

"Blew out three technicals."

"How did they react?"

"They didn't exactly muster into squads

and secure the perimeter. Lot of confusion. You're still on the southwest side."

"Correct."

"The sentry —"

"Took care of him. You looking at me?"

"No. Watching guys on the hill above the trucks. We think one's Wizard, but we can't be sure. If they come your way, we'll pick you up again. Give me your coordinates so we know exactly where you are."

Wells did. "Don't confuse me with the sentry. He's maybe eighty meters closer to camp."

"He's still alive?"

"Didn't say he was dead. Said I took care of him."

"Like a massage, you mean."

"Any read on where they're keeping the hostages?"

"Not yet."

"Tell me exactly what happened after the bomb hit."

It was then that Shafer recounted the meeting, and Wells told Shafer his plan: *Wizard should be ready to deal . . . and if not I'll take him out.*

Shafer wasn't so sure Wizard would give up the hostages, but they'd long passed the point of no return, so he didn't argue.

"What now?" Tomaso said when Shafer

hung up.

"Keep tracking the commander."

"Right. Got good news on the weather too, bro. Rain's passing within the hour. We'll have better visuals even before the sun comes up."

"Bro."

"Sign of respect."

The three shapes walked away from the fire, toward Wells. The Reaper followed and along the way made a pass over camp. "Can't be sure, but I'm guessing the hostages are in those western huts," Tomaso said. "Lot of activity over there."

Close to Wells. Maybe a lucky break. If he could take out Wizard clean and quick . . . and the Reaper's Hellfires killed the guys in the open and Wizard's lieutenants were among them . . . and Wells reached camp and found the hostages before someone put a magazine in them . . . and they escaped and the remaining White Men didn't want to risk the Reaper and decided to let them go . . . Four big ifs. Each might have a fifty-fifty shot of breaking for Wells, which meant the overall odds of a rescue were one in sixteen. Not even ten percent.

But then, Wells didn't like to play if the game was easy. He didn't want to win by twenty. He preferred the ball at his own five, down six, two minutes to go. He put himself in these situations intentionally. Though he would never own up to that truth. He was a thrill-seeking killer, a father who'd abandoned his wife and infant son, an operative who lied with ease to further his mission. He was also the bravest man Shafer had ever met. He never blamed anyone for the decisions he'd been forced to make, or asked for relief from the memories he carried. He judged himself, and his verdicts were as harsh as any the world could offer.

John Wells was awfully simple and awfully complicated.

Now Shafer saw him, or a dull reddish blotch that represented him, on the thermal screen. The three Somalis had arrived near the sentry. They all burned a brighter red than Wells.

"Why's he look so washed out?"

"Likely he's covered in mud. Dulls the heat signature." Tomaso clicked on Wells and a blue border appeared around his figure. Blue for friendly.

The Somali commander went to the sentry. A minute later the sentry stood and walked back to camp, leaving the commander and the two soldiers alone on the hill. For several minutes Wells stayed in place, downslope from the Somalis. Shafer wondered if they were yelling to one another. Or maybe Wells was waiting in silence, gauging the moment to attack.

Then a surprise. Wells stood and walked directly to the commander as the man stepped down the hill to him.

"What's he doing?" Tomaso said.

Shafer wondered, too. Without audio, he couldn't guess. No way the Somali could have seen Wells. He hadn't needed to surrender. Maybe he'd traded his own life for the hostages. Maybe Wizard had tricked him, though Shafer couldn't see how.

Wells walked toward camp, the Somalis around him. Tomaso kept the cameras on him until he entered a hut beside Wizard. "What now? Want me to look for the hostages?"

"Let's stay on the hut."

Then, disaster.

In the form of Vincent Duto, DCI. He laid his thick hand on Shafer's scrawny shoulder as Shafer stared at the screen. Shafer didn't flinch. He pinched the skin of Duto's hand until Duto released his grip.

Duto was wearing a gray suit that accentuated his shoulders and a shirt whiter than any piece of clothing Shafer had owned in his life. He looked like a politician. A winning one. "Vinny. Meet Augustine. One of your landsmen."

"What'd I miss?"

"We hit the technicals. Now Wells is in camp."

"He snuck in."

"He walked in with three Somalis."

"Captured."

"Didn't look that way," Tomaso said. "Looked like he came in under his own power."

"Come," Duto said to Shafer.

"It hurts me when you talk to me that way. Like I'm a dog."

Tomaso snorted.

"Greaser," Shafer said. "Anything happens, you find us."

"No need to take it out on him," Duto said.

"That's where you're wrong."

Duto led Shafer to an empty conference room and waved his magic director's key card to unlock the door, let them in. The high-security basement suite of offices where the drones were managed had its own dedicated air-conditioning to defeat the heat that all the computer equipment produced. Arctic jets of air swirled from a half-dozen vents and converged on Shafer's bald head.

At the far end of the room, strings of software code covered three whiteboards. The drone program had more than its share of comp sci Ph.Ds.

Duto reached into his inside suit pocket, came out with a silver-dollar-sized piece of black plastic. He laid the device on the table. A light on top flashed green and red before switching to a steady green.

"You're seriously worried someone's listening to us, Vinny? Getting paranoid."

"Why'd Wells give himself up?"

"Truth. I don't know. I'm guessing he's working out a deal."

"If he's trading himself for them, he's even dumber than I thought."

"I believe you mean braver."

"Has he said he's seen them yet?"

"Not yet."

"Okay. So I've gotten some expert advice, and as long as he doesn't tell us he's seen them with his own eyes, we're still in hearsay mode and we happy three have a free hand."

Expert advice. Which meant Duto had talked to a lawyer. Presumably to ask what he risked by not immediately telling the White House that Wells might have found the hostages. Shafer wondered if Duto had gone to the CIA's general counsel. Probably not. Probably he'd asked someone who would answer to him alone. "Inside or out?"

"You think I'd stay inside on this, you're also dumber than I thought. Justin Lerer."

Lerer had been a federal prosecutor specializing in national security and terrorism cases before leaving the government. Now he was building a reputation as the best kind of lawyer, the kind who made problems go away before they reached a judge, but who could go to court and win if necessary.

"Know what he said." Duto wasn't asking. "That if I wanted to be sure I was clear, I ought to call the White House soon as I hung up with him. I told him that I couldn't do that yet. Not until we know where John stands."

"Now you want me to believe you're worried about him."

"He deserves a chance, that's all." Duto seemed almost defensive, as if he feared that caring about Wells might be a moral failing. "He's given a lot to this place."

"You want a medal for not listening to a lawyer? Waiting a couple hours to make a call. Scared little toad. You belong in the Senate."

"Keep pushing me, Ellis, and I will call the White House. Let them take over. You want to take your chances with that?"

Shafer didn't need to answer. Wells had no use for politics, and presidents of either party rarely went out of their way to help anyone who wasn't useful to them, much less anyone who disdained their power and its trappings. Wells didn't even have the protection of celebrity any longer. After his first major mission, he'd become a public figure. But he'd done everything possible to keep his exploits private in the years since. CIA and Special Forces officers still knew his name, but civilians had forgotten. Besides, his three most recent missions weren't the type anyone wanted to remember.

So Shafer couldn't count on the National Security Advisor or anyone else at 1600 Pennsylvania caring about Wells. Whether or not they said so, they would view him as one more ex–CIA operative skulking around Africa for his own reasons. The President's men wanted the hostages back. Some of them wanted an excuse to invade Somalia, too. As for Wells, he'd have to fend for himself. Duto's history with Wells was often unhappy, but at least they had a history.

Shafer shivered, and not just from the air-conditioning.

"So when you told Justin Lerer you were striking a blow for truth and justice —"

"He gave me this fig leaf. Long as we

don't have direct eyes-on confirmation of the hostages, either from Wells himself or from the Reaper, we don't have to call the White House. It's still rumors and speculation. The fact that things are moving so fast helps. And the fact that nobody's ever heard of Wizard. And, yeah, the Reaper's up, but it's only bombed trucks."

"For this you paid eight hundred bucks an hour?"

"Eleven hundred. And worth every penny."

"I'd have to agree. He tell you how long you'd have to make the call once we do see the hostages?"

"Expeditiously, he said. I asked what that meant and he said —"

"Fast."

Duto didn't smile. "He said fifteen minutes. Which will still give your boy some time. He also said that we can't put our finger on the scales, can't tell Wells what to say. If Wells tells us he's seen them, that's it."

"So are you hanging around down here? Tell me you have a fundraiser."

Duto swung his head like a prizefighter loosening up. "No no no. I'm looking forward to spending some quality time with you, Ellis." Shafer saw that the DCI was enjoying himself. And why not? The hostages were at risk, and the United States might still wind up sending soldiers to Somalia, but Duto had protected himself neatly. As always. If everything went wrong, Duto would say Wells had insisted on going in. Duto couldn't stop Wells, so he'd ordered a drone to monitor the situation.

Duto pocketed the bug zapper, turned to the door. "Let's see if your boy can pull it off."

Shafer's phone buzzed. He didn't need to see the caller ID to know it was Wells. He didn't want to answer, not with Duto here. But Duto heard the hum. He opened his hands: *What are you waiting for?* And Shafer knew he had no choice.

26

Lower Juba Region

After Wizard dismissed Gwen, she trudged across camp, hoping the storm would wash her clean. She knew Wizard could have punished her far more brutally than he had. Still she hated him for the way he'd made her shame herself.

At the hut, she found Owen leaning against the dirt bike she'd ridden, his thumb against the starter like he wanted to see for himself how she'd messed up. The AK was still strapped across his chest, Yusuf's blood glinting off its butt. Owen didn't say a word when Gwen explained what Wizard had said. He fiddled with the rifle, his new favorite toy, flicking the safety. Like he'd known all along that Wizard wouldn't let them out. She wondered whether he'd sent her out simply to humiliate her, but she was too tired to ask.

She sat against the back wall and ran her

hands across the dirt floor, sifting the soft grit through her fingers, a strangely comforting feeling. A few feet away, Yusuf lay under the shredded motorcycle poster. A dribble of blood leaked down his face as he mumbled to himself. Gwen had brought a water bottle from Wizard's hut. She handed it to Yusuf now. "Drink."

He looked at her blankly and raised the bottle to his mouth and sipped, his lips working it like a baby's. The skin on his temple flapped loose, exposing the bright pink flesh underneath, intimate and terrible.

"What are you doing?" Owen said. "He's the enemy."

"He's scared out of his mind. We need to let him go."

"Then what leverage will we have?"

"Drop it, Owen," Hailey said. She sat near the doorway, peeking at the men guarding them. The three of them were staying as far from one another as possible, Gwen saw.

"Now you're on her side," Owen said.

"Tried your way."

"If she'd known how to ride like she said, we might be in Kenya by now —"

Gwen stopped listening. She didn't understand how Owen had turned into a man who wanted to deny this boy water. They were molting, all of them, shedding their skin and finding a rougher underlayer. Though the change had some benefits, at least for her. A week ago she would have been crying at this moment, indulging herself in the pointless luxury of tears. Instead, she wasn't even bothering to defend herself. She knew she'd done her best with the bike. She didn't care what Owen thought.

Hailey came over, sat beside her. "Truth is, he just doesn't want to admit how stupid his idea was."

"The truth is I wanted to get us out of here before —"

An explosion tore through the night to the east. The hut's walls shook. Owen grinned at her like a scientist who'd predicted the end of the world for years and finally had the thrill of seeing the cataclysmic asteroid coming. *We're all going to die, but at least I was right.* Gwen felt nearly serene, nothing like the panic that had come when Wizard raised his knife. Getting blown to bits would be quick and painless. So she hoped.

"Before something like that happened." Owen hopped off the dirt bike and looked out the doorway before striding back to her. He reeked of sweat and testosterone and mud and blood. Gwen felt a wholly inappropriate warmth between her legs. Now that he was a grade-A jerk, she wanted him? She and her libido needed to have a serious talk.

"Looks like a third-grade fire drill out there," Owen said.

"What was that?" Hailey said.

"I think it was a bomb. And I think it was one of ours. Felt too big to be anything else."

"They found us here in a day when they couldn't in Kenya for a week?"

"Maybe they've been looking for us here all along," Hailey said. "Maybe they didn't look in Kenya, they figured we had to be in Somalia."

"Which would mean Wizard did us a favor after all," Owen said.

"So why just one bomb?" Gwen said. "A warning?"

"Or they were trying to calibrate it or something," Owen said. "Either way, if the SEALs or whoever did it, they have to know we're here. And they've got to be close." He stood, put his hand over his heart. "God bless America, land that I love —"

Gwen couldn't decide if he was terrified or high on hormones and sleeplessness. "If they line us up and shoot us, how will you feel about spending your last few minutes in full jackassery?"

"They line us up and shoot us, Ah don't suspect Ah'll care." In a mock southern accent. "Let me tell you something about Wizard, Gwen. He's a moron. He thought if he got us to Somalia nobody would come for him. How's that working out?"

"You know, with Scott gone, you could have gotten some if you played your cards right," she said. "A pity lay for all those hours you spent mooning over me. From the way Scott described your equipment, it really would have been pitiful."

The cheapest of cheap shots, especially since Scott hadn't said anything of the sort. But Owen looked down at his crotch like it had betrayed him. Forget the very real risk they wouldn't see the dawn. He had a bigger worry now. Did his junk measure up?

Men.

Outside, Wizard was yelling. After he stopped, Gwen snuck to the doorway. Wizard was gone, but Waaberi and his men watched the hut from three angles. They weren't smiling. One of them, the tall one who had caught her by the latrine, saw her looking. He nodded and then slowly, distinctly, passed his fingers across his throat.

She wanted to scramble away. Hide in the corner. Last week she would have. Not now.

They would do what they would do, but she wasn't going to give them the satisfaction of knowing that they frightened her. She stared right back.

She could hear the hens clucking and the goats scraping at the mud in their pen. They'd had as long a night as everyone else. She felt the most profound fatigue she could imagine. But when she closed her eyes, they fluttered open on their own, as though her mind knew it couldn't risk sleep. So she sat against the wall, waited, as the rain lightened and the clouds thinned.

But she did sleep, she must have, because time leapt forward without her realizing, and when she opened her eyes she saw Wizard coming out of the darkness, and beside him a tall man covered in a coat of mud so thick that at first she couldn't tell if he was white or black. As he got closer she recognized him, not from his face but from the size of his shoulders and his arms. He was the white man Wizard had shown her on the cell phone the day before, in the Land Cruiser with the black guy. Gwen had asked if they were looking for her, and he'd said, *If they are, they won't be much longer.* In his cool Wizard way. But he'd been wrong about that, along with everything else.

The man didn't seem to be a prisoner. His hands were free. He wasn't hooded. Owen and Hailey stood beside her and watched as Wizard led the man to his hut.

"Maybe he's here with the ransom," Hailey said. "Maybe that pack is filled with money."

"Why they dropped the bomb, a carrot-and-stick thing," Owen said. "Luca Brasi making an offer even Wizard isn't dumb enough to refuse."

Gwen wondered what he was talking about and decided she didn't care. Behind them, Yusuf groaned. She turned just in time to see him pull himself onto all fours and vomit a stream of clear liquid.

She went to him, tucked herself under his bony left arm, straightened him up. His skin was sticky and feverish, his eyes unfocused. He stank of grease and sickness. The top of his head barely reached her chin when she pulled him to his feet. He couldn't have weighed much more than she did, which was lucky, because when she edged him from the wall, he sagged onto her.

"Hailey —"

Hailey came over, put a thumb under his chin to lift his head.

"What's wrong with him?"

"I'm more at the holding hands while the nurse gives you an ouchie level of medical expertise."

"We're getting him out of here."

"Nobody out there can do anything for him, either," Owen said.

"It's too hot in here and he's scared. We're taking him out."

Owen put a hand under his rifle. He wasn't exactly aiming it at them, but he wasn't exactly pointing it away, either.

"Planning on shooting us?" Hailey said. She came under Yusuf's right side and lifted him. Together she and Gwen walked him past Owen. He took his hand off the rifle. His mouth was notched open, like he couldn't quite believe what he'd just done.

Gwen and Hailey reached the doorway and stood with Yusuf between them. The rain had stopped now, and the clouds were lifting. A few stars shone weakly. Gwen sensed that the sun was close by, ready to banish the night.

Three White Men trotted over and took Yusuf, squawking at him in Somali. "What you do to him?" one said in English. He spat at her feet. Gwen wondered if she'd made a mistake, if Owen had been right that without Yusuf they were defenseless.

While she tried to figure out what to say, Wizard and the white man came out of Wizard's hut. Wizard shouted at his men, and they backed away from Gwen unwillingly, like dogs that didn't want to listen to their master. Owen put down the AK and stepped forward. The three of them stood side by side, a welcoming committee, as Wizard and the white man walked up to them.

"I'm John Wells. Nice to meet you." He'd washed his face, though mud still caked his clothes.

He had a low laconic voice, easy and confident. She wanted to put her arms around him and not let go. As she looked closer, she saw he was sick, shivering under his muddy clothes in the cool night air, his eyes red-rimmed. Still, she'd gladly take her chances with him.

"This man come to take you home," Wizard said.

Before Gwen could exhale, before she could exult over that word and everything it meant, Wells raised his hand. "It may not be quite that easy."

27

They looked okay, under the circumstances. About what Wells had expected. Gwen was drenched and filthy, her hair streaked with mud. Hailey's cheeks were hollow, her lips painfully chapped. They'd both lost weight. Owen seemed healthy enough, but his eyes were dark and angry, rising to meet a challenge Wells hadn't offered. Wells wondered whether Owen was remorseful for killing the guard . . . or confused because he wasn't remorseful for killing the guard. Either way, his return to civilian life would be tough.

First Wells had to get him there. Wells didn't hug any of the three, or even shake their hands. He didn't want to rile the soldiers. The volunteers might not realize, but they were lucky for the rain. Under a baking sun the Somalis wouldn't have been so patient with wazungu who'd killed one of their own.

"Come with me." Wells led them east as

Wizard walked back to the center of the compound, yelling to his soldiers, directing them into a loose circle near his hut. No one stood too close. They'd realized big groups made ripe bomb targets. Wizard ducked into his hut, came out with the bag of cash from Wells. The White Men cheered when they saw the bag, and Wizard shouted as enthusiastically as a presidential candidate in a swing state. Talking to Wells in the hut a few minutes before, Wizard had seemed exhausted, almost ready to quit. He'd made a remarkable transformation, one that made Wells nervous. A man who could swap his emotions so easily might betray the promises he made just as fast.

Wizard raised the cash over his head and his soldiers cheered again. Wells wondered if he was promising that the money was merely the first down payment on a future ransom. He pointed northeast, toward the Dita Boys.

Wells led the hostages far enough from Wizard that he wouldn't be heard. "It's good to see you three. I'm sorry about Scott, but with any luck within a couple of hours we'll be back in Kenya."

"Who are you?" Owen said.

"I used to be CIA. Gwen's family sent me. I tracked you to the camp in Kenya and then here."

"What's going on here? Who dropped the bomb?"

Wells wanted to explain the situation his own way, but he had to calm Owen. "The bomb came off a CIA-controlled drone called a Reaper that's circling the camp. We were trying to convince Wizard to let you go. He's agreed, if we'll help him with another militia leader named Awaale."

"Help? Like how?"

"Awaale has said he'll attack if he doesn't get you by the time the sun comes up. Wizard says he's got three hundred soldiers. They're called the Ditas."

"So Wizard is giving us to this guy Awaale?"

"Owen. No one's giving you to anyone. Wizard just set a meeting with Awaale. Close by. He promised to hand you over, but it's a trick to get Awaale and his men into the open so the Reaper can take them out."

"One drone can kill three hundred men?"

"Besides a bomb it's got four missiles called Hellfires. The Ditas will be clustered up and the bomb is big enough to take a lot of them out. Each Hellfire can blow up a technical — that's one of those pickup trucks with the machine guns. Wizard says

Awaale's men aren't well-trained. Once they see him get splattered, they won't hang around. And Wizard's going to attack as soon as we drop the bomb. That's what he's telling his men now."

Owen stepped close to Wells, almost chest to chest. "You obviously know he killed Scott?"

Wells nodded.

"Left his body chained to the wall to rot. We watched him do it. Then he took us. Now you're *helping* him?"

"To set you free."

"If the CIA knows we're here, why doesn't it just rescue us, make these guys lunch meat?"

"This all happened in the last few hours. The Reaper and I are all we've got right now. But my read is that trying a full-on rescue would be a mistake anyway. Wizard's men would kill you before anyone could reach you."

"Your read?"

Wells hadn't anticipated this particular difficulty, a hostage ungrateful for his rescue. He shivered, felt the sweat on his back. Fever and chills. No worries. Once they reached Kenya, he could be as sick as he liked. "I have a little bit of expertise."

Behind Wells, Wizard's shouts reached a

new pitch. Someone yelled, "Wizard!" and other voices took up the cry, "Wizard! Wiz-ARD! WIZARD!"

"What about right now," Owen said, "with them all standing around yelling? I'll bet the Deltas or whoever could rescue us right now."

Suddenly, you're an expert on close combat. Wells wanted to flatten Owen, end this nonsense. Or at least point out that if Owen hadn't killed the guard, Wizard might have agreed to let them go already. Wells made himself relax. Owen was exhausted and scared. Getting angry with him wouldn't help.

"I'll say it again. There's no team in the air right now. And if you look around, you'll see at least five guys have AKs on us. Two by Wizard" — Wells nodded over his shoulder — "two behind us. One over to your right. All close enough to kill us all with one magazine. Maybe the Air Force could bring in three or four Reapers for multiple simultaneous Hellfire strikes to take all those guys out. But the timing would have to be perfect. Then at least two Special Ops squads would have to land quick enough to kill everyone else before they got to you."

"Would that be riskier than this plan you've cooked up?"

"Having your captor let you walk is always the best alternative. I know you're mad about what happened to Scott, but I'm not interested in the highest possible body count. I want to get you out alive."

The men around Wizard cheered, a long joyous *oooh.* Wizard pointed his pistol high over his head. *Crack! Crack! Crack!* The shots echoed through the empty sky, the stars gone now, the clouds, so heavy an hour before, now wisps. The sun was still invisible, but it wouldn't be much longer. "What about justice?"

"What about Samatar, Owen?" Gwen said.

"That was an emergency —"

"I need to know that you'll do what I say," Wells said. "If not, you want to wait for your own rescue, tell me now."

"What kind of choice is that?"

"Yes or no." Like most of life's big decisions.

"Yes," Gwen said.

"Sure," Hailey said.

"Fine," Owen muttered, like the word was ash in his mouth.

The White Men, the volunteers, Wizard, and Wells walked east, past the latrines, up the hill, into the pall of smoke and gasoline from the smoldering technicals. At the top of the path, Wizard shouted. His soldiers ran for the undamaged pickups, whooping and hollering.

"You got them going," Wells said.

"Tol' them the truth. We got the secret weapon on our side, we gon' smoke Awaale once and for all. Make this whole province ours." Wizard led Wells and the hostages to the Range Rovers, hidden under a tin sunshade that was camouflaged with sticks. They were beautiful vehicles, their white paint nearly glowing. They looked like they belonged at a country club that the Somalis would be strongly discouraged from joining. Wells remembered an old British joke about Range Rovers, courtesy of none other than Guy Raviv: What's the difference between Range Rovers and porcupines? Porcupines have pricks on the outside.

Wizard clicked the key fob. The Rover's locks popped up and its alarm chirped off, an absurd and satisfying sound in the Somali badlands. When Wells pulled open the door, its weight tipped him. "Armored."

"Doors and windows." Wizard slipped into the driver's seat, Ali beside him. Wells went to the back door, but Wizard raised his hand. "Them three go with us. You in the other one."

"We stay together."

"Awaale see four wazungu, he get worried. This way you hidden. That Rover got the tints. You be right behind me. Beri driving."

"Beri?"

"Waaberi." Wizard nodded at a hard-eyed man a few steps behind them. "Been with me all the time from Mog. Trust me, trust him."

Exactly the problem. But Wells feared that if he insisted on sticking with the hostages, Wizard might call the deal off. Anyway, if he had to, he should be able to handle Waaberi.

"He knows I'll be using my phone."

"Yah."

"And you know that drone will be watching us the whole way."

"Counting on it. That magic mzungu bird. It gon' be fine, John Wells." Wizard spoke the name like it was one word, *Johnwells.*

"Drive carefully." Wells closed the armored door with a heavy *thock.* Waaberi waved him into the front passenger seat of the second Rover. Behind them sat a tall man, heavily muscled, with a scar that girdled his neck. Wells wished for his Makarov or Glock or even the AK he'd taken from the other camp, though rifles were tough to maneuver inside a vehicle. At least he had his knife, strapped to his leg. Wizard had taken his guns but never properly searched him. Sloppy.

The Rovers rolled out, mustered up with the five pickups and lone technical that had survived the Reaper's bomb. Wizard had left only a couple stragglers as camp guards. The other sixty or so men sat or stood in the pickup beds, AKs slung across their chests. They wore pristine white T-shirts and white bandannas across their faces. They poked and yammered at one another, as high-spirited as seniors tailgating on a sunny fall Saturday.

Rangers or Talibs or Somalis, men readied themselves for battle the same way. They pushed fear from their minds until the fight was so close that the frank risk of death could be ignored no longer. Then they grew grim and settled. Until the shooting started. At that moment adrenaline and fear brought them to a place that no drug could, an extraordinary 360-degree awareness that only extreme athletes like free climbers glimpsed in civilian life. They went from high to low to the ultimate high. Then crashed as the battle ended and they were left to tally wounds and deaths. No wonder some soldiers turned into junkies, for war itself and afterward for cheap chemical highs.

Wizard ordered the technical to lead the convoy, then three pickups and the two Rovers. Two more pickups brought up the rear. They rolled out slow and steady. Waaberi drove with two fingers on the wheel. The Rover was in showroom condition inside, too, its leather polished, its air-conditioning strong. It made Wells want a bath.

The sun breached the horizon, its equatorial rays turning night into day with all the subtlety of a nickel slot that had just hit triple sevens. In the light the land was flat and empty, aside from the low hills where Wizard had set his camp. The rain had left pools of muddy water that were already disappearing, shrinking into the dirt.

The convoy moved east-northeast, almost straight into the sun. Wells raised a hand to shield his eyes, wishing for his Ray-Bans. But they were in his backpack, which he'd foolishly left in Wizard's hut. He wondered if he'd ever see those glasses again. He missed them, and the woman who'd given them to him.

He reached for his sat phone, dialed Shafer. The call went to voice mail. Wells counted to ten, redialed. One ring . . . two . . . three . . . four . . . Finally, Shafer picked up. "Sorry. My internist says I have a generous prostate."

"Tell me you're joking, you left the room to hide from Duto or whatever —"

"Get to my age, you'll see. I would literally have pissed myself —"

"Enough. Are you back?"

"I'm running back now. Just a sec." Shafer sounded winded. He was old, Wells realized. Somehow in the last year Shafer had gone from late middle-aged to flat-out old. "I'm back."

"You see us."

"Yes. Count eight vehicles in your convoy."

"I'm in the second Range Rover, sixth overall. Front passenger seat." Wells leaned forward, waved.

"You're waving. It's a little lame, but yes. Hi, John!" This last in a mock-girlish tone.

"I guess the optics are as good as advertised."

"Better. I can pick out every finger. The volunteers are in the other Rover?"

"Correct. Wizard's driving that one."

"You're separated."

"We'll see if it's a problem. But he knows he needs the Reaper to have a chance. Speaking of, how big's the welcoming committee?"

"Last pass was ten minutes ago. We

counted two hundred–plus armed men. AKs mainly, some RPGs. Twelve technicals."

"Twelve technicals."

"Correct."

Too many. The heavy machine guns the technicals carried could tear up Wizard's men in one burst. Even the armor on the Rovers could stop those rounds for only a few seconds.

"Give me the setup."

"Main element has four techs side by side. At least one hundred men in that area. Two more techs spread wide to left and right. Four behind, a reserve element and also guarding against any flanking move by your side. Those four will need to be moved up to have an open field of fire. Pilot thinks he can disable the main element with the GBU, take out all four techs and maybe fifty percent of the men. More or less simultaneously he can fire Hellfires at two of the spread technicals, but then he'll have to circle around to hit the other two."

"So absolute best case, he takes six techs out right away, but at least two will survive that first round of fire."

"Yes."

"Then he'll come around, take out the other two technicals that have an open field of fire. But after that he's got no Hellfires left. So those last four technicals, the ones in reserve, Wizard's going to have to deal with those on his own."

"Any chance you can bring in additional Reapers? Or even the Pentagon?" Wells knew that asking for help ran contrary to everything he'd done in the previous twenty-four hours.

A profound silence followed. Wells wondered if Shafer had hung up. "Is that what you want now, John? Because that's a little different strategy than we've been discussing."

Now a new voice spoke. "We've informed the White House that you've found the hostages." Duto. "They're looking at putting a SEAL team in the air. And the Air Force is launching at least four MQ-9s" — Reapers. "But the minimum ETA is five hours."

Too late, as they all knew.

"If we'd had a little more time. If you'd given us a little more time."

"Miss you too, Vinny," Wells said.

"Last thing," Shafer said. "We're considering ourselves cleared to drop soon as Wizard gives us a PID" — positive identification — "on Awaale. He knows what to do, right?"

"Yes. He asked you to give him at least

one minute. He said he's going to move a bunch of guys up after he meets with Awaale."

"He say how? Because I can't believe Red Team would allow that."

"I didn't ask." But Wells realized that Shafer was right. He didn't know how Wizard would get armed men forward when he was more or less surrendering to Awaale.

"Doesn't matter. We'll see it if it happens. So we'll give him that minute, but he's got to know that the bomb will be most effective when the other side's all clustered up."

"He knows."

"And you know if things set up good, we're not going to give you a heads-up. Be ready."

"Fantastic tip. Where would I be without you?"

"I know why you've made it this long, John. You're too big a prick to die."

"Roger that. Over and out."

Wells wondered if he ought to tell Wizard that they were headed for twelve technicals. But the Somali would go ahead even if Wells told him they were facing an entire mechanized brigade. He'd roused his men and he couldn't back down.

Wells would just have to seize his chance when it came. And remember that his responsibility was to the hostages, not the White Men.

In the Rover ahead, Wizard made his own calculation. He'd promised to let the wazungu go home to their families. He would keep his word. He had no choice, anyway. Too many people wanted them. But the man who'd come for them was a soldier. He'd come on his own, even offered to trade himself for the three.

Wizard decided to take the man up on that offer. After he destroyed the Ditas, he would set the others free. But not this one. A single hostage would be easy to hold. Wizard wouldn't make the same mistakes as he'd made before. Handcuffs and hoods for him. Wizard would sell him back after a few weeks. Maybe not for a million dollars. But even a hundred thousand would be enough with the Ditas gone. His men would see Wizard had destroyed their enemies and found another mzungu to ransom. Wizard relaxed in his seat, hands loose on the wheel, eyes smiling behind his sunglasses. This new mzungu had arrived at just the right moment. Wizard didn't feel a twinge of remorse for betraying him. The man had killed four of his soldiers.

The sun rose, filling him with its power.

Wizard realized he'd been a fool to lose his confidence. How could he have imagined his magic would leave him?

28

Langley

Shafer and Duto stood side by side behind Tomaso's workstation, watching the convoy chug northeast through the empty plains. Wizard and Awaale had set their meeting at an abandoned watering hole ten kilometers from Wizard's camp. They were less than three kilometers apart, close enough that they would soon glimpse each other through the scrub that covered the pancake-flat land. Tomaso dialed back the Reaper's main camera to pick up both the White Men and the Ditas simultaneously.

"The God view."

"The Old Testament God," Shafer said. "All-seeing and vengeful and loaded for bear."

"Just wish we had a little more ammo."

"A B-52's worth, yeah."

"What's a B-52?"

This kid. "Ever heard of the Cold War?

Dr. Strangelove —"

Tomaso grinned. "Messing with you, Ellis. Course I know what a B-52 is."

"I hope you choke on your hair."

But the joke was on them both. Maybe they didn't need an eight-engine bomber, but they could have used an A-10 with a full load of depleted uranium shells. The gap between the two militias was painful to see.

The Dita Boys had showed up at the meeting site a few minutes before Wells called Shafer from the convoy. As Shafer had warned Wells, the Ditas had come with a dozen technicals, enough to keep four in reserve in case Wizard tried to circle and attack from the rear. Each technical was mounted with a 12.7-millimeter NSV machine gun draped with belts of copper-jacketed ammunition. Shafer recognized the NSVs immediately. They had been the Red Army's frontline machine gun during the seventies and eighties. They were sleek, nasty weapons that fired thirteen rounds a second. They were easily lethal at five hundred meters, and capable of serious damage at three times that distance. A skilled NSV gunner could take out a light plane.

The Ditas didn't bother with unarmed

pickups, either. Their soldiers traveled in three open-topped five-ton trucks, the same troop transport that real armies used. At this distance, even their uniforms were convincing, the mismatched jumble of their camouflage blurring together.

Meanwhile, the White Men looked like a bunch of recruits on their way to their first day of basic training. Or worse, kids headed for camp, with those ridiculous Range Rovers that belonged in a Connecticut suburb. *Coach said if we were good we could ride with him after practice.* Their lone technical was a couple hundred meters ahead. The rest of the convoy was bunched close, running single file down the track, spinning up mud.

Shafer had worried that Awaale might set an ambush near Wizard's camp, trapping the White Men before the meeting. Instead, the Ditas hadn't even bothered with scouts. Shafer could see why. No doubt Awaale saw the meeting itself as all the trap he needed. The technicals gave the Ditas an overwhelming advantage. Once Wizard brought his men within firing distance of those machine guns, Awaale would decide whether they left.

Whether the White Men survived this battle or not was irrelevant to Shafer. The alliance between Wells and Wizard didn't even deserve to be called a marriage of convenience. It was more like a one-night stand. But if the White Men were overrun straightaway, Wells and the hostages would be captured. Wells might be killed on the spot. For them to have any chance at all of getting away clean, Tomaso would have to land the Reaper's five-hundred-pounder perfectly and Wizard would have to move instantly in the chaos that followed.

Duto tapped Shafer's shoulder. "Come." Duto had been furious since Wells asked for help, confirming what they all knew anyway, that the White Men were badly outgunned.

"This is not the time."

"Now, Ellis." Duto kept his voice even, walked out loose and easy, like he was inviting Shafer for lunch. But once they were outside the operations center he grabbed Shafer's arm and pulled him back to the ice-cold conference room.

"You should have found a way to slow this down, given us time to bring in more drones."

Like Duto hadn't signed off, too, making his own selfish calculations.

"You keep forgetting, Vinny. That guy on the ground, Awaale, gets a vote, too. And he wasn't waiting on us."

"If Wells hadn't been so in love with doing this himself, we could have put guys in the air hours ago."

"Funny. I didn't see John in your office with a gun to your head to stop you from telling the Pentagon about this. Anyway, what are you worried about? You made the call your eleven-hundred-dollar-an-hour lawyer told you to make. You're protected."

"Not the point."

They were standing close now, and Shafer took some small pleasure in seeing the row of tiny pimples high on Duto's forehead. Duto was appearing regularly on CNN and Fox News and Sunday-morning talk shows, raising his profile for his Senate campaign, and he had the bad skin that came with television makeup. Duto could have his teeth brightened until they were supernova white and wear two-thousand-dollar suits, but he'd never be handsome. Shafer knew he shouldn't care, he was hardly the best-looking guy in the room himself, but he took some small pleasure in Duto's ugliness. "That's always the point with you," Shafer said.

"You let him gamble with these hostages."

"You're so upset, I almost forgot it's his ass on the line out there and not yours, Vinny."

"We put ourselves in this corner for no reason. Because you couldn't talk him down last night. He ran all over you. Like he always does."

"We both know he's earned the benefit of the doubt. Maybe you should save the blame game until we see whether he pulls it out."

"This crush you have on him —"

Shafer felt his cheeks sting like Duto had slapped him. "Loyalty. A word I know you can't imagine." He brushed past Duto. "If it's all the same to you, we should get back, see what's going on over there before you write John's obituary."

Back at Tomaso's workstation, they watched in silence as the convoy edged closer. On screen, the technical turned off the track, rolled through a pool of rainwater. The rest of the convoy followed. Fifteen hundred meters from Awaale, the lead three pickups spread out and rode side by side by side, the Rovers single file behind them.

Shafer couldn't tell if Wizard had a tactical reason for the change or if he simply hoped the T shape might make his force seem larger than it was. Either way, if the White Men tried to charge the Ditas in open pickups, the technicals would tear them apart before they got close, as Wizard surely knew.

Tomaso's hands never stopped moving, adjusting the cameras, making sure the Reaper was flying smoothly despite the weight imbalance that came from having a five-hundred-pound bomb on one wing and not on the other. He looked up at Shafer.

"The air looks good. Unless you object, I'm going to go brain, fly autopilot on a two-click hold around the Red Six. That way I can focus on the payload. But we'll only have partial visuals on the friendlies."

"In English," Duto said.

Tomaso's eyes slid to Duto, like he'd just remembered who his real boss was. "We have smooth air right now, nothing the software can't handle. I want to set the Reaper on autopilot to circle at a two-kilometer radius around those four technicals in the middle. We're assuming that's where the enemy commander is —"

"Awaale —" Shafer said.

"Awaale is. That way I don't have to worry about keeping the Reaper in the air, I can focus on putting the GBU and the Hellfires on target. Only downside is that we may lose visual contact with the friendlies."

"Sounds fine," Shafer said.

"Great," Tomaso said. But his eyes stayed on Duto until the DCI nodded approval.

29

Lower Juba Region

The convoy emerged from the last of the scrub and the White Men fell silent.

Even from five hundred meters away, the technicals loomed over the empty plain. They were Toyota Hilux pickups, crew cabs with wide tires and roll bars, built to be indestructible on the world's worst roads. The White Men drove them, too. But each of the Dita Hiluxes carried a machine gun, its long steel barrel poking over the top of the cab. Three men stood in each pickup, one to aim and shoot, one to handle the ammunition, and one in reserve.

If Wizard had commanded the Ditas he would have turned around half the Hiluxes so that the guns could shoot out the open bed of the pickups for maximum visibility and flexibility. But the Ditas didn't seem worried. Wizard couldn't hear them, but their hands told the tale, loose and relaxed.

Awaale stood in the center, a head taller than most of his men.

Wizard wasn't surprised. In truth, this meeting would have been suicide for the White Men if not for the drone. Even with it he would need every bit of magic in the world. He slipped the Range Rover behind his pickups to give it a few extra seconds of cover if the Ditas opened up. When the Ditas opened up.

The hostages had been silent during the drive. Now Gwen leaned forward.

"Be careful," she said.

Just then Wizard knew he would never see her again, whatever happened in the next few minutes. He'd be gone, or she would. He missed her already, her and her magic, the magic of her blond hair and blue eyes, the magic she'd won just by being born in America. In his pocket he found a plastic bag that held a sheaf of miraa. The bag was mostly empty, the miraa growing stale. He had nothing else to give her. Nothing else she could possibly want. He handed it to her. She seemed to understand as well as he did.

"You tell everyone at home about Wizard."

"You know it."

He popped his sunglasses back on, stepped out of the Rover. His men leaned against their pickups, their sad naked Hiluxes. Their feet sank into the mud as they snuck glimpses at the technicals.

Wizard faced his soldiers one final time. "What I told you before, it's still true. You acting like these Ditas got tanks. Look over there."

One by one, the White Men lifted their heads.

"You see tanks? I don't see no tanks. I see technicals. And I see a bunch of boys never could be White Men. Stupid boys. Weak boys. We the ones with the secret. This all gonna look different soon. So different." He turned to the Donkeys. "You know what you supposed to do, when you supposed to do it."

"When you wave," Donkey Junior said.

"Right. Keep it tight and keep coming. Everyone else, when the shooting start, remember, it the Ditas gonna be scared. Not us. They not expecting this. Done and done."

"Done and done," his men said without enthusiasm. Wizard knew that if the bomb didn't hit quickly, many of them would lose their courage and run. Without further delay he took off his pistol and held it high where Awaale could see and handed it to Donkey Junior. "You ready to give this back to me,"

Wizard said.

He started the long walk toward Awaale. The sun stared into his eyes, but he stared straight back, wouldn't blink even as his eyes sprouted tears behind his sunglasses.

Awaale was taller than Wizard remembered. He stood with arms folded across his chest like he was posing for a statue of himself. Leader of the Dita Boys, Savior of the Somali Nation. He wore a pistol on his hip and the shiniest mirrored sunglasses Wizard had ever seen. He had a new gold bracelet, too, thick and shiny. His men stood close, their AKs trained on Wizard, their lips full of miraa.

"Awaale." Wizard extended a hand. Awaale looked at it like it was made of dung. "Shake my hand, Awaale. Man to man."

Back at camp, the American had told him to touch Awaale, nod while he did. *Then the people watching with the drone will know they have the right target,* he said. *They can see that from the drone,* Wizard said. *They can see that. They can see everything.*

Awaale's lips formed the briefest of smiles, as if to underscore the meaninglessness of the shake to his soldiers. *We're making peace with a man who's already dead,* the smile said. He extended his big right arm. Wizard clasped Awaale's hand in both of his and nodded to the sky.

"So these you new boys," Wizard said. "They good for anything but eating?"

"You find out soon enough. You got the wazungu in your Rover?"

"Yes."

"You tell them they coming with me?"

"Two conditions first."

Awaale shook his head. All around them men snapped off safeties.

Showy fool. You think you in control, but you backwards as ever. Death up there in the sky, coming for you.

"Just hear me before you say no," Wizard said.

"Quickly, then."

"First, you take men of mine who want to come with you."

"Soldiers leaving you, Wizard? White Men quitting you?"

"Traitors begging to join your rabble. I don't want them anyway."

"How many?"

"Twenty, twenty-five maybe."

Awaale hesitated. Then he seemed to see that Wizard was giving him a cheap way to build his force and that he could always shoot the ones he didn't like. He grinned.

Wizard knew he'd taken the bait. "All right. I show your men mercy, even though they stupid enough to let you lead them." His smile broadened. "But not you, Little Chicken. I won't have you."

"You think I gonna play your slave. Second, you give everyone else one day to break camp, leave the province. We never fight again. You win. Just let us live."

"You giving up."

Wizard nodded like it hurt him too much to say yes.

"Say it, then."

"Yeah. We giving up. I giving up."

"And I get all you vehicles. You be walking out of this province."

"Take the pickups."

"Think I want them pickups? The Rovers."

"No."

"Come to me begging for your life and then say no. All balls and no brains, Little Chicken, only you no balls, either."

"All right."

"All right, what?"

"All right, you get the Rovers, too. We walk back to camp, take our stuff, leave."

"Go to Dadaab with the rest of the women."

Wizard shrugged.

"You know what, Wizard? I in a good mood this morning, now that you roaches not bothering me no more. Gonna let you live. Can't take anything, though. Can't go back to camp. Soon as you leave this field you gone to Kenya."

For a moment, Wizard wondered whether Awaale might mean to keep his word, let him live. Then Awaale looked over his shoulder and nodded at one of his men and Wizard knew he was lying. He and the White Men who didn't defect would die within the hour.

"Thank you, Awaale. Thank you." The words stuck in Wizard's throat. Even knowing they were a lie, he could barely force them out. "I tell my men who want to come to you, split from the rest of us, walk over."

"No tricks. Or we shoot all everyone."

"I swear, no tricks. You too much for me."

"And the wazungu?"

"Told you. In the Rover. You going to hurt them? Sell them to Shabaab?"

"No business of yours, Chicken. They mine now. Like them Rovers."

"I tell you they much much trouble."

"Maybe for you." Awaale patted Wizard on the cheek. "What happened to that magic, Wizard?"

Wizard was thankful he'd left his weapon

with Donkey Junior. He had the desperate urge to put it to the big man's chest, squeeze the trigger. He knew the drone would do its work so soon. Still his fingers itched for the pistol. A bomb was too sudden, too quick. Wizard wanted Awaale to know that Wizard had killed him.

"Go on," Awaale said. "Wasted too much time. Send me my wazungu."

Wizard turned, walked back across the field. "Everyone who want to go with Awaale, his no-teeth Ditas, walk now," he yelled.

Men stepped forward, until two dozen walked across the field toward him, heads down in defeat. The Donkeys led the way. If Awaale had known the White Men, he might have wondered why Wizard's most loyal soldiers were defecting en masse. For his part, Wizard screamed abuse at his men.

"Traitors! Wizard protected you, looked out for you, now you quit me! Awaale gon' shoot all you fools!"

Step. Step. Step. Mud caked the bottom of his pants. He wondered if even now Awaale was getting ready to open fire. He didn't look back. Nothing to do but play the role of the defeated commander. He hoped the Americans would wait long enough to let his men get close but still drop the bomb while they were outside the blast area. He trudged through the mud, shoulders slumped.

Halfway across the field when he passed the first of his men. Of course, it was brave, stupid Donkey Junior. "Junior," Wizard said quietly.

"Wizard. It okay?"

"Keep walking."

Then Wizard heard the sound he'd been waiting for, the whistle that meant the drone had let loose its magic egg —

He turned and grabbed Junior and pulled him down and —

30

From across the field, the blast didn't look that impressive, a boom that shook the Range Rover's windows and kicked out a white cloud that was quickly overtaken by a flood of inky smoke. But in the seconds that followed the damage became clear. Fire consumed the four technicals around Awaale. Men's screams carried to Wells across the muddy flats.

Wizard and his men had flattened themselves before the bomb hit. Now they picked themselves up, their white T-shirts dripping with mud. Wizard grabbed a pistol from one of his soldiers and raised it over his head and fired like a starter at a track meet. His men howled and charged. They had the field to themselves, facing not a single return shot as they ran. The air above them sizzled and two bright streaks torched the air, the Hellfires. The missiles registered more as blurs than physical objects until they connected with the two technicals on Awaale's right flank. The explosions that followed spun the Toyotas onto their sides and sent up waves of black smoke and flame.

The two undamaged Dita technicals on the left flank opened fire, raking the field. But the White Men were widely scattered and only three went down. Then the White Men's lone technical fired a long rattling burst that tore open the windshields of the Dita technicals and sent the men in back diving for cover. The Dita machine gunners had made a basic tactical mistake. They should have disabled the White Men's technical before aiming at the men on the field. Lightly armored vehicles were great on the attack, but nearly useless once they came under sustained fire. Now the White Men's technical edged forward, firing shorter bursts now at the Dita vehicles, pinning them without wasting ammunition. Textbook.

For the first time since Wizard had walked across the field, Wells thought they might all survive.

Wizard and his lead soldiers reached the crater where Awaale had stood. The thick black smoke from the burning technicals screened Wells's view, but he heard sustained return fire. The Ditas were responding at last. Wizard waved his men forward, into the cloud. The White Men had to keep attacking. The Ditas still had more soldiers, and they had those four technicals that Awaale had kept in reserve. Awaale wasn't around to order them into the fight, but his lieutenants might be. In open ground like this, a charge could look completely successful until the moment the enemy counterattacked.

The rest of the White Men jumped into their pickups and rolled across the field, shouting as they bumped through the mud. Only the two Range Rovers and four White Men remained. One sat in the Range Rover with the hostages. Another stood beside it. Waaberi and the guard in the backseat had stayed with Wells.

Wells unbuckled his belt, reached for the door handle. Waaberi put a hand on his arm.

"I did what I promised," Wells said in Arabic. "It's time for us to go."

"They go. You stay."

Wizard planned to hold Wells hostage. One last double-cross. Wizard should have been happy Wells had given him a chance to live. But he couldn't quit. A trait he and Wells had in common.

So Waaberi and the guard would die.

Wells lifted his armrest, shifted left in his seat. The Rover had a wide console between the two front seats. Driver and passenger could sit side by side without ever touching accidentally, or even acknowledging each other's existence. Very English. Wells looked over his left shoulder. No surprise, the guard sat in the middle of the backseat, legs splayed wide, the pistol loose in his right hand. Wells waved and the guard shook his head blankly. He nodded the pistol at Wells: *I'm watching you.*

Wells wasn't sure of his next move. He'd hoped to reach down for his knife, come up, put it in the guard's belly in one quick motion. But squirming from front seat into back was a slow and awkward motion in any vehicle. And these Rovers had generous backseats, plenty of space. By the time Wells came across the console, the guard would have enough time to get the pistol up. Another reason to hate luxury SUVs.

Waaberi leaned over the console, put a hand on Wells's shoulder, pushed him back. "Enough —"

Just that quickly, Wells knew what to do. He leaned into Waaberi for a moment, pushing against him. Intuitively, Waaberi shoved back —

And Wells twisted his body away, and forward, toward the dashboard. As he broke contact with Waaberi, the Somali slipped toward him. In one fluid move, Wells swung his big right arm around Waaberi's shoulders, used Waaberi's own momentum to pull him out of the driver's seat and slide him across the console. Wells was fully out of his seat now, crouched under the windshield, his ass against the dashboard. The guard lifted his pistol, but too late. Wells put his right hand high on Waaberi's back and shoved him over the console through the space between the front seats. Waaberi's body shielded Wells from the pistol and blocked the guard from moving his arm any further —

"Stop —" Wells yelled in English, the word simply a diversion. Before the guard or Waaberi could wriggle away, Wells reached down with his left hand, pulled the knife on his right ankle. Waaberi tried to push back, but Wells was braced against the dash and pinned Waaberi against the guard. Then with his left hand he lifted the knife over Waaberi and down onto the guard's right shoulder. His left hand was his weak hand, but Wells kept stabbing, deepening the wound with each cut. He twisted the knife and the guard screamed and blood spurted onto the Rover's pristine cream-colored leather seats. Now the guard's right hand was useless and the pistol wasn't a threat.

Wells didn't want to kill these men, they weren't his enemies, but he didn't see any other option. He shoved Waaberi aside and raised the knife again and slashed crossways across the guard's neck. The bright red arterial blood pumped out, and Wells suddenly found himself back on that mountain in Chechnya. The guard shrieked and tried to squirm away and raised a hand to his neck, but the blood kept coming through his fingers, too much blood, fountains of it.

Now Waaberi reached down into the well of the backseat, scrambling for the pistol the guard had dropped on the passenger-side floor. Wells followed him into the second row and switched the knife into his right hand and pushed Waaberi down against the blood-slicked leather with his left. Waaberi lifted the pistol —

And Wells raised the knife and buried the blade in Waaberi's back, nearly between the shoulder blades, cutting his spinal cord in one vicious stroke. Waaberi didn't scream. His body twitched and went soft and his bowels and bladder loosened and death filled the car. Wells pushed off him and twisted back to the driver's seat, and as he did, he heard someone yelling. The guard who'd been outside the other Rover was just a few meters from the passenger-side front door. He lowered his AK —

Wells twisted the key in the ignition and the Rover's engine rumbled to life. The guard stepped forward and pulled the trigger. He was so close that Wells saw spent cartridges pouring from the rifle. Wells could do nothing except wait for the 7.62-millimeter rounds to tear him up —

He'd forgotten the Rovers were armored. The window cracked into a spiderweb but didn't break. The door beneath it didn't even dent. Wells put the Rover in reverse, gunned the engine, spun the wheel left. When he'd turned so that the SUV faced the guard, he stopped and jammed on his seat belt and shifted into drive and floored the gas pedal. The guard fired until he had no rounds left and flung himself out of the way. Wells let him go, didn't even try to clip him. He wanted the other Rover, which was broadside to him.

He accelerated across the mud. As he closed in, he saw Owen clawing at the second Rover's driver from the backseat. Wells corrected his course, aiming for the vehicle's engine block. Then the driver shook free of Owen and the vehicle leapt ahead. Wells leaned back in his seat, held the wheel loose, waiting for contact —

And smashed the other Rover side-on, metal crunching metal, glass tearing. Wells jerked against his seat belt and flew at the steering wheel as the airbag popped to embrace him. The corpses in the second row rolled forward and smacked into the front seats and somehow, a joke of physics, Waaberi's right arm wound up in the center console like he was reaching out for the radio.

The airbag deflated. Wells took stock. His seat belt had bruised his chest and he'd banged his left arm into the window, but otherwise he was fine. With the armor the Rover weighed more than three tons, and its engine block, its stiffest and heaviest piece, had taken the brunt of the impact. Its hood was crumpled and its grille smashed, but Wells thought it would survive long enough to get them across the Kenyan border.

The other Rover was more seriously damaged. The driver's door had caved, pinning the driver against the steering wheel. He was moving, feebly, but Wells didn't think he'd survive without trauma care, which wasn't available within a thousand miles.

Somewhere in the black smoke on the opposite side of the field, two technicals exploded. The Reaper pilot must have fired his last Hellfires at the Dita technicals back there, rather than the ones that Wizard's own technical had disabled. Smart. The White Men were winning this fight almost too quickly. Wells and the hostages needed to go before Wizard found out Wells had killed his men and played demolition derby with his precious Range Rovers.

Wells stepped out, ran around the other Rover just as the rear passenger door swung open. A trickle of blood drooped down Gwen's forehead. Her eyes were dull, concussed.

"Over there. Now." Wells pointed at the other Rover. She walked unsteadily toward it. Wells reached inside, helped Hailey out.

"Owen's stuck," she said. "Really stuck."

"Get the bodies out of the other Rover. I'll handle him." Wells stepped into the backseat. Owen's left leg was pinched by the rear door. Wells looped Owen's right arm around his shoulder. They were face-to-face, nearly touching. The kid's breath stank of ten days without toothpaste. His cheeks were pale, lips set.

"My leg," Owen said.

"This is gonna sting."

Wells braced his left foot against the back driver's-side door and pressed, using Owen's trapped body as leverage. Owen screamed like a fire alarm in Wells's ear. The door gave and Wells felt Owen come free. He kicked with every fiber of muscle he had and —

They slid across the seat. Wells lifted Owen out. His left leg from midcalf down looked even worse than Wells had feared, a bloody pulp. An amputation for sure.

"It's fine. Just don't look." Wells carried Owen to the other Rover. The bodies of the Somalis lay on the ground.

"Get in," Wells said to Gwen and Hailey. He half expected them to argue. The backseat of the Rover was bloody as a slaughterhouse. But they stepped inside without complaint. Wells set Owen in the front seat.

"Lucky me," Owen said. "Shotgun."

The keys were still in the ignition. Wells reached for them. The Rover's engine grumbled, hesitated.

"Oh, come on," Hailey said.

"Please," Gwen said. "Please."

Wells killed the ignition, tried again with the briefest flutter of gas. The engine kicked into life. Wells put the Rover in reverse.

Metal screamed and tore.

Then they were free.

Epilogue

Wells knew the media storm they would face when they came back to the places that called themselves civilized. As he bounced the Rover toward the border, he helped the hostages unkink the story of the past twenty-four hours. Of course, they were welcome to tell the truth, the whole truth, and nothing but the truth, he told them.

But as far as he was concerned, no one needed to know Owen had killed a guard. Or that Wells had made a deal to help their kidnappers attack another militia in return for their release. Simpler was better. The United States had found where they were being held and bombed their camp as a CIA team helped them escape. Simple. And almost true. Not entirely false, anyway.

"A team," Gwen said.

"A small team."

"You're sure about this."

"Reporters don't need the details. You're

heroes. Let the world see you that way."

"Reporters? People are paying attention to this?" Hailey said.

Wells glanced at her, wondering if she was joking. But, of course, she didn't know. "It's the biggest story in the world. I'm not exaggerating. Pays to be pretty."

"What about you?" Gwen said. "What will you tell the reporters?"

Wells rubbed his thumb against his fingertips, flaking off dried blood. "Better if they don't see me at all."

He checked the rearview mirror, wondered whether Wizard would give chase. For now, anyway, the mirror was empty. He edged down on the gas. The Rover's engine churned and bits of metal and glass shook loose from the grille. Even so, Wells thought they would reach the border.

"There's still one problem —" Owen said.

"Only one?"

Owen didn't smile. "You know who set us up?"

So much had happened in the last twenty-four hours that James Thompson had slipped Wells's mind. "Moss Laughton's good buddy Jimbo. And the driver." Wells fought fever and exhaustion for the name. "Suggs."

"Scott, too," Hailey said.

Scott. Wells hadn't put that piece together. "You sure."

"He was yelling for Suggs when Wizard attacked the camp," Owen said. "He knew Suggs was there even though none of us had seen him."

"But we all think James sold Scott on the idea," Gwen said.

"He has to pay," Owen said.

A couple years back, Wells had tried to rescue another hostage. The man ultimately responsible for that kidnapping was still free. He lived in Saudi Arabia, protected, cosseted, unimaginably wealthy. Unless he made the mistake of leaving the kingdom without his bodyguards, Wells couldn't touch him.

This time Wells would have justice. "A Kenyan jail would do for him nicely," Wells said. "He'd be lucky to last a year."

"That works," Hailey said.

"What if the Kenyans decide they don't want to go near it?" Owen said. "What evidence do we have for them?"

"Not much," Wells said.

"We can't take that chance," Owen said. "Will you take care of him? Let him get back to Houston, let it all die down, and in a few months stuff him in a swamp somewhere?"

"Down on the Cancer Coast? Awful quiet resting place for a man who likes to talk as much as Jimmy." Wells imagined what he'd do in nursery-rhyme form:

> Grab him, hood him, toss him in the trunk
> Drive him down the highway to the bayou stunk
> Stab him, shoot him, wrap him in concrete
> Dump the body in the water for the gators to eat

And that's how we commit murder one, boys and girls! Assassination was a line Wells had never crossed, but he supposed Gwen and Hailey and Owen had earned the right to ask. James had killed his nephew as sure as if he'd put the pistol to Scott's chest.

"You sure about this? All three of you?"

"No," Gwen said. "I won't."

"Won't what?" Owen said.

"No more eye-for-an-eye. He goes to prison." Her voice quiet but firm. "Mr. Wells said we had to agree. And I don't."

"All right," Wells said. "That's out, then." He felt an unexpected relief.

"How do you propose we make sure he goes to jail?" Owen said.

"We make him confess —"

"Brilliant, Gwennie.

"Let me finish," Gwen said. "We *know* he did this, right? Whatever the evidence, we have no doubt. So what we'll do is we'll go to him — he's at the camp, right?"

"As of yesterday," Wells said.

"And tell him that Scott confessed before he got shot, that we all three heard it. And he's got two choices. Either he gives himself up to the FBI — here, not in Houston — and goes back home in their custody, or we make sure the Kenyans arrest him."

Silence, as they worked through the plan.

"What do you think?" Hailey said to Wells.

"You better get the story straight before you see him. But I think if you stick to it, all three of you, he'll believe you. Since he knows the truth, too."

"Owen," Gwen said.

Owen shifted in his seat to look at her. Pain slanted his face but it couldn't hide the surprise underneath. "Who are you, and what have you done with Gwen Murphy?"

"Is that a yes or a no?"

"All right. You win."

And that was that.

"One other thing," Gwen said.

"What's that?"

"About Wizard and the deal you made. He promised to set us free if you helped him with the attack."

"Yes."

"So did he lie? Was he planning to keep us?"

Wells wanted to lie, but she deserved the truth. He couldn't doubt the bond that she and Wizard had formed in the last twenty-four hours, however strange it might seem.

"I think he meant to set you free. He was double-crossing me, planning to hold me hostage."

He caught her gorgeous ice-blue eyes in the rearview mirror. He couldn't tell if she was disappointed in him, Wizard, or the world.

"It never ends, does it?" she said.

"It hasn't yet."

Considering what had happened to his leg, it only seemed fair that Owen would get to speak to his parents first. Gwen and Hailey played rock-paper-scissors to see who would be next. Hailey won. Gwen waited.

She closed her eyes and imagined what she'd say to her mother and father and sister, the shock in their voices. Until finally she heard Hailey say, "Mom. We only have one phone and it's Gwen's turn . . . Okay. I love you. I love you so much."

The phone was slick with Hailey's tears. Gwen took it, laid it carefully on her lap. Her fingers trembled as she punched in the numbers and heard the ring —

At Langley, Tomaso had focused on the main battle area until he launched the last two Hellfires. By the time he turned the cameras to the field's west edge, Wells was speeding off in the Rover, leaving two corpses in the dirt. Shafer had always known what Wells could do. Seeing it, even on a monitor seven thousand miles away, was another matter. One Somali's throat had been hacked nearly in half. The other had a knife so deep in his back that it seemed to be part of his body.

"It's almost a miracle that he hasn't gone insane," Shafer said.

"You think he's not insane."

"You're lucky he likes you, Vinny."

"He likes me?"

"No."

"Looks like he has all three hostages with him. Should I follow them or go back to the battlefield?" Tomaso said.

"Follow them," Shafer said. "I'm worried Wizard will come after him."

"Makes no difference."

"I don't know if you've gotten entirely senile, Ellis, but we've got no Hellfires left. No way to stop that technical."

"Don't need a Hellfire. We've got the Reaper."

Tomaso understood first. "Dive-bomb it into the technical. I like it."

But the White Men didn't chase the Rover. Maybe Wizard didn't want to challenge the Reaper. So they had nothing to do but watch as the big SUV bounced west toward the border. No need for a compass or GPS. Just keep the sun in the rearview mirror. Every few minutes Tomaso updated the distance to Kenya . . . twenty-five kilometers . . . twenty . . . fifteen . . .

"Time to tell the White House to call off the dogs." Duto said when the Rover was ten kilometers out.

"Let the Kenyans know, too, so they don't shoot anybody."

At the door, Duto stopped. "Thank your boy for me. This has got to be worth at least ten points with the undecideds, don't you think?"

"If God exists, you'll have a stroke."

"I'm glad you're an atheist, Ellis." Duto left.

When the Rover was three kilometers from the border, Shafer tapped Tomaso.

"One last thing." Shafer explained what he wanted.

"You sure it won't freak them out."

"They'll get it."

"Okay," Tomaso said. He adjusted the Reaper's flaps and throttle and the drone suddenly went into something close to a dive. In two minutes, it pulled in front of the Rover even as its altitude dropped from fifteen hundred meters to five hundred.

"I'm going to bring our speed down, and then I'll bring it up here as he comes across."

So it was that the Reaper buzzed the Rover low and slow just as Wells and the hostages reached the border. On screen, Shafer saw Wells lean forward as the Reaper drew close. Wells frowned — this close, the Rover's optics were so good that they could see not just his nose but each nostril — and then he seemed to understand the message: *Welcome home.* He nodded, waved.

Shafer found himself foolishly, joyously, waving back.

ACKNOWLEDGMENTS

The team at Putnam never quits. Thanks to Neil, Ivan, Leslie, Tom, Kate, and everyone else at 375 Hudson. To Heather Schroder, the agent next door. To Jeffrey Gettleman, foreign correspondent extraordinaire, and J. Peter Pham, for answering all my dumb questions about East Africa's politics. (Mistakes are mine alone.) To Martin and all the other Kenyans who introduced me to one of the world's most beautiful and fascinating countries. I hope to return many times. To my family for their counsel on this book and so much else. And of course, to my beautiful and talented wife, Jackie, and Lucy, our little girl. May she be the best of both of us.

If you got this far, you've earned my email address, which is: alexberensonauthor@gmail.com. I welcome all comments and suggestions. For seven years now I've responded to every email I receive, and I hope to keep that string alive. Meantime, see you on Facebook and Twitter.

'Til next year.

ABOUT THE AUTHOR

Alex Berenson was born in New York in 1973 and grew up in Englewood, N.J. After graduating from Yale University in 1994 with degrees in history and economics, he joined the *Denver Post* as a reporter. In 1996, he became one of the first employees at TheStreet.com, the groundbreaking financial news Website. In 1999, he joined *The New York Times.* At the *Times,* he covered everything from the drug industry to Hurricane Katrina; in 2003 and 2004, he served two stints as a correspondent in Iraq, an experience that led him to write *The Faithful Spy,* his debut novel, which won the Edgar Award from the Mystery Writers of America for Best First Novel. He has now written seven John Wells novels and one work of non-fiction, *The Number.* He left the *Times* in 2010 to devote himself to writing fiction, though he still contributes occasionally to the *Times.* Alex lives in Garrison, N.Y. with his wife, Dr. Jacqueline Berenson, their daughter Lucy, their badly behaved dog Maggie, and Maggie's dog Teddy.

The employees of Thorndike Press hope you have enjoyed this Large Print book. All our Thorndike, Wheeler, and Kennebec Large Print titles are designed for easy reading, and all our books are made to last. Other Thorndike Press Large Print books are available at your library, through selected bookstores, or directly from us.

For information about titles, please call:

(800) 223-1244

or visit our Web site at:

http://gale.cengage.com/thorndike

To share your comments, please write:

Publisher
Thorndike Press
10 Water St., Suite 310
Waterville, ME 04901